THE UNSEEN

By James McKenna

JAMES McKENNA

THE UNSEEN

First published by AuthorHouse in 2008

This edition reissued by

Lone Cloud Publishing in 2012

Unit 1 Betjeman Close, Cowper Road, Harpenden, Herts AL5 4XH

ISBN-978-0-9569723-4-7

lonecloudpublishing@live.co.uk

THE UNSEEN

Visit lonecloudpublishing or jameswmckenna.co.uk for more
books by this author,interviews and comments.
You can sign up for enewsletters so you always hear first
about new releases.

Other book:

The Uncounted

Books soon to be released:

Final Justice

Global Raider

wwwcrimefiction-jamesmckenna.co.uk

Thanks to Kevin for his cover design and

Virginia for her hard work and tenacity

CHAPTER 1

Stella had no defence against Caswell's gaze on her body, nor his predatory thoughts which she sensed creeping through her clothes with invasive lust. Beneath her business smile came an uncharacteristic tremor of nerves. Familiar with appreciative glances, she occasionally encouraged them, but this guy made her feel like meat. This guy stirred fear.

"If you would follow me, Mr Caswell." She indicated the stone steps and led him from the terrace of Casco Bay Villa towards a rocky headland on the Maine coast. Looking towards the sea and Atlantic swell, she heard his overbearing presence follow her.

"I expected this meeting to take place at Head Office in New York," Caswell said.

"Head Office is wherever Mr Wileman resides," she replied over her shoulder, conscious his eyes now devoured the minute quiver of flesh beneath her fitted skirt.

"Does he always have such good looking young women around him? You must be really useful to him, an old boy like that."

Stella compressed her lips and continued in silence, trying to distract with thoughts of her boyfriend, of the progress on her thesis, trying to lighten her descent so her breasts did not shiver with each footfall on the hard steps.

"I mean, lot of the top guys I mix with got personal assistants resembling dragons beyond their sell-buy date. But you, you got something else, including one peach of an arse with legs stretching way up. I see you've no wedding ring. Fancy dinner tonight?"

Stella squared her jaw and wrinkled her nose. "Thank you but I have a previous engagement. And I am not Mr Wileman's PA, I am researching for my PhD in computer technology."

"Brains and beauty, now that I like. You ever need a job, come work for me. I got a special position in mind."

Stella took a turn in the downward path and allowed silence for an answer, her thoughts finding sanctuary amidst the gulls circling on outstretched wings. The sight calmed her annoyance but did little for her uncertainty as to why Wileman had summoned her, why her instructions included escorting Caswell from the villa. She assumed Wileman wanted to learn about her research. After all, he paid for it. The Wileman Foundation had lifted her from childhood poverty, had schooled her, put her through college and university and now paid a salary while she wrote her doctorate thesis. Wileman had opened all the doors, this had to be important, least for her. She didn't know about the guy screwing her butt. She just wished he was someplace else.

The path turned to an outcrop of trees, then became lost as it wound down to the beach cove and summerhouse. Wileman sat on a bench overlooking a small cemetery with white picket railings. Sea air brushed his wrinkled face while his gaze remained on the distance, as if lost amidst the sounds of surf and gulls.

"Mr Wileman," Stella called. "The British executive, Richard Caswell. You said to bring him." She stopped by the bench and pushed strands of loose hair behind one ear. She sensed her face was glowing and her brow moist.

Oscar Wileman looked between them before offering his hand, only then did Caswell remove his eyes from her. Still flushed she gave full attention to her boss, fingers clasped sedately, hoping for something good. Wileman stayed silent for a moment then indicated she sit beside him. Expensive clothes draped his thin body, his spiky hair standing oblivious to the breeze as he examined Richard from behind rimless spectacles.

"Pretty girl, ain't she?" he said, as if she was not there, his face without animation, his blue eyes bright and cutting.

"Exceptionally so," Caswell smirked.

"Stella," Wileman said her. "I've asked you here because your future work will have direct influence on Richard's project."

"As you wish, Mr Wileman."

"Oh I do wish, Stella. You're a bright young lady with a bright future. I have things planned for you."

Stella felt relief and shuffled her feet. Maybe this was her big opening.

"She has a Masters in flash advertising on computer screens. It's there for seconds, then gone, not dissimilar from what you do," Wileman said. "Her brain and body are wasted here, but I like to have intelligent and pretty girls around me. It's a privilege of wealth." Wileman turned back to the fenced graveyard. "I bury my animals in this plot. Dogs, cats, a bear, even a llama. Plus a few other creatures. This is my pets' cemetery."

"To have kept so many you must love animals, Mr Wileman," Caswell said, Stella loathing the false smile on his round, chubby face.

"No. I amuse myself by training them. I do so by feeding their ambition and greed. In return they give me obedience. As Stella will give. Because of it she will do whatever it is you intend to ask of her."

"Mr Wileman, please." Stella sat up sharp, putting hand to bodice. "I will always follow your wishes, but I'm not sure I understand."

"It's simple, Stella. I need your total obedience no matter what I ask. And this assignment will be proof of that obedience. When I picked you and others from the gutter, when I educated you, I did so for a reason, for possession of your soul. And I if I say lie down and roll over, I expect just that. You got a problem, you can leave right now, leave my company and my payroll."

Stella felt her mouth open as she twisted on the bench, felt her gaze drop, felt fear creep to every fibre of her body.

"I ... I." Her eyes closed and moments passed.

"Witness, Richard, the control of wealth. Witness and learn. If you want money, Richard, this is your opportunity, but first, like Stella, judge which is more important, morality or ambition."

Stella stared between the two of them, hating both, hating her inability to leave, her weakness in not speaking out.

"My morality is yours, sir," Caswell said, his eyes on her breasts.

"Good, because I'm talking about control of America, control of the financial world and all the power that acquires. America's vast debt and the infighting of politicians over solving it puts this country and, indeed, mankind on the brink of collapse. If you cannot pay the army and the police, you cannot rely on them. The result, chaos, anarchy, a return to the primeval."

"I'm with you, boss." Caswell nodded his head and Stella watched his intrusive gaze give way to self-righteousness. "If you have ability to influence the politicians, you have ability to control the people."

"And make a lot of money."

"I assume you refer to my work on subliminal psychotic induction," Caswell said.

"SPI over computer screens directed at the right people could put our country in the direction we require, indeed, we could influence our whole civilisation."

Caswell curled his fingers into a fist. "Covert control by the unseen. Money, just think of all that money."

"Which is why I'm closing you down."

"What?" He stepped back, sagging, his arms splayed.

Stella sat motionless, teeth clenched, trying not to gloat over Caswell's demise. What game was Wileman playing?

"Such controversial research is highly volatile. Any connection to my company would be disastrous. Your programme is terminated forthwith and you are dismissed from Starways."

"You're kidding me? I've proved what we can do." Caswell raised both hands in bewildered question.

Wileman remained looking out to sea, his expression bland. "At this point, Richard, note the extent of my power over your bank account. Then listen to my requirements." He paused. "You listen too, Stella, because your research is not dissimilar. WorkWell, our new business and office support application, will soon be ready for integration into the Starways operating system. In England you will set up a company and using what Stella sends over, you'll develop WorkWell so it accepts coded SPI viruses. In other words, install a facility which will interpret certain coded viruses as updates from a source provider."

"That would corrupt your own software."

"You misunderstand. What I want you to develop and incorporate into the WorkWell programme is a means whereby a virus from an unknown source, but carrying the right code, is accepted by the software as legitimate. These viruses will lie in a server or PC as a Trojan horse. They will not damage or cause a problem. Their only function is to send subliminal messages to the terminal user whenever there is screen movement. Within two years SPI, subliminal psychotic induction through our WorkWell application, will influence the world, will influence the money markets and politicians. Think of that, Richard."

"But why England? Why not here, in America?"

"Starways must never be involved. If we were ever accused of experimenting with SPI it might be interpreted as an intention to influence individual or public opinion. The media would slaughter us. That's why this meeting is private and witnessed only by Stella, who in turn chooses to prove her loyalty and obedience beyond question."

"But why go to England?"

Stella felt her breath, sharp and short. She swallowed and watched Wileman turn hard eyes on the Englishman before raising a bony finger. "It is illegal to use SPI on the public. If the government found out they would confiscate our research for themselves. They too would like to influence, the Senate and House of Representatives. Perhaps even now they watch us, waiting to intercept and steal our programme and they would use it, Richard, believe me." He shook his head. "All done while the courts crippled us with a fine of billions. No, security is paramount, that means out of sight and out of mind, somewhere in Britain."

"Employees would talk."

"Not if you pick only those who share your morality and ambition. Pay them well, the same way I do Stella, then you'll have their silent obedience," he said and squeezed her hand. "You will start a cover company known as PKL. Starways own the rights on two computer games, Princess Kay-ling and Killing Fields. PKL will pick up those rights very cheaply. You'll infuse both with the SPI research already developed. Over the Internet you can then send SPI out to these games as a virus and use the British population as guinea pigs. As a British firm, you will also be a listed sub-contractor on the WorkWell application. But the sole purpose of your involvement will be to adapt the application to accept SPI which had been developed through the games. For every other appearance your work is to create an SPI firewall provided as an upgrade."

"For user safety," Richard added.

"Diplomatically put. But our insertion must be designed so no-one can trace the source. At all times we must remain the unseen."

"Starways will fund the whole operation?"

"Starways will have no involvement. Your set up funding is in place via Russian contacts. Thereafter PKL should make enough profit to fund itself. I don't want you drawing attention. Use any excessive profit to keep trusted employees silent. Your reward will be waiting here when you return and that reward will be substantial."

"I have a free hand?"

"Stella will use her research programme to covertly pass you information, otherwise no-one this side will come near you. Insofar as Starways is concerned, you'll be a minor British non-entity and totally deniable. But there are three provisos. You must stay clean and you must stay hidden. Keep PKL as a family game, that's where the money lies."

"You're on, Mr Wileman."

"The third proviso is, when finished, you remove all traces of research in the UK, then via Stella you will personally deliver the results of your work to me, here at Casco Bay. On no account must you transfer anything relating to Starways by e-mail or let any other party have a copy. The result of failure in this would be unpleasant for you. Stella will monitor your progress and be your only contact."

"Have no fear, Mr Wileman, my ambitions will always be at your disposal."

"Excellent. Go down to the summerhouse and wait for Stella. You may use her as you please. She won't like it, but she'll accept. She also has ambition and once she sacrifices her integrity to that ambition, then I will trust her loyalty."

"Mr Wileman, what's going on here?" Stella said, watching Caswell saunter down towards the beach. "Listen, listen please. I'm not a whore and I see no logic in what you demand. You already have my loyalty."

"Do I, Stella? Well, I demand more. I need your hatred of Richard Caswell, your ruthless determination to destroy him if required. I need your anger, your contempt. The path you have chosen is the building of power for the purpose of self. It is a path without morals and to that end we are all whores. Your mind and body are but a means to an end. Greed has placed mankind on the edge of destruction; only control by the strong will save the human race. Do you wish to be amongst the strong? Because if we fail what will occur over the next hour may well occur every day of your life. I know Caswell, I know his past, his lack of morals, but I chose you to stand with the inner circle, with the unseen."

When Stella entered the beach house Caswell had stripped to his shorts, the hang of his gut folding over the stretched waistband.

"Can we talk this through," she said, moving from the door and circling the open plan floor as he came towards her. "Wileman has this notion that if I let you make love, there'll be some kind of bond."

"Love, Stella, who's talking of love? I don't want love, I want absolute control. I want you suffering and humiliated."

"Listen Mister, you're crazy." She put the couch between them as he crossed the room. "I'm not some floozy and I ain't gonna let you fuck me like some pig."

His movement and precision came much faster than she expected from a middle-aged slouch. Stepping on the couch he grabbed her blouse and a handful of hair simultaneously, pulling her over the back so she fell head down to the cushions, her legs flaying the air.

"I don't intend to love you, Stella. I intend to rape you, to fuck you purely for my pleasure. Have you monitor my progress, some chance. You don't know half of it. Soon I'll have power over you as I have power over Zoby, eventually over Wileman, power over everyone who uses a computer." One hand reached into her skirt, grabbing and yanking at her pants, while the other ripped open her blouse.

"You bastard, fucking get off me. Fuck off." She thrashed her arms as his overweight body pinned her full length on the cushions. His hands seemed everywhere, ripping, pulling, grabbing. Reaching her nails to his neck, she gouged in primeval retaliation, clawing until the back of his hand smacked hard across her face. For moments her sight fragmented then another blow hit her mouth. In the dazed cloud of pain she laid comatosed, feeling his full weight flop over her, feeling him probe then enter her body, feeling him heave and squirm, then in seconds roll away.

"Bitch," he said and began to dress.

Stella lay as left, conscious the blood from a split lip wet her chin, staring at the ceiling, her mind swirled in self-contempt, then loathing and hate for the animal now leaving the house. Tears mixed with the blood, tears driven by all-consuming rage. Wileman had been right. Hate came so easily, hate for the hand which fed her, for the one who had abused her, but mostly hate for herself.

Time passed, she had no idea how long, time meant nothing. Then a face appeared above her, a friendly, female face with motherly concern.

"I'm Diane Hopper," the woman said. "You're safe now. I've brought a doctor and one of our security personnel. We need to take some DNA swabs and your statement. Need to get that lip cleaned up. Rape is a serious crime. Caswell could spend his life in jail should a complaint be made."

"You knew this would happen, what this guy would do?" Stella sat, lowering her legs and pulling at her skirt.

"We know nothing, only our orders. So let's get started." She beckoned the doctor.

Stella remained wrapped in self-loathing, complying with instructions, signing the sworn statement, allowing treatment to her lip. The clothes Diane Hopper produced from a case represented a full outfit with price tags Stella only dreamt of.

"Welcome, Stella, to the House of Wileman. I'm instructed to inform, you now have a new position, Head of UK Research and Development. Mr Wileman said by now you would understand the need for past events. He also said be careful. Richard Caswell is a very violent and dangerous man. Oh, and Stella, don't report anything to the police. Starway's security will handle this."

When they had gone, Stella dressed, cold to the caress of the expensive lingerie, the silk blouse and business suit. All fitted perfectly, all had been planned. Staring into the mirror she examined her puffed lip, her bruised cheek and discoloured eye. Yes, she understood. She had been used. Wileman now had the threat of a rape charge over Caswell and her hatred of him. Hatred enough to kill. She shivered. If they were capable of doing this just to trap Caswell, what might they do to her if she failed them? Yes, she understood. With hatred came self-loathing and fear.

CHAPTER 2

Her back to the door, Danielle fussed over the kitchen worktop not realising Sean had entered. For seconds he surveyed her trim outline, then joined Rebecca, his hormonal fourteen year old daughter, at the table.

"Hi Dadda," she said, not looking up while frantically scribbling homework.

"Breakfast!" Danielle called. "Eat now or be late for school."

"I've gained half a pound," Rebecca said. "I don't do breakfast."

"Half a pound for a young woman is nothing, please eat your cereal, it's slimming." Danielle placed croissants and coffee before Sean as Rebecca scooped cereal onto a spoon, holding it in the air while still scribbling with her other hand.

This appeared to satisfy both and Sean glanced between the two, his gaze slipping slowly from Danielle, her slight smile, her boyish face and pageboy hair cut always a pleasure to see. At forty he figured maybe he had started suffering middle-aged fantasies, for he never failed to imagine a sensual presence in her eyes, same time he also saw a barrier forbidding him to cross. Something about her stance, her manner and strong will made him suspect. Camilla, his ex-wife, had found Danielle through friends. Sean had no objection, she kept house, cooked his meals, looked after Sophie during the week and both girls when Rebecca visited weekends. Not that male desires had ever nudged him to cross the unspoken line, but he suspected Camilla was vindictive enough to have deliberately set him up to share house with a mature twenty-nine year old PhD student with preference for her own gender. Who cared? She was a great cook. Pity she had handed in her notice, her study time in England having run its course.

Sophie strutted in, posing at the threshold, one hand on her hip, the other against the frame. She wore her new prep school uniform, box-pleated skirt, white blouse and primrose tie. Sean felt pride and love brush the world aside.

Danielle clasped hands. "Oh Mademoiselle, vous êtes elegant et si belle. What style, what poise – please to join us for breakfast."

Sophie's model walk was not textbook. Sean kissed one cheek, Danielle the other.

"So my first week at boarding school," Sophie said. "But I am taking my computer games." She drew a yellow play station from her skirt pocket.

Sean placed an arm to encircle her shoulders and Sophie leant her head against him. For seconds he closed his eyes. All Camilla's demands for private schooling in exchange for unrestricted child access were worth such moments.

"My eight year old little girl is growing up, leaving home."

"But I'll be back next weekend, every weekend we're not visiting Mum. So just watch out."

"Yeah, well I'm going to be a real meanie. When Danielle leaves, the housework gets left so when you two visit you'll be scrubbing, washing and cooking."

"Dadda." Rebecca looked up, chin on curled fist. "Don't fib, you wouldn't do that. You're the biggest softy going. And we love you for it"

"Children, who would be a father?"

"You would Dadda." Sophie hugged him. "Because we know you'll get a lovely housekeeper to do everything while you take us to the theme park. But if you really want us to work ... but you wouldn't, would you?

"OK so I get a housekeeper, but who's going to look after you, my little sweetheart?"

Rebecca shuffled books into a briefcase and stood from the table. "Don't worry, Papa, she's got big sister to mind her." She came round the table, her fitted skirt high over mid-thigh.

"That skirt's too short," Sean said, sitting straight.

"Father, get real." She helped herself to a Ryvita. "I'm wearing 70 denier black tights, they're the decency item. The skirt's simply for school rules. Tell him, Danielle."

"Les filles seront toujours des filles et les pères, toujours des pères. Eat and be happy. Tomorrow skirts maybe long and computer games a bore." She sat sipping coffee while the girls ate. Concentration lasted two minutes.

"Dadda, take us somewhere special next visit, please. You know Bradley took us for lunch at the Park Lane Hilton in his new Mercedes, then to the cinema. So you gotta do better."

Sean grimaced at visions of his ex-wife's partner, a pink shirt, highlighted hair. "Let's be original. Let's sightsee London top of a number 9 bus."

"Cool." Rebecca cracked another biscuit and moved from the table. "Can't wait to tell my friends."

Danielle stood and started stuffing textbooks into a monstrous shoulder bag. "OK, mademoiselles, we are late. Cases in car. Make sure you have your school work."

Sean watched his two daughters gather equipment as they hurried from kitchen to hall, assembling coats, cases, sports bags and carriers. He hated this moment. It was Camilla's method of absent torture. The school was only forty minutes away. Danielle could have fetched and carried, she had time. He rose when Sophie came for her hug.

"Miss you already, Dadda," she said, clinging around his waist.

"Miss you too, little sweetheart. Have a good week." She stretched on tiptoes as he bent to kiss her.

Rebecca came next, embracing with both arms, her cheek against his chest. Silence said more than words. Sean kissed her head. "Take care, my lovely. Call mid-week."

"Rely on it. Bet flash Brad's never been on a number 9. Love you, Dadda." She returned the kiss.

Sean watched them depart in Danielle's ancient Citroen. He felt sadness. His girls were growing up, soon they would be growing away, vulnerable to what lay out there.

* * *

The new warmth of early spring and the tranquillity of the English countryside gave Sarah little comfort. For the first time in her career she was perplexed by indecision; to tell her partners of Richard Caswell's unscrupulous behaviour in marketing PKL shares, or join in his deceit. Torn between conscience and ambition, even on her walk she found indecision over which path to follow. Her normal route to the right led through pine and dappled sunlight, the left fork traversed meadowland to Rattlers Wood, a place of dark and heavy deciduous trees, a place never visited.

She chose the left fork. Logic told her it was foolish, she would be late back for her meeting, late back to reveal that for two years PKL had used subliminal psychotic induction to influence sales and make their games the best selling in Europe. With substantial shares and sale distribution rights, her company had much to lose.

"This way gives me time," she spoke in whispered excuse as she walked, her hands thrust in pockets, her gaze on distant sheep. Inside her jacket she clasped her mobile, occasionally turning it in her fingers. Why walk to a place she did not know if not to gain time? She put her indecision down to conscience and a desire to escape. Since reaching level ten of the PKL video game and entering Princess Kay-ling's Garden of Serenity, the compulsion to visit Rattlers Wood had grown steadily. She enjoyed walking into the unknown to explore where the inhibited feared to tread. Like the use of Ben, her young gardener. Why shouldn't she satisfy the licentious frustrations of a single woman nearing middle age? It kept her slim and conscious of appearance. She desired more eccentricity in her life than addiction to a computer game, even if such addiction had resulted in making her a wealthy woman. PKL was heading towards becoming the best selling computer game ever; providing they didn't get caught. She picked up a stick and thrashed the grass.

"How could you be so stupid, so greedy?" she said aloud, as if Caswell was beside her. Five days ago she had felt pride on reaching level ten. The first person ever, the first person to walk through the gate into Kay-ling's Garden of Serenity. But for the first time also, the screen showed graphics without action. Without the distraction of moving characters, her keen eyes became drawn by the flickering pulse of words which read the same as the constant thought in her mind. Buy PKL shares. Realisation and anger came immediately. Throughout the hundreds of hours playing PKL, Caswell had influenced her to buy PKL shares. She held thirty percent of their stock. To tell the truth would cripple her finances plus those of every shareholder.

Richard's denial had come with sharp anger.

"Rubbish. Absolute fucking rubbish," he had shouted. "You're losing it woman, becoming addicted with visions of fantasy. It's a game, not real. Maybe we should check your distribution contract for a mental health clause."

But when she downloaded the following programme, the Garden of Serenity had been overwritten. More suspicions; and still he had not agreed to an investigation.

Ahead of her, at the boundary of Rattlers Wood, raucous crows tussling on the ground caused her to hesitate. Go into the forest or turn back?

Puffball clouds dotted the sky and the air was still, perfumed with the scent of spring. Sheep dotted the meadow. Looking one way she saw the perfect rural setting but looking the other way she found more crows sitting on the wire, all watching her with bright, hard eyes. Those on the ground fought over the carcass of a dead ewe, the victim of some rogue dog. They picked out its eyes, flapping their wings and squabbling while plucking putrid flesh.

Sarah turned away. She wanted the solace of rural England, not its dark side.

A fence post gave support as she braced herself to precariously straddle long legs over the wire, finally hauling herself onto the far side. She had no right to be there. Rattlers Wood was private land, the property of some trust or forestry company. The sort of place she liked to visit with Ben. Sex had always been a favoured indulgence, particularly with someone fifteen years her junior. Sex gave a break from computer games, from the stress of business and money. It gave the woods new meaning and a reason for her to explore new places. Somewhere here was a spot for future use. She had visualised it in her mind, a vision which had been there for weeks, as if in a dream. It was a Kay-ling kind of place, a circle of trees where grass lay open to the sky. A beautiful and secret place, a place of sanctuary.

Without sheep the grass grew calf deep and then gave way to new bracken interspersed with areas of flat leaf mould. The smell of budding foliage grew intense. Within minutes of moving from the boundary she was totally enclosed by trees. Her sense of isolation became overwhelming, as if the world outside had been severed, her thoughts and conscience free to decide. Accumulation of wealth could not be used as an excuse, she thought. She had morals, ethics. Children and young people played these computer games. Subliminal psychotic induction had the premise of evil.

She found the clearing within three hundred metres of entering the forest. It was as she had imagined, tall grass and warm sun in a surrounding wall of leaves. She had seen it many times. Where? She thought, how?

"Buy shares, visit Rattlers Wood," she whispered. "Oh dear God! No."

A branch cracked and bushes rustled. Sarah stood motionless, listening to a second single crack of dead wood, realising she was not alone. She saw him over her left shoulder, a square faced young man, clean-shaven, his mouth open, his eyes staring, no movement, no expression, as if a wax dummy.

"Knew you'd come," he said. "The Colonel is always right. I've been watching you, waiting days for you to get here."

"What do you want? I don't carry money," Sarah said, unable to prevent a quiver in her voice. Should she run? She was no longer fit, instead she fumbled for her mobile.

His speed was startling. As he closed the gap between them she screamed, her feet slipping on damp leaves. Next moment she was thrown full stretch on the ground. One of his hands pinned her throat, strangling her voice as another hand unfastened her trousers. He was immensely strong, stronger even than her terror. She thrashed, punched and kicked, her half-choked cries startling crows out of the trees and into the sky. The next moment he twisted her over, her face rubbing into leaf mould as he lifted her legs, yanking her trousers around her ankles.

"Welcome to Zoby's world," he said, pressing her shoulders to the ground. She screamed again, screamed to the crows and the empty forest, feeling the brutal pain of him thrusting inside her.

CHAPTER 3

Traffic jostled for position both sides of the motorway, never allowing Sean to test the five-year-old Mercedes allocated from the motor pool. Cars were constantly swapped between team members so no outside observer knew which vehicle belonged to whom. The front hubcaps were missing, one wing was re-sprayed, but the engine purred to perfection. He allowed an hour from his home in St Albans to the team's covert operations office in Cricklewood. An hour of thought and contemplation, mostly on his work, but frequently on his ex-marriage and access to his daughters. Camilla claimed her infidelity had resulted from his neglect and constant absence at work. His crime, she insisted, and counter-accused with accusations of his own infidelity. Though innocent, he knew such accusations from an operational view point would be hard to disprove. In the balance lay unrestricted access to his daughters. For certain Camilla stayed determined to play the offended bitch and kept a constant presents by her insistence on Danielle to innocently intimidate and frustrate with French charm, beauty and sensual presence, a temptation from which he stood forbidden; plus her insistence on private education to cripple his finances. The rewards were no legal recriminations, no open court battles to twist his daughters' love, instead he had them most weekends, had their happiness and the chance to see them grow.

Such thoughts drifted between car noise and the constant ring of his mobile, mostly from his office in Cricklewood, but this time from Cobbart, his boss.

"Sean, have something for you, urgent."

Sean drove straight to the Serious Organised Crime Agency headquarters in Pimlico. The message had been urgent.

His chief's office lay in its usual shambles of organised chaos. Files were piled high, the desk littered with notes and computer printouts ready for shredding.

Chief Superintendent John Cobbart sat in an untidy bundle of pinstriped suit, dandruff and half-rimmed glasses, his manner gentlemanly, his expression inscrutable. Sean gave respect to the man, he even liked him, but the divide of seniority always remained.

"How are those girls of yours?" Cobbart asked, waving him to a seat.

"Growing fast." Sean sat. "One already thinks she's a woman."

"Ah, for days of long ago," he paused. "You remember Superintendent Sammy Sinclair?"

"He had a bad end." Sean visualised the man, balding, red-faced with a gut bulging from an enlarged liver. He had once lectured when Sean was a cadet at Hendon Police College. The man had shown a sharp-witted brain; drink only kills so much of a person.

His boss pushed the papers on his desk and looked uneasy. "He was a good copper, one of the Old Boys. And that particular club are unhappy with the way he was treated."

This is Masonic, Sean thought uneasily and said, "Suicide is a lonely, desperate act. The man drank himself to hell."

"He had his reasons, though I question whether he made his own exit."

"The coroner said he did."

Cobbart's expression changed and for the first time he looked human enough for Sean to realize the man suffered emotions.

"Sammy had a daughter, Lizzie, from a marriage long in pieces," Cobbart said. "Lovely child." He shifted in his chair, eyes downcast. "She was my goddaughter. A year ago Lizzie was murdered. I want you to investigate it along with another unsolved murder. At the same time, I want the true circumstances surrounding Sinclair's death. I'm certain they're linked."

"SOCA doesn't do murders."

"Not officially, not unless they're involved with organised crime." Cobbart cleared his throat. "If you solve the tragedy of the Sinclair family I can guarantee the Old Boys will be forever grateful. Don't under-estimate that gratitude or their power."

"I'm a new boy on the block, John. I'm not a Mason, not part of the Old Boys' network and I never will be. Besides that, I've Operation Back Door in progress."

Cobbart's big white teeth appeared in the troll smile from which he earned his nickname, a cynical smile edged with devious interpretations. "Operation Back Door is looking at the trafficking of assassins for use by organised crime, correct?"

Sean nodded. The guy knew it was correct.

"Perhaps one of those assassins has been used in these murders."

"Unlikely."

"But possible. Therefore I'm letting Operation Poor Girl run in tandem with Operation Back Door. I've even managed to get limited funding."

Sean sighed. He had no doubt of the power and influences that Cobbart and the Old Boys represented. He also had no doubt he was being thrown into crossfire between the politically correct paper fillers and the Old Boys' Club. From either side he was on dangerous ground. At the same time, Cobbart would not have placed this on him without absolute trust in Sean's loyalty. Shit.

"What of the other murder?" Sean asked by way of acceptance.

Cobbart's expression showed brief satisfaction, then darkened. "Like Lizzie, the other woman was attractive and successful. When Sinclair retired on medical grounds, he investigated his daughter's death and linked both. Each killing was extremely brutal; both women were computer buffs. Both the killings were in London and both are on the shelf. That is totally unacceptable."

Sean clenched and opened his fist. Gangland killings were one thing, psychopathic butchery something else. What made it more difficult were the logistics. If Cobbart had managed to open and fund two abandoned cases and encroach on a third without consultation or approval of the original investigating teams, then he was probably on the very outer edge of the official system. Poor Girl was going to upset people and tread on toes. "I'll need access to the case notes," he said. "That means liaising with the Met. Whether or not these murders are open or shelved, the CID won't welcome my interference."

"Have no fear, I can guarantee the investigating officer's full co-operation."

"Who's he?"

The man sat back and for the first time smiled with real pleasure. "She is Victoria Lawless."

Sean sagged. "You sure pick 'em, boss," he said, visualising her face, attractive, intelligent, pushy, an expert in the use of a beguiling presence. Cobbart would have been no match for her. "I heard she made DI in the Met."

"Briefly. Her boss was Charlie Creech."

"She worked for that arsehole?"

"I'm glad you share my sentiments, but she's a tough lady. She investigated both London murders and might have solved them if Creech had not ordered her to arrest the wrong man. Lawless resigned, as she resigned on principle from SOCA. She's now a spook with MI5 and equivalent to chief inspector. Creech's suspect walked free but Creech became a tabloid hero by accusing the courts of weakness. Hence he shelved both files as solved but awaiting justice."

"Then I can count on her co-operation?"

"Better. When I took these files from Sammy's house I used the Met's CRIS computer to check a few facts. Somehow she got knowledge of it because two days later she was sitting in this office flashing those big dark eyes and showing enough leg to gain an old man's full attention. She has downtime and is free to help."

Not a good idea, Sean thought. He kept his expression bland when Cobbart pushed two A4 files towards him. Clearly Victoria's tactics remained consistent, as did her understanding of male gullibility.

"Try this contact number." Cobbart passed a card. "Her contribution will be invaluable and, more pertinently, it gives her a golden opportunity to shaft Creech."

You and her both, Sean thought, but said instead, "I trust she will accept this is my operation?"

For the first time Cobbart looked uncertain. "You're handling an SOCA investigation, she's MI5. Both female victims suffered the most appalling violations. For Victoria this will be justice for her gender. But I'm sure two senior officers like yourselves will find an amicable solution."

CHAPTER 4

Mark hunted on the streets, his stride positive, his bearing military. He took pride in knowing he was the best, always pristine, pressed grey slacks, well-cut blazer and regimental tie. He wanted to feel good this bright morning but the pressure was balling inside his skull, imploding into a black void of frustration. He blamed the blonde girl on the dance floor. She had laughed, had walked away calling him a liar, had left him cut by the jagged edge of her scorn. Bitch. To get himself right he tried to distract himself with images of Cindy Bradshaw. He visualised her beautiful face, her beautiful body, the firm swell of her breasts beneath his hands, but all he got was the blonde girl laughing. One day he would kill her, like he had killed the others, like one day he would kill Cindy if she ever became a hostile. But he knew that was impossible. Last time they met, Cindy had smiled at him with big blue eyes. She had touched his shoulder, her breasts brushing his arm. Cindy was the perfect female and one day soon, Cindy was going to be his. What he needed in the meantime was enemy action, an interrogation or some close-quarter combat. On this bright morning, somewhere near, there had to be a hostile.

He found her in the Strand near Trafalgar Square. She sat on a rolled up sleeping bag begging from passing office workers. She had tattoos here, there and everywhere. She wore rings in her upper ears, rings in her lips, studs in her nose and tongue. Mark wondered if maybe he should melt her down. He smelt her body, a sharp, rancid odour. A small rat dog lay beside her.

"When did you last have a bath?" he asked.

"Don't get personal, mate. A quid will do."

The imperfections of this creature brought a sense of nausea. Was she a hostile or a potential recruit? He had to test her, change her and restore his faith in female perfection. He had two hours spare before work, also a place in which he could secure her and later practise his techniques in training and obedience. "Want to make real money?" He heard the tone of sincerity in his voice, sincerity gained from lessons at drama school. He felt confident in his ability to deceive.

"I don't do sex," she said, her lip curled.

"From where I'm standing, you don't have sex to offer."

"Piss off." She reached for the dog which growled in guttural menace.

He would have kicked her, but at 8 a.m. the pavements were getting busy with early workers. He smiled a little and tried to keep his brain cool as he produced two, twenty-pound notes. Her punishment could wait. "I'm looking for eyes, not tits. I'm not interested in what's under your clothes but what's in your brain."

She drew up her legs and wrapped them with her arms, hiding what figure lay beneath two T-shirts and baggy jeans. "You're standing on my patch, geezer. Either give, or fuck off." She looked away.

Mark dropped a twenty-pound note at her feet, nodding in satisfaction when she snatched it with the speed of a darting lizard. Her expression changed from bored indifference to cunning.

"Plenty more where that came from. No sex, I just want you to beg, and watch."

"While you jerk off, bloody weirdo."

Mark felt the vacuum of a black void hollowing into his brain. Now he would make her suffer, truly suffer. She would end up screaming. He elevated the situation to live engagement. Objective one - penetration of hostile confidence. His smile widened. "Lady, I got a hard shell and you are rightly suspicious, that's good. I wouldn't be interested in a sucker. Truth is, I'm recruiting for MI5."

Then she laughed. The noise was a screech on stale breath that soiled the very air he stood in. For Mark it confirmed his suspicions, she was a hostile. No Brit woman would smell the way she did or foul the air with her stinking breath. Cindy's breath was pure and sweet, the kiss of an angel. This smart arsed bitch was an alien whore. He let his smile grow wide.

"Not so far-fetched as you think, miss. Street people are perfectly suited for unobtrusive surveillance. If you watched the building across the road, who would notice? If I stood here for even five minutes, I'd be sussed immediately. It's twenty minutes walk to Thames House, Milbank, MI5 Headquarters. You get forty pounds for the walk. Fifty pounds for an interview. Your country needs you, lady."

"You kidding me?"

Mark shook his head and held up the remaining twenty. "I kid you not. You any idea how many terrorist groups operate here?" he said, and watched her stand, watched her come up for the bait. She was maybe eighteen, maybe older, definitely female in a scrawny sort of way.

"We're gonna stay on the pavement, always in full view of everyone?"

"Down Whitehall, past Parliament, past Lambeth Bridge to Thames House. Straight through the middle of law and democracy."

"Give, and you're on." She reached for the twenty.

He drew the note backwards, enticing her hand to follow, ensnaring, playing her on the line. This was so easy. "When we get there. You're not stupid, neither is MI5."

"Don't mess with me. I want a tenner now before I go anywhere."

Mark tore the note in half and pushed the Queen's head into the neck of her T-shirt. Would she scream as she died, would she not? "You get the other half on arrival, plus an extra twenty for expenses."

The rat dog shifted round to her feet, staring upward, one paw raised, waiting on its mistress to decide her move. Mark had confidence, money always swayed the disbelievers no matter what bullshit he gave. Something for nothing was a great persuader.

Mark started to walk away. Inside he could hear himself laughing, hear the boy who was hiding where no-one could see. His prick was rock hard. Would she follow? He heard her call, heard the dog bark. A moment later she was beside him, sleeping bag slung over one shoulder. Using mental monotone, he spoke to the Colonel over the combat radio inside his head, a radio that had been there since he was a boy. "Stage one successfully accomplished, Colonel. Hostile defence penetrated. I will now consolidate position ready to secure prisoner. Anticipated interrogation time, two days."

"Go to it, Zoby." The Colonel's answer also came inside his head, came back over the combat radio fastened permanently into his brain, a radio which had been there for as long as he could remember.

"Name, rank and number?" he asked her, but the words came out as, "What's your name?"

"Me mates call me Sisshy."

"What's your real name?"

"Does it matter? Sisshy will do fine. What's your name?"

"Darley," he answered. "Captain Jez Darley." He put a guiding arm to her shoulders as they crossed the corner of Trafalgar Square, dodging traffic until safely in Whitehall. He felt the thin shoulder blade beneath her T-shirt and wondered how it would crack. Her odour was pungent, a dank smell of stale clothes and body. He hated an unhygienic hostile. When they got to the flat, he would scrub her, scrub her with a hard brush until she came out militarily clean. He would curry the dog, make the girl beg for her food. He smiled at the idea but did not report it to base.

Again she laughed, that hoarse, screeching laugh that was instantly irritating. "Jez Darley. What sort of ponce name is that? Sounds like some dickhead celeb's name."

"Ex-regiment. I was SAS." He quickened his pace. The black void was back in his head, spiralling incessantly through his thoughts, cutting communication with the Colonel. "Before that I attended medical school." He spoke in a clear, clipped voice mimicked from speech therapy tapes, hoping the hostile would not realise his radio link was down. He had to play cool, had to play steady.

"A spy, a doctor! You'll be a bloody prime minister next." The ass screeched laughter again.

He hated her, this filthy shank of female meat that never stopped talking, rattling in his ear like an incessant drone. Soon he would teach her the purity of restraint, gouging her body as she screamed her life into silence, the same way his mother had screamed into silence. But then his mother always screamed. Screamed more when she lay burning, too drunk to rise from her bed, too drunk to move while he fed the flames with vodka, his back raw from her scrubbing. "Bitch!" He stumbled. The dog yelped.

"It's a dog." The girl was there again. "Don't kick my dog."

He was lathered in sweat. They were passing Parliament. He remembered nothing of walking down Whitehall. "MI5 keeps this place clean," he said. "We check each member for terrorist connections."

"Bastard politicians." The girl flicked two fingers. "Least I'm an honest beggar. What do those sods do but fiddle their expenses?"

Again Mark tried radio communication and failed. The vibes from this hostile really screwed him. He was speaking, he heard his voice clear and distinct. "Ask not what your country can do for you, but what you can do for your country. If you undergo the test, lady, if you pass, you can do a lot to put these bastards down. I've fought in Afghanistan, Africa, Iraq. I've undertaken covert missions from the Colombian jungle to the Arctic."

"What test?" She stopped on the pavement, then trotted to catch up.

"The usual to join any organisation. Medical, IQ. Then if you really want to go for it, selection. If you do that, you're on a grand a day." As he hoped, beyond Parliament and

Victoria Tower Gardens, away from shops and offices, pedestrians gradually thinned to none. To their left lay the black swathe of the Thames and the far embankment.

"A thousand a day?" Once more she stopped, the dog also. "If you're fucking with me, I really know how to embarrass a bloke in public."

Mark looked back at her and tried to decide. They were alone here, the pavement deserted, but if he gave her a good kicking, it might draw attention from passing cars. Better to get her to the flat, stay with mission schedule. The owners were holidaying for two weeks. He could gag her, enjoy her for days before she died. He smiled, hoping to convey reassurance. "That's what I'm on. It takes time to get there, but serious money can be made once you complete training. You start off as a watcher then end in T Branch, counter-terrorism, or maybe K Branch, serious crime and espionage."

When she caught up he crossed the bottom of Lambeth Bridge. He loved this spot, this place so close to MI5. "There it is." He pointed to Thames House, keeping on the opposite side of the road as they walked the tree-lined embankment. He felt certain of re-establishing communications here. He always managed communication outside MI5.

"OK, gimme," she said, holding out her hand, following along the stonewall dividing pavement from river.

"When we get to the flat. That's over Vauxhall Bridge in Kennington." He passed the last of the trees and looked across the river, along the embankment on the opposite side, to MI6. He was waiting on a call from MI6, waiting for acknowledgement. He was the universal soldier, it did not matter what agency employed him.

"You think I'm going to some flat, you're out of your box." She came behind, her voice rattling, irritating, seriously getting him annoyed.

"OK." He turned to her and produced the second half of the twenty-pound note. "Here. If you do the interview you get another fifty and the bonus I promised."

"You're having me on, ain't ya? What's your game?"

He hated her. He wanted no more questions. She was a hostile, he wanted her obedience, he wanted her to understand discipline, the rigors of combat, of interrogation and pain. He had suffered, she must suffer. The beatings, the humiliation. He wanted her in pain. "Come to the flat and find out, you get fifty for the test. That's seventy quid, plus what you got already." He tried to smile but the pressure inside his head left no strength for animation. She was before him, hand out, begging, offering her stinking body.

"You ain't got seventy quid, have you? You're all mouth. You were never in the SAS. MI5, my tits. You're a dickhead."

The void dissolved as the Colonel spoke with clear and precise orders. "Immediate action, eliminate hostile."

He was surprised at her lightness. Clutched by the chest and crotch, she went up like a beanpole, her rattling voice turning to a scream as she sailed over the embankment wall. It took seconds. He was unable to see her fall all the way. The cessation of her shriek came when she entered the dark water of the Thames below, then silence. The dog started yapping, nipping sharp bites to his ankles until he scooped its twisting body and hurled it out over the river. Then he had total silence.

"Hostiles down," he repeated loudly to the Colonel, watching a car which had stopped by the kerb.

"You bastard." The passenger door began to open. A fat woman stared at him. "You threw a dog over that wall. I saw you."

"She annoyed me. You going to do something?" He moved towards her. The woman shouted and slammed the door as the car moved off.

Mark sucked on a forefinger where the dog's teeth had bitten. Smart-arse bitch, who cares about a couple of dogs? He ran to the wall, hoisting himself to look over. Twenty feet below, brackish water rushed in tidal current, its surface unbroken, empty of life. "Enjoy your bath, Sisshy," he repeated aloud and dropped back to the pavement, suddenly annoyed. What right had she to leave him? Now he had no-one. No one to play with, never anyone to play with. In the end they all went against him. "Returning to base." He spoke to the Colonel on the combat radio in his head. He wrapped a clean handkerchief around his finger while walking back towards Parliament and the West End. "Returning to base," he reported to no-one. "Combat proficiency proven. Zoby is number one."

Richard Caswell sat in the PKL conference room hearing the traffic from below, his elbows on the polished glass table, his fake smile encompassing the development team. For the first time in his life he made serious money and the last thing he wanted was a bunch of nerds going moralistic on him. Before him were some of the best creative minds in the business, minds that covered programming, psychology and graphics. He wanted their skills but their professional ethics he could do without, and for that he relied on their greed. They were paid double the salaries given by competitors. Richard had an unshakeable faith in greed. Wileman's prediction had proved correct.

"Listen, guys." He kept his arms on the table, his hands open as if he was embracing them all, yet speaking to each individual. "PKL is a computer games company. We keep our edge by being first at the research frontier. That costs money, so we contract out to others. Part of that research contract is in subliminal psychotic induction for security purposes. We send that research to our clients across the pond. It belongs to them, not us."

"It's illegal," Joan Hincks said. She looked at him from a pinched face, her hair in a straggly knot, her figure loose and sloppy beneath ill-fitting clothes.

Richard improved his smile for her. Hincks was important to him. Ever since her recruitment to PKL he had consistently remained the absolute gentleman in her presence. That and his city suit style all helped his impeccable image as the hardworking entrepreneur.

"I'm aware of that, Joan," Richard said and glanced through the glass at her knees. "The use of SPI is illegal. Our client, Dr Stella is using this research to form barriers she can offer against the unscrupulous use of SPI by rogue outfits. Look at it as a vaccine. You use a virus to protect against a virus."

Dr Klass with beard and sockless feet tapped his fingers on the table. "We are currently experimenting with an image lasting one hundredth of a second. There is no brain in the world able to consciously read that. But subconsciously, yes it does. It's dangerous."

"My point exactly. So we need a computer to read it also and lay a defence, and that's what this is about."

"But we are sending it over the Internet as a virus. Don't you realise the implications?"

Richard smiled at the chubby bearded doctor and longed to punch him in the face.

"That virus is sent to targeted volunteers, people who are aware of what is happening. You yourself volunteered as a guinea pig, Dr Klass." Richard turned to Snibbard, his project manager. "What was this week's colour?"

Snibbard looked through his folder. "Green," he said. "Next week's colour is yellow."

Dr Klass looked down at his green shirt and pursed his lips. Others round the table smiled.

"That's the extent of our influence, Dr Klass. For the last days, SPI over your computer has been suggesting you wear something green. Nothing sinister in that, and you did volunteer. Jill, you were a target this week. How about you?"

Jill Faulkner gave a tight grin and crossed her long legs. "That's a secret between me and my hosiery."

All laughed as Richard winked and tapped his nose. "So it should be. I see other guys wearing green, some who don't." Richard opened his hands. "Proof that what we do is harmless. Every person at this table had been sent SPI suggesting that they wear green, but every second person also had an anti-virus sent with built-in defence. Hence half of you wear green, while half don't."

Klass raised a pedantic finger. "But if used by a trusted supplier, one of the global networks, it would enable them to bring subliminal induction to mainstream software. Users would have no defence."

"Doctor, our trials and research are used by Stella in defence of any unscrupulous body doing just that. All the big anti-virus software companies are probably researching the same. You notice the increase in flash advertising on our screens. Some may believe they can just step further, then further. We need to be prepared, we need defence. Buy breakfast cereals is one thing. But what about pay your taxes, vote fascist, obey the police?

We're talking about Western democracy here. And it's that ideal which Stella is looking to defend. Do you honestly believe a global provider with the wealth of a third world country would do anything to tarnish reputation and hence profits?" Richard sat back looking round the table deciding it time to play avarice against principle. "Our research facility is unique. I've a dozen PhDs on line everyday looking to join us. We're a fun company bringing joy to people through games like PKL and Killing Field. Loosen up, guys. In two weeks our work will be finished and there's a five million dollar bonus riding on the outcome. That's five million dollars shared between each person around this table. Anybody want out? The choice is yours."

"Providing we stay within the law and the ethics of our professions," Klass said.

"No problem." Richard sensed his smile spread over clenched teeth. "In return, I emphasise the binding terms of confidentiality and non-disclosure written into all our contracts. Should anybody think of breaching that confidentiality, their professional and financial demise will be draconian. Mention SPI research in conjunction with PKL and you'll be financially dead." He leant forward again and opened his hands. "So before I confirm payment of your five million dollar bonus structure, do we have any dissenters?" He watched them squirm. "Then all are agreed. Part of a five million dollar bonus will be paid to each who stay the course. But our research must be fully operational and with a single master copy on flash drive within one week, that's our deadline, the bonus hangs on these conditions."

Richard watched Klass shuffle with sheepish capitulation and felt gratified that there was nothing like greed to set the right moral tone.

"OK ladies and gentlemen, back to work.

The meeting over, Richard flexed his thumbs behind braces and looked out the window of his Shoreditch office. The sixties building was not his idea of a grand palace but it served well as a city business address. He had a three-month lease left on two floors, plus a flat, coupled with a six-month lease on PKL's industrial unit out in Milton Keynes. For the purposes of respectability, cost and administration, both buildings were ideally sited.

Snibbard approached as the others left, his exophthalmic eyes veiled by thick spectacles.

"You watch that Klass," Richard told him. "You're the project manager, arseholes are your responsibility."

"Don't worry, Rich. He wants the money." Snibbard spread both hands, his eyes staring from a pale face beneath a domed head, his body sagging round the waist. "They have no idea about the hotels or what I put into the end-product."

"For both our sakes they'd better not. We're on to a good number here, Snibbsy. Design and marketing are mine, but programming is down to you. Don't get fucked up by some moralist prat. Certain parties would not be pleased. Oscar Wileman likes his research kept very confidential. If he even suspected what we really did, well I wouldn't want to think about it."

Snibbard shrugged. "Don't worry, it's no problem. The Stella woman's got no clue of our venture in Brighton. All programmes can be overwritten within four hours. In three months we'll be multi-millionaires. We won't need Wileman, like we stopped needing Sarah Finch."

Richard felt a brief clutch of false emotion. "She's dead. Don't say anything against the dead, Snibbsy. That girl was special."

"She knew."

"That was your fucking fault."

"I can't hide SPI if there's no screen movement. You're the artist and graphic designer. To reach level ten you need eyes that could see a speeding bullet. She saw it."

"Is that why you did her, to shut her up? If for one second I thought you had any involvement, Snibbsy, then old friendship would be tested." Richard pointed his finger watching the other visibly cower.

"On my life, Rich. I told you, told the police. Never. I was here when it happened. So were you. How could it have anything to do with PKL or her discovery of SPI? She met some nutter in the woods. She was in the wrong place at the wrong time."

Richard put a hand on Snibbard's shoulder. "Buying a thirty percent stake in PKL showed her as gullible, too gullible. Sorry for my suspicions."

"I feel too, Rich." Snibbard's hooded eyes blinked. "But no player does anything they don't want to. I only put in the suggestion. SPI, that's all it can do, suggest."

"The world is full of weak minds, Snibbsy. It's also full of greed and lust. That's why we'll make a fortune. But sharp eyes see, so we gotta stay loose. Be ready to cut and run."

Snibbard stretched his lips in imitation of a smile. "Well, I meant to mention that, Rich. Sharp eyes have given us another little problem. I loaded a new virus into the Garden of Serenity but because the garden currently has little action, I slowed exposure from one in every twenty-fifth of a second, to every half a second. In all the trials no-one saw it, but they had normal, human eyes. This girl isn't human. She opened the gates of Serenity, same as Sarah. If anyone does that, next time they go online, my station is automatically flagged, like it was with Sarah."

"Don't tell me she's seen something?"

"She sent me an e-mail asking why she had to buy shares. Your design, Richard. If a player opens the gate, it's pulsing right in front of their eyes, every half second for a twenty-fifth of a second. What are we going to do? I never thought another person would get there. She's the fourth."

Momentarily Richard covered his face. This was not part of his plan. "Overwrite it with; you win PKL shares. Then email her a prize, plus a programme to reformat her hard drive. I'll get publicity to arrange a presentation."

"That may be difficult. She's a bloody nun, in Ireland. What if she goes to the police?"

"Maybe she's corruptible. Nuns who play PKL ain't ordinary. What do you bribe a nun with?"

Katherine glanced across the convent library to ensure she would be undisturbed before starting to copy the final level of Princess Kay-ling on to a flash drive. Once complete, she then removed the copied file from the hard drive as she did every night.

Later, alone in her room and huddled beneath bedclothes, headphones on ears, she rattled dextrous fingers over a play console sneaked into the convent a year ago. Time and again she planned to replay her final triumph at reaching level ten and the gates of Serenity. Now the flash drive was successfully loaded, she went back to the Kay-ling chat room and entered her password.

Crystal's elfin figure appeared at the edge of the screen and his words in the box.

Welcome Sister Katherine, and once again, congratulations.

Don't call me sister. I've told you, I'm a student, not even a novice. She typed.

But you are devout, young and beautiful.

Crystal, I shall get cross if you say such foolish things. Katherine again glanced across the convent library, fearful the silent words might leap from the screen and shout deceitful presence. She took comfort from Bridget and Teresa, both bright eyed and industrious, their fingers tapping over keyboards, pale skin reflecting the light of Holy Scriptures. Katherine hoped the same light reflected on her own countenance. By the window, Sister Beatrice snoozed in the glow of a warm Irish sun. Katherine's attention returned to the Internet and the PKL website. Crystal's answer had appeared.

You are only the fourth female to reach level ten. How do you feel?

Sensing pride and ignoring her guilt, Katherine typed expertly. Unbelievably happy, like I've completed a marathon. She glanced across at the nun who shifted in her chair, fingers laced over ample belly. But I am perplexed and cross. When I finally reached the Garden of Serenity, the gates opened and in their centre words were flashing repeatedly. I only saw them because there were no moving graphics. I could not decipher them at first as they flashed so fast. But when I concentrated long enough, they became clear. Buy PKL shares. Ever since I started PKL I've wanted to buy shares, but I have no money. Has this message always been there? Why should I buy PKL shares?

The return words appeared almost instantly. They should have read – you have won PKL shares. They are part of your prize.

I don't understand. What prize? Katherine looked fleetingly to the room fearing someone might see the small elfin figure sitting in the corner of her monitor.

To reach the Garden of Serenity means you have extraordinary concentration and skill. Download the final episode to flash drive. It will contain instructions to claim your prize. You must have your photo taken. You have only one more test.

Katherine slumped. There was always another test. Since downloading the first game a year ago she had spent hundreds of nocturnal hours battling the enemies of Princess Kay-ling. PKL had become like a spiritual drug. She didn't really want to do it, she shouldn't do it. But, something compelled her. She was hooked, she knew it. Staring at the screen, she tried to reconcile her faith and her unfathomable obsession to win. She had blamed innocence and lack of knowledge. But now she was uncertain. Could flashing images affect the mind? She realised something fundamental had shifted in the structure of her subconscious. During past weeks, Princess Kay-ling had stayed in her thoughts day and night. During prayers, during mass, through tutorial and calligraphy practice to devotions and evening prayers. Each night she could not wait to resume the game. Crystal had materialised from nowhere the moment Katherine had first entered her e-mail address, enabling her to download PKL for free. He came as a tiny elfin figure with gossamer costume. Always he appeared over the edge of a buddy-box or lounging round the screen. Should she believe him?

Are you a virus? She had typed.

I'm from the game. I'm part of the game. I am Crystal, companion and messenger to Princess Kay-ling. But I am also your mentor and servant, Katherine. When you downloaded level one you passed back your e-mail address and I was assigned to you. I came with the file. When you e-mailed your picture, I knew how you looked. On level two you filled in details for your combat clearance. Age, height, gender, occupation, clothes' size, remember? I thought we were old friends

Katherine managed a smiled. Very clever to play on my emotions. Do you promise me what I saw was a genuine mistake? Should I report it?

You have, to me. Now I know your concerns I'll be able to deal with them. I have sent you the last episode of Kay-ling's battle. This will overwrite your last download.

What about all the other copies I have? I can't play on the library computer so I take them to my play-station upstairs.

Are there many?

Lots. Everything from start.

You're not supposed to download them.

I'm not supposed to play them either, but I do.

You must bring them to me when you collect your prize, trust me Katherine. I will send Zoby for you.

By the window, Sister Beatrice snorted herself awake and looked with benign eyes to her three students before rising to her feet.

I must go, Katherine hurriedly tapped the words.

Download tomorrow night, you must meet PKL face to face. You must accept her reward. Saturday would be good.

Katherine came out of the private chat-box and went straight to the site for Trinity College, Dublin. She clicked her mouse over the departments and onto the Book of Kells. By the time Sister Beatrice reached her shoulder Katherine studied detail of the illuminated manuscript.

"Such devotion, my child, does you credit," Sister Beatrice said.

"Is it not beautiful, Sister?"

"And available through the wonders of this machine. But, I thank God I'm too old for its complications. They baffle me."

"I can show you, Sister. It's easy when you know how, and you can reach the world."

"I thank you, child, but no. I prefer the cloisters of God's walls. Come now, it is time for prayer and supper."

"Sister, my hands are causing me pain again. I need to visit the chiropractor in Dublin. My father will pay, of course. Do you think maybe, next Saturday?"

"I'll talk to Mother Superior, but I'm sure it can be arranged." She displayed her own small, withered hands. "Pain in the fingers is the bane of a good calligrapher. To illustrate a manuscript is to give suffering to Christ."

"My time of suffering is yet to come, Sister, I'm sure."

Katherine completed shutting down the computer and rose from her seat, brushing the skirt of her convent uniform. On her cheeks she felt the fusion of heat, in her pocket the newly loaded flash drive.

Crystal sat back from the keyboard and closed his eyes on visions of Sister Katherine. She knelt before the altar, her naked breasts and long, white limbs bathed in candlelight. He laid back his head, his breath coursing over wet lips, his fingers splayed. He had seen two of the others naked, but not this one. When she became his cyber slave, then he would see her stripped and tethered by Zoby. For moments he shivered, waiting for licentiousness to pass. Eventually he returned his attention to the office computer.

The file he selected contained Princess Kay-ling's final quest, the whole four hour sequence infused with a strong, subliminal psychotic induction pulse to obey Crystal and trust Zoby. He attached both as files and emailed them to Katherine along with a note.

It is imperative you return to and re-enter the Garden of Serenity. Kay-ling awaits you. She will send her trusted charioteer, Zoby. Do as he asks and you will end in God's grace while obtaining two thousand euros for your convent and three thousand shares in PKL. This goes to all contestants reaching level ten. A just and rightful reward. He signed it Crystal. When the e-mail had been sent he deleted it from file and started a second message to a different address.

Zoby. Immediate action required to secure and interrogate hostile. Subject young, beautiful and claiming purity. Need to confirm virginity. Acknowledge mission acceptance. He signed it, the Colonel.

Crystal sent, then deleted his message, switched off the computer and left the office. He returned again at 6 a.m. the following morning. Zoby's response sat waiting in a chat-box.

Mission accepted.

Crystal tapped on the keys. Look for photograph, money and mission schedule in usual drop-box. Digital footage required as previous. Mission start, immediate.

I await your orders, Colonel. Zoby sent back.

Colour identification, yellow. If she's fully indoctrinated, she'll have something that is yellow. Mission code, Clean Cut. Again Crystal sent, and then deleted the message from file before closing down. At six in the morning no-one saw him drift through the empty Shoreditch office. Should there be any future incrimination, the use of PKL's main office server via terminal 3 would only add confusion. He felt safe, confident.

On this bright morning, Mark Harrison strolled the pavements resplendent in blazer and grey slacks, his shoes polished, his shirt pristine. He saw the people around him, ordinary people, the kind he hated. He hated the shit heads who had turned down his application for Sandhurst, who had failed him on selection to the Marines, on selection to the

Paras. He hated the dumb idiots who had failed him first year in medical school. He hated the headmistress who had expelled him for fondling young girls. He hated the probation officer who had sent him to a psychiatrist. He hated his mother whom he had burnt alive when he was ten years old, but most of all he hated his soldier father who had never acknowledged him. Then he saw Cindy outside Travelpath, his agency situated under the towering American Stock and Commercial Bank. Mark let the miasma of hate slide from his mind. For the first time that week he felt OK. Cindy sure had a lush figure, soft, round and slim. She was everything he wanted; beautiful, rich, a market-maker on the trading floor, a real wheeler-dealer. He tried not to think of her husband; her husband made him angry.

"Miss Cindy." He tapped her shoulder. She turned, startled. He saw surprise in her eyes, or maybe fear. He didn't want her to be afraid, not yet. He wished he could squeeze her breasts, he longed to squeeze her breasts. "I was going to phone," he said. "I managed to book the Lake District's most charming yet secluded cottage. Got you a good deal with boat hire thrown in."

"Mark, that's so neat." She squeezed his arm and he flexed his muscle.

He loved the way she said, that's so neat. "Specially for you, Miss Cindy."

"My husband will be delighted. This is our first anniversary. The chance of a few days together is so rare."

Mark tried to keep his smile. "I did it for you." He hoped her husband fell out the boat and drowned. He was going to kill him anyway. The day after the jerk got back, he would kill him. "I did it for you," he repeated. "Everything just as you wanted, spent hours on it."

"And it's appreciated." Again she touched his shoulder. He thought she would kiss him. Her eyes were shining, big, beautiful, blue eyes. He bet she wore really expensive lingerie, silk or satin, designer stuff. He couldn't wait to get his hand in her knickers. "If you e-mail your credit card details and address, I'll get the whole package hand delivered to your home."

"That's so neat, thank you, Mark."

He watched her smile. When the time came he knew she would submit, they all did. She waved and headed for the bank, merging with the crowd who entered the glass and marble hall. Smart, snappy people with money and ambition, Mark knew he could take them all. He had reached grade ten of Killing Field. Mark reached grade ten on all the video games Crystal sent him. Mark knew he was top-dog, and wouldn't Cindy know it soon. But first, he had his mission.

CHAPTER 5

Sean climbed the stairs in an unmarked warehouse off Cricklewood Broadway. The building had almost become a second home throughout the Back Door operation. The Serious Organised Crime Agency fronted it as a pharmaceutical sales company; the neighbours believed it. When Sean entered the central office, DC Heidi Greenshaw, the administrator for Blue and Red Teams, sat tapping computer keys.

"Hi, boss." She looked up at him, her plump little face cherub and pretty.

"Where is everyone?" He indicated the empty room.

"All beavering some place."

Sean checked his watch. "Call them. I have something real nasty. First briefing at 1700 hours. I want everyone here."

Sean entered his cramped office at the back of the unit and threw the two files for Operation Poor Girl on his desk. Letters and memos were stacked neatly to one side by Heidi. Sean sat and opened the top file. The photo showed the mutilated corpse of a once beautiful woman. He visualised the blank face of a spectre in darkness and weariness was replaced by determination. He had a target; a person who shouldn't be on this earth.

Sean gave full concentration to the tragic demise of both women, each attractive, intelligent and ambitious, each forced to a degrading and violent death. Sinclair's obsession for justice became understandable, as did his frustration over the lack of police co-ordination. Sean observed an absence of notes leading to the days before Sinclair's death. Notes missing, or never made. Periodically he heard the comings and goings of Red Team who occupied the same building, the starting crank of motorbikes, car tyres squeaking over concrete in the shared vehicle pool below, the occasional laugh, blasphemy, chirping ring of numerous mobiles. Twice he phoned the contact number for Victoria Lawless, both times finding her unavailable. The second time he left words on her voicemail. Whatever his own incoming messages, Heidi deemed them unimportant because she left him in peace. When he entered the Ops room at 1700 hours, the whole of Blue Team waited expectantly. He carried with him copied files of Sinclair's suicide and the two murders comprising Operation Poor Girl. Inside he felt totally focused. Cobbart had given him a specimen that made the assassins from his other operation look saintly.

"In case you were feeling overworked, the troll has landed us with a possible suicide and two murders."

"We don't do murders," the voice came from Detective Constable Sims. With choir boy looks and cheeky eyes he would have passed in school uniform as much as in his seriously casual clothes.

"For the record, we're searching links to organised crime and the possible involvement of an imported hit-man." Sean looked to the corner where Sims sprawled in his chair. "Off the record, it's a favour for the Old Boys' Club. They want to reactivate the files independently of CID, more pointedly, independent of the Creech mob in East London. After reading current information, my mind is open, but off the record, we have a gut-ripping serial killer."

Sean glanced to the faces of the nine men and women comprising Blue Team. Some wore jeans, some were booted and suited.

"Can we assume Poor Girl and the Back Door enquiry are linked?" DS Diane Sutton spoke from the rear, arms folded over a full bust, her body heading past its best.

"Yes. John Cobbart is crusading for his old friend Sinclair. Cobbart was Godfather to his daughter. In that respect he'll give all the help he can but funds are tight so any time given needs positive results. We give Poor Girl priority for three full days, then after we've gathered initial facts, you'll only come in when needed. I'll do the rest. We begin with

Sammy Sinclair's suicide. It's nothing to do with organised crime, least not on the surface. So no-one say it, just do it."

"I thought he was a piss-head," Ali Hussein said.

"One of the murder victims was his daughter. She also died in Stoke Newington. In fact, father and daughter died within a hundred metres."

"That's Charlie Creech's manor again. He ain't gonna like us." Jan Rice stretched her long legs. Lean and small busted, with a boyish ambiance, Sean figured maybe she and Danielle had something in common.

"Consider him the enemy. Sinclair publicly accused Creech of incompetence. Probably for that reason, on Sinclair's demise, Creech sent only one junior DC to investigate the scene. Maybe the lad picked up everything, maybe not. Ali, Bob, I want you to find out." Sean moved across the room and handed a file to Bob Howells. "Sinclair believed there was a link between the two murders, also that this killer operated under external orders. If so, it's organised crime in our back yard. Unfortunately, he gave no reason and some of Sinclair's papers are missing. If we can prove Sinclair's death was the result of defenestration, we have ourselves a case. Bob, Ali, try and find out. "

"What if Creech blocks us?" Ali asked.

"Go behind his back, use the crime report information system at Bramshill. Get an excuse to interview the DC. We're the Serious Organised Crime Agency, Charlie Creech is an outdated head-banger lost in a 60s TV script. OK, first case Helen Carter. You may have heard of her, TV presenter and journalist, mainly on high tech and new innovations.

Again she had all the attributes of Lizzie, looks, personality, yet also a private person. She was a declared lesbian who welcomed and received full media attention because of it. Jan," he walked over, holding out the file. "I'm not being sexist, but you're the best informed to have insight into her mind."

"Thanks, boss." She raised her eyes and took the file. "Always knew dykes had a use."

"More than that. When you prove Charlie Creech wrong, your knee in his bollocks will be twice as painful."

"That's bribery." She grinned and opened the file on a picture. "Fucking hell." She slammed the cover closed. "What bastard did that?"

"The person we search for." Sean looked to the room. "Helen Carter was stripped, tied and whipped, repeatedly raped, then finally beheaded while kneeling on the floor of her own living room. Both ears were cut off. Her ordeal lasted three days. Chad," he looked to the West Indian. "You work with Jan."

"Pleasure, boss." The velvet roll of his voice passed on an audible smile. "I just love to cuddle with Jan."

"I have a good reason to choose you, Chad. Helen Carter was of mixed race. Her mother is from Trinidad and stayed her closest confidante. From the report, the lady doesn't take kindly to white policeman."

"No problem, boss. Little black ladies are my speciality." Chad's grin widened. "Hey, Jan. This time we smoke your fags."

"This time you keep your hands off my butt."

"Enough," Sean cut in. "I'll look into Sinclair's daughter Lizzie myself. But for general information this is the brief. Another quiet academic girl, close to gaining her doctorate in Information Technology. Her murder took place in Abney Park Cemetery, Stoke Newington. Again, turf belonging to Charlie Creech. For those who don't know, Abney Park is an overgrown Victorian shambles favoured by foxes, rabbits, winos and the dead. What Lizzie was doing there, nobody knows. She lived in Hampstead. June eleventh last summer she was stripped, raped then cut up over a tombstone. The press linked it to devil worship. The investigating DI for both London murders was Victoria Lawless who, some of you may remember, was once a sergeant with SOCA"

"That prissy petal working for Charlie Creech?" Diane said. "I don't believe it, the girl was political."

"Going from SOCA back to the Met CID is not easy. She was looking for an opening, he was looking for someone to tread on. She ran both the Carter and Sinclair files, she believed both were murdered by the same man, but was never allowed to finish her investigations. Under media pressure, Creech dragged out a convenient scapegoat, one Edward Mears, a convicted burglar and rapist. The evidence against Mears was purely circumstantial backed by a confession under duress. In her usual, bolshie manner, sweet Victoria resigned in protest. Mears, of course, walked free, but Creech played to the press as the hard-nosed copper let down by a soft judicial system. He made it obvious the killer had been caught and set free. The tabloids loved it. Creech became a celebrity and our gods promoted him to superintendent. He's now behind a desk but controls his manor like an outdated warlord. Both murders went to the back shelf."

"What of the beautiful Victoria?" Jan asked. "She'd be spitting venom at Creech. She's got info we need."

"Victoria quit the job but got taken by MI5. She's now a spook with the equivalent rank of DCI. And you're right, she's eager to shaft Creech. She's agreed to help our investigation."

"More likely wants to run it," Diane said

"If she's a spook, she might well have other motives." Simmy spoke without his usual smile. "She could fuck our security."

"Leave Victoria to me. If she's here to play games, I'll soon find out."

Victoria Lawless sat in a Spartan room and observed the woman opposite. Alice Sibree had the exterior of a professional bureaucrat, her tailored outfit and bland face able to fit on any committee or board of enquiry. To receive her total concentration was unnerving. Victoria shifted in the chair and uncrossed her legs, wishing she had a worn a longer skirt, hoping the trickle of sweat down her back would not show through her crisp white blouse. She had dressed for smart comfort on a hot day and had bound her thick dark hair into its customary French pleat, knowing the style gave boldness to her small, classical features. She wanted to impress. Alice Sibree did not sweat or wear makeup. A protracted silence hung between them before Victoria spoke again.

"You're asking me to go beyond the pale."

"It comes with the job. Occasionally every industry demands its pound of flesh. The Secret Service is no exception. But from past involvement, on this occasion your flesh is the most suitable."

Victoria sensed a second bead of sweat course down her lower spine. The older woman was asking her to enter a web surrounded by predators. She saw it as a possible compliment to her operational skills, or her use as cannon fodder. "What if their killer strikes again?"

"Leave him to the police. From start the real objective of this operation is deniable. If, as I believe, Starways is involved, its financial, legal and political defence will be formidable. MI5 will not spend resources defending a hopeless position. They will close the door, Victoria, leaving the sacrificial victims outside. That's you and me. I may be the temple priestess, but my throat will be slit along with yours. Alternatively, with success, the rewards to your career in MI5 could be significant. Your loyalty will not be forgotten. You will be giving to your nation the ability to infiltrate and control without the subject's knowledge. We can spread a lot of good. Think of the positive directions in which we might guide the inmates of our prison services, our citizens on benefit, our hoodies, our rioters, those who should know better."

Victoria shifted in her seat. Those who should know better could equally mean the civil service, the security forces, the politicians. She swallowed and stayed silent. "What exactly is the brief?" she asked.

"This operation is to manoeuvre events, minimise police damage and covertly lift the WorkWell research ahead of anyone else. That includes our American cousins, the CIA and the FBI. No doubt they all watch, but I want our finger in the pie first. This is your golden opportunity, my dear." She smiled but Victoria saw no sincerity.

"I would be directly answerable to you?"

Alice nodded. "Only me."

"OK," Victoria said. "But on condition that, if the killer is one of them, I have the right to terminate."

"Not if he's the principal player. It might compromise our objective."

"You would allow another woman murdered?"

"You have a sharp brain, Victoria. Don't cut yourself on it," she paused. "As in all nations, those who govern and control our country have an inner sanctum, the Community. That community has much to offer those who go the extra mile. Keep that fiery temper of yours under control and leave vengeance to God. He's never far away. Your time will come when our objective is secured."

Victoria re-crossed her legs and felt sweat catch on the back strap of her bra. She suddenly realised if the room did not rate the air-conditioning switched on, no-one had booked the room out. The meeting was off record.

Sean agreed with Victoria's suggestion they should meet in an Italian café off Church Street, Stoke Newington. He considered it close enough to the crime scene and neutral enough for neither to lose face. The clink of spoon on cup, the scrape of a chair and hiss of espresso steam, along with the chatter of echoed voices, gave no chance for eavesdropping. Mothers, kids, workers, students, all gave the place normality. Victoria presented the same image he remembered, a good figure, smart clothes, her eyes bright and inquisitive. It was the same image that had tempted him two years ago to love the person beneath. In the first seconds of eye contact he realised her appeal had not diminished.

"I recommend the cappuccino," she said, and without waiting for a reply called his order to the counter.

"Black coffee," he countermanded and sat in the chair opposite, watching the twitch in her smile.

"When we did our undercover training together, you always drank cappuccino." The smile became warm and seemingly innocent, if he hadn't known her from old.

"Times change. You still sleep in clam-tight pyjamas?"

"Only when I'm on operations with a large hairy male beside me. Other times I have a preference for silk." She paid the waitress three pounds. "My treat." She smiled again, raised carefully plucked eyebrows and snapped closed her purse.

One up to her, he thought and felt himself mellow.

"How are the girls?"

"Rebecca's in rocket mode. I swear her skirt hitches higher by the hour. Sophie, thank goodness, is still a child."

"Trouble is, little girls grow bigger every day. Hope they're not giving you too hard a time."

Sean sipped from his cup and detected the sensual smell of her perfume over the aroma of coffee. "I have a mature nanny, she keeps house and looks after the girls with best friend love. She's French and her cooking is magnificent." Victoria's eyes widened in mock surprise. She knew that, he thought, and wondered what else she had researched on his personal life. That his bank balance was always stretched by school fees, his clothes past their throwaway date and his mortgage hovering on arrears. "How's it with you?" he asked. "Hear you left the job."

"Principles are hard to live with. I'm now a spook; K Branch, serious crime."

"Active or administrative?"

"Covert mainly. Not a lot different from SOCA." She sipped coffee then touched a napkin to her lips.

"And this operation?" Sean watched her eyes come up, big, brown eyes that locked onto his. Cups clattered on nearby tables and the espresso machine again hissed steam.

"Business ... in a very personal way. Like it or not, MI5 hacks all main police computers including the Met Crime Report Information System. When Sinclair, and then Cobbart, lifted details on my casework, I got an automatic e-mail. Out of the blue came an opportunity to clear the record. I talked to Cobbart, made downtime, and here I am."

"You want to screw Creech?"

"In a most unsavoury manner."

"So, where do we start?"

"Sinclair was murdered," she whispered, glancing at those who sat nearest.

"No proof."

"He was a serious alcoholic and probably suffered from acute depression, but you must remember, he was also a member of the old school. A good Mason, in the right lodges; a good club member, and for most of his career, a good copper. He may have shot himself, may have taken a long swim out to sea, but jump from the window of a derelict council flat in Stoke Newington, never."

That's what the Old Boys would think, Sean thought. That's why they started this. "Still need proof though," he said.

"No one took a serious look."

"Two of my lads are there now."

"It gets worse, now I have another case for you. A woman has been murdered in Suffolk, the similarities too close to ignore. The murder of Sarah Finch occurred a few days ago. An attractive, charismatic and successful businesswoman in her late thirties. "Big country house, smart car, substantial bank account. She lived a full social life, but her men friends were all kept at arm's length. She was a private, independent person. At the same time, she had eight computer cash and carry warehouses plus a vast army of sales agents spread all over the country. She shifted more computer games than any other dealer. For her, everything was business. Her one weakness was a young lad who looked after the garden and who confessed he was her toy-boy."

Sean watched her eyes momentarily close as she shuddered, then let go of her breath while looking round the bustling café, looking to the people lost in the buzz of conversation over TV, football, the price of petrol and the scratch on their car.

"He cut open her stomach, disgorged her entrails and cut off her breasts. Suffolk CID believe he tried to imitate Jack the Ripper. However, so far they have drawn a complete blank. Over one thousand people have been interviewed, including all male associates, all possible enemies. They have no linkable forensic evidence, no prints, no comparable DNA, no hate-mail, no stalkers, no nothing. Their conclusion is she met her killer by chance. Someone who then slipped back into darkness."

"Suffolk won't like our interference," Sean said.

"We play hoping for their help with shared info. SOCA going to the local boys for assistance is good for their image. SOCA pushing in will make you no friends."

Sean glanced as the café door burst wide under power of a baby buggy. It preceded a woman wearing a short T-shirt and baggy tracksuit, her blancmange body quivering with each movement. She occupied one hand with a cigarette, the other with three, pre-school children, all of them whinging.

"Poor woman," Sean said.

"Stupid woman." Victoria rose to leave.

"You ever talk to Sinclair?" he asked, when they emerged into the warm sun, heading for Abney Park Cemetery.

"On the phone. He grew to be a nuisance, always telling me how I should run the investigation. I know the girl was his daughter, but the man became obsessed. In the end I refused to accept his calls. An assistant faxed him weekly. When Creech arrested the wrong suspect and looked no further, I think it broke Sinclair. That's when he started his one-man crusade."

They passed through high cemetery gates, into an area of clipped lawn sprinkled with winos and the homeless. Sean let his solid frame guarantee their disinterest. Beyond the inner gravel path lay mausoleums, crosses and marble angels, a necropolis overgrown with vegetation and stunted trees. Nothing was visible of London save at the far perimeter. A council block thrust its roof above tree level.

"Jesus, this is ghost forest," he said, looking either way along a track which followed the walled boundary.

Victoria hoisted the strap of her shoulder bag. In bright sunlight he noticed she shivered. "London cemeteries are a world within a world." She started to walk. "This one is no longer used except for the occasional family interment. The council has no money. They can't look after the living, never mind the dead. But it's patrolled occasionally."

He followed along the path. They saw no other human being, only scraggy shrubs and graves. Even noise of traffic failed to penetrate save as a distant rumble.

"You came here, without protection?" he asked.

"Only once. I got flashed within twenty seconds. We may appear to be alone, but I guarantee there's a concealed masturbator every ten yards. Necrophilia is in vogue at the moment." Victoria turned from the main path to a sidetrack, hitching her skirt to step carefully between the undergrowth. "Grown back a bit since last year," she said. "I should have worn trousers."

Sean was tempted to take her hand and offer easier balance. Instead he side-stepped in front and trod down the brambles. He observed nice legs, her feet stepping delicately to save her tights. Either side, graves lay amidst tangled creepers that snaked over stone and marble. Nothing lay visible beyond the immediate surroundings. At the path's end, remnants of a hacked out area gave moveable room around a flat, granite top sarcophagus. Disregarded police tape still marked the crime scene.

"This place is macabre," he said. "I can't believe a bright, intelligent girl completing her PhD would run a gauntlet of winos and wankers to come here. Even to meet someone."

"That's one of the mysteries and unfortunately, graveyard tossers don't make voluntary witnesses. We carried out twenty interviews and kept a presence here for a month, undercover cops playing at winos. Everyone disappeared. It really did become a place for the dead. My guess is, she came with someone she trusted. I interviewed all her known male friends, even girl friends I judged bi-sexual or suspicious. All volunteered DNA, none matched her rapist."

"Maybe she picked someone up," Sean said, glancing to dark stains discolouring the lichen-spotted stone.

He watched Victoria shake her head, her lips pressed tight.

"She died between 9 a.m. and 11 a.m. She had no known association in this area. Even prostitutes stay out."

"Maybe an all night party, a one night stand. Let's do it on a grave before breakfast. Girls are bold these days."

She grimaced. "Possible, but out of character. Lizzie was a good-looking young lady, but her interests lay solely in gaining a PhD. All her girlfriends, her boyfriends, spoke of her as dedicated. She didn't smoke, drink, party or go clubbing. Her only relaxation was interactive computer games, but then they were the subject of her thesis."

"Same as Danielle, my housekeeper," Sean said. "She's into the physical stimulation and mental influences imposed by intense concentration. According to Danielle, computer games can be as addictive as drugs."

"Friends say Lizzie spent thousands of hours on games. She was highly ranked, British South East champion. PKL, the game-makers, even funded a portion of her PhD. She went to head office to collect and made the national papers."

"These companies have leagues? I didn't realise." Sean surreptitiously looked her over but had a sense of reciprocal observation, her eyes on his hair, face, hands. She was weighing him, judging what, if anything had changed. He wondered if she recalled lying beside him in bed when they had played Mr and Mrs undercover, she locked tight in pyjamas, he in a tracksuit. She Miss Cool, he ready to explode as he strained against base instinct.

"They have leagues for everything," she said. "And before you ask, my investigation into PKL was incomplete, except I found they do minor research for Starways, the American systems provider. Creech closed me down before I got further. Starways probably operate sixty percent of all computer systems worldwide. That makes them ultra clean, and by association, PKL also."

Sean shrugged. "Still doesn't answer why she came here."

"I doubt we'll ever know."

"A walk in solitude, like the Suffolk girl. If the place was full of weirdos, it could have been a chance encounter."

"Again, possible."

She held herself and he recognised a gesture of self-protection, as if she felt unconsciously threatened. It gave an insight. She was not so detached as she pretended.

"If it was chance, it led to her being raped and butchered," she said, and paused. "Disembowelled, each organ cut out and placed separately. This guy knew female anatomy. Parts were missing, taken by the killer or some animal, no-one knows. The same thing that happened with Sarah Finch and Helen Carter."

Sean lifted both hands from the embellished stone and the dark stains. "Poor girl. No one saw, no-one heard; here in the middle of London." He indicated the council block, its top windows facing where they stood. The rest of the building was hidden by leaf-heavy branches.

Victoria followed his gaze. "The place is being emptied for demolition. Top flats have been deserted a year. The window you see is the one Sam Sinclair supposedly jumped from. Unbearable grief as he looked down on the site of his daughter's death. That's what Creech put forward. I've checked the whole building. It's the only place where you can see the crime scene. Lizzie had been put out by chloroform, gagged, tied then spread-eagled, her clothes cut off. If consciousness returned she would have been helpless. And if someone saw, they're saying nothing." A tight grimace appeared. "I have one factor though. One very definite, very positive identification. The DNA sperm sample from her killer matches that found at the Helen Carter crime scene."

"Why wasn't that in your report?" he asked, trying to fathom what lay in her mind. "You telling me no comparative DNA tests were run through records?"

She shook her head again. "Did you ever stop to think why I left the police, why I'm so angry? When Creech shut me down, the analysis results were still away. For reasons unknown, the system took eight weeks to complete tests. I assume because it would have proved Edward Mears' innocence and Creech a fraud. They never got to the National Crime Facility and I only made the comparison once in MI5. Sarah Finch also matches. That shows interference or incompetence beyond belief."

"You rifled police files?" he asked. "Without authorisation?"

A twist of smile appeared. "MI5 is part of the Secret Service, you know. And I enjoy that kind of thing."

"We have a serial killer."

"We have a number one juice-head, and I want him, Sean. That's why I'm here, and I'll do anything to get him. I want him for Lizzie, for Helen, for Sarah. I want to stop him before he kills again. And I want revenge for the disgust of all women who fear and wonder how this happens in our society."

CHAPTER 6

At 6 p.m. Mark parked his moped outside Cindy Bradshaw's home which occupied the ground and basement floors of a converted Victorian house in Lambeth. Pretending to be confused, he went first to the basement entrance beneath the canopy of the building's main steps and found it reasonably hidden from the pavement. The door was heavy and contained three deadlocks, one above the other. Mark tapped the frame. It was modern, relatively new and made of softwood. He thought Mr and Mrs Bradshaw sure seemed concerned no-one entered their neat little home; but Mr and Mrs Bradshaw had so weakened the doorframe by hollowing out lock-keeps, they made means of entry, just so neat.

"So neat, Cindy baby," he spoke aloud, and climbed back up steps to the front door. He whistled as he posted in their package from the Travelpath Agency then returned to his moped. He figured they would leave anytime after 0700 hours next day, which gave him plenty of time to pick the place over.

When he burgled the Kennington flat, first rummaging produced only a credit card and a small amount of cash. In disgust he defecated on the bedroom floor, then looked on top of the wardrobe.

"Can't fool me," he said, on discovering a passport plus driving licence with photo ID in the name of Jez Darley. He figured it his best find ever. The guy was medium height and compact like himself, round faced with not dissimilar features. Easy to copy. The credit card was six month old but in pristine condition, which probably meant its purpose was to hold a long-term debt at zero rate. A dangerous card to use because it might well be full, but it was handy with the driving licence and passport. He disregarded all else. Photos of the couple showed a plain woman.

"Sexless cow," he said, looking into her underwear drawer. "You gotta be 'A' list to get my interest."

Switching on their PC he found their passwords on auto-admittance, so read a few emails and got to know them better.

"Can't hide from me," he said. "You hide nothing from Zoby." They weren't married. She was Sue Raybert, her friends called her Bunny, a lawyer, he discovered. That made her more interesting. He went back to her lingerie drawer, picked out a pair of black lace knickers and pushed them into his pocket. Now he had power over her.

The ride on his moped to Willesden cemetery took forty minutes. He found the cut grass and symmetrically placed headstones gave him a sense of well being, mainly because the ground held his dead mother.

The mailbox had been his own idea. It gave a purpose for her existence and an occasion for him to stand on her grave. The black marble chips, long sullied by grime, held deposits of moisture which allowed the establishment of moss and weed. The grave bore no headstone, no identification of its occupant, just a small, inconspicuous disturbance of the surface, as if some animal had buried its faeces, or some hand clawed from beneath.

Mark whistled as he scraped away the chippings and extracted a sealed, waterproof wallet. He weighed it in his hand, rubbed fingers over the thick wad and nodded satisfaction. The Colonel could always be relied on. He had hidden once, waiting for the Colonel to arrive. When he did, he knew it was Crystal masquerading as the Colonel. It did not matter, so long as he received his money. He had watched Crystal without being seen and followed him to the tube station. He disliked Crystal, the man was not built like a soldier and Mark much preferred the Colonel, except the Colonel never came. Perhaps one day they would meet, soldier to soldier.

Inside the wallet he found one thousand pounds in twenty pound notes, full details of his mission, plus photos and ID of his target. A nun; his first. The adrenalin rush was instant, his prick became rock hard. He felt elated. The white cloth of her wimple enhanced her face to give an unblemished and simplistic beauty. He couldn't wait to find what lay beneath, what goodies would be his as he consumed her purity. Between Sister Katherine and Cindy, August looked like being a good month. Mark began to whistle and felt the sun was shining on his day. OK, time to go to business, he thought, time to organise itinerary, the logistics and acquisitions. He pocketed the wallet and removed his mobile. Walking back to the cemetery gates he dialled Travelpath. Stratton, his boss, would be dealing with after-hours customers, people on the way between work and station, pavement cattle looking for escape. Stratton was on the line within thirty seconds of connection. Mark knew he'd oblige. Mark was his best salesman and sold more holidays than the rest together.

"Bad news, Mr Stratton. I just visited my mother. She's has a serious condition. The doctors say it's irreversible."

"I'm sorry to hear that, Mark." He listened to the man's pause, his indecision. "Will you be working tomorrow?"

"'Fraid not, Mr Stratton, it may be four, five days. Cancer is like that. You never know where you are." Again the pause.

"You must do what is best. We're very busy, I have to go. Call me when you're free."

"Thank you, Mr Stratton, I knew you'd understand." Mark hung up. Stupid arsehole, he thought. Then the man was gone and Sister Katherine entered his head instead. He tried to image her naked, pristine and untouched. He began to whistle again and found a spring in his step.

Mark divided his flat between operational and living quarters. Communications and combat room lay on one side, the kitchen, his bed and trophy room the other. In the combat room he stored various equipment including a Samurai sword. He practised daily but had used it only once operationally, to behead Helen Carter. Discovering the keenness of its blade, the sudden and awesome consequence of its use had been stunning.

He recalled every detail. Sweat soaked his naked torso as he stared down at her, knowing after three days and two nights of interrogation he had her compliant. Face to the floor, her wrists tied to her neck then hobbled to her knees, she could not lift or move other than to crawl butt up. He removed her gag.

"One sound and I will whip your arse 'til raw. You want out of this then you better be totally obedient. Understand?"

"Yes." He heard her whine, heard the gargled shiver of her voice before she lapped water from a bowl. It was then she had urinated, destroying what he saw as the perfect ambiance of her submission.

"You bitch, that's against military regulations. For that you'll suffer." He replaced the gag, muffling protest as he velcroed the straps behind. He pulled up her head by the hair. "A good whipping, I think." He removed his belt, dangling it before her. "Lesbian, ha. But now you know a real man I guess you think different."

"Nummhh," she begged and shook her head, eyes wet and wide.

"And if you make one sound, I'll use this." He picked up his sword. In the Victorian flat amidst the leafy suburban streets how he had loved the way her body trembled, the shiver of her skin, the total hysteria of her muffled pleadings.
He had not planned to kill her, but kneeling at that moment she looked so vulnerable, so perfectly placed. The movement came before he realised. The sword severed her neck in one clean and precise strike so that the body sagged while still retaining its kneeling position. The head rolling sideways onto the blood sprayed carpet, its eyes and mouth open.

The Colonel loved his home movie and gave Mark a bonus of two thousand pounds. Mark cut off her ears as a keepsake and put them in his trophy room.

Combat training lasted an hour. Then dressed in fatigues, Mark cooked hash browns and beans before switching on his computer. Whistling, he downloaded the latest interactive games Crystal had e-mailed and spent the next six hours fighting Princess Kay-ling. By means he didn't understand, Crystal had given Kay-ling Katherine's face. At 0200 hours, he had beaten her to submission. His reward was her total capitulation. He felt good then, his body lathered in sweat. Mission completed, combat proficiently proven.

"OK, bitch. Time to pay the price of failure," he said and clicked the reward button.

Crystal's computer-generated animations were the best, totally different from those in the regular game. So lifelike was the presentation of his victim that Mark sensed her terror, begging for his mercy before he killed her. It felt good, but now for some reason he wanted to kill Sister Katherine for real. Her image came constantly to his mind, a perfect female face combined with the aura of virginity. When he slept that night he dreamed of her. The Colonel's instructions were explicit. Operation Clean Cut would commence 0500 hours the following morning. Mark loved that name, Clean Cut. So neat.

"Do you ever surf the Internet?" Katherine asked, her mind burdened with secrets. She pulled her legs onto the single bed and leant back against the wall. Teresa sat at the small worktable, absently doodling on a pad. She was plump, her face round and her smile radiant.

"Of course, for research," Teresa said.

"I mean, looking for other things?"

"We're not allowed to."

"I know, but do you?"

Teresa shrugged, her bright cherry lips pouting to a rose. "Sometimes," she said finally.

"I do, every evening."

"I know web addresses for sex sites." Teresa dropped the pen and swivelled ready for telling. "By accident, of course," she added.

"Of course." Katherine smiled and giggled with her. She swivelled her body, leant forward, their heads close. "Not sex, computer games," she whispered.

"I've never played," Teresa also whispered.

"I'm Southern Ireland champion, I've won first prize in the Kay-ling finals; money." Her breath felt short as she sighed with the relief of confession.

Teresa stared back, her mouth open. "How much?"

"Two thousand euros."

"What will you tell the Sisters? They might expel you."

"I'm telling no-one, no-one but you. I've wangled treatment for my hand this weekend, in Dublin. I'll collect the prize and give it straight to my parents. They've spent so much on me. The Sisters need never find out."

"You're a sly one." Teresa took her hands. "And me thinking you were Holy Jo herself. You're so daring."

"I arranged it with Crystal. I meet Zoby this Saturday at Trinity College in Dublin, and if I take my old files they will give me new ones. I downloaded final instructions this evening in the library. I'll play them tonight."

"How?"

Katherine pulled her bag from under the bed and lifted out the games-console. "Don't tell, please."

"Never. How's it work?"

"Best in the dark. I use headphones for the sound. This game, Princess Kay-ling, it's all loaded on flash drive. It's complicated so I'll show you when I come back. I have it set up now, ready for tonight."

"I can't wait to have a go."

"Don't tell, promise?" she repeated.

"Cross my heart." Teresa leant close, her voice hardly audible. "I have a satin suspender belt and stockings, I wore them last Sunday to Mass."

"You minx." Both giggled their voices half-choked with gasps of suppressed snorts.

An hour later Katherine drew the curtains and fitted her headphones. Crouched beneath bedclothes, she viewed the play-screen and moved hips with the strutting sway of Princess Kay-ling. When she switched off two hours later, her mind held conviction she must meet Zoby near the inner entrance of Trinity College, 11 a.m. Saturday. She needed to wear something yellow and take all her old files. She had never felt such exhilaration and confidence. She could trust Zoby, Crystal said so.

CHAPTER 7

In his warehouse office, Sean sweated hours over the Poor Girl file becoming more and more certain. He wanted this guy, wanted him in a box or a cell. He began to understand Victoria's emotional involvement. She had been hunting a human misfit who viewed women as objects for his sadistic gratification. Sean channelled his own anger. It was a professional necessity. While Victoria investigated the London murders, he knew she would have done the same, but forced to turn away, her anger had now become raw and deep. Even worse, it had become personal.

Without Victoria's DNA information, the Sinclair and Carter murders had only circumstantial connection. Although both carried evidence of rape, abuse and butchery, after Carter's decapitation, except for the ears, the body had not been touched. In contrast, Lizzie Sinclair had been systematically cleared of all primary organs. The Suffolk woman had her throat slit and her torso hacked open in a frenzied attack of stab wounds. Pieces were missing, but evidence showed disturbance of the remains by forest animals. He e-mailed the Forensic Science Service for the conclusive DNA match. If proof could be established of involvement by organised crime, SOCA had an ongoing op and a vicious killer, but he doubted there was a connection. Gangs rarely mutilated except to demonstrate power of punishment. This kind of savagery produced no profit. The only other link not investigated was their individual involvement with computer technology, something Sinclair had started to look at just before his death. From the page numbering, most of his notes on this were missing. Sean put it down to drunken negligence. Jan and Chad looked in at 8 p.m., enough excuse for a gathering in the pub.

One beer and thirty minutes later he headed for home. The car CD played Rachmaninov's No 2. It cleared his mind of murder, but not Victoria Lawless. He pondered on her re-entry into his life, her considerable attractions and, more alarmingly, her failure to inform on vital evidence. He reasoned the woman had allowed contempt of Creech to cloud her judgement, or more deviously, she played a political game not yet apparent.

Sean switched off the car lights and stepped out onto the cobbled drive of his detached home. For moments he stood in cynical pleasure of ownership. He no longer resented the house, just accepted the place as a burden of fatherly love.

Danielle sat cross-legged in the family room, her figure draped in a pink wool tracksuit. She waved from where she sat before the laptop, momentarily shifting her concentration from the video game she played. In her moment of distraction she was zapped.

"You're getting worse than my daughters," he said, from the doorway.

"A new business opportunity to help my thesis." She smiled and switched off. "Part is on the psychological affect computer games have on children and young adults. For some it becomes an obsession with sub-psychic influences. Because many games have no social contact, the players may become isolated and detached from reality. For certain minds drawn into deep concentration, there exists the possibility of subliminal psychotic induction. I believe this is a possible means of corrective education, particularly for computer-orientated delinquents."

"Sounds scary. You got my kids involved?" He returned her smile and watched the round, soft movement of her body as she stood.

"Sophie and Becky are keen to help." She eased past, heading for the kitchen. It left him with the sweet aroma of a woman just bathed. For brief seconds he closed his eyes and imagined.

"And the business?" he questioned, placing his briefcase in the hall and following the lure of her scent.

"Through Finch Distribution I am now a home agent for PKL Computer Games and Starways Software," she said. "I sell their products and make small money to help pay university fees."

"PKL came up in a meeting today."

"Now, monsieur, I am also part." She poured red wine for them both, placing his glass at a single setting on the table. "I discover and apply two weeks ago. Now I am accepted, they give me my own website, half price games-console and lots of free software. I will put it on your PC. The girls can also play trial games for Princess Kay-ling II. Everybody wins."

He watched her dish potatoes and casseroled beef. She placed his plate on the table then turned to the sink. "Camilla phoned, she goes this weekend to New York with Bradley. She asked if girls could stay again. I said, OK."

Sean watched her movements, watched the taut stretch of her tracksuit bottoms. "Nice casserole," he said, and began to eat, realising celibacy was no longer compatible with domestic harmony. Victoria smiled into the vision of his mind. He drew back and looked again at Danielle.

She hung up the tea towel, collected her wine glass and came opposite. He glanced up as she sat and saw the subtle smile of a scheming woman.

"I have a present for you, monsieur." She drew an envelope from her pocket and slid it across the table. "A chance for you to take your girls somewhere Bradley would never think of. A little gift before my departure."

She was looking at him over the rim of her glass. He had seen Camilla look that way. He slit the envelope with his finger. The contents took away his suspicions.

"A complimentary, half-price weekend reservation for Morrison Hotel, Brighton, one family room for Saturday night. That's great," he said, searching for excuses to reject.

"It came free with my PKL business package. They have some franchise deal. If I introduce a friend, there is free invite. So I do it over the Internet and put your name, but you must go this weekend. It is in Brighton, so you have the seaside. There is also free gym, swimming pool, sauna, and most important, the latest cyberspace games room."

"Danielle, you're very sweet, and I'm touched, but it's not for me. I have work." He placed the invitation back on the table and smiled into her eyes, hoping she wasn't upset.

Momentarily she squeezed his hand, something she had never done. He felt himself weaken.

"Think of what the girls will tell Camilla and Bradley. Swimming pool, sauna, Jacuzzi, disco. The games room has the most advanced virtual reality systems in Europe. It can only be used by invited hotel guests. The girls will love it; Bradley will hate it. My gift to a good father."

Sean reasoned with a large gulp of wine. "You're some sales lady. How can I refuse?"

Danielle stood and walked around the table. "As a French woman, I understand honour and pride, monsieur." She kissed his cheek and retrieved her wine glass. "I go back to my computer game, leave you to eat in peace." She crossed the floor and he watched the sway of her departure. In the doorway she turned. "One thing I forget, the weekend, my friend may come, it's OK to stay maybe, two nights?"

She had conned him so shrewdly Sean felt only admiration.

"Sure," he smiled reluctant consent. "Just make sure he doesn't leave smelly socks."

"Not him, her. And I'm sure her stockings will stay secure."

Realisation of macho jealousy was enough to make him think perhaps he had been alone too long. "Put the girls together, use one of their rooms," he said.

"No need. My bed is big enough for two." She blew a kiss.

Mark opened his eyes and listened, his body gripped by panic as a harsh exhalation of coarse breath disturbed the stillness. His mouth closed and the sound stopped. For moments he peered around the room, glad nobody was there to see his fear. Glad nobody was going to hurt him. He was alone. Always he found himself alone. Except today he had Cindy and tomorrow, Katherine. He saw her vision, her body cloaked in white, waiting.

Mark rose from his bed, he had a mission. At 0500 hours precisely he began his daily training and worked up a heavy, grunting sweat. Twenty minutes were spent at martial arts, ten on muscle toning. Showered and towelled, he stood in his boxer shorts before a full-length mirror. He liked the mirror, he understood perfection. Beside him, open shelving held theatrical makeup, wigs, body padding, face distorters and coloured contact lenses. He prided himself on his ability to camouflage, to slide through the city jungle without visible recognition. That meant voice change too. The voice gave persona to image and misled people's interpretation of whom they saw. During preparation he played speech tapes and practised the accents for his chosen character. He considered it essential to blend, to become a shadow within shadows.

At 0815 hours, Mark presented a beer-gutted and balding man at the intercom shared with Cindy's ground and basement flat. A male voice responded from above, clipped, impatient.

"National Water," Mark spoke into the speaker. "Bradshaw's got a leak. Might 'ave to turn yer water off, OK mate?" He wore a black T-shirt under overalls. A plastic ID card around his neck identified him as authorised fitter 304. Mark believed in giving a justifiable presence. It eliminated chance discovery and satisfied inquisitive hostiles over noise and intrusion.

"That's inconvenient." The voice became authoritative. "Do you have a key? Who gave you a key?"

"The Bradshaw's left 'em wiv the office."

"The main stopcock is under the basement steps but don't turn anything off until my wife leaves for work. Is that understood?"

"No problem, mate." The intercom went dead. Arsehole, he thought. He returned to the pavement, went round the basement railings and down steps. Under the canopy formed by the main entrance, he set down his tool bag and switched on his head radio.

"Commencing entry," he spoke into his mind-radio and checked his watch.

"Op time zero, eight, one eight," the Colonel answered.

Mark drew on surgical gloves, removed a short builder's prop from the bag and dragged out its telescopic head. Using a block of wood to spread pressure over the three deadlocks, he wedged the base of the prop against the brickwork under the pavement and pushed home the retaining pin. With the flat steel plate against wood, he began winding the screwed shaft, expanding the telescopic length of the prop until he heard the first splintering of the inner frame. Careful not to cause too much external damage and cursing in case the door was bolted, he put a further four turns on the handle. A section of the weakened frame twisted sideways, snapping cleanly where the door-keeps had been cut into the wood. Forced simultaneously, all three locks and their steel retention-keeps came free from the splintered internal frame so the door swung open.

Mark immediately released tension, folded the prop and returned it to his bag. "Entry accomplished," he spoke into the head radio and again checked his watch.

"Operation time two minutes thirty seconds, you're on schedule," the Colonel answered. "Fastest yet. You're flying, Zoby."

Mark smiled, his confidence high. The Colonel always used his nickname on a mission. He re-twisted the splintered section of doorframe so at a glance it appeared undamaged.

"Find it OK?"

The voice cut Mark's isolation and he jerked startled, recognising the nasal clip of the arsehole from upstairs. The idiot peered down over the railings, his face pumped up with class pretension. Mark relaxed, he could take him anytime. The man was nothing.

He rubbed the padding of his belly. "Any chance of a cuppa before I graft?" He stared upwards. Would the prat comply? No chance.

The man stared as if observing some incomprehensible idiot. "I think not. My wife will inform you when the water can be turned off."

"No problem, mate." Mark carried his bag into the flat. When he looked back the man had gone. "No problem, I'm just too good for you shitheads." He wondered what the wife looked like, wondered if she was worthy of special attention. He considered the possibility of paying a call. Maybe she had more to offer than tea. He closed the basement door and wedged it with his bag. For a few moments he stood imagining her submission.

"Zoby! The purpose of this operation is acquisition of mission funds. Stick with priorities."

"Sorry, Colonel." Mark smiled at the soft reprimand. "Operation proceeding."

The area gave access through to the back garden, the block floor narrowing where stairs descended from the front door and hallway above. The first room housed a small gymnasium containing a treadmill, weights and steam box. Mark stood on the threshold and allowed his mind to fill with images of Cindy pumping iron. He saw her legs spread either side of the bench. He sure hoped Cindy obeyed when he came to take her. He would hate it if she turned out to be a hostile, hate it if she deceived him. Standing there, thinking of her, he felt the mist come down and settle on his brain. He had no comprehension of how he got to the next room, but he was there, standing by French windows and looking out onto a neat garden. Light threw oblongs of sunshine and shadow over the floor and a giant, king-sized bed. The quilt and pillows were still rucked, the sheets smelling of her perfume, of her body. Her nightdress lay at the bottom. Black, long and gossamer thin. His penis swelled.

"Zoby, proceed with operation objectives," the voice sounded dry, without compromise.

Oh, oh. Colonel's getting edgy. "Yes sir." Mark dropped the nightdress underfoot and went to the bedside cupboard nearest the door. "Search commencing, sir." He rifled with practised skill, his latex-gloved fingers shuffling the contents and searching between layers. He found no money, no cards. Disappointed he started on the adjacent drawers, working from the lowest upwards, always returning everything to position. He ignored all items of value, a gold watch, cufflinks, ID bracelet. He wanted only cash or cards. Nothing.

"Shitheads." Mark fought his growing irritation and tried to dislodge the black void pushing into his mind. Where did they put their credit cards? The first cupboard he tried held Cindy's clothes, so did the second. On the third he smiled at a row of suits. Starting one end, he frisked each garment with dextrous speed, finding a wallet in the seventh jacket. The contents were a clutter of assorted dockets and scraps, but it also held thirty-five pounds cash, two credit cards and a photo of Cindy on a beach. She stood naked, immodest with hands held high, her expression one of mock surprise. He felt shocked. He did not like her posing nude in public. He would punish her for that. He tried to console himself. Maybe she had left the photo for him to find, letting him know what was rightly his. He placed the photo into an inner pocket along with the money and cards, then went back to searching.

Her dressing table came next, the top clustered with bottles either side of an oval mirror. When he pulled a side drawer, his breath slid over his tongue, catching at the back of his throat so it sounded like escaping gas. His hands hovered, then closed amidst a jumble of panties, bras and suspender belts. He shivered, fingers pushing down into the perfumed cluster, touching, testing, selecting white shorts with lace front and back.

"Told you Cindy, told you I'd get my hands into your knickers." He fondled the gusset, testing between thumb and forefinger, his tongue extended, fanning hot breath over the material pressed to his face. A small sound quavered in his throat, his groin ached so he could barely stand. Leaning forward, he clutched her underwear against his erection, his breath forming clouded circles on her makeup mirror. He wanted her so badly, wanted to enjoy her now. At that moment she came behind him and reached around to undo his zip. Her breath coiled with his own and he felt her hand in his trousers pulling him out. Her mouth had formed a scarlet O, bright with lipstick, a ready and willing mouth. She fondled him, slowly at first, then more vigorously until he saw her face, saw her laughing, and realised she was a hostile. She was trying to distract him, jeopardise the mission.

In the clear, stark silence, the sound of a key in the door and the opening latch sliced into his brain. Cindy's image vanished and he was suddenly alone. In the bright, sunny bedroom he shuddered the result of his ejaculation into the white lace held between his fingers. Twitching, he couldn't stop twitching. Hell, he was exposed, vulnerable. They had tricked him. They had returned deliberately to catch him. He threw the underwear aside and extracted an eight-inch folding serrated knife. This was his opportunity. He would kill the husband, interrogate the whore. Both were now proven hostiles, it was his duty. He tidied himself then went quickly to the stairs, the blade behind his back.

"There you are," a female voice spoke down at him. It was not Cindy. This one was stout, blonde, her hair held by an Alice band, her skirt pleated, her figure full. From the low angle, he looked upwards to the underside of her breasts. Good breasts, breasts he could do things with. "You can turn the water off now. Did you find the main stopcock under the entrance steps?"

Zoby mounted the stairs without hurry, trying to smile, trying not to frighten her. She was solidly built, she would be strong and would struggle. He needed to get her down on the floor, get her naked quick as possible.

"Mum, taxi's here." A boy of perhaps ten appeared at the flat door which had stayed open onto the common entrance hall. He stared at Zoby in silence. Zoby could see him staring. Children unnerved him, they were aliens from his past. Before becoming a soldier, he had been one of them. He knew the boy could see inside him, see him hiding inside, knowing he was there. Zoby hesitated.

"Well, did you?" The woman insisted. The boy ran off. Now Zoby was uncertain. If he stripped the woman the boy might come back, snitch on him, tell everyone where he was hiding and jeopardise the whole mission.

"Yes," Zoby answered. "Leak's in the bathroom."

"We look after each other's flats. Cindy never said you were coming. I suppose she was in such a rush with the holiday."

"Only called us yesterday." He moved closer to the last step turning the knife in his hand. "While I'm here, perhaps I can do something for you?"

"Mum! The taxi's waiting." The boy's voice carried from outside.

The woman was stupid, he could see it, deserved what was coming. He came onto the landing.

"Leave a card on the hall table. A reliable plumber is difficult to find. And make sure you lock up." She turned away from him, closing the door as she left.

Zoby waited till the building grew silent and hollow, then refolded his knife. When he re-entered the bedroom, Cindy had still not returned. He slid the drawer shut and looked around him. The room seemed oppressive. Everything weighed in on him, hating him, telling him to go. He kicked the bed. Next time, she wouldn't get away so easy. Next time he would keep her for a week.

Tool bag in hand he left, ensuring the outer door stayed wedged back into the splintered frame with no obvious sign of entry from outside.

"Operation accomplished, cards secured. Exit achieved," he reported into his head, confident the burglary would remain undiscovered until Cindy's return. He wondered if she would find his little gift, wondered if she would wear them. He couldn't wait to put a gift inside her. He whistled as he walked away.

"Operation time, zero, eight, three, eight. Return to base," the Colonel ordered.

Thirty minutes later Zoby entered a cyber café and using Darley's credit cards and the Darley e-mail address, he booked car hire and return flight from Luton to Dublin, using the three digit number on the back for security. He kept the Bradshaw card for emergency.

Zoby packed with careful consideration for his mission, particularly in camouflage and disguise. To him Ireland remained hostile territory. On a mission deep behind enemy lines, concealment within the indigenous population was imperative.

After using Darley's passport to check in, Mark spent an hour in the airport's departure lounge familiarising himself with mission requirements. Other than to destroy her files on flash drive, he found no word of what to do with Katherine, but it wasn't necessary, the whole scenario seemed as a film set laid out in his brain. How it came there he had no idea, but the vision always materialised after playing one of the Colonel's games. He guessed it was transmitted secretly over the combat radio in his head. Probably covert, Special Forces equipment, the best. Mouth open he watched people pass his seat. Families, business people, a group of girls all dressed in pink heading for some hen night. Under the floating noise of tannoys, crowd chatter and clinking cutlery he considered joining them. Fucking nine girls would be fun.

In the gents' toilet, he flushed torn instructions down a WC pan and then examined himself in the mirror while washing his hands. He saw another man there, Darley, but Mark knew he was hiding behind the face, hiding in the shadows.

I'm the strongest, he thought, because I can make you do anything I want. I could even make you kill your own wife, Bunny. Yeah, he nodded and Darley nodded back in agreement. I might just do that, after I've dealt with Cindy.

He used Darley's passport to check himself on to the plane, huddled in amongst others on the economy flight. Who would guess, he thought, looking round him. Who would guess I'm on a mission? During time spent flying he went through the facilities of his digital video camera. The Colonel would require photographs, close-ups of every detail. Zoby always enjoyed the photo session.

Zoby observed the small, square-shaped girl at the car hire company and felt the claw of nerves which came with first enemy encounter. He watched as she tapped computer keys with adept skill. He handed over Jez Darley's driving licence and passport taken from the Kennington flat. The transactions were precarious. Should Darley's credit card be full, then the driving licence would be useless. Both had to be valid or it meant drawing cash and starting again. Even worse, she might tip off security and that would mean a fast exit. She took notes from the driving licence and handed it back.

"Do you want additional insurance to cover excess and theft, Mr Darley?"

"No," he said, his accent county Irish. Excess would require additional use of the card.

She continued to tap, then swiped Darley's card through the machine. "If you fill up the tank before returning you won't be charged." She checked her watch then stared dreamily from the office window, waiting for the hire document to clatter out of the printer. When it stopped halfway, Zoby picked up his bag. In minutes he could be back in the terminal, mixing with crowds.

The girl opened the printer drawer, slammed it shut and watched it restart. Seconds later she twisted the document for him to sign.

In squiggled loops, he executed a perfect replica of Darley's signature. It could have been any name. She checked briefly with the back of the card, then placed hire agreement documents and keys on the counter.

"Blue Honda Civic, bay 43," she told him. "Have a nice day and thanks a million."

"And yourself," he said, letting her realise he looked at her breasts, letting her know his power. These cluck heads were as dumb as the dipsos back home.

Thirty minutes later he drove into the underground car park of Tomlins hotel, Dublin Central. He let them take a swipe of Bradshaw's card and then retired to his room. Alone, he switched on his head radio.

"Enemy lines penetrated, safe haven secure," he said into his mind.

"Roger, Zoby. Acquisition of ordnance to commence ASAP."

"Will do, Colonel. Over and out."

The room was basic, bed, cupboard, utility bathroom. Two pictures on the wall showed old Dublin. Zoby unpacked and hung equipment in neat order, surgical rubber boots below the overalls. Once all was stowed he checked the list of ordnance still needed. He decided to start with meat slicing requirements, then preparations to secure a quality car for the operation.

Forty minutes later he drove on the outskirts of Dublin, his imagination on the tailoring scissors just purchased. He saw them cutting soft fabric, revealing delicate white skin for his new knives. He thought maybe he would leave the veil, leave the vision of purity as he fucked her. "Fuck a nun," he said aloud, and began to laugh. He couldn't stop laughing and knew it was the boy inside having his joke. Soldiers did not laugh, they only killed.

He picked St Julian's Golf Club from a magazine, primarily because it looked expensive. The car park stood full of Jaguars, Mercedes and BMWs. The place had wealth. No recession here.

Wearing a blond wig, dark glasses and golfing gloves, Zoby sought out the pro in his shop. The pro looked pure designer with everything and anything for money.

"I need five, twenty minute lessons. You got 'em at fifty a lesson."

"The earliest slot is two weeks," the pro said, his mouth opening when Zoby dropped a hundred euro note on the table. "But I see here a cancellation, 11 a.m. tomorrow, OK?"

"I need changing room facilities," Zoby said and watched the pro write out a receipt.

"Show this to Reception. She'll take care of things."

Zoby whistled as he drove and felt the sunshine on his day. He bought a guidebook on nearby country houses and found what he needed on his third visit. Standing in the parking area late afternoon, he surveyed the near deserted ground and surrounding forest, then hoisting a large holdall, he began to explore. At the end of a side path bordered by trees, he came to a walled garden with derelict greenhouses. The place looked neglected by estate workers; a lonely place, closed and silent save for birds.

Standing for a moment, he listened to the harsh escape of his breath. "This is it, Katherine," he whispered aloud. "The place where you get to be a woman. Mind, you got to show me your spirit first. Show your fire and what you got."

Under the lichen-coated glass of the furthest greenhouse he set to work clearing a space and hammering in four heavy wooden stakes, he whistled as he laboured, as tuneless as his thoughts. He hid the bag behind potting trays. It contained the scissors, the butchers' knives, protective clothing, rubber boots, rope and masking tape. It was everything he needed for interrogating a hostile. That evening he went early to bed, went to sleep thinking of Katherine and her white veil.

Next day continued its sunny, balmy weather. Zoby felt calm and confident. Dressed in blazer and flannels, his face disguised, he presented himself at the golf club reception desk. His acquired day-pass gave access to the changing room, a clean, timber-clad place with a rear exit to the first tee. He nodded greeting to a couple of elderly members then sat fussing with his bag of kit, waiting for them to finish dressing and leave. Forty seconds later he had broken into three lockers. He felt the jagged rush of adrenalin as he searched. People were outside, people who could catch him. He found a heavy bunch of keys but as a precaution, he opened two further lockers, feeling in pockets, locating another car key then a third. At the first sound of voices from the corridor, he retrieved his bag and exited by the course entrance. He felt lucky, felt his breath calm as he approached the car park and pressed unlock on the first key. The hazard lights of a 3 series BMW blink their greeting and brought his contempt. "Too small," he sneered. The second key flashed the lights of a Mercedes S Class 500. "Yes!" Zoby raised his fist and switched on his head radio. "Transportation for mission secured, Colonel. Making strategic withdrawal." A minute later he was on the road to Dublin. He whistled as he drove, the mission was looking good, the Mercedes gliding like glass.

CHAPTER 8

Sean grunted, his eyes closed, his fingers resting against his forehead as he assessed and collated evidence relating to Poor Girl. Something sick had crawled from the darker side of humanity. It was his job to eradicate it. He drew on professional detachment to keep rational, but it didn't stop a powerful desire to put a bullet in this person. He would not fail on this one, must not fail.

The first progress briefing was at 10.00 hours. It was a relief when the time came.

Blue Team sat in silence, emitting an odour of cigarette smoke, beer, perfume and close body confinement. Across the room Victoria Lawless leant back to wall by an open window, her expression flickering defensive hostility. How she had found their address or gained knowledge of the meeting from clamped-jaw Heidi, Sean found a credit to her ingenuity.

He placed his briefcase by the Nobo board and sat on a table. "Welcome team to this bright and sunny morning. For those who have never met, may I introduce our MI5 Liaison Officer, Victoria Lawless."

The response came in a shuffle of chairs and a few grunts.

"Hi," Victoria answered, her hand sweeping to the assembly, her expression unchanged.

Sean cleared his throat and tried a different approach. "As a DI with Met CID, Victoria investigated the London murders. She's volunteered information vital to our operation. Please consider her a team member."

Again a chair scraped.

"If it's any consolation," Victoria said. "I do buy my round."

"On this team, bribery gets you everywhere," Jan winked.

Victoria smiled. "Spooks at MI5 can be useful," she said. "Mistrust and rivalry lead to a lot of cross-references being neglected or hidden. During this op I'd like to prove co-operation and trust between services can work for the benefit of all. I've been Wendy on the beat, CID and SOCA. The game rules at the Box, MI5, are also tight, but they have a different field of play. Off the record, I can access information this team would normally be denied."

"And buy your own round, sounds too good to be true." Simmy stretched long legs towards her.

"Prove it," Diane said.

"There's a positive DNA match between the sexual assaults on Helen Carter, Lizzie Sinclair, and Sarah Finch."

"How come it's not on record?"

"Ask Creech."

"I'm asking you."

"Spooks have secrets, as I'm sure you have too, Diane."

"Thanks for sharing yours."

Sean watched Victoria lean to retaliate and intervened. "It's on record now," he said. "Victoria has saved a lot of groundwork and given this enquiry a head start. Which means you can spend more time on our other objective, Operation Back Door. In all honesty, I don't think Poor Girl is involved with organised crime. These murders are too savage. Unless of course, we have a sado-psychopath as hit-man. It is not unknown. We roll with Sarah Finch. Diane," he called and waved her to the floor. She rose, arms folded over her bosoms.

"As expected, Suffolk CID regarded us as city posers. However, after Simmy bought two of them lunch and a couple of pints they did show us the file."

"Simmy spent his own money?" Jan was pointing, mimicking shock. The others clapped.

Sean waved all to silence and let Diane continue.

"The file revealed little, but we did lift names and addresses. We interviewed two of her girlfriends, plus Ben, the boy who did her garden. He was, and still is, prime suspect. My first impressions say he's a good-looking, but harmless country boy. Sarah was the kind of woman Simmy dreams of - model looks, intelligent, successful and single. Her house will sell for over two million. She had tennis courts and a Ferrari. The business, Finch Distribution, is valued at seven million."

"The car," Simmy said. "Men are suckers for a fast car."

"Perhaps because of guys like Simmy, she had no known close relationships with any men. She satisfied basic instincts using the gardener, though I doubt her circle ever suspected. For a better insight, I pushed the gardener on sex. He told me one thing the Suffolk boys didn't get. Sometimes Sarah liked to go out of the ordinary, way out. Role-playing, but mainly sex in the open, places where others might see. The boy complied, anything she wanted. But he wasn't invited on her last trip. His alibi is ninety-nine percent. My point is, this unconventional trait of Sarah's may have been the reason she went alone to Rattlers Wood, maybe looking for unusual sex in unusual circumstances. Maybe she met someone over the Internet. Outside of sex and business, all other energies were spent on horse riding and computer games. She was the principal sales distributor for a number of leading software companies, including Starways Systems and PKL, for whom she distributed through a network of home-based agents. According to her parents, she spent hours playing PKL computer games. She became league champion. But then she also sold them, so her efforts could have been for publicity. Starways you probably know of. PKL stands for Princess Kay-ling, reputedly Britain's number one bestseller. They have a second, Killing Field. Half the kids in England play PKL."

Sean wrote PKL on the Nobo board but his thoughts were on Sophie and her yellow game box, on Danielle and her agency connections. For a moment he hesitated, not speaking, caught in a vague sense of unease over links between family and crime. Too remote a connection, he thought. A thousand games outlets and half the kids in England gave PKL a squeaky clean guarantee.

"No one knows why Sarah went walking alone in the woods," Diane said. "But my guess is, she met someone over the Internet, someone she came to trust."

"That could link with Lizzie Sinclair's visit to a derelict graveyard," Sean said, and wrote Internet and trust on the board.

"Sarah Finch was aware of personal safety," Simmy added. "Her house was seriously alarmed. She trained in unarmed combat. Didn't take chances."

"Nice day, solitary walk. One of life's pleasures," Jan said. "If she was confident in her physical defence, tripping a little sex amongst the bluebells might appeal."

"I'd ask another question." Victoria's voice came from the back. "She was a horsy lady, if she wanted solitude, wouldn't she have been riding on a horse? If she wanted excitement, how about Lady Godiva? It's a lot safer than walking to meet a stranger."

Diane nodded. "Agreed. I just can't see a woman of that intelligence going to meet a stranger. If the toy-boy is out of it, whomever she met spent a long time building her confidence. It was someone she trusted."

"Did you see her diaries?" Sean asked, glancing between the two women, hoping he saw amnesty.

"All on a laptop. Suffolk CID had a look, nothing suspicious."

"Then we'll look."

"Parents have it," Simmy said

"Sweet talk them. What's on Helen Carter?"

"The Creech mob refused entry passed the gate," Jan said. "We went straight to the mother. You wouldn't believe Chad had such a honeyed-tongue. She even gave him tea and biscuits."

"I told you, Jan. Little old ladies are my speciality." He grinned at her. "I could sweet talk you, if you wanted."

Jan flicked two fingers and continued. "Helen Carter had a degree in public relations, had television beauty, a healthy bank account and a luxury house in Richmond. Declaring herself lesbian brought a lot of media attention and hence contracts. Her mother said she was simply waiting for the right man, but in truth she always had regular girlfriends, had planned for one to stay over the fatal weekend, but cancelled. It was her last known contact. She suffered three days of sexual abuse and torture. You mentioned earlier a psycho sadist. That's a bland description of the person who killed her."

"The mother is still deeply affected," Chad said, smile absent. "But she volunteered the names and telephone numbers of Helen's best friends, all women. Several admitted relationships but more interesting, all said Helen's main relaxation was interactive computer games. She played for hours. Computer games go right through this whole enquiry, boss."

"Can you get hold of her personal computer? We need to look at hard drives here."

"If the little old lady has it, I'll get it." Chad grinned.

Sean wrote computer games and put a times three. "Ali, Bob, what did you find on Sinclair?"

"Asking Creech for his bollocks would have been easier," Ali said. "With us and Jan at his door, the portcullis came down, end of story. The caretaker at the flats however, thought we were part of the Creech mob. Sinclair's death provided his fifteen minutes of glory. We got the grand tour – description of the blood, the gore, where Sinclair fell, how he found him, his need for counselling. The flat that Sinclair went out of is still unoccupied. Gets the odd dosser and the estate head- bangers, but generally remains as left. The windows are partially boarded, part broken, as is the window in question. When asked about it, the caretaker went quiet, as if we should know. That's when he realised we weren't who he thought. Says something about the Creech influence. The window is centrally pivotal, but removable. The guy said it was fixed at the time. You wouldn't fall accidentally. To jump you'd need to go sideways or push up on the sill to tip headfirst, not the sort of window a suicide might choose. A suicide would stand or sit face to the drop. That's not possible with this window, unless, of course, you were drunk and thought you could twist around. Or you were pushed."

"Any reason why he would be there?"

"Caretaker said Sinclair had visited several times. He thought the guy was suffering from drunken emotions. From the flat you look down over the graveyard. You can see the clearing where his daughter died. Real sad."

Richard Caswell wore a wide-striped city suit. Sitting in the display hall of his Milton Keynes industrial unit he watched potential shareholders tilt and swing in the twenty game seats occupying the central floor. Synchronized shrieks from players came with each sudden sway of their chairs, their faces hidden by wraparound DVD visors, their hands working controls set in the broad armrests.

Faulkner, his programme director, moved between players and without their knowledge, observed any female whose skirt was too immodest to cope with the chairs' tilting gyrations. Richard kept his own eyes on Mrs Zellar. She wore trousers but she had spoken of a possible one million investment. To Richard that was far more interesting than all the other punters together.

A combined shriek from the people before him signalled the DVD ending, their seats momentary tilted high and sideways. Behind their visors, quadraphonic sound blasted their senses while they sat locked in the virtual reality of a fighter plane, its spiralled flight flashing them through canyon, fire and tempest. It was a good show, he had spent three hundred thousand of PKL's profits on the computer generated animation. He watched Snibbard, lean forward, the little wanker's eyes fixed above the hemlines of three teenage girls whom he had guided to seats directly before his control desk.

"Two positive," Snibbard said and smirked. "Very tasty." He marked their seat numbers on a pad.

Richard guessed them to be lottery winners, too young for anything else, all of them gullible. One wore a yellow top. No need to look at her knickers. Snibbard stayed transfixed by the exposed view of their thighs. The guy was so predictable that Richard had no reservations about Snibbard's involvement in the overall plan. A combination of lust and greed made him the perfect patsy.

Faulkner walked back to the control desk. "The women in chairs nine, twelve and seventeen have yellow underwear." He moved off ready to help the female guests undo their harness.

"The new programme looks good. How many do you think we pulled?" Richard asked Snibbard.

Snibbard mused. "A load of them are wearing this week's colour, yellow. Idiots don't know why they wear yellow, but it sure gives insight into our SPI and their impressionable minds. The fighter sequence has an exposure of two prompts per second demanding immediate discussion, so let's see who starts talking and if they're wearing yellow. I suggest this afternoon we give a one-hour viewing of our new Princess Kay-ling. Again two prompts per second with the buy virus. Any who don't come over, we give flash drives to take home, then download the buy virus over the Internet. After a week viewing a few more are bound to cough up."

Richard signalled a technician to switch off the DVD show. His audience of twenty immediately ceased movement and started to take off their VR visors. Snibbard sat back in his seat. Women patted hair to shape and pulled at their skirt hems. The men tried to look macho and above it. People were smiling, a melee of voices started in unison. Only a few stayed silent and none of them visibly wore yellow. Richard pressed his monitor screen allowing cameras to survey the room and identify dissenters. He reckoned the prompt for immediate commentary had worked on at least fifteen people.

In a back room his secretary would be watching, putting names to faces, changing place-cards on the lunch table set in the pub nearby. Those who had not reacted to subliminal suggestion would be isolated. Non-receptives got eased out; the eager were given a taste of honey.

Richard stood and raised a hand for silence. "That's our product, ladies and gentlemen. What do you think?" He listened to the sounds of approval, the flurry of clapping. On a swift calculation, apart from Mrs Zellar, he judged a take of maybe eighty thousand. Influencing the greedy was so easy.

"Glad you approve." He pointed. "Because this afternoon we have a full hour of the new Princess Kay-ling game. Give this tape your maximum attention. Soon it will be in forty percent of British homes. The potential is massive, and remember, PKL is only one of ten games currently planned. Our next bestseller, Killing Field, has already topped a hundred thousand in global sales. Cinema, television, will soon be history. Interactive graphics displayed in cyber real-time along with quadraphonic audio will sweep the world."

Richard felt his adrenalin rise on the spontaneous applause. This he loved. "Our growth potential is awesome. Our market share continually rising. The new share issue for PKL II will be limited to investors like yourselves, the ordinary men and women who play these games. The mental and visual environment in which you were enveloped was created right here in Milton Keynes. No camera crews, no props, no actors, just computer generated animation at minimal cost."

The clapping came again and he threw his baited line. "Capital requirements are rapidly reaching target. Shares in the new PKL will go on a first-come-first-buy basis. Minimum investment, five thousand sterling. DVD games are the future, and PKL is the best. This is your opportunity to join us, to substantially increase your investments. You have everything to gain and nothing to lose. Ladies and gentlemen, transport will now take you to our local pub for lunch."

Richard bowed to the applause, gave Zellar the once over and watched her smile in return. For a million he'd give all the attention she wanted. She reminded him a lot of Sarah Finch. Except he figured Zellar was probably laundering for some East European mafia.

Faulkner came back. "The fat woman in chair eight has a yellow bra on." He grimaced and handed over a list of chair numbers and names.

Richard stood. "If our home-induction tapes prompted them to turn up naked, I wonder how many would?"

Snibbard grinned, Faulkner grimaced again. "We want their money not their flesh."

"Let's give it the hard rub," Richard said. "Increase the afternoon tapes to a suggestion rate of three per second."

"That's pushing it, Richard." Faulkner shook his head. "The conscious mind could pick up influence and direct it straight into thought process. The subjects might question the idea's origins, talk amongst themselves."

"Give it full throttle. We need to experiment."

Faulkner shrugged and followed after his guests who were heading for the door.

"He's right. They could realise," Snibbard said, scratching his belly.

"But they could never prove it. I want this wrapped up quickly. Any time someone might realise PKL is crap. We need their money now, Snibbsy. We can't get away with this forever. Meanwhile I'll pay attention to Mrs Zellar. She's worth all these other jokers put together." Richard looked down to his subordinate who stared across the room, his hooded eyes on Zellar's honed body. "If you want to fuck a woman like that, Snibbsy, you either got to get rid of that gut or get money."

"So what good does that do you?"

"Watch your mouth." Richard pointed, then lowered his voice to whisper contempt. "I can take a pill, Snibbsy, but no woman will accept that fat-faced body of yours, unless of course, you rape 'em, like you did Sarah Finch."

"Not me. I swear on my mother's life, Rich. I couldn't." Richard kept his finger pointing. "You forget I looked after you in Glasgow, Snibbsy. I've looked after you ever since. Don't fuck with me, because I know what lies underneath. This morning I looked at our office hard drive. I was worried about the nun. And guess what? Someone used your terminal number three to send cross-reference e-mails between Zoby and the Colonel. No staff member would have done that and the last time that happened was just before Lizzie."

Snibbard's jaw went slack, his eyes round and wide. "We better tell her, the nun."

"Tell her what, because she discovered SPI she's going to get raped and cut up? A lot of good that would do us. What I want to know is, have you been talking to Faulkner? Did you tell him anything?"

"No. I promise."

Richard pressured his finger against Snibbard's flabby chest "What if he's Crystal? What if he controls Zoby? How safe does that make us? You want to end up with that fat gut all over the floor? When we have to skip, I always thought of you and me setting up again, Snibbsy, maybe in America or Tokyo. But if Faulkner is holding something like Sarah over us, that's going to be very difficult. Think before you open your mouth, Snibbsy. Think what you are saying. You have a masters in computer technology, yet you ain't got the brains of a dead fish. Now," he looked across to where Mrs Zellar lingered by the door. "I think we'd better join our guests and just pray your nun stays whole."

CHAPTER 9

Sean worked past 7 p.m., the little office hot and stuffy, his mind clogged with detail. The Poor Girl case file had increased to a point where a weekend with his daughters was rapidly fading. It did not help when Victoria phoned.

"I've been through all my old notes on the Sinclair and Carter enquiries," she told him. "I'd forgotten some of the conversations I had with their various friends. When computer games were mentioned, all of them referred to the interactive game, Princess Kay-ling. All confirmed both played that particular game above all others, but then they would need to, it runs for thirty hours and demands intense concentration."

"Mind blowing. What do you suggest?"

"We look through them. The fact all three victims put such effort into winning may have a connection. I've acquired a complete set, plus a games-console. I suggest you do the same. They retail in most computer shops."

"Victoria, how can a DI of the Serious Organised Crime Agency possibly justify thirty hours of police time playing computer games? We have a high-tech branch, they can look."

"You going to tell them what for?"

"I don't know myself."

"Exactly, and if you don't look now, will you ever? Just thought I'd let you know. Also the office here has a sudden situation. I'll give Poor Girl what time I can but it's difficult. The good news is, next week I'm completely free."

"I look forward to it." He hung up, wondering if he had spoken words more truthful than he cared to admit. He went back to work. Thirty hours of computer games … he shook his head. Time was valuable. He already had a case for each murder to be reopened in a combined operation. If time or politics prevented SOCA from bringing someone to justice, it would go back to CID; Creech most likely. That dismayed him. Creech had no passion for truth, only personal glory. Sean picked up the phone and dialled CID's Stoke Newington office. He needed to meet, to find the full facts on Sammy Sinclair's death. Creech was unavailable. At 7.30 p.m. Sean's mobile rang.

"Hi, Dadda, it's me."

"Hi, little sweetheart. How you are settling in?"

"My bed's by the window. I share with three other girls. Julie's next to me. She's even older than Becky. Becky sends her love and would talk but she's watching Eastenders."

"Is the room nice?"

"Yes. We have yellow trim on our pillowcases and duvets and Miss Nathan gave us yellow ribbons for our teddies. She's the housemistress. She's yellow everything at the moment. Julie has a teddy too and the most amazing computer games. She's also got a laptop, she's going to show me."

"How about homework?"

"All done. Have to do it straight after tea. Julie's good at English, she helped me. She's got a PKL game console, and guess what? It's got full Princess Kay-Ling on."

Sean sensed the same tinge of unease he had experienced during the briefing. PKL was squeaky clean, Diane said half the kids in England played the game, games sold on every high street. Yet three adult players were dead. Coincidence? That quantity of public exposure would have revealed any dangers long ago. It's not the games, he thought. So what connects it with murder? He shrugged, money was the great motivator, then sex, then love. "How do you have access to PKL? Does Brad buy it?"

"No, Julie's dad has a shop. But you can download samples off the Net. We're allowed to go on providing we have a prefect in the common room. PKL give loads of free downloads."

"Do your teachers know?"

"Dadda, I'm no longer a baby. Our teachers show us how to do it. Miss Nathan showed me. If you look closely, she's got a moustache. Do you think I should tell her?"

"No, sweetheart, say nothing. Listen, this weekend Danielle will be looking after you." He listened to her long silence. Someone had been talking.

"Mum said you were taking us to Brighton. She was going to New York and we were going to Brighton. I've told everyone."

Sean pictured her face, jutting lip, terse eyes. Life was not kind. "It's work, sweetheart. I'm running an operation almost single-handed."

"Are you?" Silence.

"Sophie, if it were possible, you know I'd go."

"Would you?" Again the pause.

He knew then she had been watching her mother, knew the timing, knew just when to jab the barbs.

"My new friends were green with envy," she said. "I told them my Daddy was the best in the whole world because he was taking us to the Morrison Hotel, Brighton. Do you know it has the latest interactive virtual reality games room? And you only get there by special invitation. Kids everywhere want to go."

"Do they have Princess Kay-ling?"

"Dad, she's the best. Of course they have it, all thirty hours. But now I'll never be able to see it, never be able to watch over a VR visor with quadraphonic sound."

For a moment Sean thought he was listening to his ex-wife, but then he figured one problem might solve another. "Listen, sweetheart. I'm going to make a few calls. See if I can shift some workload, then I can come to Brighton. I'll text you soon, OK?"

"OK, as you're the best Daddy in the world, I'll trust you." She hung up.

Sean dialled down to see if Heidi was still there. "You should have gone home hours ago," he said to her

"Who's going to turn out the lights? What do you need, boss?"

"I'm researching PKL computer games. Phone Morrison Hotel in Brighton, pretend you're Mrs Fagan, say the family has a reservation this weekend but due to business only your husband and children will be there. Ask what access guests have to their video room and are all their games suitable for children, including Princess Kay-ling. For your own curiosity, I'm visiting this weekend, researching games linked to Poor Girl. Also taking my kids, but it's really work."

"I believe you, boss. Give me ten minutes."

Sean dialled out once more and connected with SOCA's high-tech unit. Researching PKL was one thing, exposing his family to unknown influences was another. He had to be certain. "Is Steve Rawlings on duty?" he asked, hoping his one-time college chum might help. That man he trusted.

"His shift starts at 0600 tomorrow."

"This is DI Fagan. I need some info. Want all you have on PKL software, anything sinister?"

"You're looking at a brand leader. We play it at home. Basics are family stuff. Higher levels are more demanding, it takes an adult. That said, granny could play. Steve might tell you more, phone in the morning. I'm the paedophile officer. We got a new ring trafficking children from Asia."

Sean put down the phone. Minutes later Heidi was back on line.

"They're really sorry I can't make it, boss, because Morrison Hotels are truly family hotels. However, Mr Fagan and daughters will be welcome. Because of the popularity of the virtual reality room, depending on how busy they are, each guest is allowed one hour a day. However, if you sign up to join PKL as an agent, you get unlimited access and free games. Everything's for free."

Sean felt cynical. "Sounds like they want to get you hooked."

"Friend of mine went in for it," Heidi said. "She does OK. The games are really good, I've played."

"Anything that could harm kids?"

"Only pride if they can't reach high levels."

"I was thinking of letting my own kids play."

"They'll enjoy it. No worry, boss."

When Heidi rung off, Sean sent a text to Sophie. Brighton here we come. Pack bucket and spade.

Ten minutes later he returned along the motorway listening to Mozart's Violin Concerto in C major. He did not hear the finish, did not realise he was home until he switched off the car engine. PKL still troubled him. Higher levels were reached only by adults, which left the kids safe but what about young women?

* * *

Sean woke early the following morning and went down to make coffee. Ten minutes later Danielle drifted by, her feet bare, her hair ruffled and her face soft from sleep. For minutes, Sean allowed himself the pleasure of witnessing the diaphanous effect of morning sun through her cotton nightdress. Some complications in his life, he figured, were more pleasant than others.

On his shuffling drive to London, Camilla phoned. He clipped his mobile to hands free and tried to remain polite in his response. Traffic around him condensed to a solid jam. The woman in the car beside was talking into her mobile with heated animation. He watched her.

"Are you listening to what I'm saying?" Camilla's voice rose an octave over his phone.

"Sure." The woman in the car seemed oblivious of her surroundings and stayed when other cars shuffled ahead.

"I'll pick up the girls from school. You collect them from my house by ten this Saturday morning. That's the latest for our taxi to the airport. Are you listening?"

"Sure." He thought of Danielle's words from the previous evening. Intense concentration by the young is capable of producing physic obsession.

"Now, when you go to Brighton, both girls are to dress properly for dinner. No jeans or T-shirts."

"Sure." Pride and the obsession to achieve drives them to higher levels.

"Don't let Rebecca sunbathe, she has delicate skin and Sophie must wear her teeth brace at night. Right?"

"Sure." Intelligent women spending thousands of hours dedicated to one game.

"I'll pick them up again from school the following Friday evening on my return. As usual, I do all the collecting and carrying. Are you listening?"

"Have to go, Camilla. Woman in the next car just swallowed her mobile."

"Don't let Sophie chew gum. My children are not street kids."

"She's trying to reach it through her ear."

"Do you understand what I said?"

"Sure, Camilla. Have a nice trip."

"Remember, Bradley and I will collect the girls from school a week Friday."

The phone switched off. The woman in the opposite car kept talking, even though the traffic was well clear in front of her. In his mind he saw Danielle crouched over her game console. A harmless game played by thousands is suddenly an obsession with three women who are later murdered. Why?

Sean looked with concern as Steve Rawlings' twenty stone slouched down on his chair with the threat of impending disaster. Scattered over the desk before them lay components from Helen Carter's and Lizzie Sinclair's computers, both units stripped to basics and interlinked by a mishmash of cables. If anything lay hidden, Sean knew this man would find it. Save for football and family, the guy lived and breathed computers. All around the room hummed with activity amidst the rattling clatter of terminal keys punctuated by ringing telephones.

Steve stroked a trim goatee beard as he spoke and Sean could see he had lost none of his shy and nervous disposition.

"The PKL games on these hard drives are different from those bought on the high street or downloaded from the Net," he said. "My guess is, the recipients were targeted."

"From where?" Sean asked.

"Can't tell. What I do know is the games were different insomuch as they were susceptible to a certain virus. The virus went through firewalls so possibly it came from a trusted supplier. Possibly even PKL."

"Why would the management put out a virus?" Sean asked. On screen he watched Princess Kay-ling's lithe and supple figure leap from the claws of a crouching dragon, her sword poised ready to strike. Steve pressed a key which froze her in mid action.

"Unlikely the management, could be sabotage," he said. "Possibly a staff member with access to systems. In truth it's not a virus because the game accepts it during auto-upgrade which overwrites everything before it. Afterwards it sits in the operating system and does not come to life until use of specific programmes. Only then does it take on the mannerism of a virus, even though it remains benign. See," he pointed at the screen.

Sean peered at the four words that were concealed within the frozen graphics. Obey Crystal, trust Zoby. "Who the hell are Crystal and Zoby?"

"Characters from the game. You're looking at subliminal psychotic induction. The players of these games were pulsed once every three seconds, that's twenty times a minute over hundreds of hours play. The suggestions would have become hypnotic."

"For what purpose? If subliminally they obey Crystal and trust Zoby, what does it do? Improve their game?" Sean could see a quagmire ahead. Convictions came from hard facts, this did not look like court material.

"That is one possible use. I suggest another. What if they then received e-mails from Crystal telling them to go to a forest, or a graveyard? And trust Zoby when they met him there."

"Three dead women." Sean felt his skin prickle and tried to rationalise. What Steve suggested was horrendous. "Even under hypnosis nobody does what they don't really want to," he countered.

"True, but being so involved maybe they wanted to trust. It's only a theory." Steve shrugged and indicated the screen. "I've a long way to go before I can prove it. Equally sinister, these viruses are programmed to disappear as each level of game is achieved. If the computers had been left in use, all SPI suggestions would have been overwritten – gone without trace."

"We have a two-man team, Crystal and Zoby?" Sean asked.

"Men, or women. Or maybe they're one and the same. I've a ton of information to lift yet. This is kind of unofficial and it needs a lot of time."

"What about the public playing PKL? What if a hotel had a private games room?"

"Wouldn't be dangerous. A system that size would have special security. These viruses came over the Internet to individuals, possibly sent by some crank or student. Neither is it unfeasible for someone to do it on a world-wide scale. Could be young women are set up to obey Crystal and trust Zoby from Britain to China."

"In PKL games?"

"These viruses clearly have a connection. My worry with this particular one is its ability to breach the computer's security. It's not a normal virus, it's accepted by the system without question."

Leaving Rawlings' office Sean realised the investigation now headed for uncertain ground. Subliminal psychotic induction and murder were an unlikely match, but the consequences if ignored appeared terrifying. He needed something more solid. The council estate in Stoke Newington slapped him back on the ground.

Malcolm appeared from the caretaker's flat in floral shirt and shorts. Pink-framed glasses and sweet cologne left no doubt. He wanted immediate recognition.

"You're a big policeman. What can I do for you, dear?" He glanced at Sean's warrant card.

Sean gave his nice-guy smile knowing it intimidated. "I'm looking for a few facts."

"The fact, my man, is that this estate is full of head-bangers, druggies and dealers with whom you people do nothing, but because I am open about natural inclinations, you're always in my face."

Sean retained the smile but removed any benevolence. "Malcolm, you've been done twice for drug dealing, three times for indecent assault and six times for soliciting"

"Everyone a total miscarriage of justice."

"Creech also tells me you're an informer."

"Absolute lie."

Sean saw the flash of apprehension and knew he'd found a truth. "The injustice, Malcolm, is what would happen to you if the dealers found out. Don't make this a bad day. Did Sinclair come here often?"

"Perhaps, I don't know."

"Spill, Malcolm. Tell me, prevent another injustice."

"I saw him twice, no more. But he may have come other times, at night. Strangers are always here, dealers, hoodies. They frightened Danny away, he never came back." Malcolm's lips pursed. He looked either way along the flats and hugged himself.

"Who's Danny?"

"No one. He slept in the flat, for favours." Malcolm shrugged.

"Was Danny here when the girl got murdered?"

Again he shrugged, not looking up. "I don't know, they frightened him away."

"Who?"

"Creech."

"Be scared if you've told lies, Malcolm. I'll be back."

Sean watched the door close then headed towards the crime scene of Lizzie Sinclair's murder, waiting on proof of Malcolm's connection with Creech. It came a few minutes later when two large, shaven-headed young men stepped from a car and walked immediately in front of him. Two more stepped from a doorway behind, a third pair came onto the kerbside. Sean realised he was boxed and though they looked like thugs, he also recognised the style. The leading man stopped before the entrance to a café.

"Boss wants to see you, Mr Fagan," he said.

With no way to side-step, Sean went inside. Creech sat in a corner, his head shaven, his suit dark. When Creech's boys came in behind, the few other customers left while the proprietor disappeared to a back room. "Still modelling yourself on the Krays, Superintendent?" Sean said, sitting opposite Creech.

"And I see you're still modelling yourself on Inspector Clouseau." Creech smiled as his boys took seats by the door. "What are you doing on my manor, scaring my people, putting your finger in my pie? First your little people come snooping, now you."

"Trying to find the truth."

"The truth is often misleading, Inspector Fagan."

"Sinclair never committed suicide. Not through that window," Sean said, watching the man's reaction. Too many lies had spun out of this fellow.

"Let me put the facts. The autopsy showed Sinclair to be six times over the limit. Maybe he didn't jump, maybe he fell. He's dead, verdict, misadventure or suicide. Who cares?"

"I do, Superintendent. Lizzie Sinclair was murdered by the same man as Helen Carter and Sarah Finch."

Creech clasped hands over his stomach, chin drawn down to a cynical smile. "I know. His name is Mears."

"No matching DNA."

"There never was."

"You want to bet?"

"So, pretty Victoria's been stirring. The case is closed. Bring me new evidence, I'll consider it." Creech stood, his boys with him. "The next time you intrude on my manor, Fagan, do me the courtesy of asking first."

"Stick a guy named Danny on your lists," Sean said as he entered the office. "An occasional dosser round the council estate and possibly witness to murder."

The team grunted or waved acknowledgement, some sprawled around the outer office, some bent over reports, others cradling phones. Sean rubbed hands. Details were pointing to a full-blown operation with the possibility of it gaining more resources. Heidi came across and passed a message to phone Steve.

"I've got a whole load of SPI influence stored on the hard disks of each victim," Steve said, when Sean called him. "The source is PKL, Shoreditch. I'm not saying it's the company. But both games and virus were e-mailed over a line registered to that company. Could be anyone with access, officially or unofficially."

"You're a diamond. Give it what elbow you can, Steve." Sean hung up and said to the room in general, "I want everyone with time to look at PKL. Anything that can give info."

"Got something from my interview with Sarah Finch's mother," Diane said. "PKL are constantly seeking new small investors. Sarah held a thirty percent share and got a good return on her money. Share buying could possibly give you a way in. You need a minimum of five thousand pounds."

Sean returned to his back office and contemplated what lines his investigation needed to follow. Subliminal psychotic induction and the PKL establishment looked prominent. Nothing showed any risk to the general public, but somewhere within the PKL structure, something was emerging as a target, and Diane had found the perfect opportunity to examine it. Time to stir the Old Boys and drag the troll into battle, he thought.

Sean was answered on the third ring. "I have positive links on the Poor Girl victims," he told Cobbart. "Also an area of enquiry with direct lines to each victim, PKL computer games. Could be nothing, but my hunch is otherwise. My line of enquiry requires I go undercover as a potential investor. I need funds, enough to get serious PKL attention. Say five hundred k."

"Don't ask much, do you?"

"I also need Steve Rawlings in High-Tech to be given resources and time."

"The whole idea was to keep this low key. Other forces are involved, there is a political side."

"We have a serial killer in our midst and you sent me out to hunt. This will only get bigger before it's finished." He listened to Cobbart's grunt of dissent and knew he had approval.

"Leave it with me," the troll said. "That sort of money takes time."

Sean stopped outside MI5 and watched Victoria cross the busy road. "I've got five minutes, maximum," she said, sliding onto the passenger seat and closing the door.

"You said the Box could tap where we couldn't. You must have a huge resource file."

Victoria nodded. "All sorts of goodies."

"What about subliminal psychotic induction?"

"Used and banned years ago." She paused, her eyes steady. He thought maybe she was ahead of him. She said finally, "Commercial companies used it to encourage sales. Images were flashed on TV screens and in cinemas. Words, pictures, all designed to produce a subliminal impulse in the viewer."

"Could it be used over the Net?"

She shrugged, twisting in the seat to face him. "Possibly. The implications would be immense. But I think it very unlikely. You would need to be in deep and with high resources."

"Mass indoctrination or individual targeting, my question is, could SPI be targeted at certain people so they behave without questioning what they do? Like maybe, go alone into the woods or open the door to Zoby?"

Behind her dark eyes she seemed to hesitate. "You think that's what motivated those girls?"

"Could be. All three of their hard drives had SPI messages. Obey Crystal, trust Zoby. Can you go into records and see what's there?"

"Sure." She checked her watch. "Meet on Monday. I can give you full time then."

He watched her climb out. "Victoria," he called. She leant to the window. "I may need a partner to go undercover next week. My plan will look better if there's a Mr and Mrs."

She smiled and twitched an eyebrow. "Then I'd better find my woolly combinations. Meanwhile, get a good look at PKL this weekend. I'll be doing the same."

He watched her walk back across the road to Thames House and wondered what she knew that he didn't.

A Harley Davidson motorcycle with French number plates was parked next to the Citroen. A big, heavy bike, definitely one for the boys. Sean found the owner drinking wine with Danielle in the kitchen. He guessed the visitor at least six two, saw broad shoulders and a flat stomach, but not a boy. Shapely backside and hips wrapped in a stretched micro-mini skirt indicated otherwise. Her breasts needed no uplift. Sean sucked on his teeth.

"Monsieur Fagan." Danielle poured him a glass of wine. She was wearing a new, soft, button-through lilac dress. Minimal buttons fastened at the front gave flashes of what lay beneath. "Please meet Francesca, but friends call her Frankie." She smiled softly for Sean.

Frankie stood, hip jutted, balled fists at her waist. Her hair was short, her eyes blue, her nails and lipstick crimson. She took the glass from Danielle and handed it to Sean.

"Welcome home, Monsieur Fagan, and thank you for allowing me to stay." Her smile gave challenge, while her eyes remained confident.

"She stays two nights, Sean, this OK?"

"Sure." Sean accepted the wine, slowly realising Danielle's dress was not a casual display but a visual message. He saw the work of Camilla and bet she realised from Danielle's first interview.

Frankie went beside her, midriff bare save for a silver chain and a stud in her navel. She put an arm round Danielle's waist and placed her long firm fingers over Danielle's hip. Frankie raised her glass. "You are so kind, Monsieur Fagan, when you go next to Paris I would love you accept my hospitality. I am bodyguard for celebrities. I know many good places."

Sean sipped at his wine and looked between the two - and he had thought himself a detective. He grinned acceptance and saw both women relax. "Do I get fed?"

"But of course." Danielle blossomed in smiles. "The best of French cuisine. We cook together." She went to the stove. Frankie helped serve his dinner. "Now we leave you in peace." Danielle placed pans in the sink. "Tomorrow I clean. We go to watch TV in my room." She took Frankie's hand, leading her to the stairs.

"Goodnight, Monsieur."

Sean bet Frankie had a hidden tattoo. That night he dreamt of Victoria.

CHAPTER 10

Richard had sat next to Mrs Zellar throughout lunch and stayed dutifully attentive for the rest of the afternoon. Listening to her broken, mid-European accent describing the jet-setting, money-motivated world in which she lived, he found her mature years becoming more attractive and her slightly exaggerated dress style enticing enough to consider giving her sex. That she would be a willing participant was all too evident in her body language, particularly when he described his privileged background, his Eton and Cambridge education, his contacts amongst the political and wealthy. Bullshit had always been his forte. Dressed in city suits, with the right accent, hairstyle and manner, he had always prided himself on extracting money from the gullible. Her million would be child's play. Pity he couldn't rape her as well.

He left Snibbard and Faulkner to deal with the others and drove Zellar back to Shoreditch in his leased Mercedes. During the journey Mrs Zellar became Jovana and Richard began to wonder if he had enough Viagra for the weekend.

At 6.30 p.m. the office was empty and while he clicked on lights she walked across the main open-plan floor and stood looking from the window towards the city.

"So, Richard, you bring me here to show your empty office or for other reason?"

"To collect and fill in your share forms, of course. Were you thinking of something else? Maybe you would like a drink first? My flat is upstairs. Comfortable, convenient."

She laughed. "Deal money first, Richard. It is my rule."

"OK. A million sterling. If you want to give a cheque I can make out the necessary papers right now." He put a hand to her waist hoping to consolidate his position. A million kept it from going further.

"Negotiate, Richard. That is also my rule. By morning I could double my investment."

Richard removed his hand. She was several year his senior with the scrag-end appearance of the everlasting bimbo, but for two million he'd go down to her smiling. "Why not two million now? As I've said, within a year you would have doubled the value of your investment. Maybe more."

"Not my investment, Richard. The money I spend belongs to others."

He smiled without mirth. "You're laundering," he said, eyebrows raised. Who provided the money was no concern of his, so long as it ended in his account without causing problems.

"Laundering has become such a dirty word, Richard. I am investing for those who wish to place their funds beyond reach of unscrupulous tax agencies. Offshore, legitimate business. Kids games, Richard. Perfectly safe, perfectly respectable." She smirked, showing little white teeth.

"Good as blue chip." He maintained the grimace of stretched lips. "So, deal done. Whose name you want them in?"

"Tomorrow, I tell you tomorrow. You also bring twenty thousand worth of shares in the name of Jovana Zellar. Free. Maybe I can increase our transaction. Maybe much higher."

Richard kept his smile. Under the bullshit this one was a true, grabbing little scrubber. He put his hand back on her waist. "How much more?"

"My shares?"

"OK," he said, considering the shares nothing. Money in his account was the priority. "What do you intend to spend?"

"Two million plus."

He shrugged. "You arrange for two and a half million within forty-eight hours, I'll arrange for Mrs Zellar's shares."

She checked her watch. "I give you the address of my hotel. I must contact my principals. That will take time. In two hours bring my shares and we will arrange a day for our main transaction."

"You that eager for your cut?"

"No, Richard. I'm eager to see if you can put a smile on my face with your tongue."

In the flat above his office Richard removed a Remington 870 pump action shotgun and a 12-bore side-by-side from the back of a cupboard and expertly took both to pieces. He placed each component on the table before him, glanced at his watch, then put in a call to Oscar Wileman in America. He queued fifteen minutes for his turn to speak on a scrambled line. While he did so he oiled both weapons and checked his supply of cartridges.

When Wileman answered Richard dispensed with any pleasantries. "Our research for the required inclusion in the WorkWell application will be finished within five days. All will be contained on one set of flash drives."

"You must deliver them without suspicion or problem of any kind." Wileman's voice rebounded down the line in monotones.

"I'll ensure my end is clean. But if I need to disappear I'll be looking for cover."

"Don't worry, Richard, just deliver the goods. I'll give you deep and total sanctuary."

Richard hooked the phone to his chin and began to reassemble the guns. "Have you tried what I sent already?"

"I have, covertly on our own staff. Like getting into work early, working longer hours, obeying company instructions. The results were remarkable. You've done well, Richard. Governments will definitely be interested. And that's where my concerns lie. If they have any inclination, they will also be watching. You must take detailed precautions. Destroy everything other than the master copy. And that you must deliver by your own hand."

"Stella still working for you, Mr Wileman?"

"A trusted and proven employee, I'm sure she will welcome your arrival."

"Don't worry, Mr Wileman, I've taken care of everything."

"You better have. Just image what Al-Qaeda could do with this on air traffic controllers. What a paedophile could do with kids. What a manipulator could do with the stock exchange."

"Just imagine," Richard repeated, aiming the shotgun to darkness beyond his windows.

Katherine sat on a bench inside the main courtyard of Trinity College, Dublin. The sun shone warmly on her face and for moments she closed her eyes in the luxury of summer joy.

When she looked again, a young man stood before her. He was smartly dressed in blazer and flannels over a neat, compact figure. She found him handsome and hoped he didn't detect the momentary flush on her face.

He bowed, a sharp, heel-clicking gesture she thought dashing.

"You must be Zoby," she said.

"I am indeed, Sister Katherine. Here to drive you to the photo session in a nearby country house. Princess Kay-ling and our PR management are waiting with your two thousand euros and share certificates. May I?" He reached for her yellow plastic carrier bag.

"Thank you, but I'll manage." She picked up the carrier which contained her lunch and ten prayer cards of the Virgin, brought to give as presents, also her old flash drives. All but the last one. New for old was too good an opportunity to miss.

Zoby ushered with his hand and she walked beside him out of the courtyard. She could trust Zoby and was happy to enter the Mercedes. He said little during the drive and shyness kept her from asking questions. This was her first time alone with a man for years. Thrill of the adventure was enough. The journey lasted forty minutes before they entered the woodland car-park of a country house. People lounged in the Saturday morning sun. Some looked towards her and she sensed her blush again. It was strange to feel important.

Zoby flicked down on the car key causing a flash of yellow lights. A thud of locks disturbed the woodland clearing. It dismissed all others with panache.

"Our picnic," he said, showing her a cool bag. "A little pleasure for when labour is finished."

Clutching her own yellow plastic bag, she followed him along a path into the wood, feeling the soft pine needles beneath her feet and the gentle pounding of her heart. She wondered who would play the part of Princess Kay-ling, wondered if Crystal would be there. Crystal said to trust Zoby. So peaceful here in the woods with Zoby. When finally he opened a door in a high brick wall, she stepped through. This, she thought, must surely be the place. Not quite what she expected, neither was the hand that began to fondle her breasts. For a moment she stood in utter disbelief, then a blow stunned all her senses.

Zoby guessed her weight about fifty-five kilos, nice size, not fat, not thin. Lifting her bodily, her head and arms trailed downwards as he carried her to the greenhouse. In the chosen spot, he placed her carefully on the ground. He didn't want her bruised. I have to keep her perfect, just perfect, he thought. Then he went back for her carrier bag and searched the contents. He kept the flash drives as the Colonel had ordered. With no interest in the rest he discarded each item one by one on the greenhouse floor. Standing over her, savouring his power, he began to sweat. Everything in his body was pulsing, trembling over what he intended. Kneeling beside her, he carefully spread her arms and ankles ready to tie. She smelt of sweet vanilla. Her mouth was partially open, her teeth white, one with a filling. He placed a finger on her tongue and felt it moist. He shivered. Once he had her spread-eagled and tied between the four wooden stakes, he adjusted her veil so it framed her unblemished face. He had never felt this excited with a girl before, a nun, a virgin.

"Now for the purest of the pure," he whispered and lifted the hem of her long, wide skirt, dropping it in a cathedral arch around waist and legs. "Bitch! Goddam bitch." He stared down at the satin suspender belt and stockings. "Why the fuck do you always spoil it. No nun would wear those." He switched on his head radio. "Colonel, the prisoner has been classified as a hostile. I repeat, the prisoner is a hostile."

"Go to it, Zoby. Give the enemy what she deserves."

Zoby threw off his clothes and stood with clenched fists, his penis and body rigid. When his rage could no longer be contained he came down on her, ripping the crotch of her underwear, yelling in brutality on entering her body. Her eyes opened. Inches away from his face she was staring at him. He saw the disbelief, the pain, the horror and disgust. Her mouth came open, he felt the swell of her body as she drew breath to scream. He slapped his hand down, this was combat, he'd practised, knew exactly what to do as he grabbed the masking tape. She managed only a squeak when he spread the three-inch band from cheek to cheek, slipping his hand away as he smoothed it across her lips.

He got up then to watch her thrash and twist, her eyes wild with terror. He took photographs. Then he cut off her clothes with the scissors, revealing the white skin beneath, her limbs, her breasts, her body. He left the veil. She looked better with the veil. Halfway through she stopped her twisting and just stared at him. He knew it was disbelief, the onset of trauma.

"Hostile has ceased resistance," he reported over his head radio. When she was finally naked, he prepared himself for a second thrust. She was shivering. He liked that.

He wallowed, letting self-gratification consume his senses. She never moved or made a sound through her gag, just laid with her head to one side, but he knew he possessed her, and in that moment he let himself go. Silence followed, she hardly seemed to breath. He pushed himself up from her white, clammy skin and saw she was crying, her eyes red, her face flushed with long rivulets of tears. Mucus seeped from her nose. She wouldn't look at him. He smirked, sensed triumph and rearranged her veil. Standing to the side he watched her all the time he dressed; first the overalls and surgical outfit, then the rubber boots. Her face was still turned from him, staring at the green, algae-coated glass. Boy, was he going to get her interest. Kneeling beside her, he unrolled the butcher's knives. She looked then, eyes wide, her body shaking.

Zoby felt confident about this and knew exactly what he would take from her, but first he needed to discover if she had someone hiding inside. He smiled and made his first incision. "Don't worry, I used to be a doctor."

Tongue out over his lower lip he worked on her for an hour. First with his knee on her chest, ignoring the muffled screams, until after ten minutes she became still. Then he knelt beside her. He took photographs throughout. Afterwards he considered what was left and felt it was his best operation; particularly his trophy. Naked once more, cleaning took thirty minutes, much of it spent on his hands and face. He was careful to return all chemical and blood-soaked cleansing tissues along with other equipment to the bag.

Finally dressed in his blazer and flannels he whistled as he left the garden. He wondered who the people saw when he drove away the Mercedes. He knew it wasn't him because he was hiding in the shadows, hiding where nobody saw him, where nobody could find him. He was disappointed no little girl had been hiding in Katherine.

Behind a sprawling council estate on the outskirts of Dublin, Zoby removed the cool bag from the passenger seat. He poured a flask of petrol over the interior of the Mercedes and another into the boot, then flicked in a match. The walk to where he had left the hire car took ten minutes. He considered it enough distance to avoid connection. Across the fractured air came the incessant wailing of fire engines. He smiled and reported to the Colonel over his head radio.

"Mission accomplished, heading for base." At the hotel, he showered and placed all clothes worn in the Mercedes to a small zipper bag. On his way to the airport he tossed the bag into a skip.

The flight was no problem. Three hours later he knelt by his mother's grave to bury a sealed plastic wallet amidst the marble chippings. Inside was proof of mission, flash drives from her computer, a card from the digital camera with photos of the hostile during interrogation, during her execution, of the mess that was left afterwards. Zoby switched on his head radio. "Mission, Clean Cut accomplished, Colonel. Returning to base. Unit ready and combat proficient." He knew the Colonel wouldn't answer. The Colonel never answered after a mission, but Zoby was confident he would be back with another. He whistled tunelessly as he walked and felt the sun shine on his day.

CHAPTER 11

When the girls appeared from Camilla's house dressed in their finest and clutching a bunch of CDs, Sean knew he faced suppressed rebellion. The drive to Brighton took two hours, the car's speakers blasting incomprehensible pop music while Sophie and Becky bopped and rattled on the back seat, discarding their pristine clothes for jeans and T-shirts. He figured best they let it out in the hope of a quiet weekend.

First sight of Morrison Hotel gave him the impression of a people factory, a big block of a place set back from the sea front, the exterior all shiny and flash. Kids were everywhere. Sean carried Sophie's bag to reception while she clutched an assortment of teddies and comics. Becky trailed behind portraying "just-flew-in-from-Hollywood".

In the plush foyer a display of PKL Investment portfolios was prominent, another advertised for sales agents. Sean smiled for the receptionist and received a slick grimace of teeth when he handed over his complimentary voucher. He signed a false address into the book, considering it prudent to stay hidden. The receptionist passed tickets for the games room. Sean let the girls lead to their family room. Once unpacked they headed instantly for Princess Kay-ling.

The place was at full capacity with every hotel guest seemingly playing or queuing. Scores of kids and assorted parents sat with DVD visors wrapped over their faces, their fingers punching on buttons set in the chair arm, their ears clamped by headphones. The constant squeal of children and the amplified music of Princess Kay-ling's battle hymn blanked all other sound. To enter the room was to enter its heart. Waiting in the queue Sean felt his apprehension fade, these people were having a good time. This was mass, family entertainment. Sophie was already dancing with other kids around her, all doing the clenched fist stomp which appeared the current PKL routine. Becky linked his arm and put her head against him, trying to stay above it while she tapped her feet. By instinct Sean found himself watching people. Their entry and exit was controlled by a short, stocky woman who kept order with two hassled assistants. He felt peeved when she led a pretentious couple to the front and allowed them preference for seats. He hesitated on the verge of complaint. Both stood displaying their privileged position, both wore articles of yellow clothing. Maybe it's the yellow club, he thought, but sensed the detective twitch.

"You have one hour, sir," the assistant said, finally guiding Sean to a seat. "After 9 p.m. it's £10 per session, but over eighteens only. Half price after midnight. Press the right-hand buttons for choice of PKL or Killing Field. Controls are in the arm. Enjoy."

Sean eased himself into a seat and saw Becky and Sophie doing likewise. Earphones automatically clamped his ears as he pulled down his visor. The screen before him shimmered in colour, then Sean pressed for PKL. In virtual reality, a wide-open desert appeared from nowhere, the sun high over distant mountains. He heard the wind, felt it brush his face and saw it stir the desert floor. He had a sense of being there and heard himself exclaim in spontaneous amazement. Across the desert, dust rose in a long brushed line as a chariot raced towards him. Hunched over the reins a handsome adolescent urged the horse forward. On the chariot platform the tall, graceful figure of Princess Kay-ling stood clad in bodice and skirt, her arm raised to throw a spear. Sean jerked in reaction at the sudden appearance of a monstrous dragon. He pressed what he hoped was the fire button, missed and watched the chariot being destroyed beneath the monster's feet. When the dust had settled a small elfin figure appeared.

"Hi, I'm Crystal, councillor for the Princess. As a new fighter it seems you need instructions. Obey my commands and eventually you will succeed in reaching the Garden of Serenity. The Princess has her trusted charioteer, Zoby, but she needs your skill and concentration. Listen to my words, and obey me."

The princess reappeared with Zoby. This time she stood before a target. Zoby handed her a spear.

"Under your left hand you will find a ball control set into the arm rest," Crystal said. "Swivel this to direct the Princess's aim. Press the button under your right index finger to fire. Now practise."

Sean did as instructed and made Princess K hit the target edge. Zoby handed her a second spear. For moments Sean examined his face but saw nothing sinister. The youth was clad in Egyptian style armour, simple and unadorned. His ambiance was honest and appealing.

"You can trust Zoby," Sean whispered. Zoby paid no attention other than to his princess. Sean achieved a near centre on the second shot and a bull's-eye on the third. The princess smiled for him and climbed back into her chariot. Crystal, who had been watching, turned to face him.

"Well done, good friend. Let us now journey to the Garden of Serenity. Onwards."

From across the desert a chariot came racing. A sense of elation hit him when he killed the dragon. Demons followed, then ferocious beasts and warriors. The vision faded in mid picture when his hour was up. Sean lifted the visor. In the chair along side, the man from the posing couple did likewise.

"Get far?" he asked.

"Level 3," Sean said, the man's bright yellow shirt hit him like a beacon. "How about you?"

"Level 5."

Smug bastard, Sean thought and smirked his congratulations. The girls waited out front, Sophie holding up a games voucher.

"Me and Becks won prizes, an extra half hour for high scores. Have to play before nine tonight. Did you win a prize?"

"No chance, just can't zap 'em like you guys." He followed them out passed the hotel boutique. Sophie lingered there. Most of the display held yellow clothes. Sean recognised the poser's shirt priced at £10. Cheap, he thought, looking over the display. All yellow items were cheap compared to other colours. Again he sensed the detective twitch and knew something he should see was staring out at him.

At 7 p.m. Sean led them in to dinner, the girls in best jeans and T-shirts. The room enveloped him with the babble of family noise and the smell of hot plate food. A waitress with plastic earrings guided them to a table. Sean wanted this over quick. The place was a gilded works canteen. The food looked as if it matched. Mr and Mrs Poser sat near, their two kids immaculately dressed, all talking in loud, overbearing voices, all wearing yellow items of clothing.

"Dad." Becky touched his arm. "It's not Danielle, but it's not school dinners either."

"Brave girl. Let's wade in." They placed their orders.

The girls chatted as they ate, Sean gave half attention to the conversation, half to the room. On the far side a lacquered representative of PKL circulated amongst the guests. She stopped at any table where someone wore yellow, always handing over a PKL Investment portfolio from the bundle in her arm. It left Sean thinking.

"Dad, this food is disgusting," Becky said, pushing a half eaten hamburger and chips aside. "You cook better than this. Mind if we go back to the games room and use our vouchers?"

"We'll take you to the disco, after," Sophie said and ate a last piece of sausage.

"You mean that, you really want to see me rock?"

"No Dad, we're being polite. You're too old."

"That's a relief. If I'm not around, bed by eleven."

Both made to leave, came back and kissed him.

Sean's mind went immediately to work. The lacquered PKL rep intrigued him. When he caught her eye he waved her over and asked for a portfolio.

"Did you play PKL today, sir?"

"Is it a requirement?"

"I recommend it." She handed him a folder and moved on.

He bought a large whisky from the bar, found a comfortable seat and started flicking through the sales literature. It offered two opportunities. To become an agent for PKL in the manner Danielle had, or an investor in PKL games. Investments required five thousand but allowed the privilege of touring PKL at Milton Keynes and testing the latest games equipment. He figured the promise of a hundred thousand should get someone's attention.

"We've won more prizes." Sophie came up behind and threw arms around his neck. "A trial set of the new PKL game."

"And we've had our photos taken for the prize-winners' annual," Becky said, flopping in the chair beside him. "Everything will be sent to our email address."

"Girls, I've told you." Sean pointed to emphasize. "Don't give personal addresses to anyone without sound reason. That's home address or e-mail address."

"Dad, you big silly. It was the PKL receptionist, the lady on the desk. You can trust PKL. We're going to the disco." He was left with two more kisses.

"Trust PKL, trust Zoby." The words stuck in his mind. Time to find out about Zoby. Sean drained his whisky and went to the games room. He stayed long after midnight. The game constantly became harder, constantly demanded all his concentration. In time he reached level six, but learnt nothing about Zoby except he was reliable and trustworthy.

In sleep he dreamt of Princess Kay-ling dashing over the desert with her young charioteer. He woke up thinking about it and went down to breakfast convinced PKL a good investment.

The girls were chatting about their disco night and the prizes they had won. Sean considered re-mortgaging the house to raise money. Two tables away, Mr and Mrs Poser were signing papers presented by the lacquered PKL rep. If they bought in, why can't I? Sean pondered this, then found his mind locked in sudden realisation. He took careful stock of people around. Sophie was chattering in the background. Everyone was smiling, everyone had that big, life-is-so-nice smile. Unnatural.

"Dad." Sophie shook his hand. "They got some great Princess K sweatshirts in the shop, would you buy one for Becks and me?" Sophie had her best, try your luck smile.

"What colour?"

"Yellow."

"Any reason?"

She shrugged. "It's our house colour."

"No." He felt mean but adamant. "Listen girls, I thought we'd go swimming, then maybe a walk on the beach. Meet me by the pool in thirty minutes." He stood and surveyed the room amidst a babble of noise, the clatter of cutlery, plates, the drone of voices, everything as it should be in a big family hotel. Obey Crystal, trust Zoby. "I have calls to make," he said, and left the table.

He phoned Steve first. "Sorry to wake you on a Sunday but I need urgent info."

"Kids woke me two hours ago. It's football in fifteen minutes – shoot."

"Can SPI be downloaded without the recipient realising?"

"If it came as a virus and the recipient had good anti-virus software, then it might be difficult. But if it was a trusted source, the AVSW would accept the input as supplier material."

"How about a hotel chain? How about one specialising in cyberspace entertainment?"

"No chance. They'll have individual play-stations all networked to a secure server. Any virus would be stonewalled. Alternatively, if someone had connections to the system provider and made a rogue insertion by giving a trusted source code, then the virus would enter and lie undetected like a Trojan horse."

"Steve, I think I've just pulled something grimy out of the water."

He phoned Cobbart next. "I need to know if our undercover fund is in place."

The man was dry-toned. "One hundred thousand will be deposited by Monday morning. Just don't even think of writing a cheque." He gave bank details. "Finding a suitable undercover house in case the opposition check up is taking longer. Perhaps by tomorrow. There is a recent development in Watford which looks promising."

Sean went to PKL reception and told the woman he might consider investing a hundred thousand pounds in PKL. "We won the lottery a month ago," he qualified. "But I want to do this quick, and I want to talk to a director." He watched as her fixed smile slide to oily smooth.

"You won a lot, sir?"

"Five million plus, but we're investing in small packages."

"Very wise, sir. But for that amount PKL would ask for bank references. We only act as commission agents here. All your transactions would be done direct with PKL head office in Shoreditch."

"No problem."

He phoned Victoria on his way to the pool. "What did you find out? Is it possible for SPI to influence someone against their nature?"

"Afraid not. It's possible to confuse them but you won't get the blonde to kiss you if she doesn't really want to. On the other hand, if the blonde is undecided, she can be influenced to your way of thinking, but nothing outside her natural inclination. More alarming is that SPI can awaken basic instincts and emotions. Underneath our civilised veneer there's a savage in all of us. For some, that's only skin deep and easily ruptured."

"But it could influence people to wear yellow or be happy?"

"For what purpose?"

"To give an indication of whose mind is open to influence."

"Very possible."

"Victoria, I think I know why Sarah Finch walked into a forest, why Helen Carter opened her door to a murderer and why Lizzie Sinclair visited a graveyard. What I said while we were outside Thames House about you playing Mrs Fagan, you want to go active?"

"With such an ingenious chat-up line, how could I refuse?"

An hour later the PKL rep sought him out by the pool. Mr and Mrs Fagan were invited to visit Milton Keynes. Arrangements could be made for them to stay at a local hotel if need be. Their bill at Morrison's had been waived.

Victoria sat for ten minutes before she phoned and had no love of herself when she did so. Alice sounded ruffled, clearly her Sundays were precious.

"Fagan's moving closer," Victoria told her. "He's on to SPI, its use in the hotels and its source. If you wish to take precautions, now is the time."

"Can he prove anything?" Sibree asked.

"No. But that won't stop him. He works from logic. The proof is fitted in later. He wants me to go undercover as his wife."

"Then do that, Mrs Fagan. Draw close, encourage him to confide as only a good wife can."

CHAPTER 12

On their arrival from Brighton the previous night, Danielle had greeted them with a warm, blustering welcome; Frankie had been dressed in a black leather mini skirt and transparent Cossack blouse. Becky had gazed in open admiration, Sophie in awe. Sean still had a fantasy vision. Monday morning Frankie stood strident in full biker's leather while Danielle fussed barefoot and brave faced.

To stay would intrude on their farewell. He grabbed toast, kissed both on the cheek and left. He had already kissed his girls goodbye, Sophie's embrace hard to let go of. Sometimes he hated Camilla. Before he made the car, Steve Rawlings' call jerked his brain back from anger.

"An SPI directive in the last five games Sarah downloaded from PKL told her to explore Rattlers Wood. Part was overwritten by new material but part remained on the hard drive," Steve said. "An SPI message given in the final game, the Garden of Serenity, told Helen Carter that Zoby would be calling. The game had been downloaded by file transfer protocol from the PKL website a week before she died. They have a work unit in Milton Keynes and a head office in Shoreditch. I'd say both are now priority search areas with Zoby and Crystal the main contenders for questioning."

"I already have a visit arranged to Milton Keynes," Sean answered. "But Zoby and Crystal are cyber characters. How do you question them?"

"Question the person who put them there. The difficult bit is not to alert them."

Cobbart's call came next. He had found a house, now he wanted to set the scene. Victoria was on her way. Sean felt the adrenalin surge. At last he could go hunting.

By 9 a.m. Victoria sat beside him, Cobbart opposite.

"Short notice," Cobbart said. "But as you are going to probe and stir PKL, we must expect them to probe back. I've managed to set up a rented place in Watford. That way at least it's halfway between Milton Keynes and Shoreditch. Four weeks ago you had a five million joint win on the lottery. The bank has been briefed and will back the account. Just don't use it because there's only a hundred k which is not to be touched.   PKL have already e-mailed them for references so you're covered on the financial front. You're new partners, not married. If they look further than Mr and Mrs Fagan, this way we cover Sean's visit to the hotel, his daughters being from a previous marriage. Plus it gives a reason for your individual names and circumstances."

"Sounds cosy." Sean smiled at Victoria without response.

"Milton Keynes is the main animation studio, exhibition and display venue," Cobbart said. "The head office is on two floors of a sixties block in Shoreditch. Richard Caswell is Managing Director and also has a flat there. Outwardly, Caswell's main occupation centres on selling shares. Their value has increased four-fold in six months. It's a bubble ready to burst. The availability of your fortune will be very attractive to him. We don't have much information to show exactly who runs what, but other directors are listed as Sidney Snibbard and Derek Faulkner. Both highly qualified in their fields."

"They're on a scam," Sean said. "They're using SPI to influence investors. We should widen our investigation to both murder and fraud."

"No." Victoria shot the word out and plucked the neck of her blouse. "This is strictly an investigation into murder. Divert activities by opening another front and we'll end in a quagmire."

Sean watched her expression and judged it didn't gel with her words. He felt perplexed as to why she wanted limitation. A second front would allow Cobbart to increase manpower and speed up the investigation. They had links, a positive lead. No one could deny progress. Victoria shifted as if for better defence.

"Murder and fraud could be linked," Sean said. "I suspect Morrison Hotels have SPI in their games. Our victims were also influenced by SPI. The two operations could be combined."

"SPI is still an unproven supposition," Victoria said. "Conflicting activity may cross and then alert our killer. Let's keep this low profile, at least 'til we have a positive target. Say, two weeks. I suggest we work undercover alone and use your team only if we require outside activity."

As Sean expected, Cobbart chose neutral ground and ignored both.

"For the image of new moneyed people, I've arranged a metallic gold Jag. Log book in Sean's name. Also joint chequebook. But for Christ's sake, don't write any cheques. Covering for one hundred thousand put the accountants into meltdown."

Sean turned slightly and smiled for the full attention of Victoria's eyes. He saw no give, just adamant self will, the Victoria of old. She was making excuses to keep the operation covert and contained. She knew something he didn't. He figured confrontation would dig her in, so decided on subtlety.

"SPI proven or not," Sean said. "When we go in, a hundred thousand should get us serious attention. If they believe we have a lot more spare we can dangle it for a detailed inside view. The dangers are, Victoria and wealth. Sarah Finch was a wealthy woman and attracted our killer. Likewise Helen Carter. Victoria may do the same. We need to take precautions and have a team ready for immediate action."

Her nose twitched.

"Sounds feasible," Cobbart said.

"Let's get professional here." She shook her head. "First, I'm a big girl and I've been trained to bite back. Secondly, my time here is off the record which gives me licence you guys don't have. The last thing I want is big policemen bounding through the window and queering my patch. On the first encounter we gather intelligence, then withdraw. On the second encounter, Sean plays from the front while I go covert behind their backs, right into the heart, if need be. Once I've identified a target I'll extract. How I do that is down to me."

"Settled then, but as a precaution I'll put Blue Team on standby, just in case," Cobbart said and answered his phone on the third ring. The troll smugness became concentrated. Sean glanced at Victoria who stared petulantly out the window. He thought her beautiful.

"Get back to this Liam Haggarty," Cobbart spoke into the handset. "Tell him we have useful information, but I want to trade. I want our own man to visit, I want shared intelligence. I'm positive he'll realise the benefit of mutual co-operation, particularly if they can blame a Brit." Cobbart hung up and rubbed his jaw.

Victoria had turned back to look at him, her expression as if she knew what was to come.

Cobbart exhaled. "That was our man at Criminal Intelligence. They've had a request from the Irish Garda in Dublin regarding the brutal murder of a young nun. There are similarities to the Poor Girl murders. Looks like our boy's been travelling."

"How do you know it's him?" Sean asked.

"Has all the hallmarks. The girl's vagina and uterus were cut from her body. Whoever did this took them away."

Sean felt his rage and condensed it into a hard knot. Victoria had her eyes closed, hands balled to fists.

"Liam Haggerty, he's the Garda in charge?" Sean asked.

Cobbart nodded.

"Tell him I'll be over. I need him on our side." Sean called Heidi on his mobile. "Book a ticket for Dublin." He checked his watch. "Quickest you can get to leave in one hour thirty minutes, sod the cost. Return by 0900 hours tomorrow. Central accommodation for one night." He looked at the troll. "Boss, I need a fast car to the airport."

"Include me," Victoria said.

"No." Sean stared into the flare of her eyes and continued before she could protest. "Someone has to take a briefing from Steve Rawlings. We need to know more about SPI, we need to know about its transmission and covert use. We need to know what you and I face at PKL headquarters. More important, what you might face when you get further involved and I might not be there."

"I've investigated both London crime scenes, I know details you and Haggarty don't."

Sean stayed with eye contact. She was stubborn, without compromise.

Victoria hid smugness when she placed her ticket on the check-in desk at Luton Airport. Sean had outmanoeuvred her in Cobbart's office with the retention of Blue Team, but he could not deny the logic for her going to Ireland. Zoby had killed again. This time she was determined he would be sanitised. In the departure lounge she gave Sean her best pretty-girl smile and made excuses. "Need to buy things for overnight," she said and received a grunt for her effort. She crossed to a discount arcade and hid behind shelves selecting underwear, then a toothbrush, her mobile pressed to one ear.

Alice Sibree sounded sympathetic, Victoria doubted she was. "I can't stay passive on this, Alice, not if it's Zoby again." She listened to Sibree's hesitation.

"Let's not do anything rash. Zoby's demise will come. It's a prime objective. But we need to protect our operation and secure copies of the merchandise. Then we extract before the police close in. I've had word, Wileman's people are also watching. It must appear to Wileman that he is the sole beneficiary of SPI or the covert use of our own viruses will be compromised. If you find Zoby, eliminating him before time would bring media involvement and jeopardise our objectives. Your opportunity will come. Wait."

"And what of Crystal, he's equally guilty?"

"How does one kill by remote hypnosis? The difficulty of proof is his saving grace, and for the moment ours. Keep in contact."

When Victoria returned, Sean stood waiting, his head and shoulders above the others like a rock in a human river. She saw him aloof, isolated, scowling. He looked so lonely. She maintained her best pretty-girl smile.

"Cobbart was on the phone," he said to her. "The man follows Cheltenham Gold Cup. So does half of Ireland, including the Garda. As a result he has good contacts. A car has been arranged for our arrival and Haggarty will be at the crime scene. All you need is to win him over."

You and him alike, she thought, and followed towards the departure gate.

Sean shook hands with Garda Fitzgerald who held the door while Victoria slid into the back seat.

"First name's Cory," Fitzgerald said. He was clad in jeans and leather jacket, his hair was cropped and two studs were fastened in one ear.

"Terrible," Cory said, as he manoeuvred through Dublin's outer traffic. "Would you believe a pure wee nun. Just a young girl, no older than my own sister. The whole of Ireland is shocked." He floated the car into a roundabout and headed out the other side on the N3 to Navan. "We'll get the bastard though. Word is he's Brit. Is that right?" He looked into the rear mirror, to the guilty foreigners.

"Could be," Sean said.

"We'll get him, mind. Terrible, a nun and all. No older than my sister. No one's safe."

Twenty minutes later they pulled into a tree-lined car-park. Victoria extracted herself and Sean watched her tight expression as she looked towards the white overalled

Forensics team who dotted the weed infested vegetable garden.

Cory indicated a neat, bespectacled man in cords and wellies who came under the tape.

"Liam Haggarty." The Irishman extended his hand to Sean, looking at Victoria. "It's okay. They've moved the remains," he said, over her hesitation at the tape.

"I put away his last two victims," Victoria said in a bland lifeless voice. "And I never move into another person's crime scene unless invited."

"I appreciate that." Haggarty nodded and lifted the tape. Sean waved her forward. She had won the guy's professional respect, now she needed to stay emotionally detached. "We're of the same school, Inspector," she told him. "If we have the same killer, we're basically involved in the same operation."

All three stopped at the greenhouse entrance. Sean looked inside. Streaks of blood discoloured the glass. It was flecked out in spidery tendrils and had dried to a mottled brown. Flies had settled. Victoria faltered and visibly paled.

"The spray of blood patterns shows she was alive when he started," Haggerty said. "Staked out, her mouth heavily taped. She died from loss of blood and trauma."

Sean watched Victoria repress a shiver and waited until she found her voice. "The killer our side tied and gagged his victims before cutting them. He started with sexual assault, then graduated."

"This one's the same. Cut off her clothes, leaving only her wimple. Does that suggest anything?"

"That suggests he wanted to keep her as a nun," Victoria said. "The man understands purity, perfection. His past victims were what you might call elite, beyond the reach of many. He thinks of himself in the same way."

"Any DNA?" Sean asked.

"It will take time. The corpse was a mess. Fingerprinting useless. He wore surgical gloves the whole time. Blood splashes show she struggled, bruises indicate he knelt on her chest. He must have been covered. He emptied the whole inner cavity of her body, including the uterus and connecting genitalia which he took away. Psychologically these continue his possession of her."

Victoria was looking down at the earth. Congealed furrows were littered with bloodstained prayer cards. This time she stayed silent.

Sean said, "What about the car, clothes? Someone who must have seen him?"

"I have teams out searching. Initial evidence suggests he visited twice, first time to prepare, possibly leaving a change of clothes and stuff to clean up with. The second time he brought the girl. I have one witness who saw a man in a blazer helping her from a Mercedes car. They gave a poor description I'm afraid"

"Then she trusted him, same as our victims. Did she use a computer? We have strong evidence all the victims played a computer game called Princess Kay-ling."

"Katherine was a skilled calligrapher and studied the art of illuminated manuscripts at one of our best colleges. Most pupils there go on to take Holy Orders. I can see computers, but not games." He raised his hands. "But then my sister's a nun. They can play the devil if they take a mind to."

"It's Zoby." Victoria finally spoke. "I know it. Zoby removed genitalia from Lizzie Sinclair. Our man is your man, Inspector." Haggarty looked up, his relief visible behind the glasses. He was no longer alone.

"I'll share evidence," Sean said. "But I need insight into Katherine's mind and background. I need to talk with her friends."

Haggarty checked his watch. "I have a woman detective sergeant at Katherine's college now. Kilkenny is a good two hours drive, maybe more, unless young Cory takes you."

"It's okay." Victoria raised her hand. "Your men are needed here. We'll hire a car."

"If I share evidence," Haggarty said. "And if you catch him in Britain, I want him afterwards. One day they'll let him out of your jail, but he'll die in ours."

They reached Kilkenny City and the 16th century teaching convent in late afternoon. The DS from Dublin CID stepped from an unmarked car and introduced herself as Finola Kelly. Victoria edged Sean aside, this was women's ground and he let her lead.

"The sisters are in a state of shock, I can hardly get a word out of them," Finola said.

"Did you talk to her friends?"

"Her close pal is Teresa. I've tried to interview her, but she keeps crying and the Mother Superior won't leave us alone. Getting information here will take patience."

"We have a return flight tomorrow morning," Sean said. "If Katherine used a computer, if she was in contact with anyone over the Internet, we need to know."

Finola gave a grimace of apology. "To be honest, I don't think men are welcome at the moment." She glanced towards Victoria. "If we two try by saying you're from England, Mother Superior may give us ten minutes."

Sean waited in the car for thirty minutes, lost in speculation of why Zoby had killed in Ireland. Was he trying to prove his capabilities or dilute the search over two countries? If so, perhaps he didn't realise he had opened a corridor. Passing between borders meant passing through security. It gave a reference point for the operation to search. The other avenue was Crystal, if only they knew what part Crystal played.

When Victoria finally returned through the heavy doors of the convent, she was followed by DS Kelly and three young students, all were carrying computer equipment. The three gathered round the boot of the Garda's car and placed their burden inside. Victoria shook hands with DS Kelly then crossed to Sean's car.

"Wow," she said, once inside. "Never knew nuns could be so scary. Given the chance, I think Sister Deirdre, the Mother Superior, would have scourged both of us on the spot. She's not a woman to mess with, so I hit hard. Told her if we didn't have her and Teresa's help this guy would kill again. We would all have blood on our hands. That broke the barrier."

"Well done." Sean glanced at her and wondered if that was her motivation, the thought of blood on her hands through failure.

"She let Teresa walk with me in the garden. The poor girl let it all pour out. Katherine was computer whiz kid of the convent. Her parents kept buying her the latest equipment. Katherine secretly downloaded and played Princess Kay-ling every night. She was Southern Ireland champion."

"The convent never knew?" Sean asked.

"Young girls are young girls, convent trained or not. Teresa admitted most students had hotmail addresses. It was innocent fun to them, sending messages to friends and parents. The girl said in her opinion, if God did not want them to access modern technology, he would not have provided it. From what I saw of the older nuns, I doubt they even know how to switch a computer on. They have four PCs in the library, all supposedly used to research illuminated manuscripts on a worldwide basis. It also brought the temptations of the world to the heart of their community. Last Thursday Katherine downloaded the Garden of Serenity, the final level of Princess Kay-ling."

"Did it have SPI?"

"Finola will find out, she's taken all Katherine's equipment for analysis. Last Saturday, the poor girl went innocently to collect a two thousand euro prize. She went to meet Zoby. She told Teresa she could trust Zoby."

On the return drive to Dublin, Sean stayed with his own thoughts, glad that the dark scenarios which whirled through his head were frequently interrupted by the ringing of his mobile. If Crystal and Zoby could reach to Ireland, they could reach to Australia, America, Russia.

Heidi had booked them separate but neighbouring rooms in Jury's Hotel. Sean felt better after a shower and use of the hotel toiletries for a shave. Spruced, he went down with Victoria to meet DI Haggarty and Finola in the bar.

"They'll have information from the hard drives tomorrow," Haggarty said. "We played the one flash drive found in the girl's room. Crystal and Zoby are integral characters in the PKL game. On the surface they seem OK."

"Slow them down and you'll find subliminal suggestions, obey Crystal, trust Zoby," Sean said. "Messages are sent as viruses and downloaded onto the game. They encouraged Katherine to obey instructions. What we're looking for is the origin of any e-mails, anything connected with her last journey."

Haggarty leaned away, apologising as he answered his mobile. It created silence. When he finished he leant back and scratched his stubbled chin. "Local Garda have been checking over a burnt out Mercedes. Seems it holds partial remains of a bag containing knives. The vehicle was stolen two days ago and fits the description by our witness. I have a team on it now." Haggarty rose to leave. Sean stood also.

"We'll come with you."

"You look after the Brit side, I'll look after mine. Stay in touch. Enjoy your dinner and have a safe journey home."

"I think we've been told our limits," Sean said, watching them leave.

She looked good, even in clothes crumpled by the long day, but then Sean knew he wasn't looking at the clothes. She had untied her hair from the French pleat so it fell dark to her shoulders, shining in the candlelight. He went back to the menu.

"Share oysters?" she asked.

"Sure." The night was good for sharing. He thought better of saying it. Both ordered steak and Sean picked a good-bodied Syrah he hoped she'd like. The alcohol played its part after a hard day. While they ate he received two text messages, one from Sophie, one from Becky.

"They're good kids," Sean said. "Worried about their Dad in foreign parts."

"Kids reflect their parents." Victoria's red lips sipped at her wine and left a smudge of lipstick imprinted on the glass.

"Jesus, not their mother." He closed his eyes, then looked back to her. "No, I shouldn't have said that. Her heart is good, we're just not compatible. Living with a policeman is not easy."

"Guess that's why we're alone. We're too selfish outside of professional endeavours."

He ate slowly, wondering if he should dig. "You never married?"

"No." The word had a hollow, final ring creating a line not to be crossed.

Sean waited and finished his meal while she ate sedately. "I should never have married, but then I love my kids. They give life meaning," he said.

"Exactly." She sat back, her ambiguous half smile suddenly bewitching, her eyes beautiful. He wanted to sleep with her.

"We have an early start tomorrow." She checked her watch.

"Tempus fugit. Day after, we'll be Mr and Mrs Fagan."

"How respectable." She gathered her bag and stood.

Sean followed her to the lift and waited in silence as they rode to the fourth floor. He was conscious of her absolute power. Outside her room she stopped to face him. She made to speak, then kissed her finger and touched it to his cheek.

"Good night, Mr Fagan."

"Good night, Mrs Fagan."

She hesitated on closing the door. Her touch lingered until sleep came.

They split at the airport to collect fresh clothes. Within two hours Sean arrived at the undercover house. There were six properties in a square-shaped cul-de-sac, each property a twee little box trying to seem more pretentious than its neighbour. Sale notices were still up with only two sold. Few could afford the price.

Jan waited with the Jaguar keys.

"Houses either side are still empty," Jan said. "Wouldn't mind one myself. Nice patio and kitchen." She handed him the morning post. "Gas, electricity and telephone bills, just in case you want something to dump for snoopers. I put an answering machine on the phone. Before your lottery win you were a welder. Victoria ran a pub. In case they check with the hotel, the girls were from your previous marriage."

"The place was full of kids. Can't see anyone's interested in mine. If the bank gave this address, that's all we need. These people are after money, not my family tree."

Jan nodded and moved away when his mobile rang.

Steve Rawlings was buoyant. "The hard drives on their computers all show e-mail activity from the PKL Shoreditch web address. All originated from PKL3 which suggests it's terminal three on the main office server. The sender signs as Crystal and makes frequent references to Zoby."

"What about SPI?"

"It's in virus form and the message is always simple. Obey Crystal, trust Zoby. Be there at 11.00. Get into the car. Let Zoby enter. One appears every three to ten seconds."

"They have an effect?"

"Providing they are simple, and these are, yes, they can have an effect. Yesterday we experimented. We sent SPI messages to the screen of a volunteer WPC. She only drinks tea. We told her, buy coffee. This morning in the canteen, she asks for coffee. She immediately realised, didn't know why she bought coffee and changed it. She was subjected to three hours. If we had hit her for thousands of hours, what of the effect then?"

Sean listened to the quiet draw of his own breath. Trust Zoby in the forest, in the graveyard, your house, your convent.

"Steve, what do I need to look for at Milton Keynes?"

"Computer-wise that's difficult without raising suspicion. Any person with access could originate these things. Cobbart found us a court order to hack their lines. We're set up to intercept all e-mail traffic. What we need to discover is who's using T3, then link them with timed e-mail transmissions. That won't be easy."

Victoria packed, choosing clothes to fit her role while trying to convince herself that deceiving Sean would eventually bring good. Minutes before she left for the cover house she phoned Alice Sibree.

"Sean Fagan is closing in rapidly. I suggest we lift the WorkWell programme now, or it may be too late."

"I require more time. Those above can't possibly act through official channels. One whiff of this to the media and they'll descend like savages. Our source inside PKL informs us the rogue components accepting SPI codes remain incomplete. They require three more days. Caswell will then pass the flash drives containing these components to Wileman. In turn his trusted technos then need to incorporate them into the WorkWell application before any SPI message from either him or us will be accepted. Delay Fagan."

"Alice, when the time comes, Fagan will go in like a sledgehammer and nothing I do or say will stop him."

"Then work on Caswell. You must get close to him, close as you can in the time available. If possible, steal a copy of the WorkWell files without anyone realising."

"And just how do I manage that, Alice?"

"Use your cunning and your charms, my dear. You're very good at it. It's why I picked you." She hung up.

Thank you Alice, Victoria thought. This was probably what the Witch wanted all along, to steal, off-record illicit research that could never be placed on record. But for whom, a government agency? Certainly not one that was making its self known.

Sean watched from the living room as Victoria's BMW pulled into the drive. He went to greet her and help with the case. She was dressed in a fitted blouse and tight trousers, her hair tidied by an Alice band. She looked the exact part of Mrs Publican, turned Mrs Wealthy Suburbia.

"It was the show house," he said, carrying the case upstairs. "Fully furnished, Cobbart has leased it for three months though I doubt we'll need it a week." He pushed open a door and placed the case inside. "Master bedroom. What do you think?" He indicated the made up bed.

Victoria placed a briefcase on the dressing table and folded her arms. He watched a half smile appear. "I hope it's comfortable for you, but I won't be sleeping here tonight. Mrs Fagan resides, but only sleeps with Mr Fagan when the enemy watches. And that won't be 'til after we visit PKL headquarters."

"How one must suffer for duty." He shrugged as she brushed aside his hopes.

"Any news from Ireland?" she asked, opening the case to place bottles on the side and hang clothes in the cupboard.

"Haggarty phoned. Items found in the burnt out Mercedes held evidence of Katherine's blood. Looks like Zoby is getting over confident and careless. The car was stolen from a golf club previous day. The thief made a pretence of booking lessons, fortunately on that first visit security cameras got the licence plate of a hire car from Dublin airport. Forensics commandeered and took the car apart. They found traces of Katherine's blood on a seat. Hire details give a British driving licence, one Jez Darley. They checked hotels. One Brit did a runner without booking out, but they have a credit card swipe in the name of a Martin Bradshaw. Haggarty faxed details to the office. Heidi's is checking for addresses."

"Licence and cards sound stolen."

"Hundred percent certain, unless our target's completely stupid. I have Jan following through. She's a good street lady and knows her way."

"Just warn her not to visit any suspect. Zoby likes untouchable ladies. An attractive, lesbian policewoman would be his ideal victim."

"So would an MI5 lady, so take that advice yourself. Three women trusted Zoby, went to meet him and died. What I don't understand is, where does Sammy Sinclair fit? Someone knows. Because SPI wouldn't work on an alcoholic." He waited on her reaction. She had been close, she had to know something.

"I never found out," she said and dropped underwear in a drawer before opening her briefcase. "MI5 goodies." She handed him a mobile. "These mobiles are under constant surveillance and no-one can listen in."

"Except MI5."

"I said, no-one listens." She folded her arms and nodded to the briefcase. "I also brought bugging equipment and surveillance cameras. Shall we go to work?"

Sean looked at the brand new bed and the pristine sheet, then headed for the stairs.

On the drive to London he slotted a CD of Mozart's Adagios into the stereo and listened without talking. They were now Mr and Mrs Ordinary amongst the traffic. He felt amazed by that, to have an attractive and charismatic woman who pretended to be his wife, who would kiss him in public if required, but not in private. Heidi's phone call interrupted his thoughts.

"Bradshaws are in Lambeth, boss." She read the address. "Darley in Kennington. He and his wife returned from holiday yesterday. Their alibi is sound. The place was burgled. He's there now if you want to see him. Forensics have finished."

Sean thanked her and headed the car to Kennington.

"Look at the mess." Jez Darley gestured to his immaculate flat. "The whole place is ruined, my wife is distraught and forced to stay in a hotel."

Sean ignored Darley's posturing. He wanted simple information. The rest of Darley's life was his own affair. Victoria stood across the room as if casually admiring the flat's contents, her face bland.

"Was it only the doorframe he broke?" she asked. "Nothing else?"

"Only!" The man turned on her, his bald head glistening, his designer shirt and jeans perfectly tailored. "Our spiritual space is corrupted. And where were you people? I exhaust myself at work, pay my taxes, take a well-earned break and you allow this to happen."

"Did he steal anything other than the card, passport and driving licence?" Sean asked.

"Isn't that enough? I'm furious." Darley folded his arms and drew down his chin.

"He could have shit on your bed," Victoria volunteered, her face still bland.

Sean flexed cheeks to control his smile. Victoria screwed her face a little. "Normally they trash the place, crap everywhere and break what's of value." She flicked a hand towards the original paintings, porcelain and Eastern rugs. "Lucky you had cheap stuff."

Darley's jaw slackened. "The contents of this flat are insured for a million pounds."

"The last burglary we looked into, the man was raped by two creepers. That's thieves who break in at night. He was sore over that, really had it in the butt. Sometimes it's lucky to be out."

"This is outrageous." Darley stormed three paces then turned. "You don't think he'll come back?"

Victoria stayed silent.

"Who knew you'd be away, Mr Darley?" Sean asked.

"Friends, but they would never, never."

"You were turned over by a pro. He left no prints, no visible signs of disturbance. He was looking for cash, credit cards, items which had immediate value. My colleague is right, you're lucky."

"Do burglars come back? They do, don't they?"

"Did any trades people know the flat would be empty? Did you book through a travel agency or over the Net? Did you give the dates of your holiday and address over the Net?"

"No. I booked through Travelpath, a highly reputable city firm. Their service is impeccable. Should I have additional locks fitted?"

"Bars on the windows," Victoria said.

"But I'm on the fourth floor."

"They abseil from the roof."

In the street outside, Sean unlocked his car. "Are you that hard on all witnesses?" He watched her smile appear.

"The guy annoyed me. I was thinking of Helen Carter. I just compared how lucky Darley and his wife really were. He was out to give us nothing. Now he's spooked enough to give whatever we ask."

Sean held the door and saw logic in her technique. He admired the curve of her figure as she slid onto the seat and wondered when if ever, they would again make love. To distract himself he phoned Jan.

"What's on the Bradshaws?"

"Still away, back early this evening. The flat's been burgled. I called the local Bill and they've put a seal on it, but we can't touch 'til the Bradshaws give consent. The good news is, the neighbour spoke to a guy. A bogus plumber, fat and balding. They're doing a photofit now."

Sean recognised the fading of Cindy Bradshaw's tired happiness. She had maybe planned a bottle of wine and a pizza, or a homecoming fling at some favourite restaurant. Now her face became apprehensive, her husband taking her hand. Police waiting was bad news. Who's dead? What's destroyed?

"You've been burgled," Victoria said, her tone sympathetic.

"Did they do much damage?" Cindy put down her case and unlocked the door.

"Bastards." Her husband went straight to the living room. "I don't see damage."

"He stole a credit card and used it during another crime. A more serious crime."

Sean closed the front door. "Your neighbour saw him," he said. "A bogus plumber."

Her husband was already on the stairs, Cindy behind, Victoria followed.

"I hide an emergency card in a suit pocket." The husband went straight to a cupboard. "I left only one, a gold Visa."

Sean watched Cindy's jaw tighten and saw a woman losing her privacy. "We went in a hurry," she said, moving to pick up her nightdress. "He's handled this?" She turned to the dressing table.

"Card's gone," her husband said, flicking through the wallet.

"Anything else?" Sean asked.

"No." He looked to his wife and his face said he lied on her behalf.

Cindy gave a small, tight shout of rage. "Pig! He's been through my things. Bastard!" She pointed to the defiled briefs on the floor.

Sean thought the husband good. He went straight to her, cradled her and let her shed silent, angry indignation.

Victoria produced an evidence bag. "May we take these, Mrs Bradshaw? It would seem they might hold DNA evidence."

"Take the whole damn lot. He's dirtied everything. Christ, I think I'm going to throw up." She pulled away from her husband, not stopping until she was behind the bathroom door.

"What kind of perverse creep would do that?" Bradshaw said.

"Burglars are sick; slimy misfits of society." Sean saw bright anger in Victoria's eyes, anger which said, if you defile the modesty of one woman, you defile all women. He understood then a little of her personal involvement. She shook her evidence down into the plastic bag and sealed the top, pulling the snap crease with firm, definite fingers. "I'll hand these to our lab."

"It could have been worse, Mr Bradshaw," Sean said. "The more serious crime involved a woman's death. Until your door is repaired, a uniformed officer will remain outside in case."

"Are we in danger?"

"I don't think so. More probably you've just been used. Who knew you were away?"

"Neighbours, a few friends."

"No trades people or services you use or cancelled?"

He shook his head. "None I recall at this moment."

"How did you book your holiday?"

"Travelpath. I've used them before. They're a good firm."

Victoria's eyebrows were up. "What happened here would upset any woman. I can understand Mrs Bradshaw's disgust. If she wants counselling, I can get someone."

"Thanks, but my wife's a strong lady, we're also good friends. We'll handle this together."

"Mr Bradshaw." Sean passed him a card. "If you think of anything you feel relevant, please call. Forensics will be here shortly. It's best not to touch anything until they've finished. I'm sorry this has been such a bad homecoming."

Cindy Bradshaw emerged from the bathroom, pale faced and red eyed. She sat on the bed. Bradshaw went to her. Victoria nodded Sean towards the door.

On the street outside Sean clenched his raised fist. "Travelpath, it has to be the link. This calls for a full team."

"You realise this will split our operation," Victoria said. "We now have two lines of enquiry. One into PKL, one into Travelpath. You deal here, I'll deal with PKL."

"No chance." He let her into the car and went round to the driver's side. "Remember your own advice to Jan. In PKL you become a potential victim. You don't go in alone. We've still time to see Cobbart." Sean checked his watch. "I want things rolling here. Could be a late night."

"Drop me at the nearest tube. Do what you have to. I'll be at the cover house at ten tomorrow morning, not late tonight. Let's not tempt fate, Mr Fagan."

"For a sideline operation you're causing a lot of expense," Cobbart said. He sat in his shirtsleeves amidst piles of paper, a disgruntled crease to his brow.

Sean gave him facts. "I need my team active not just on standby in case Zoby appears. If the Old Boys want justice, resources will have to increase substantially."

"Your own team is no problem, but diverting others from outside operations may be difficult. Who's Zoby?"

"Our target. It's my belief SPI was used to make four women trust Zoby. Someone in Travelpath knew the burgled flats were empty. Maybe Zoby, maybe someone who knows Zoby. I want my team to start surveillance while I'm at Milton Keynes. I want photos of all employees at Travelpath. We need to work out the numbers involved. Then I'll need extra people to start whittling the numbers down to serious suspects."

"Request what equipment you need. Extra manpower," he shrugged and pursed his lips. "I'll try."

Sean knew then that his day was done. Until men or equipment materialised he could not put a plan into action. Travelpath was closed. He drove to Cricklewood. Heidi had turned out the lights. No one was in the local pub. An hour later he was in the cover house staring at a big empty bed, an Indian takeaway downstairs on the kitchen table. He figured the day had been good. The op had gained momentum and direction with Zoby was a step closer. But what he needed now were faces

He slept fitfully, woke before dawn and was in the office by six. His first objective was to draft a list of requirements to Pimlico; a long wheelbase van with periscope facility and camera equipment, traffic warden uniforms, body sets for group communication. At seven he heard the first car roll into the motor pool, by seven-thirty, members of Blue Team sat in readiness.

"Jan, Diane, get yourselves over to Westminster Traffic Division and kitted out with uniforms," Sean said, shuffling his sheaf of papers. "You patrol as wardens outside Travelpath. Simmy, Chad, you carry out surveillance from the van. I want photographs of all staff members, let's see if we can get a match with the photofit of Bradshaw's bogus plumber. Build up what character traits you can on the manager. If we can lift him and bring him on our side it will make life easier. The agency has twenty branches. Heidi, find where head office is and what other outlets they have locally. Mike, make a visit on the pretence of booking a holiday, go back as often as possible. Get a feel for the staff inside. Ali, Bob, you start tailing and eliminating suspects. One of them may well be Zoby.

"Victoria and I visit PKL early afternoon and hopefully follow up on their Shoreditch office tomorrow. Could be we'll find something dark in PKL's administration, but my instinct is Zoby is someplace else, probably working in Travelpath."

Sean left them at 9 a.m. and was waiting for Victoria by 10.30. She wore a fitted business suit, the skirt short and the jacket open. The kind of outfit she wore when dangerous.

CHAPTER 13

Richard sat nursing his 12-bore shotgun as he waited on Wileman's call from America. He reached for the instrument at its first ring.

"The line is scrambled," Oscar Wileman said. "I trust everything is coming to a conclusion?"

"Everything is as I planned, Mr Wileman. How was my research received at your end?"

"Certain parties showed keen interest but they're concerned over any hint of publicity. Should that happen they, like myself, will retract and then condemn. So make sure you clean away all evidence and your team are suitably silenced. Return here with the single copy immediately your programme is complete."

"Rely on it, Mr Wileman," Richard said, holding the phone to his ear as he walked to the window and looked out across the city. He imagined the little arse counting his money and thinking of his future world influence. But it would never match the influence Richard Caswell would have on world stock markets. He needed only an extra million from Zellar and he would be gone into the unknown, a covert copy of the SPI disks hidden for his own use.

"How long before you finish?" Wileman asked.

"Three days."

"Just be careful. If it ever got out, SPI would be dead on the ground and your future with it."

Richard felt his smirk grow naturally. "Don't worry, Mr Wileman, I've planned meticulously. There's only one niggling worry."

"What?"

"You clearly haven't heard the news. Zoby's been at work in Ireland." Richard listened to the long pause before hearing Wileman's pained exclamation.

"I don't wish to be involved in your security. Sanitise everything."

"The problem is, with SPI, it's easy to create a new Zoby. There are thousands of psychos out there. I suspect one of my partners conditioned a second one."

"Then get rid of both. Get your house in order."

Richard listened to the click of Wileman's receiver thinking, that scared the little shit. He replaced the shotgun into its cupboard along with the Remington pump action then headed downstairs to Snibbard's office. The man sat at terminal three.

"How's it going, Snibbsy?" Richard put a hand on his shoulder.

Snibbard rattled his fingers over the keyboard. "I've just sent a sample of our latest SPI over the pond by special courier."

"Nothing serious, I hope?"

"No, just enough to keep them panting."

"Little bit at a time, Snibbsy. Just like we did in Glasgow. Remember how we started at Glasgow University?"

Snibbard nodded and to Richard's satisfaction lowered his head. Mention of Glasgow had become a deliberate goad. It reminded Snibbard of the female students and Richard's intervention to save him from the police.

Richard looked down at his friend with Machiavellian benevolence. "The very start of SPI over the Internet. Three girls, Snibbsy, we got three out of five girls into the woods. And who was waiting there? Not the teddy bears' picnic."

Snibbard looked nervously across his shoulder to the open office door.

"A long time ago, Rich. And you set it up. You were watching, remember?"

"Assessing the experiment, Snibbsy," Richard said. He patted Snibbard's shoulder. "But now for the good news. Zellar's going to put in a million. Providing, that is, I give her a good seeing to."

Snibbard grinned, then frowned. "But you can't. You're ..."

"Don't say it, Snibbsy boy." Richard pointed his finger. "They've got pills nowadays. But it's all in the line of duty. Anything for our partnership."

"What are we going to do about Faulkner?"

"He'll have his cut of PKL."

"He'll end up in prison."

"That's why we're leaving, Snibbsy, so we don't. But someone has to take the blame."

"Poor sod." Snibbard tapped a key and swivelled in his char. "But then he shouldn't be greedy."

"Quite right, greed is a bad thing." He moved his hand to the back of Snibbard's head and gently stroked. "You still have only the one set of flash drives, don't you?"

"In the main safe as agreed. Why do you ask?" Snibbard looked up through hooded eyes, clearly suspicious.

"I just want to make sure Faulkner can't get a copy," Richard said as casually as possible. "I don't want anyone fucking it up. Bad murder, that one in Ireland."

Snibbard's eyes went wide. "It's not me, not us."

"She reached level ten. I told you, who did you tell?"

"Only Faulkner."

"Best watch your back, Snibbsy. If Faulkner is using SPI to control another Zoby, then he's a dangerous man. Especially as we're about to drop him in the shit." Richard winked and went to see Patricia, his secretary.

"Any punters today?" he asked her.

"Two A1 investors, Mr and Mrs Fagan from the Brighton hotel. You're to meet them at Milton Keynes, eleven o'clock. Their contribution could be substantial. They're lottery winners. After that you have Mrs Zellar again."

Richard checked his watch. He didn't want Zellar alone, didn't want any repetition of what he had performed in her hotel room. The same time her promised millions were within his grasp, he had to keep her eager.

"If she phones, tell her I'm arranging shares and will be in contact."

The Jaguar was brash, its metallic coating a hideous gold. Richard judged the Fagans suitable material. She was attractive enough to play with, he was all brawn and clearly out of his depth. He doubted Mr and Mrs Fagan had much brain between them.

"Richard Caswell. I'm MD of PKL." He extended his hand, deliberately glancing over the husband before dismissing him. Only a numbskull wore a union tag in his jacket lapel. He smiled for her. She looked far more interesting, and by her direct eye contact, the one who led, and so ultimately controlled the money.

She smiled back and opened her jacket. He took that as a positive invitation.

"My wife thinks PKL is a top investment," her husband said.

"And I'm always right." She took a step forwards, lingering extra seconds on their handshake.

"Confidence is the sign of a knowledgeable investor," Richard answered, and waved through to reception.

Sean followed behind, this is what they had agreed during the journey. Victoria would take the lead and Caswell's attention whilst Sean concentrated on staff and the buildings. To authenticate their roles he wore a tie with yellow stripes, while Victoria displayed a yellow-ribboned bra beneath a tight fitted shirt. She had also given him an MI5 goodie; a metal lapel badge with an embossed cogwheel designed to tell any who cared to look that he was a member of the Amalgamated Engineers' Union. Except that the embossment was in fact the miniature head of a digital camera, its lead pierced through the material of his jacket to a camcorder beneath. Victoria wore a brooch with a similar device pinned to the shirt above her platform bra. He was to play dumb and quiet, she was to play dumb and pushy.

Dangerous, he had told her, but she insisted. Until he was off the suspect list, she wanted Caswell's undivided attention.

"You get a lot of investors?" Victoria asked.

"All the time. People like yourselves who recognise a good deal. They all come here, play on our machines, investors, distributors, journalists. We like to keep open house, keen to show our product. Seeking private funding from small to medium investors has allowed expansion without bank interference. The results are adventurous and impressive. PKL will revolutionise home entertainment. The games realise a five-fold return for investors."

Sean nodded and tried to look impressed. Caswell half turned to look back at him while walking close to Victoria.

"I'd like to have a go, try out the product," Sean said.

"Our viewing room is next door. Perhaps you would try an hour on PKL II? It's impressive."

"I'd rather look around." Victoria smiled at Caswell.

"I'll look at the games," Sean said, knowing the sooner they split up the wider their surveillance pattern.

"No problem. While you play with the Princess, I'll show Mrs Fagan our technical and administrative areas." Caswell smiled white teeth.

"Call me Vicky," Victoria said, and touched Caswell's arm.

Vicky, she hated that name, Sean smiled inwardly. He just hoped Caswell wasn't connected with Zoby.

In the main exhibition area Sean climbed into one of the twenty automated chairs.

"We'll be back in an hour," Caswell said and lowered the visor. Sean was left with the image of Princess Kay-ling striding towards him.

"Now, what can I show you?" He heard Caswell ask Victoria.

"Everything. How you put it all together."

"My pleasure."

Their voices faded and the sound of Princess Kay-ling's battle hymn filled Sean's ears. After several minutes he lifted the visor. The room was empty. Glancing round he saw no visible CCTV cameras, but that didn't mean he was not being watched. Careful to maintain the behaviour of someone unaware, he walked up to the control desk, his expression disgruntled, as if he was searching to install a different game. The desk held a half dozen CD ports. He opened the port marked five that matched with his chair number and surreptitiously slid the game DVD inside his jacket pocket. If it contained SPI, he had enough to raid the place and make arrests. From a plastic case on the desktop he slotted a replacement disk into the port he had just emptied. The closed case he shuffled back amongst others. With luck no-one would notice. Still casual, he stood from the controls and went out to the corridor. No one from security turned up to stop him. Time to explore, he thought.

Victoria was conscious she bounced with each step, the movement beneath her blouse keeping Caswell's close attention. His hand was often at her back when he opened doors and he stood close while they bent over computer screens. He had that confident, public school arrogance which patronised lesser mortals. He did all this with a sickly, white-toothed smile that at best was patronising and at worst, creepy. It created an overwhelming desire for her to knee him in the groin.

"You husband does not seem interested in the production or administration of PKL," Caswell said.

Victoria flicked dismissively with her hand. "He's a welder with a welder's mentality. That's tits and the sports page. You'd think five million would change his life, but not a chance." She shook her head.

"Five million?" Caswell echoed, his voice dropping an octave.

"Split between us, of course."

"And how much were you thinking of investing here, Vicky?" He opened the double doors for her and for once his hand did not touch the back of her bra strap.

Victoria put her head to one side and lifted an eyebrow. "I'm told by insiders you can quadruple my money in one year. On the surface, it's too good to be true. But it is very tempting, that is, if I am tempted."

"I have a special portfolio for high investors. Were you thinking much over a half million?"

"Talk right and it could be a million."

His smile changed, becoming wide and extra toothy. "Just how can I do that, Mrs Fagan?"

"You could explain more about the business prospects, maybe over lunch or dinner?"

"And would Mr Fagan attend also?"

"I'm sure he'll be too busy reading page three."

"I'll make arrangements, Vicky."

She smiled at him, drew breath and strained the buttons on her shirtfront. Sean wouldn't like her going off alone, but this man used SPI to make money. If he also used it to murder women, then she wanted him terminated.

The staff were mainly young, academic in appearance and absent in their expressions. No one paid Sean much attention, even when he stopped behind someone to covertly film their computer screens. Security was clearly minimal, until he went to the first floor. At the top of the stairs he was faced by double fire-doors and a sign which read "Research staff only. Keep out. That means you." Sean walked right in. A front corridor led off to various individual rooms. Sean entered the nearest door.

Four computer terminals were occupied by employees older and clearly more experienced than those below. The deep hum of other electronic equipment in the room mingled with the rattle of keyboards beneath dextrous fingers. At the far end a young guard in a blue uniform was collecting a signature from a tall, shaven-headed guy. Sean was halfway down the room before they saw him.

"This area is restricted, sir." The guard came towards him, his arms outstretched to apprehend.

"I'm looking for Richard Caswell." Sean took a step back and played thicko. "He's showing my wife around."

The guy who had signed his signature came also. "My name's Faulkner. I'm a director. Will you please go with security. He'll find your wife." He took hold of Sean's arm.

"You mustn't walk the building alone, sir," the guard said, escorting Sean down to reception.

Within minutes Victoria came from the depths of the building with Caswell.

"Until tomorrow," she said to him, and led Sean out into the sunshine as if he were some errant schoolboy. The whole visit had lasted forty-five minutes.

"Did you get to the first floor?" he asked, once they were in the car. "That's where they keep the restricted stuff. I saw at least four staff. If they're all working with SPI, prosecution witnesses will not be difficult."

"We agreed not to deviate," Victoria said, buttoning up her jacket. "Let's concentrate on murder. We can deal with any SPI factors once we have Zoby and Crystal."

"Ever thought that Crystal might be running Zoby through SPI?" He produced the stolen disk from his pocket. "We can't ignore the technical implications. I'll have this analysed. If we find evidence we can go back with a full team. We can raid the hotels at the same time."

"Sean," she swivelled to face him and he momentarily glanced from his driving. She was biting on her lower lip. From old days he knew that was a sure sign she was troubled, or about to be devious. "Let's get this straight," she said. "The person I want is Zoby, followed by his controller. So I'm deliberately pushing myself as bait. Caswell is very greedy for money, mine at the moment. When I turn him down he'll get angry. We'll see then what happens. We give it two weeks, OK? If we go your way and have them for fraud and SPI, Zoby and Crystal might slip the net. I can't allow that."

Sean twitched his nose. "You walk a precarious path. For all we know, Crystal and Zoby might be the same person. That person could even be Caswell. If SPI is run as a sting to gain shareholders, Caswell will know it's only a matter of time before he's clocked. If he's shrewd, and I think he is, he'll have an escape route set up. He's a wide-boy and won't call it a fair cop. He'll try disappearing to the Bahamas or some such place."

"When that time comes, then you block his escape. But until then, don't interfere with my approach. At the same time, there is no harm in you being close."

"What if it's not Caswell?"

"Then we look at the other two suspects, Snibbard and Faulkner. Snibbard was once arrested for rape. Faulkner has convictions for Internet card fraud."

Sean turned down onto the M1 and headed for Watford. "You've been doing your homework."

"Not me, Alice." Victoria turned back into her seat. "I'm not the only one involved in this."

"And you believe Alice would let you walk in as possible bait for Zoby?"

"On this one, she'd expect it."

Richard sat in his small office on the top floor of the Milton Keynes industrial unit, his fingers absently twiddling a gold-plated pencil. He felt smug, spoilt for choice. Who did he screw next, Jovana or Vicky? Both of them offered serious money. Maybe they'd do three in a bed. He smiled at the thought and considered how many Viagra pills he would need to sustain himself for the duration. The pencil stopped in his fingers and he sneered. Decision time. Who would die immediately? Who would die later? Money. He picked up the pencil again. Whoever produced the money first would be the witness; the one who hesitated, would die. If he sexually goaded both on the way, it would make testimony to his bravery that more galling for the survivor. Afterwards he would give her to Zoby, or maybe, even himself. He had always found female subjugation most satisfying to his masculine problem. He would particularly enjoy it in Zellar's case, on account of the demands she had made in promise of her money.

For a moment he watched the pencil turn in his fingers. It was a habit borne from concentration, the slow twiddling of his pencil, his talisman. It was the single item he retained from the life of Harry Woods, a ten-year-old who had won a scholarship to Westminster. It remained his first and only prize. In two, maybe three days time, Harry would need to re-emerge from the shadows. Without raising the bank's suspicions, he had already transferred most of his assets into Harry's New Jersey account, including half the funds from PKL. To draw on that account Harry had a legal passport and no current history to hinder him. The only thing that Harry did not have at present was a body.

The ringing of Caswell's mobile brought him out of thought. Faulkner spoke.

"Richard, we might have a problem. That Fagan fellow, he's nicked an in-house DVD with SPI on."

"So what, he's a pleb. That's the sort of thing they do. He'll never reach level ten, never see it."

"Possibly, but I've just run through the CCTV security tapes because he was wondering round the building, then I checked what he did down here. He nicked the induction DVD with the 'buy more shares' prompt, then replaced it with another disk. If he was just stealing, wouldn't he have nicked a complete set rather than an odd disk?"

"Extra thick people do that sort of thing."

"And extra clever people bluff that way as a cover up. If he just wanted to play games, why was he wandering round the building looking at computer screens?"

"I'll be down." Richard stood and headed for the display floor. He had taken little notice of the husband, only a rich woman flashing her tits and legs.

Faulkner sat at the control desk tapping his finger on the software box. "What do we do? Working people are mainly polite and respectful, they don't go walking through doors marked 'keep out'."

"OK, let's assume they are police. What we research here is legit providing we don't use it on the public. The guy's stolen a DVD. That's no evidence for a court," Richard said, his mind suddenly in survival mode.

"They came here as members of the public. If they're police, then we're fucked. This is serious, Richard, very serious." Faulkner shook his head. "I suggest we start cleaning the system now."

"OK, if you're that worried," Richard said, trying not to show his own concern. "Go onto the Net and download our sanitising code to all public outlets. Phone the hotels; tell them all games are offline due to a virus and system failure. No one will argue it's bullshit. Then activate our cleaning programme. We need all hard drives reformatted then overwritten with clean material."

"That will take hours."

Richard shrugged. "Say they are police, and there is no proof of that, by the time they've had the disk analysed and obtained search warrants, it will be days before they're back. By then PKL will be saintly clean. Fagan could never prove that DVD was shown to him here. Neither could they prove it was shown to anyone else. It may hit PKL, but so what? We got plenty money. You and me, Derek, we'll just start again." Richard grinned.

Faulkner put hand to forehead. "I knew this would happen. We couldn't scam it forever."

"Philosophically taken." Richard slapped Faulkner's shoulder to express solidarity, then leant back against the control desk. For a moment he swallowed. It was time to start the endgame, time to move out. "The downside is Snibbsy. I hate to tell you this, mate, but you'd better start watching your back. You're in charge out here and Snibbsy might blame you."

Faulkner looked baffled. "Why? I've done nothing."

"I know that, but Snibbard's got a funny mind. I should have told you earlier. Snibbard may behave like a perverted little wanker, particularly where women are concerned, but underneath he's a total freak. He thought Lizzie Sinclair was going to cough on us so he did for her. Once he got the taste he followed on with Helen Carter and Sarah Finch."

"Fuck off will you? Never."

Richard shrugged again. "Well, I know for a fact he raped those girls in Glasgow, because he told me."

"Sidney Snibbard! That bloody toad wouldn't have the nerve." Faulkner shook his head again.

"But he did. And the last girl, if you remember, was stabbed. That frightened him. But I believe it also gave him the taste for blood. There's an evil side to SPI and Snibbard's been using it. He's found a psychopath whom he's nicknamed Zoby. It wouldn't be difficult through private chat-boxes to flush out a total shit-head. Apply SPI and you have yourself a remotely operated killer. Snibbard wouldn't have the nerve, true. But he could remotely use someone else to rape and kill."

Faulkner was looking at him with open mouth, his head shaking slowing from side to side.

"It's difficult to believe, I know. I would not have done so myself unless I had positive proof," Richard said. "I found a memory stick amongst our master files, hundreds of digital photos of the murdered women."

"You're fucking having me on, tell me you're having me on. Why would he put them there?"

"To blame us. I didn't place them there, you didn't. I've never raped a woman, you've never raped a woman. Snibbard has. He's the only other one with the combination to the safe. He's the only one perverse enough to have those women killed in the manner they were. I don't have to tell you how close I was to Sarah Finch." Richard brushed his brow, looked away as he took a sharp intake of breath. "She helped me in the early days. We even talked of marriage." He sighed, shook his head. "I believe you went out with Lizzie and got friendly with Helen?"

"You don't think for one moment I had any involvement in their deaths?"

Richard looked back as if shocked. "No, Derek, of course not. And I'm only telling you about Snibbard because I have a high regard for you."

"We should go to the police."

"And fuck up everything we ever worked for? You would be incriminated, I would be incriminated. Snibbard would blame us for the murders and the SPI. You may have noticed from the papers that miscarriages of justice are quite common in this country."

"Fuck."

"In a nutshell, that's why I'm saying, watch your back. If you have any doubts, I'll show you the photos that Snibbard left in the safe."

"I'll come to London with you."

"No. You've got work to do here. I'll clean up at head office and we'll meet there tomorrow. If that pair are police we'll come out of this clean. Then we'll deal with Snibbard."

Faulkner's face was ashen when Richard left and drove back to London. Now he had put his plan into motion he needed everything to fit perfectly.

Share value and interest in PKL was only maintained through SPI. With that gone, the sales would plummet. Zellar could have all she asked for, so could the Fagan woman. All he wanted was their money followed by their bodies. If Vicky was a policewoman then she could be the witness. Zellar could be the sacrificial offering; her price for feminine depravity. He had twenty-three of the twenty-five

WorkWell flash drives containing SPI in a safety deposit box plus a copy on his laptop. The final two programmes would be ready in the next two days. It was vital Wileman had the full complement to officially put the WorkWell programme worldwide. Then Harry Woods, using his secret copy to portray him as a trusted supplier, could send SPI influences wherever he wanted. Richard was confident the stock markets would soon turn his few millions into billions. It all depended on Snibbard. Poor Snibbsy, poor Faulkner. As for Jovana and Vicky, "Got a mission for you, Zoby," he said out loud as he headed down the motorway. "Except you ain't going to have the fun this time, this time it's mine."

Richard arrived back in Shoreditch after the office had closed and went straight to terminal three. Using the main server he brought up the public relations info and tapped in Fagan. He was thinking if the Fagans had come from the Brighton hotel, would they have gone there under cover as police simply to get access to Milton Keynes? He doubted it. There were quicker routes to PKL investment, it was still possible they were genuine. He hoped so. It meant a million pounds of Fagan's money remained available.

The monitor flicked through categories before stopping on a list of potential investors. There was only one Fagan on Saturday at the Morrison Hotel. He had given an address in Watford.

Richard checked with the phone book then connected to the hotel's PKL rep. "Lucy, it's Snibbard here," he said. "I need some information." He listened to her silence.

"Mr Snibbard from Shoreditch?" she questioned.

"PKL project manager in person, Lucy. Last Saturday you had a Mr Fagan who showed interest in investing. Did he have his wife with him?"

"Let me check my records, sir." He heard her tap on keys and waited. Her voice came back seconds later. "I've no record of a wife but there were two daughters, Rebecca and

Sophie Fagan. Both won new player incentive prizes, a trial set of PKL. We have their e-mail addresses. One for the prize-winners and one where the original hotel vouchers were sent. The hotel register does not tally with the address given with the bank details."

"Is there a reference number for the original hotel vouchers?"

"Yes they had to give that for their prize details." She read off the number. "We also have photos of the girls for our magazine."

"OK, so I want everything e-mailed to terminal three, Shoreditch, now." He switched off then brought the PKL agents' list up on screen. He checked on incentive schemes then typed the voucher number into the allocations.

Miss Danielle Pointu came up, c/o S Fagan. This time the address was St Albans. A man of property, Richard thought. Or maybe one of them belonged to Vicky Fagan. This did not sound like police, certainly not if children were involved, but there was no harm in getting inquisitive. He had to know whom he was dealing with. Rebecca and Sophie sounded the most interesting names. If Vicky came over with the money, no problem. But if they were police or some other concern, then Zoby could have a field day. Operating him from America would be a very interesting experiment.

When Sean entered the Watford undercover house he sensed the atmosphere as empty and soulless. No human spirit had yet left its mark, no history coloured its atmosphere.

"We weren't followed," Sean said, placing the supermarket bag onto the kitchen worktop. "I kept a careful watch on the motorway, and a careful watch in the supermarket."

"Didn't think we would be." Victoria dumped more carrier bags beside him. "But after I've met Caswell tomorrow, he might get more nosey. OK, I'll leave you to put away. I'm going to sort the spare room for you."

"I thought we were meant to be married," Sean said, putting beer cans into the fridge. He looked over to her, eyes wide and hopeful.

"If I thought the opposition might peep through the bedroom window, then I'd sleep with you. But as that is highly unlikely, you can sleep in the spare room. However, as you are a lottery winner, you can first take me to dinner."

He lifted two bottles of white Rioja from the bag. "Who wants crabby restaurant food? I'll do better. I'll cook you dinner. Halibut in white wine with olives, capers and a tossed green salad, or maybe you'd prefer peppered steak?" He extracted a bottle of Monsterio, Calatayud, red. "Or ..."

"It won't happen, Sean. Our lives are too far apart and too busy. I can't let it happen." She remained by the door, staring at him, her arms folded as if she were trying to hide.

He placed the bottle onto the kitchen worktop. "I remember four magnificent days in Cornwall. Four days where you and I played undercover for real. I remember one night when something so wonderful happened, it has stayed in my mind and heart ever since." He moved towards her.

"No." She raised her hand. "It's a memory. A beautiful memory I agree. But let's keep it that way. Let's not complicate our lives. Marriage never worked for you. Even partnerships don't work for me. This is business, Inspector Fagan, not a casual fling."

"That might be, Agent Lawless. But you're still beautiful."

She stared for long seconds. "So are you," she said and walked out the room.

He finished unpacking the groceries and laid two prime halibut fillets on the cutting board. His granny had always told him to persevere. Maybe he could tempt her with his culinary skills. Maybe. Upstairs he heard the shower. The night was early and Mrs Fagan had set him a challenge. Were their lives really so distant and far apart? His mobile rang and Diane spoke.

"Just reporting in, boss. Travelpath is big. We estimate there are at least twenty staff on the premises. Others come in on a shift basis. The boys are building up photo IDs, mainly males, but it's possible a female worker might be passing on information."

"Unless we hit a match with our burglar, there's no easy way out of this. We need to start following people home, see who their friends are."

"You're looking at manpower."

Sean heard the click of her lighter, heard her draw in smoke. "Cobbart would want firm results first," he said. "I have a disk nicked from PKL and a camcorder film which needs to be taken to Steve Rawlings. If you have a team member anywhere near they could collect them. Otherwise I'll deliver tomorrow. But if we can prove mass fraud, Cobbart will sanction more men."

"I'll phone round, boss. Be in touch." Diane switched off.

His isolation interrupted, he took the opportunity to check his text messages. Becky said hi, and yes, she had done her homework. Sophie informed him she had reached level 3 of Princess Kay-ling. Sean texted back. Don't forget your mum's birthday this Saturday. He put down the mobile. Don't do what I did, forget. He went back to preparing dinner.

Maybe Victoria was right, each of them was so wrapped up in their work they had no time for personal things. But every now and then they could at least recreate that same magic they had once shared in Cornwall. No commitment, just blind, passionate lust. He washed the fish, peeled the potatoes and set them on the stove. For a moment he paused, realising that was the crux of their problem. They hadn't simply shared sex, they had made love. Something must still lie deep, something to re-awaken.

When everything was ready to cook Sean went up the stairs. The door to the main bedroom was shut and his clothes left in a neat pile in the spare room. It removed any excuse for him to knock.

He used the main bathroom, showered changed and went back to the kitchen. Sean heard the deep-throated roar of the motorbike cut out on the driveway moments before the bell rang. The guy on the step wore full leathers and looked like some mechanical robot but with tiny waist and hips. When the visor was lifted, Jan looked out.

"Diane said you had an urgent collection. I'd just followed a suspect home to Radlett so I shot over here."

Sean gave her the disk and the camcorder film taken via his lapel badge. "Take 'em to Steve at High Tec. What's new at Travelpath?"

Jan shook her head, her deep brown eyes looking back at him through the elongated slit of the helmet. "Just leg work."

"What we need is the manager. Set up a lift for tomorrow, Jan. Tell the others."

"Will do, boss."

Sean closed the door and called Steve. "I'm sending you a disk from PKL. Also a camcorder film. Could you let me know if they contain usable evidence?"

"Will do," Steve said. "At the moment we're intercepting heavy e-mail activity, most of it's coded. It'll take time to crack, but my guess is, they're scrubbing hard disks and over-writing with new programmes."

"Who are the recipients?" Sean asked, turning back to the kitchen.

"Morrison Hotel, Brighton is the main one, but there's other stuff going out on multi-transmission. Probably to sales agents. If you open files from a trusted supplier containing a dedicated instruction, it would bypass any checks and covertly download a cleaning system."

"So we raid the hotels now, get what evidence we can?" Sean spoke with visions of Victoria in Cobbart's office, her lips compressed, her eyes unyielding. What did MI5 know that he didn't?

"Too late," Steve said. "By the time we're on target everything will be clean. It will only blow our cover. Somewhere, someone won't open their file instruction. We need only one lead, one staff member to start talking. One agent or investor with a suspect file."

"I know just the person. Keep at it, Steve." Sean redialled and waited on Danielle. "If you receive e-mails from PKL, the girls' prize, possible business information, don't open them."

"But my research. What must I do?"

"As I tell you."

"Les hommes!"

Sean listened to the silence as she switched off. If PKL were cleaning files then they suspected unwanted interest. He couldn't see how his lifting of the DVD had compromised their operation, but it was possible they were edgy after the Irish murder. Which also meant whoever cleaned was a participant.

He returned to the kitchen and started to cook. If their cover had been blown then any contact Victoria now made on her own would be dangerous. She would need backup and if MI5 wouldn't provide it, then he would, whether she liked it or not, whether she knew or not.

When Victoria appeared, she had clearly made an effort. A top and long skirt flattered her figure but in a totally discreet manner. Her makeup was light, her hair loose.

"You look stunning," he said.

"Thank you." She smiled and folded her arms staying near the door. Her expression had a mixture of sadness and determination which he thought was perhaps the reason for her extended absence. She bit on her lower lip.

"Sean," she looked up at him. "I don't want sex for the sake of sex. I always thought you and I had more than that. And in truth, I'm scared of facing it. I'm thirty-six-years old with three failed partnerships. I don't want children, and yet,

I do want children. Same time I don't want commitment outside of my job. That places me in a vacuum cocooned by a veneer of resolve. To make love with you would dent that resolve. And that frightens me."

"Like it or not, what you just said means we have a whole future. So maybe I could start by tempting you with something more interesting than sex." He scooped a halibut fillet from the pan. "Good food and wine. Perhaps a little Classic FM on the radio?"

She smiled. "Try to understand, Sean, for us."

"I'm trying, for us."

End of mission, Zoby cleaned and stowed reusable equipment. Cards, driving licences and soiled clothes he destroyed. His trophies were the memorabilia, items considered keepsakes of war. Not even the Colonel knew of his trophies. He had to trust the Colonel, the Colonel had always been there, always in command; but the Colonel never knew about trophies. Zoby never told him.

The nun's uterus and vagina had kept well in the cool-bag. With the aid of a scalpel he cleaned associated body tissue and congealed matter from the black, grey tube lying on the kitchen table then washed it under the tap. He whistled quietly to himself as he set about the task. He knew a better job was possible, but it wasn't his fault. They should have allowed him to stay in medical school and become a top surgeon. Zoby stopped his tuneless whistling and started to hum the Princess Kay-ling battle hymn. Both ovaries and fallopian tubes were severed, but he figured they weren't necessary. They no longer had a use. More important was a means of display. He had in mind a flat glass tank with the whole piece pinned out. Then maybe he would give it to Tate Modern. Dead flesh in preserving fluid seemed popular with the people who ran it and he would like others to see his skills. When satisfied with its cleanliness he let the soft tissue slip through fingers into a laboratory jar of formaldehyde, his nose wrinkled at the smell. Sealed away he placed the new jar next to Helen Carter's. Her jar was small and the contents something of a disappointment. He had really wanted to take the severed head but her expression had become stretched and ugly, so he cut off her ears instead. It seemed a good idea at the time. Now they looked nothing.

During the day he had phoned the office and told Stratton his mother had died and he was arranging her funeral. Stratton sounded sincere in his condolences though Zoby doubted he was. He agreed to do some work from home and downloaded files over the Internet. That evening he went out hunting but found no suitable quarry. He was restless now, he was always restless after a mission. Staring into the mirror he saw himself tight, compact, neat. The perfect combat soldier, always ready for action. Somewhere beyond his image in the mirror he knew the boy hiding inside was also watching, somewhere way back, somewhere no-one could see. To distract himself, he worked out for three hours, then practised two hours with his Samurai sword. He considered the possibilities of taking up conceptual art for real and making himself famous. The idea of shocking people appealed to him. He would steal a baby and cut it in half. Why mess with dead animals when you could do the thing properly? Zoby spent the night thinking of that and looking up maternity hospitals. The baby would have to be new, unsullied by human contamination. Unable to sleep, he checked his e-mail. The Colonel had a new mission, immediate action, code red. He sat waiting.

At 1 a .m. Richard came out of his flat which occupied half the top floor along with the executive offices of PKL. The conference room was the first along the corridor, then accounts, then Snibbard's office with terminal three. Downstairs was the main open-plan floor of the admin section. During the day this was full of busy, well-paid young women who accepted Snibbard's grubby attentions with weary tolerance. Richard despised them for letting the geek get away with it, but then Snibbard agreed their joint bonuses and made sure they got paid. For Richard, that made them all whores.

As project manager and Richard's number two, Snibbard's office had windows giving fine views towards the city, a little fridge provided cold drinks. Snibbard had never retained a secretary for more than two weeks. During his lunchtime, he went to watch pole dancing in a local wine bar, in the evenings it was a laptop bar. While students in Glasgow it was Richard who picked up the girls while Snibbard stood around open mouthed. After some weeks of Internet contact to place both the girls and Snibbard under SPI, Richard then sent them to the woods. There he could watch in secret frustration while Snibbard indulged his lustful perversities. It built a grudging one-sided friendship. Snibbard like a bucket of testosterone with a computer for a brain but never realising he was part of the experiment. No girl had ever openly given herself to Snibbard. It proved Richards first success with SPI, but like Zoby, it was now time for Snibbard to be sacrificed.

Walking over the office floor that was partially illuminated by moonlight, he passed the mainframe server that had been activated by Faulkner in Milton Keynes. Stacked in a corner it chugged and clicked, chattering away with its sanitisation programme to erase and over-write all SPI on the Shoreditch system.

Richard clicked rapidly with the mouse. The expected e-mail from the Morrison Hotel, Brighton, contained web addresses, the digital photo of two girls taken at prize handout, hotel register address and discount voucher number. From the voucher number he re-checked files for the address of the original PKL sales agent. As before the address did not correspond with the address given by Fagan when signing the register, nor the bank. For a moment Richard was puzzled. The present Mrs Fagan would have needed teenage pregnancy to be mother of the elder girl. So the current Fagans were most likely in a second partnership. Two houses in such a relationship were not uncommon, three improbable, particularly for a welder even if he had won money. It could possibly be a police undercover operation where one true address had been inadvertently revealed. He looked at the photograph of the girls, both beaming smiles of innocence. If Fagan was police, maybe he had visited the hotel with his kids and realised what was going on. One of the addresses, possibly the agent, could be the original parental home, Mr Fagan's family enclave. But he had to be sure.

He loaded PKL in the company's prize winning format and sent a copy to each e-mail address, one where the hotel voucher had been sent, the other a hotmail address given by the prize-winning girls. He did the same with a second, special prize. While the main office server ground out files for disk scrubbing, whoever might intercept would stare at reams of print out. Until eventually analysed, a few more pages would pass unnoticed. He tapped commands giving T3 a priority external line, then entered a private chat room. As he expected, Zoby was waiting.

Mission Code Name, Termination Road. Top Quality Females. Immediate Commencement. Confirm mission acceptance.

The reply came in seconds. Combat proficient and ready. Good to be working, Colonel.

Richard had a glow deep within his rib cage, a flutter of exhilaration which caused his skin to ooze sweat. He had never participated in multiple executions, both male and female. The males were a tiresome necessity, but females had become a sweet, secondary bonus to his overall plan. The sensation of watching them killed was far greater than the sensation of using Viagra to fuck. Pity to sacrifice Zoby and Snibbard, but then the world was full of Zobys, probably full of Snibbards too. Richard was confident he'd find more. He tapped words onto the screen.

Security rating, code one. Go to pre-arranged procedures. Swapping line communications now. E-mails to follow.

If the messages were being intercepted, Richard considered the words enough to start the police on a false search to nowhere. The real fun would be here, three, maybe four dead. He plugged leads from T3 and a mobile into a laptop then dialled out on the cell phone. Within minutes he was back to Zoby on a different line.

Previous landline contaminated. Future communication via mobile, text messages and email. Mission objective. Abduction and detention of two, possibly three hostiles. Information sensitive. Receive on need to know only. Richard hesitated, his request was out of the ordinary. He needed a lure. Finally he tapped Zoby's special skills required. Respond. He waited.

Received and understood.

Richard hunched his shoulders to type. Required ordnance. Prestigious limo, isolated interrogation room, personal equipment for female hostage restraint, commandeered mobile for non-traceable communications. Number to base control ASAP. Respond.

Received and understood.

Zoby to commence mission by transmission of PKL file, obey Crystal, trust Zoby. SPI rate three pulses per second. E-mail address below. No photos yet of targets. Suffice – top quality females, easy abduction. Richard typed the address and then, Respond.

Received and understood.

His fingers hovered. Zoby would not like what followed.

Once hostages secured, method of interrogation to proceed on my orders only. He stopped typing. Never had he interfered with Zoby's methods, but control of his overall plan was essential and secondary to any gratification gained through the remote violation of women. To add incentive he typed. Cash payment one k per hostile. Respond.

Three minutes, no reply. Zoby was essential. Zoby was conditioned to obey. Zoby must obey – must.

Received and understood.

Richard's escape of hot breath clouded the screen. Zoby had never let him down. Zoby was totally stupid. To whet his appetite he entered the address from the sales agent package, the most likely to be real, the most likely house to contain a woman who might satisfy Zoby's appetite. First female. Observe only. Report on any other occupants, possibly adolescent girls. Stand to. Over and out.

Richard shut down the terminal and stood looking from the window to the moon bathed rooftops of London. He found himself soaked in sweat. So many years of planning were rapidly coming to fruition. With a secret copy of SPI installed on WorkWell programme, he would have the same means as Wileman to send SPI to any Starways user world-wide. His influence would have no boundaries. It gave such sweet excitement to kill their women and take their money. Not bad for a boy out of nowhere. Pleasure came to every nerve, filling his mouth, his belly and his brain. They would never catch Harry Woods, no never.

Sitting before Sean's PC, Danielle completed her essay and sent it to print. She yawned and waited on the first page to clatter through the machine, the inkjet was slow and her bed was waiting. Passing time she checked her e-mail in the hope of something from Frankie. She found two. Once from PKL prize department, the other from PKL publicity. Ignoring advice, she downloaded both. The first informed that Sophie and Becky had won a trial set of PKL, the second, showed a cute cartoon character, the handsome youth she recognised as Princess Kay-ling's charioteer, Zoby. It said winning the first prize made them eligible for a second, surprise package. If she entered sizes and address on the following form, two PKL sweatshirts would be despatched by return. She felt so pleased, so happy for her lovely girls. She typed as requested.

When the printer finished she closed everything down and went to her room. Beneath the sheet, she pulled a pillow to cuddle, knowing Frankie would be unfaithful. She was far away, always popular with other girls, always one of them on the back of her Harley Davidson.

"Gotta trust the Colonel," Zoby said to himself. "The man pays, the man knows." He did not care for the Colonel's interference, but then two, maybe three k was handsome compensation. One female for immediate observation. It sounded good and got his juices boiling in anticipation. Top quality, he liked that.

Zoby set to work. He sent the "Trust Zoby, obey Crystal" virus as instructed. Once opened they would spread quickly, activating instructions concealed within PKL games previously placed on hard disk. Zoby was careful with the procedures. The Colonel had given detailed instructions prior to their first mission. He was proud the Colonel trusted him with this delicate and covert commencement of an operation. He imagined a real slick female opening the file and smiling at the cute little charioteer who waved out at her.

"Hi baby, who's right behind you?" he said aloud. He wondered who lived at the address given. He liked covert watching, liked to observe the pretty ladies he would soon be on top of. He would wait for daylight, he preferred daylight. It put people at ease, made them feel everything was normal.

The electronic notebook in Zoby's briefcase provided a client list that he read in conjunction with a road map of the Home Counties. Isolated interrogation would be difficult. He also needed people away for at least a week. In the end he short listed three properties and marked each with a blue circle. Now he needed to check no family members were left behind, no pets or nosey neighbours. He figured a drive of three hours for a fast reconnaissance. He had no worry about acquisition of a prestigious limo, London was full of them.

CHAPTER 14

Sean woke just after dawn and lay in momentary peace, the covers thrown from his body, his skin bathed in filtered light. He checked his watch, 0600 hours. Within moments the spare room had closed in on him like a sterile box, a place for junk and the unwanted.

The fish had tasted good, the wine had eased him and seemed to cheer Victoria. Classic FM had provided them with Beethoven and Brahms, music enough to mellow any woman; but Victoria had kept conversation on turmoil in the Middle East and the burdens it placed on MI5. Sean respected her stance and determination. He made no suggestions, no innuendos, or tried a surreptitious touch. He had faith in his cooking as a covert means of seduction. It failed. After the meal and a period of grace, she went to bed. Sean drank more wine, listened to the radio play Bach and went alone to the spare room. Dawn always brought a new day.

In the early morning light he lay contemplating. Should he switch his mind on and be confronted by the stress and horrors of his professional life, or should he just laze in moments of peace? He heard Victoria rise and move across the floor. Moments later his door opened. Her face was soft from sleep, her eyes wide and close to tears. She was dressed in lace pyjamas.

"Good morning, Mrs Fagan."

"Sod you, Mr Fagan." She began to undo her buttons as she crossed the room and climbed under his duvet.

He always knew his granny was right, perseverance wins.

Danielle awoke at 9 a.m., nestled a few moments then reluctantly swung her legs from the bed. She threw back the curtains, ran fingers through tousled hair and stretched herself as she looked from the small bedroom window over a well-tended garden. She kept it so for the girls to enjoy, for

Monsieur Fagan to watch them play; all children together. Her witness to his poignant acceptance of her lesbianism touched a tender instinct never realised for another man. She would sleep with him if he asked, if it helped until he found a good woman.

She showered, creamed her skin. The day was hers, the sky blue, the sun shining. One essay to finish, then an hour in the garden before uni. In white bikini pants and new yellow T-shirt, she went down to the kitchen, opened the back door and stepped out onto the patio. The air was good, warm and fragrant. Within minutes she added the aroma of coffee and toast, eating a banana while passing between PC terminal and kitchen, checking her breakfast, changing her notes. She carried cup and plate to the computer, biting on buttered toast, brushing crumbs from her thighs as she tapped. Only then did she remember the e-mails from the previous night and logged on to the Internet. She entered Sophie's hotmail address.

Congratulations, Mlles, you win top prize from your hotel weekend. PKL will be in touch through Princess K's charioteer, Zoby. Sounds fun. You can trust Zoby. He's cute. Hugs and kisses, Danielle.

Once the e-mail had gone, she checked for messages in her own post-box, pouting her lips at Frankie's neglect. "Petite peste, tu ne me veux plus. You love like a man. At your convenience."

The doorbell came as a distraction. Jehovah's Witness, doubling glazing? Too early. Maybe the milkman for his money? She opened the door to peer head and shoulders round the edge, her free hand attempting to pull the hem of her T-shirt below hips.

"Seaboard Gas." The man was young, good looking had his belly not been bulbous and his hair lank.

"I don't think we are Seaboard, Monsieur."

"Fagan property? My instructions are to read the meter. Could be my supply company has taken over your one.

Happens all the time." He lifted an ID tag hanging from his neck. He smiled.

Danielle hesitated and kept her body hidden, conscious she wore little clothing. "This is not a good time," she said. "Mr Fagan will return tonight or maybe tomorrow."

The man groaned disappointment and slid a notebook from his pocket. "I've done all the other houses. It means I'd have to come back just to do yours. It'll only take a minute."

"The meters are in the garage, wait while I get the key." She sighed away the nuisance, pushed the door almost closed and went quickly to the kitchen. On her return she found the door swung wide. Without cover she had no choice but to cross the hall, returning a gaze which never met her eyes. She pushed the door to hide herself.

The man's smile never altered. "Nice morning for sunbathing." He winked.

From cover she passed the key. "Please to return it, immediately."

"No problem, love."

Daniel waited, heard the swish of the rising garage door and went swiftly upstairs. A towelling robe hung in her bedroom. Securely wrapped, she returned with less haste. The man stood in the hallway.

Zoby watched her descent, saw suppressed fear. He liked them worried. She jiggled beautifully. Top quality for sure. "Permission to commence immediate action," he whispered into his head radio.

"You say something, Monsieur? You must wait outside, please."

Zoby held up the key. "Don't have a glass of water do you, miss? It's already hot out there and I'm sure thirsty."

She half smiled but he knew it a sham, her body was retreating into itself, terrified. One kick behind and the front door would slam. No one around, he could play with her all day.

"Please wait here," she said and turned to the kitchen. Zoby followed silently. Nice long kitchen table. Ideal for fucking her. Nothing like a good slam across the kitchen table. Her hand shook as she passed the water. The other clutched at the neck of her robe. He knew the signs, had seen them many time before. He sipped, put down the glass. Time for the day's pleasure. He grinned. Her eyes narrowed. The voice came through static bursts, faint but clear over the combat radio which sounded from his head.

"Offensive action might jeopardise mission. Back off, Zoby. That's an order."

She stepped away, her expression openly frightened. "Please, I'm very busy. You must go."

"OK, no problem. Thanks for the water." Zoby turned to the front door. He waved on exit. "Enjoy the sun."

Minutes later he sat in a black transit van especially stolen for the occasion. His next stop would be the interrogation centre, a place off the A1, the last location selected from Travelpath's client list. He whistled as he drove. A French woman, now that would be fun, real fun.

For breakfast Sean cooked a light omelette with crispy bacon and Victoria made the coffee.

"I'd get fat living with you," she said. She was back in her platform bra with tight sweater and second-skin jeans.

"No way, there's more to life than food. I have a rigorous exercise routine which is best started early in the morning." He watched her smile, then watched her big dark eyes grow serious.

"I meant what I said last night, Sean. Our lives are too demanding, too complex. Breakfasts together would be few and far between,"

"So, you admit my cooking did seduce you?"

She smiled momentarily. "Everything about you seduces me, but we both live with the dark side and our world is no place to sustain a relationship." She checked her watch and stood. "I'm meeting Caswell at eleven and I've reports to write first. He tells me there is a project manager, Snibbard. Both he and Faulkner would be ideally placed to put SPI out over the Net and play at being Crystal."

"What if one of them is playing at Zoby? Going alone puts you at risk."

"Caswell thinks you're the kind of guy who hangs around betting shops and pubs. If you came, he'd be suspicious. Playing thicko has its advantages, he'll tell more to someone he believes is unaware. Also he'll spend time chatting me up as part of his male ego. Your presence would hamper that. For today, I suggest you suss out Travelpath. Zoby is more likely to be there than in Shoreditch."

Sean drank the last of his coffee. "I don't like it. Let me have Jan shadow you."

"Sean, I'm MI5, I'm trained. I have my mobile. I don't want interference. I also need to solidify our covers. I intend to talk a million pound deal, that should draw Caswell in. I also want him to bring the papers round here tonight. Nothing will happen to me if I'm promising a million, so I don't want you here, just be close." She picked up her bag and hooked it to one shoulder.

"Am I allowed to kiss Mrs Fagan goodbye?"

She threw a kiss with her fingers. "We've had sex. Let's not get involved with what follows. It's called commitment. I'll be in touch."

Sean put the plates in the dishwasher and left the frying pan in the sink. With a dirty coffee pot and cups, it made the kitchen domesticated enough to look normal. Upstairs he scattered yesterday's clothes around the master bedroom and put his shaving gear in the bathroom. More than one cover house had been burgled by the opposition to check its authenticity. He never underestimated the enemy. Ten minutes later he was heading for the warehouse in London, constantly checking for a tail. Through the bank, Caswell now had their cover address and in Zoby's circle, no-one could be too careful. No one.

His mobile rang and Sean hooked it to hands-free. Steve Rawlings spoke.

"Amongst the garbage spewed last night from PKL's main server, we intercepted messages in a private chat room. Mission, code name Termination Road, Top Quality Females. Commencement immediate. Confirm mission acceptance." Steve paused, rustling paper at the other end. "The reply read, Combat proficient and ready. Good to be working, Colonel. Then they swapped to another line of communication on which we had no tap. There were hundreds of other e-mails. Standard stuff, probably auto replies. But those stood out. I'd say your man is active."

"Females - plural," Sean said. "Christ, this is getting out of hand."

"One other thing. The amount of activity they were generating last night may have been an automatic update to all outlets. At the same time, they could have been cleaning the systems. It's just possible they're taking evasive action."

"That makes our situation more urgent. Stay with it, Steve, and well done." Sean pressed numbers for auto-dial.

Victoria's voice came softly in reply.

"I've new info in," Sean told her. "Zoby is stalking two women, possibly more. His control identified not as Crystal, but the Colonel. There are e-mails from the Colonel giving Zoby orders."

"Obey Crystal from PKL, obey the Colonel from Killing Fields. Split command sources to confuse. Could still be one person," Victoria replied.

"Take out his control and we stop him. Raid PKL now."

"No. If they're active they're more exposed. Let's keep both fronts as agreed. You go after Zoby on the outside, I'll go for his controller on the inside. Close PKL and everyone goes to ground. How do you prove murder by the Internet? Crystal, the Colonel, they're here in PKL, I know it. Played right, maybe I can draw them out. If I need to be bait, so be it. Attention on me may distract Zoby's controller from the other women."

"What if the Colonel calls Zoby to Shoreditch?" Sean asked

"He kills by remote. It would make no sense to bring his hatchet home. If Zoby comes after me, he'll do so when he thinks I am alone. It could be I am one of the women mentioned. I hope so, because I know you'll be close."

"I can't be that close. Not unless you accept backup." He waited on her silence.

"You'll be close enough, Sean. Zoby's on the streets stalking women. Shoreditch is full of staff during the day and though I didn't tell you, I have an automatic pistol in my handbag, a small concession from Alice. And my MI5 mobile is constantly monitored for location. I'm perfectly safe."

"It could be they are aware and suspicious of us. They have a lot of Internet activity going on."

"Then all the more reason to strengthen our cover. The slightest slip up on our part and they'll run. Having them believe in us will only be done by full barefaced bluff. You play your part, I'll play mine."

"Just don't end up dead."

Since winning prizes at Brighton, Sophie now went to the computer room before starting gym club. She went at lunchtime, three days a week. The other two days she practised martial arts. That way she both met her heroine and learned to fight. Julie was computer room prefect, sitting as usual with her laptop, always ready to help. Sophie now considered her a best friend, especially in the dorm where they both played PKL on Julie's games console.

"Can I check my e-mail?" Sophie asked. "Dad and Danielle send most days. So does Heidi, she works for Dad."

"OK, but quick because the seniors will be here any moment doing the same." Julie sat at the desk beside her and switched on the computer.

"I've brought your PKL." Sophie held up the DVD. "I made level three after you left last night." She leaned on Julie's arm, resting her head as the PC checked its systems. The older girl briefly stroked her hair. Sophie closed her eyes. "What's your princess doing?" she asked.

"Level Seven, fighting the Meehong Dragon." Julie nudged. "Come on, you've only a few minutes."

Sophie reluctantly sat up and clicked with her mouse to hotmail. She had two e-mails. First came from PKL prize department.

Congratulations, Sophie and Rebecca Fagan. During your stay at Morrison Hotel, Brighton, your high scores have won you PKL sweatshirts. Please give your size and address so our special designer shirts with our PKL monogram may be despatched ASAP, and if you think that's good news, then read on. You have also won a full set of PKL games which must be downloaded from the accompanying file. Please do this immediately.

Sophie nudged. "I've won a prize. All the games, a sweatshirt, everything. We have to download."

Julie leaned across and checked. "Clever girl, do it through the disk writer."

"I haven't got any clean disks."

"I've some by my bedside, go fetch them."

"There's no time, I've gym in ten minutes."

"Shift your bum then." Julie squeezed so they both shared the same chair. "I'll download to hard drive and we'll transfer after lessons." She began to click the mouse. "Just don't tell anyone or I'll be in trouble."

"What about the sweatshirt? Can I give my address?"

"You know school rules. Never give your private address over the Net. Not to anyone."

Sophie thought quickly. "But we can put the school down – have them sent to grumpy old Mr Farlane on the gate. When he checks the post tomorrow, they may be there."

"I suppose." Julie tapped letters into the address box. C/o Gate Lodge, Primrose House, St Monica's School, Ivinghoe, Bucks. "There. If it is a bomb, old Farlane can do the commando stuff he's always on about."

The instant return e-mail showed it an automatic response. Congratulations again. In the nick of time you are now entered into the PKL Grand Draw. That's a photo session with Princess Kay-ling herself, plus two thousand pounds cash. The draw takes place tonight – so watch this space.

"That's brill." Sophie edged off the chair and hugged Julie, squeezing tight. "I have to tell Becky. This is brill."

Steve's call was the deciding factor. If Zoby was in Travelpath, Sean needed to identify him without delay. If that called for pressure, so be it. In the team warehouse he called Diane who was acting as co-ordinator in his absence.

"You get my message to pick up the manager of Travelpath?"

"His name's Stratton," Diane said. "He never leaves except to close up. The first opportunity without alerting the staff will be tonight.

"Then we take a chance. Phone and tell him who we are, emphasise the need for absolute secrecy. Instruct him to go out at lunchtime. We'll meet him as he walks."

Sean listened to her confirm and put down his mobile. He put the MI5 mobile that Victoria had given him into a drawer. He wanted them to know where Victoria was, but he didn't want them to have a trace on himself. He had never trusted Alice Sibree. They didn't call her the Wicked Witch for nothing and Victoria was her protégée. That morning in bed her hunger had surprised him and afterwards her warmth was all embracing, but she was still MI5 and as devious as they come.

Heidi looked round the door.

"We have a photograph from Ireland," she said. "Car hire firm have CCTV over their compound. Bad image, but I have the photo lab doing enhancement."

"Try it for comparisons with witnesses' description from the Bradshaw burglary. Check with Haggarty and Dublin Airport for security footage covering the hours before and after Zoby's flight. Do the same at Luton airport this side. Anything out of the ordinary."

"Will do, boss. A small item just in. Steve Rawlings reports e-mail over your personal landline from PKL. It was one of thousands going all over the country."

"Danielle's an agent, it figures."

"He asks if you want the line monitored."

Sean hesitated. One hint of domestic involvement and John Cobbart would have him out. That regulation applied to everyone.

"Tell him yes, but unofficially. You understand?"

"Read you, boss."

Sean scrolled his phone book and dialled Danielle. Her mobile was switched off so he left a message on voice mail. He shook his head over any possibility of connection. The Morrison Hotel registrar would give no clue he was anything but a genuine investor. Danielle was a genuine agent. The girls had won prizes, given their hotmail address to hotel staff as genuinely expected. Routine company e-mail was inevitable. It gave no way for physical contact, no location. The hotel register held a bogus address and their cover was still good. He shook his head. Even if they made a connection he was police, they'd be running, not closing. His girls were safe at boarding school and Danielle would be at uni. In his mind he realised the onset of a policeman's phobia; the dread of criminal activity entering personal life. Unreal, he thought.

"Shit." He dialled on the mobile. "Jan, I'm looking for a personal favour. Need someone to baby-sit my housekeeper when I'm away nights."

Sean stayed close behind the target, a dapper, bespectacled man who strolled along the busy Holborn pavement. Immediately to his right Jan crawled the kerb in an unmarked car, the bonnet level with Chad and Simmy up front. Diane sat waiting in the back seat.

"Now," Sean said, over the mike of his body set. "I want him with no place to go." Chad and Simmy stopped, so the target almost bumped into them and was forced to step towards the road. Jan pulled to the kerb, Diane throwing the rear door wide. The target again looked to side-step, unable to do so when Chad and Simmy boxed in the space. Sean was instantly behind him.

"Police, Mr Stratton." Sean showed his warrant card. "Please get into the car without fuss, all will be explained." He placed a hand on Stratton's shoulder, pushing down and sideways so the man's crowded body was forced into the rear seat. He went obediently and without protest while Diane slid to the opposite door; Sean came in beside him while Chad went to the front passenger seat. A moment later Jan had them out in traffic.

Sean again showed his warrant card. "Excuse this intrusion, Mr Stratton. I'm Detective Inspector Fagan, Serious Organised Crime Agency. Could you tell me where you were last weekend?"

Stratton's mouth hung wide. "At home with my wife."

"Can you produce an independent witness to verify that?"

"Yes." He looked between them. "The woman said one of my staff has been stealing."

"Unfortunately, Mr Stratton, Travelpath and members of your staff have entered our enquiries regarding a serious crime. Two of your recent customers have been burgled,

Darley and Bradshaw. Who in your company would know they were absent from home?"

Stratton's brow furrowed and his jaw closed. "My staff are the best."

Sean grimaced. "Answer the question, Mr Stratton, please."

"I have thirty-one staff, we work shifts. Eight till eight or the last customer. Lots of different people could be involved."

"You make life difficult, Mr Stratton," Diane said. "We have some photos of your staff, but not thirty one. You have company photos, staff parties, company outings?"

"Yes, I suppose, somewhere."

Chad turned in the seat and smiled with pitted, white teeth. "Kind of you to let us have them, Mr Stratton."

"I'll have to find them first." He looked to Sean. Sean gave his best friendly policeman smile.

"No hurry," he said. "Finish your lunch. I'll come to collect in one hour. Jan." The car pulled over.

Sean leaned back and stared at the padded roof. "When you return to the office, Mr Stratton, collect what photos you can. I want a list of all staff who had time off since last Thursday. I also want a list of every staff member who had dealings with Bradshaw and Darley. Circle them on the photographs. I also want all their addresses."

"Am I a suspect?" Stratton's lip jutted.

"'Course not. That's why we're being kind. We have an interrogation cell for suspects. But I do want your silence, Mr Stratton. If you mention a word of our conversation to anyone, including your wife, we'll know. We'll wonder why you did that, why you betrayed our confidence. Then you become a suspect." He stood from the car, letting Stratton slide out. "We appreciate your co-operation, Mr Stratton. One hour."

"I'll do my best." Stratton looked at him.

"We'll be watching." Sean smiled for the man's departure. "Follow him, Chad. For all we know he's Zoby and anything he provides is bullshit." Chad nodded and climbed out, leaving Sean in the front seat. He lifted the car phone. "Heidi, ask Red Team for spare members, ask Cobbart for all the help he can send. I want every suspect followed home and put under surveillance."

"Everything as requested." Stratton passed the package, glancing either side, his voice lost amidst the chatter of sales staff and customers in the busy, open office. "The group photo is a year old. Unfortunately, about five employees are not included. Two of those are presently absent. One with flu, one at his mother's funeral. Including accounts, bookings and sales, six people in this office knew our clients' itineraries. But most of the work is done from head office in Birmingham. I've no idea how many are involved there. I trust this co-operation results in total discretion?"

"Absolutely, Mr Stratton," Sean said. "As I also trust you will say nothing to any staff member until we have identified a suspect. Staff are loose lipped. Imagine the consequences if the press discovered someone in Travelpath sent clients on holiday, then burgled their homes."

Stratton showed teeth in an uneasy smile. "I am positive my staff are blameless."

"We'll be very close, Mr Stratton."

On returning to the car Sean pushed into the back seat, squeezing Diane towards Simmy. On the kerb behind them, an unmarked van with a periscope surveillance camera held six members of Red Team. The three parking bays were suspended. Sean opened Stratton's package.

"We have two principal suspects, so we can eliminate from the top down." Sean began to copy addresses. "One, Dave Hardy, Croydon, supposedly sick with flu since last Wednesday. I want him interviewed." He handed the note to Diane. "Get down there immediately. If he can't produce an alibi, bring him in. Chad, I want you up in their Birmingham head office, I want a list of all the people involved with our two files. I want their addresses; I want them questioned. Red Team works from here." He handed Simmy the photos. "Four possible suspects are on the premises now. Have them identified and followed. If Zoby's on a mission, he's going to get active. Jan and I will check number two main suspect, Mark Harrison. Seems his mother just died."

During the drive to Holloway Road, Sean stayed within his own thoughts, grateful Jan gave him space but knowing her questions would come eventually. She drove with aggression; her long, lean body laid back in the seat, her movements wafting a light, girlish scent. On her left index finger a silver Claddagh ring showed the heart turned outwards. No romance or partner. He revitalised his vision of Victoria's soft nakedness, her body entwined in total surrender. He had no worry about Danielle and Jan. Jan was a professional. Danielle had a partner. But like it or not, he couldn't shake his worry over Victoria entering Caswell's web.

"Sleeping at your place, boss, I should know what I'm watching for. You had home contact from the opposition?"

"Nothing so dramatic. It's me being over cautious. Along with thousands of others, Danielle is an agent for PKL games. Last night she received an e-mail about some prize. The next two days look like long ones and I won't be home for at least forty-eight hours." He shrugged. "She'll be at uni and you'll be working most of the time. It's the evenings and nights I'm concerned about."

"Fine by me, boss. What about your girls?"

"Staying the weekend with their mother." He looked at her. "You watching over Danielle, it's strictly unofficial, not even the team can know."

"I understand, boss." They drove in silence. He preferred it that way.

Concrete steps led to an upper balcony and accessed one of ten, drab utilitarian ex-council flats. Mark Harrison's property was central.

"He's out." The informant sprouted a De Gaulle nose with grey bristles beneath. His face was motley and heavy with wrinkles. Sean walked to where he sat in a folding chair. Jan re-pressed Harrison's doorbell then followed.

"How long?" Sean asked.

"Since eight this morning."

"You sure?"

The man tapped his nose. "I'm community watch."

"His mother died. Did he say the funeral was today?"

"We don't talk. He's army, SAS." Again he tapped his nose. "Less said, know what I mean?"

"How do you know he's SAS?"

"His uniform, the insignia, the winged dagger."

"Have you any idea when he'll return?"

The old man shrugged.

"Was he in uniform when he left?" Jan asked.

"No. In jeans and shirt like everyone else."

"Not dressed for a funeral?"

"No. Who shall I say called?"

Sean handed over a plain card bearing just his name and mobile number, wondering if he had discovered a useful watchdog or a nuisance. He suspected the latter.

The old man scrutinised the card, then tapped his nose. "Secret Service, I can tell."

"You're sharp. I'd appreciate you letting me know when he's back." Sean winked. "Tell no-one. Not even Mark."

Jan came beside him as they returned to the car. "There's a lot to do when a relative dies, sorting legalities, family and funeral. It's all stress."

"I agree, but if he's wearing a SAS beret, he's either Territorial Army or fantasising. Soldiers go on missions, and Zoby's on a mission."

"Want a search warrant?"

"Get on to Heidi. But first we put a watch on this place. This could easily blow up in our faces. If Mark Harrison is genuinely grieving his dead mother and we raid the flat, the press will slaughter us. I don't want to be bogged into politics but I do want bodies." Sean took out his mobile and dialled up John Cobbart.

"I need at least twenty additional men, some in Birmingham. I also need people on telephones to follow enquiries, at least six, plus ghost shift."

"This is supposed to be a minor, a preliminary investigation. You've already got one extra team."

"We're a leap ahead, sir. The next three or four days we need to concentrate."

Jan clutched his arm, listening on her own mobile before speaking. "Lab boys at Forensic Science have been on to Heidi. The DNA at the Bradshaw's crime scene, it matches with Poor Girl."

Sean went back to his own conversation. "We have six lead suspects, plus a possible twenty on the fringes. Our burglar has provided positive DNA linking Poor Girl. Zoby is poised ready to kill again, no time to fuck about, John. We have to do this."

"Give me an hour."

"Appreciate it, sir." Sean switched off. Jan was leaning on the car roof, still talking. "Is that Heidi?" he asked and took the mobile. "Heidi, get on to the War Office, Territorial Army, SAS and Special Forces. Ask Records if they've got a Mark Harrison listed. I need addresses."

He listened to a falter in Heidi's voice. Stress. "Guv, I've got Jill from Red Team but our telephones are getting hot. I need more lines, I need more people."

"Cavalry's coming. Six people, plus a ghost shift. The troll is gathering forces via the Old Boys' Club."

CHAPTER 15

The Dobbs' home was a single storey gatehouse, a mile off the A1. The original old manor was converted into offices and its grounds now a sprawl of light industrial buildings scattered between unsold plots. Not the ideal setting, Zoby thought, but isolated. No other domestic buildings meant no neighbours to interfere. A hedge and trees gave shelter.

He left his van on the industrial estate and walked back along the road carrying a fuel can. He walked unhurriedly, thinking that to any observer he would appear some jackass driver who had run out of petrol.

He entered the Dobbs' place by a side gate and stood in a well-kept garden with trim lawns and weedless flowerbeds. The Dobbs clearly gave it time. Dobbs' little haven, he thought. A plaque beside the door read, Hollyoaks. Zoby spat on the black polished wood and watched his phlegm slide down over the white lettering.

Round the back, a chewed rubber ring and punctured ball meant a dog in kennels. No cat flap, no rabbit hutch, so no neighbours to call around for pet feeding. The burglar alarm was an irritant rather than a deterrent. Zoby switched on his head radio.

"Enemy base deserted, Colonel. Moving forward to test security."

"Steady as you go, Zoby."

"Steady it is, Colonel."

Zoby walked the full perimeter, checking each window and locating the bell box. He saw no phone number and recognised the logo as a DIY warehouse product. That meant the system would probably be unmonitored. At the back he pulled on gloves and using a bayonet prised loose the glazing beads on a sash window. The small double-glazed unit came out easily and he reached to unfasten the latch. Holding his breath he slid the sash upwards and broke contact on the closed-circuit alarm system. When the electronic sound went off, panic clawed his brain, the high-pitched screech piercing the air and surrounding trees. Instinctively he cowered, then steadied himself. He was combat proficient, strong. "Going to sit this one out, Colonel," he said into his head radio. "Going to see what reaction we have." Zoby walked back through the garden and returned to his van. The screeching alarm faded with distance. He waited twenty minutes for the bell-stop timer to cut in and silence the noise nuisance. To pass the time he hummed Kay-ling's battle hymn, drumming his fingers on the steering wheel and figuring what he'd do to her when he reached level ten. When the alarm finally stopped he knew that unless someone came to reset the system, the auto cut-off and the broken contact would leave the alarm inoperable. He could now return with impunity.

After thirty minutes he drove back passed the house. The alarm was silent, no police, no security firm, no-one. Zoby swung round at the next road junction. This time he opened the double gates and parked on the front lawn so the van was left hidden behind high hedges.

To be extra safe, he searched out folding steps from the garden shed, then using them to reach the bell box, he prised it off the wall with his bayonet before throwing it into the adjoining woods. Once inside the house he went to the living room and stood by double French windows which overlooked the back garden. "Enemy position secured, Colonel," he said into his head radio.

"Roger that, Zoby. Assess for provisions and ordnance."

Zoby did as instructed and checked the whole premises. "Some food in the freezer and a kitchen full of knives. But I'll bring my own, I work best with my own. Proceeding back to base." Zoby spoke into his own head and heard the crackle of static inside before the Colonel replied.

"Roger that. Crystal should have delivered your mission funds by now. Pick up when needed."

"Will do, Colonel. Over and out." Zoby was impatient for his cash. He liked to count his money. Certain it would be there, he drove straight to the graveyard. Nothing.

The black mist came down on him. He felt the pressure of it inside his skull, felt it eating his mind. "Damn you, Crystal. Where's my cash? If you want me to proceed as ordered, I want my cash." He called up on his radio. "No money or I.D. on the hostiles. What the fucks wrong?"

"Crystal must have screwed up. Leave it with me."

"Will do, Colonel. Over and out." Zoby kicked at the grave and scattered the marble chippings. "Shit head Crystal." He went back to the van and drove to his council estate where he spent ten minutes changing number plates. It calmed him, having something to do. Only when the pressure had gone did he go up to his flat.

The Nose was sitting four doors down on the communal balcony. He hated the Nose, always watching, prying. One day he would cut the Nose off.

"The police were looking for you," the Nose said, staring over the railings to the buildings opposite.

Static flared and scrambled Zoby's mind, the black mist was instantly back, filling the void with jagged images. He saw the door to his flat, its surface covered with soft flesh and mutilated entrails. He could smell the shit. He clutched the handle and steadied himself. The Nose was staring at him, mouth wide, like the stupid, crazy old fool he was. Zoby thought of killing him.

"How do you know it was police?"

The Nose narrowed his eyes. "I can tell the Old Bill a mile off."

"MI5," Zoby corrected. "How long ago?"

"Ten minutes. Sorry to hear about your mother."

"We all get to die." He pushed open the door, closing it as he clasped his head. What had he done? Each mission had been a success. The fucking police weren't in on this. This was Crystal, this was Crystal fucking up. The black void was now burrowing through statics, forming a hollow core in his mind. "Crystal, fucking Crystal," he said, his cheek against the floor. The Colonel had stopped answering his call sign.

Zoby was unsure how long he floated in the war zone but finally the static faded. He stood up from the floor and immediately switched on his head radio.

"Zoby to Colonel. Have reports of hostiles snooping base camp."

"We can't jeopardise mission, Zoby. Take for a long haul."

"Will do, Colonel."

Zoby's two bergens had cost one hundred and eighty pounds each. He figured the situation demanded both. Shifting base because of hostile activity was now routine. The pigs were always sniffing. He packed a full set of fatigues, blazer, slacks and other clothes wrapped round a dismantled shotgun. The Samurai sword was slotted so the handle protruded upwards. Laptop and game disks he pushed to outside pouches along with a stolen mobile. The bulk of one bergen he packed with cash plus a roll of hunting knives. Into the second bergen went makeup and wigs, chemicals, police uniform, police and chauffeur's caps, false number plates, waterproof combat coat, then crash helmet on top. He hated leaving his trophies, hated leaving his bulky PC. He checked e-mails then deleted everything. While packing he considered burning the place but figured the Nose would have the fire brigade around before he was down the steps. Nothing he could do about prints, but they hadn't caught him yet, and they wouldn't catch him now.

He humped one of the bergens into the back of the transit van followed by his moped. The Nose watched him leave but said nothing. Zoby knew the guy would soon be gathering his stick, taking his insect body back to his flat so he could phone the police.

"I'm going to my mother's funeral, I may be away three, four days. Keep an eye on the place will you?" Zoby asked him.

The Nose raised his finger but said nothing. Zoby hoisted the last bergen onto his back. Time to go to war, he thought. Within the hour he was back at Hollyoaks.

With a platform bra and white Lycra sweater under a fitted jacket, Victoria felt like a two-pronged bumper bar. Standing self-consciously in PKL's reception, she expected to spend the day as the sole companion of Richard Caswell. Dangling a million pound investment while dressed to give no doubt of what lay beneath and on offer, she hoped to distract Caswell enough to build psychological pointers. Faced with sexual opportunity, most men begin to stalk and in doing so, become overbold, boastful and careless. Judging from Caswell's attentions the previous day, she had no doubt of his interest and she felt safe in exploiting it. What could he do in a busy office, even if he was Crystal?

After announcing herself to the receptionist she unbuttoned her jacket and waited for her target to appear. Instead a fat-waisted man with hooded eyes came down the stairs. His gaze immediately latched onto the prominence of her nipples and remained there until he offered his hand.

"Hi, I'm Snibbard, PKL's project manager. Richard asked me to show you around."

Victoria smiled and tried to hide her disappointment as he pressed clammy skin against her palm. Of the three principal suspects within PKL, she rated this guy as second; and by his manner, it was clear he had a sexual obsession bordering on anti-social. But having set herself up, she gritted teeth and left her jacket open.

Snibbard raised an arm to usher her forwards but as she stepped passed his other hand brushed the stretched fabric of her jeans. She glowered annoyance but Snibbard appeared unaware of the contact. She had his measure then.

"I have another lady here, you'll be doing this tour together," he said, leading her behind office partitioning which divided the open floor. "Allow me to introduce Mrs Zellar."

Mrs Zellar rose from her chair and looked Victoria over with the curiosity of one assessing the opposition. She wore a smart trouser suit and about a kilo of gold in various adornments around her throat and fingers. Victoria smiled, lifted her chest in a deep breath and shook hands. Zellar was clearly a professional piranha.

"I expected to meet Richard," Zellar said.

Snibbard grinned a full set of teeth and clasped his hands together. "He's out on an emergency call to our unit in Milton Keynes. The main server is playing up and we've had to re-install some programmes. As number two in PKL, I'm deputising for Richard."

"He will not be back?" Zellar asked, looking at Snibbard as if he emitted some loathsome crepitation.

"He also has to arrange extra share certificates, Mrs Zellar. He hoped you would understand."

Victoria watched the woman's plastic smile which for moments gave the appearance of a blow-up doll. "OK. So what do you show us?" Zeller asked.

Snibbard led them back out into the main office. "I've two DVD interactive chairs in the conference room. You can view up there without interruption."

"Tell me, Mr Snibbard," Victoria said as they walked towards a staircase. "What exactly do you control here?"

"I put it all together." He followed them up the stairs, Victoria conscious of his eyes burning into her from behind. "Without boasting, everything you see in the finished products of PKL and WorkWell are the results of my engineering."

"Everything?"

"Well, plus the team of course, also there's input from Derek Faulkner who you may have met yesterday at Milton

Keynes. He's responsible for the animation. Richard is creative and administrative director but also with technical input. But I assemble and collate everything. The final effects are all mine."

Victoria suppressed a shudder and turned at the top of the stairs. "I'll be interested to see these effects."

She suffered Snibbard to help fasten her into the games chair. His arm brushed her breasts, his fingers fumbled at her waist and on her legs. She watched Zellar allow the same with an attitude of bored indifference, which for Victoria, confirmed she was there to make rather than to give. Snibbard just indulged himself. Would Crystal be so blatantly obvious? Victoria kept her mind open. At least with others around he could do no more than irritate. She wondered if that was why Caswell was absent; so Snibbard could vilify himself. Not the best way to treat potential investors. Or was he testing her?

Two hours were given to video games, mainly the new version of Princess Kay-ling. Then they toured the design office directly below Caswell's flat. Again the space was open plan with moveable screens. It housed a team of ten industrious young geeks of both genders. Victoria judged none capable of hurting a fly, never mind another human being. All appeared happy.

"All staff are eligible for a substantial bonus on account of completing a WorkWell project ahead of schedule," Snibbard said. "Richard is generous that way. PKL has researched part of WorkWell for Starways. The system will hit worldwide. By next year every institution will be affected, my work again." He smiled, chin back, smug.

"So how much work do you do for Starways?" Victoria asked, snatching at Snibbard's indiscreet revelation.

Snibbard expression became cautious. "PKL have a minor sub-contract for insertion of WorkWell updates, it's insignificant really. Our lucrative areas are PKL and Killing Field. Forget Starways, it's nothing."

"Killing Field is not exactly a name for family entertainment," Victoria said. "Who thought that up?"

"It came when we bought the licence. PKL is for families, Killing Field is for the TWs. Short for testicle wavers, that's what we call them."

You're one of them, Victoria thought, but said, "I'd like to view WorkWell and try some of the programmes. If I put in money, I want to know all your little activities, no matter how insignificant, Mr Snibbard."

"No problem," he said, suddenly distracted from her body. His face had coloured as if he realised his boasting had gone too far.

"If you could set it up for me, I'd like to discover what it's all about," she said.

"It's of no real interest." He waved dismissively.

"Let me be the judge of that." She heaved her chest at him and regained his full attention.

"I have done this already," Mrs Zellar said, and checked her watch. "I go back to my hotel. I wait for Richard there."

Ten minutes later Victoria was left in the conference room with a plate of sandwiches and coffee. She felt certain Snibbard wasn't Zoby, but he could be Crystal. Equally interesting was Snibbard's caution over her reference to Starways. It indicated he knew of WorkWell and SPI. A minor sub-contractor, who had the ability to insert programmes containing SPI, that was some influence. No wonder Snibbard had tried diverting from the subject. She switched on her buttonhole camcorder, connected it to the open line on her mobile then selected a flash drive from a wallet on the desk. The basic programme was child's play. Within minutes she knew how to download pre-designed packages. She chose one for stock control, another for traffic control. She sensed no SPI effects. By late afternoon she was satisfied with the programme's condition. With no-one to overhear, she switched on her mobile and used voice mode.

"It's clean, Alice. They've erased everything, even the games kept for visitors. You can bet the same has been done at Milton Keynes."

"The images you transmitted were not good but our first analysis suggests you are right."

"I spent hours this morning on PKL and Killing Field – nothing. The police would have no case."

"Is WorkWell complete?" Alice asked.

"According to Snibbard, yes. Either here or Milton Keynes. I have a whole wallet of flash drives in front of me, but they're not the ones we want."

"Then we go deeper. After following Caswell we've discovered a safety deposit box. My guess is, it contains a copy of the master files for his own use. The original are probably still kept in Shoreditch. Due to legalities and outside interest, we cannot touch the bank. Therefore it is imperative for us to monitor and wait on Caswell to move them. Then we intervene."

"SOCA already have an op in full swing and Sean Fagan is closing rapidly. He's crafty enough to have surveillance on this place without telling me. In the next few days, Operation Poor Girl will have this building busted. That's the time to pilfer. MI5 will be the only agency who know what to look for."

"I get your message."

Victoria paused. "OK, Alice, I've done my treachery, I want out now. I want to catch Zoby."

"Stay my dear, he's much closer than you think."

After homework and tea, with cheeks flushed, Sophie raised the DVD in her hand as she entered the common room of Primrose House. She received questioning attention. "Trial game for the new PKL. We've downloaded it," she announced. "Everyone can have a copy." She stood aside as twenty adolescent girls headed for the computers. Perhaps she shouldn't have told. What if Julie got into trouble?

Miss Nathan put down her book, placed an arm on Sophie's shoulder and followed the others into the corridor. Sophie grinned affectionately, "I won it last weekend, sweatshirts too. They should be here tomorrow. Becky and me are in the grand prize draw. We might have our photos taken with Princess K." Sophie felt pride in her news, pleased she could share it and get approval.

"Did you tell your mother?" Miss Nathan led into the computer room.

"Not yet, she's in New York. But she's picking us up tomorrow after school, Bradley too. It's Mum's birthday on Saturday."

Each of the four PC terminals had a cluster of girls all ready to make copies.

"How did you download this file?" Miss Nathan asked Julie.

"Onto the main server so everyone can get a copy."

Sophie winced under Julie's sharp gaze.

"What if it had a virus? The school network would be infected," Miss Nathan said.

"It can't have, Miss. PKL can't have a virus, it's worldwide."

"For your sake I hope so." Sophie took Miss Nathan's hand and led her to a PC. Both hovered at Becky's shoulder, watching her click the mouse through the necessary procedures. "Any sign of a virus?" Miss Nathan asked. Sophie thought she didn't sound happy.

"No." Becky shook her head. "Everything's cool. PKL downloads have a guardian, Zoby. You can trust Zoby."

After an hour the other girls deserted en mass for Eastenders. Miss Nathan went with them. It left just Julie and Becky. Sophie grew bored and pushed gently between them for attention.

"Read our e-mail, see if we've won the grand draw," she said, her hand over Becky's, encouraging her mouse to click on hotmail.

Congratulations Sophie and Rebecca Fagan. You both win the PKL star prize – two thousand pounds and a photo session with Princess Kay-ling. Due to pressure of engagements this session is scheduled tomorrow. A chauffeur driven limousine will whisk you to the rendezvous where our press and entertainment officer will be waiting with Princess K and two thousand pounds. Please indicate below ASAP a convenient place and time for pick up. The message was signed, Dr Faulkner, PKL Prize Draw Executive.

"Two thousand pounds!" Sophie stared at the screen. "We're rich."

Becky put arms around her. Sophie felt she would burst. Amazing!

"Let's tell everyone."

"Wait." Becky raised a hand of caution. "The school won't let us go. We need to think about this."

"But we're getting a limo. It's Mum's birthday on Saturday, she's here tomorrow. We can buy huge prezzies. We can surprise her."

"How do you get out before your mother arrives?" Julie asked.

"Simple," Becky said. "We tell the truth, well sort of. We tell Mum we need to buy her a present, that gets her to OK we leave early. We've only games tomorrow. Mum won't arrive until five, six, maybe. We can meet Zoby, get our prize, buy our present and everyone's happy. Cool."

"Cool," Sophie repeated.

"Where you going to meet him and how?" Julie asked.

Becky sniffed and folded arms across her blouse. "If he comes here the school won't let us go. So, we go to Dunstable as if we were going shopping and meet him in the foyer of the Red Lion Hotel on the High Street. Easy."

"Mum also collects us from there at six," Sophie said.

"And we meet Zoby at four. Loads of time." Becky sat back at the keyboard and started to type a reply. When the e-mail had gone she closed the computer down.

"Text Mum now, so we know for certain," Sophie said.

"Mobile's upstairs, plenty time later."

Sophie leant towards her sister. "Do you think it will work? Will Zoby really be there?"

"Of course. He won't let us down. You can trust Zoby."

CHAPTER 16

By 8 p.m. the ops room grew crowded while ghost shift received briefings from day shift. In the close atmosphere, Sean sat sifting through locations of possible suspects with addresses covering Birmingham, London and the Home Counties. Elimination was his current objective, it required speed in establishing who was where last Saturday. There was no further need for covert surveillance now the suspects were openly interviewed, just the collation of facts and DNA samples from mouth wipes. It was possible for the murderer to have been either in Birmingham or London, then Dublin and back again in a matter of six hours. That left plenty of time for a pre-arranged meeting with the victim. Sean also needed a face for Mark Harrison. The department artist had produced a drawing from Stratton's description which bore no resemblance to the bogus plumber. Harrison's neighbour was better, but it was still a face that mirrored an ambiguous mug shot. Airport security had responded to a request with thirty-six hours of video footage. A further twenty-four hours of footage was due from the channel ports. All had relevant times either to the air ticket or car hire paid for with the stolen credit card. At 9 p.m., Sean felt the pressure of a thousand facts and details crowding in on him. He needed a break, needed time for it all to filter. On Diane's suggestion he went with her and Simmy to the pub.

Close to the bar Simmy received a mobile call. Sean bought the drinks and passed Diane her vodka. When their fingers touched he saw her eyes lose weariness and for a moment she sparkled with a soft smile. Sean took out his mobile and dialled Danielle.

"Am I safe?" she asked.

"Sure, Jan's only a precaution due to this op having a remote but possible personal link."

"I cook her good dinner," she paused. "Jan is very nice girl."

"Don't spoil her."

"No more than you. Au revoir, Monsieur." She hung up and Sean listened to the echo of her words, imagining the two of them side by side on the couch. They wouldn't, would they? He phoned Victoria.

"How's Mrs Fagan?"

"Living the life of Mrs Fagan, sitting alone with a takeaway pizza in an empty house."

"How was your day?"

"PKL have sanitised their software. Snibbard is a grubby pervert who can't keep his hands off women. But if someone snapped back he'd run a mile. He could be Crystal, but my bet that's Caswell or Faulkner. How's it your end?"

"I have a suspect, but nothing proven as yet. For politically correct reasons I can't bust his empty flat, but tomorrow might change that. No contact your end?"

"No evil demons popping out of the shadows. I was expecting Caswell to phone, he never did. I've been left like a wallflower. But maybe that's intentional. My impression is, he considers himself a slick ladies' man, and I'm playing that angle far as possible. My beguiling smile aside, a million has to be of some interest to him, unless he's twigged us."

"Just remember, he's a prime suspect for brutal murder. Don't push your luck."

"Don't worry, I'm perfectly safe."

"I'll be back in about two hours."

"I'll be waiting, Mr Fagan."

Sean switched off and wondered how many times he had spoken similar words to his ex-wife. I'll be home before the kids go to bed, home before they go to school. Home before they grow up and you walk away. But he never was home, never there to read the signs and learn the lessons. Maybe Victoria was right – their lives were too complex and far apart.

Victoria put down the phone and returned to her half-eaten pizza. Waiting for him to come back, she thought, was really no different from waiting alone in her Maida Vale flat. Waiting for no-one. But at least alone you had peace. She had changed for him, put on a long skirt and stockings, also a more natural shaped bra under a very low top. She had revamped her makeup and opened a bottle of wine in expectation. She never did that in Maida Vale. Alone she did not sit and worry, alone she did not wait eternally, hoping he was safe. She poured more wine and sat for a moment until the sharp shrill of the doorbell cut into the silence.

Every nerve in her body went taut. Who would call? Had Sean sent Jan to watch over her, or had someone in PKL sent Zoby? She lifted her handbag and slipped the Glock 9mm from inside. She had no place on her body to hide the weapon so kept it in her left hand while she latched the chain then opened the front door. Caswell stood staring with the kind of smile which said he knew she was alone.

"I hope I'm not intruding on you, Mrs Fagan. I've been trying to get back to you all day and as I was on the M1 from Milton Keynes and passing, I thought maybe I'd drop off your contract."

She realised then why she had been left with Snibbard in a crowded office. It gave Caswell the perfect excuse to check her address and turn up unexpectedly. He had called her bluff and left her no choice but to play the part.

"Just a moment." She pushed the automatic into the pocket of her coat hanging in the hall, then undid the chain. "I wasn't expecting visitors," she said, self consciously covering her exposed décolletage with one hand.

"Remiss of me not to have phoned." He looked down at her, his expression predatory.

"My husband's unavailable, we should meet tomorrow."

"I bet he's in the pub. If I show you the contract now, then you could sign it tomorrow in my office. It's your business I'm really interested in, Mrs Fagan," he said, moving onto the step.

"In which case." She stepped back to open the door.

She led him into the living room. She could sense the bulk of his body in close proximity behind her, sense her own clutch of anxiety.

"Nice house," he said.

"We've just moved in. Everything is new. Would you care for a seat, a glass of wine?"

"I'm driving, I wouldn't want to break the law. You never know where the police are." He smiled and passed papers as she took a lounge chair opposite. Was this guy playing games with her, being clever by referring to the police?

"I like your outfit," he smiled, then stayed silent.

"Thank you." She glanced at the documents, six sheets containing details of share options.

"I like what's underneath too."

She smoothed her skirt. "Don't frighten me off, Mr Caswell. One step at a time."

"What you have there is just a start. There's ways of making millions if you know how. If you're open to a little explorative adventure." He smiled again, slick, questioning.

His expression made her flesh crawl. "Mr Snibbard was very informative, I learnt a great deal about PKL, and him. Mr Snibbard has an unfortunate compulsion to touch what he shouldn't."

"The eccentricities of genius. I hope he didn't annoy you. We tolerate him because his input into PKL has been vast. He makes us a lot of money. He'll make you a lot of money, but the man who puts together most of our programme is Derek Faulkner. That man could create any computer animation you wanted."

"Who created Zoby?"

He looked at her, his eyes momentarily dark, she felt the hair on her neck prickling, felt the goose bumps rise on her arms.

"We all created Zoby," he said. "Cute, isn't he?"

She uncrossed her legs and stood. "I'll read through your share offer and meet you tomorrow, Mr Caswell."

Caswell stood also and Victoria read indecision in his eyes. Would he make an advance and possibly jeopardise his sale? She swallowed on her sense of apprehension. To rebuff him completely and make a scene would ruin further undercover surveillance. She felt the lounge chair behind her legs as he took a step forward and raised his hands, possibly to make a point, possibly to intimidate. Was this the man who ordered Zoby to cut up women? If he thought she was police he would not be jeopardising himself, surely? Her cover was safe, but was she? She stood her ground and looked him in the eyes as she felt his fingers close over one breast. She had deliberately left herself open, offering herself as bait. She daren't show weakness.

"My husband will be home at any moment," she said, annoyed at the tremor in her voice. "When he's been drinking, his behaviour can sometimes be abusive. I'll be at your office at 11 a.m. tomorrow."

He moved his hands. "I look forward to it."

Victoria folded her arms in defensive protection, but her apprehension remained. This guy was money motivated, sex should have been secondary, yet he endangered their transaction just to fondle her breast. Something was not right.

"Don't take offence that I touched you, please. I appreciate beautiful things." He smiled. "And you are beautiful, Vicky."

"Flattery, Mr Caswell, is pleasing but don't pick up bad habits from Mr Snibbard. For the moment let's keep our business in hard cash."

"Message received." He turned towards the hall and Victoria followed, trying to cover the inexplicable fear that continued to coil in her stomach. She shook his hand before closing the door and for moments rested her forehead against the wood, listening to the sound of his car move away. Back in the kitchen she retrieved her wine glass pretending the tremor in her hand did not exist, realising she had fooled herself over her ability to ignore the phobia of all women, rape. She knew then that faced with reality, she had felt as vulnerable as any female hunted simply for her sex. For two days she had flaunted money and possible availability. But would he really have behaved that way with a million pounds at stake? Maybe she had been too blatant in her portrayal, or maybe she was seeing the first insight into Crystal's mind. Perhaps he knew she hunted him and was challenging her to back down or face him. Perhaps Alice was right, Zoby was closer than she realised.

Richard drove straight to Shoreditch and entered the flat above the empty offices. In the darkness of his spacious apartment, he banged his fist against the wall and recoiled with pain, cursing himself for his stupidity. For the sake of seeing her fear he had nearly blown everything.

"Control," he said aloud. "That's what Zoby's for. To do what you can't. Not yet, not yet, Harry boy." Richard hit the wall again. She was too cool, too icy for a new millionaire, ex-pub owner. If she had really been the person she portrayed, pushing her tits around and showing her legs, she would have welcomed him, laid down for him, given a sample of what to expect, flashing her money and her power with brassy ignorance. Not doing that showed she had no money. A policewoman would have blustered or pushed him off, but she had stayed ultra cool, even invited him to play again tomorrow. So what was her game? Maybe someone spying for Wileman. He didn't care. If she had no money, then she was meat for Zoby. Which left him Zellar. Tomorrow would not be quite the day people expected. Tomorrow would be Richard Caswell's last day on earth, whether any of them paid or not.

Richard sat on his king sized bed and lifted a mobile. Zellar answered on the fourth ring.

"I have your share certificate," he said.

"Thank you, Richard, I collect it tomorrow."

"Tonight, bring your cheque. I'll give you the twenty thousand, more maybe."

"I need signatures from my employers. Come to my hotel and tomorrow I give you cheque."

"If you want your shares, you come here, tonight. Tomorrow is too late."

"You let me take certificate away?"

"Sure, but first I'm going to leave my signature in you."

She laughed. "It is a price. You will not be disappointed. Give me one hour."

Richard switched off. "Whore." He spat the word. Another one with no money chancing her luck. Boy, was she going to get some signature.

He phoned Patricia, his secretary. He listened to her detached answer then almost sensed her sitting up from a couch as she realised who spoke. "For complex reasons, I've had to call an emergency meeting for tomorrow morning," he told her. "Snibbard's behaving real funny and Derek is getting pissed-off. I don't want any scene or scandal upsetting the staff. Could you do me a favour, ring round and inform everyone to take the day off. It's Friday so they'll be happy to have a long weekend. They've completed WorkWell and their bonus is waiting. I want no-one in tomorrow except you, I need your help. We have a big investor coming, a Mrs Fagan."

"I saw her today," Patricia said. "Attractive lady."

"I'd like you to welcome her and assure her everything is fine. I think Snibbard did something to upset her."

"Groping again, I suppose."

"Maybe worse. I don't want any staff there to hear heated accusations. A lot of money is at stake."

"I don't have all staff telephone numbers at home."

"I'll e-mail them to you. Once you've seen the lady onto the premises you may go yourself."

"Anything you say, Mr Caswell. See you tomorrow."

Richard hung up. Tomorrow Harry Woods came back into life. Tomorrow would be the start of everything.

Sean stayed in the pub for two pints then returned to the office when Diane and Simmy left for home. A woman DC from Red Team had taken over Heidi's desk. Once suspects had retired to their houses and beds, surveillance activities diminished, except for the prime suspect, Mark Harrison. The search for him had intensified. The woman DC was scanning computer records provided by the military, fitting names to the electoral role. Recent civilian deaths of any females were checked via address against a list of Harrison's on the military register. A son joining the forces was usually young enough to give a parental address. If his mother died, there would be a connection. None tallied, which made Sean more certain that Harrison lived in a fantasy world. Two other members of Red Team sat watching video footage from Luton and Dublin airports. Somewhere in the crowd was Zoby.

For half an hour he checked the files on Caswell, Snibbard and Faulkner, then at 2200 hours he left for the undercover house in Watford.

For distraction Sean slotted a disk into the CD player and listened to Glazunov Violin Concertos, hoping somehow to put himself in the mood for wine, pizza and Victoria. He imagined her smile, her lips, her body. He remembered her passionate re-entry into his life that morning, her warm embrace, the sweetness of her kiss. Was it just another brief but tantalising encounter, or the start of a hidden dream?

When he opened the front door she stood to one side pointing a Glock 17 automatic at him.

"Hi, having a tough day?"

"Sorry." She stepped back. "I'm a touch edgy. Caswell was here."

Sean closed the door and took the weapon from her hand, carrying it into the kitchen and placing it on the worktop.

"He was checking up on us, our home, our marriage, our story."

"Did we pass?" he asked, over his shoulder.

"More pointedly he was checking on me, testing me out. I think I fooled him, I said you were in the pub."

"Did he try anything?"

She shrugged. "For a woman alone his presence is unnerving, as if he's circling, hunting."

Sean poured himself a glass of wine, looked at Victoria's glass on the side and topped it up. "I warned you. Playing footsie with the enemy is dangerous."

"But is he the enemy? Or just one of 'them'. One of the male gender who see women as vaginas with extended parts." She put a plate with three-quarters of a pizza in the microwave and pressed buttons.

"Isn't that what Zoby is about? What your enemy is about?"

"My enemy." She looked at him. "That puts me in my place."

"I didn't mean it that way. Women are not so alone as some of them like to believe."

"Then don't isolate us by gender. Women are vulnerable, it's the nature of humanity. The male is meant to protect, not hunt us. We're not animals."

"Animals don't have the restraint of morals over lust. Neither do some men. It's one reason we have laws and police."

"To protect females? How sad." She folded her arms defensively.

"To protect us all. Just think, one human can now use SPI to murder another human, using a third human by remote psychotic control."

"How sophisticated we've become." The microwave beeped and Victoria removed the plate, setting it on the kitchen table with a knife and fork. "Let it not be said I don't reciprocate your cooking, Mr Fagan."

"It is noted, Mrs Fagan, along with your concerns on female vulnerability. But as you once explained, if the blonde doesn't want to kiss you, she won't and most won't. But if the blonde is undecided, outside events can influence her to do so. We are dealing with fringe lunacy. Zoby, like others, may have always suffered fantasies of killing, but restraint and fear prevented it. If the Colonel removes that restraint by SPI and then provides victims and places, it might tip a psychopath over the edge, as it might tip other seemingly normal people over the edge. And once their cravings are fed, bloodlust rises. Via the Internet, someone has a remote killing machine. Someone able to create countless killing machines."

"You mean the Colonel and Zoby might never have met?"

"Exactly. And if there is one Zoby, there could be thousands. Your neighbour, the person beside you on the tube, your auntie Dot knitting the kids´ sweaters. The populace might not be so safe as they think."

She sat down opposite him, her face creased with the potential horror of SPI.

"Look at the millions in North Korea," he continued. "How many have met the beloved leader? Yet how many slavishly obey him? SPI is only a technical extension of what's happening there."

She folder her arms on the table and hesitated to speak. "How's the pizza?" she finally asked.

For Sean, it revealed a little of what MI5 was not telling him. His directing of the conversation had worked. He ignored her question. "All four victims were computer experts, all four played computer games. What if they discovered SPI was used to sell shares? Maybe they were killed not for sex but to silence them. Using Zoby, the slayings would appear sexual and not commercially motivated. Sinclair was not killed for sexual reasons."

Victoria bit on her lower lip and sighed. "All possible," she said. "So, we stay with the three principal suspects."

"And Zoby. I'm gathering history on our three executives, all went to the same university in Glasgow. They all studied computer or related subjects. These three go back a long way. I've got Diane digging info from their past. All of them maybe guilty of using SPI. Snibbard almost certainly used it to lure and rape women in Glasgow, maybe Caswell also. Faulkner has a conviction for Internet fraud. It's possible all three are guilty of murder."

"Admitted," Victoria said. "So we go deeper, but by necessity, faster. I've arranged to see Caswell in Shoreditch tomorrow. He's expecting a cheque. I can bluff for a while but in the end I'll have to give it. As tomorrow's Friday, the bank won't bounce it until Monday. That gives us three days before our cover is blown." She checked her watch. "It's past midnight, time to switch off. Time for me to retire." She smiled without conviction and left him to eat.

Sean knew her departure covered a retreat. She knew now that he knew what MI5 were after, for the government, for themselves; the use of subliminal influence over the populace. The beloved leader wasn't far away. How they intended to lift it without anyone realising he did not know, but he was sure they had a plan, both Britain and America. That aside, Victoria was right about one thing. Dawn would come all too quickly. It was time to give Operation Poor Girl a rest.

After a while he went upstairs and relaxed under the shower. She made no reply to his knock on her door. The bedside light glowed and she looked up from the pillows with an expression which said she had waited; that this was now their time.

"Let it not be said I don't reciprocate your favour, Mrs Fagan."

"Don't make a habit of it, Mr Fagan." She threw back the sheet.

"Should I be so lucky?"

"That's what worries me, you might be."

* * *

Zoby considered the Dobbs sitting room and decided it needed interrogation space. "Gotta have room to swing a sword, stretch a woman or two," he said out loud. He began to shift furniture, whistling as he worked. He was left with three chairs and a dining table. He placed the three chairs side by side, tying the legs and backs so they formed a bench, that way he could sit the two hostiles with a gap between, or stretch one out over the full length of three seats. He'd done that for a while with the Carter woman. She hadn't like that, being stretched out while he played with her from behind. She had obeyed real quick after that.

For an hour he practised with his sword, slicing the air where their necks would rise over the chair backs or hang from the seat edge if they were prone. He had plenty rope and belts and found more cord in the garden shed. He imagined one over the chairs, another spread-eagled on the table, her thorax taut, waiting for the blade. He kept imaging them till his mobile buzzed with a text message.

Limo req for lift

Zoby switched on his head radio. "I need target location, Colonel. Two women might need special equipment, have to be prepared." He heard only static back. "Fucking combat radio." He smacked his ear. That left him angry. He returned the text message.

Where's my money?

Crystal messed up. But money safe. Women gorgeous, best yet. Trust me. Col.

Zoby put down the mobile, hit the head radio a second time so it crackled to life. This time he heard the Colonel instantly.

"These bitches are long-limbed and firm-breasted, Zoby. Top quality, hardly used. Self-willed though, need training."

"Leave it to me, Colonel," Zoby answered. "You want a limo, we get a limo."

He texted. Sending patrol to secure transport.

Zoby felt real neat in the police uniform and figured he would have made a good cop, most likely he'd be undercover, a top detective, catching those shit heads who had fucked up his life. He pulled a dark blue topcoat over the jacket and covered his head with a crash helmet. The police cap he placed in a side pannier. His journey on the moped into central London took an hour and twenty minutes. At 0200 hours he encountered little traffic. He parked up near Hanover Square and swapped helmet for cap. He strolled a little, then hovered in a doorway for covert views of New Bond Street. In the dead of night, traffic remained light with few pedestrians. He wanted a vehicle with single occupancy, a class car, Jaguar, Mercedes, preferably something with a stretched chassis. He watched for ten minutes but saw nothing suitable. When a cruising patrol car turned around the corner, he stepped back into shadow and watched it pass. The two men and one policewoman inside were chatting, passing the night while he worked. When he returned to the light, four girls, clearly drunk, went silent on his sudden appearance. He enjoyed that, power. He felt himself harden and decided to walk. If a cop car had passed it wouldn't do again for some time. He walked slowly, his hands behind his back, strolling the pavement for thirty minutes until finding the car he wanted, a long wheelbase Jaguar with chauffeur compartment. It was double parked and clearly waiting for a pick up. The driver, a bored Afro, watched Zoby leave the pavement and walk to his window.

"This your car, sir?"

"Just waiting on customers, man." The driver smiled white teeth, his hair grey.

"Do you mind stepping out of the car, sir." Zoby checked the road. No one was nearby.

"Listen, man, I'm only waiting. They're African diplomats. They don't walk."

"Out of the car, sir," Zoby said, and opened the door, sliding an eight-inch length of lead pipe from his pocket.

The driver had one foot out, his head coming up when Zoby struck. He made no sound and his body fell sideways when yanked onto the road. Keys in the ignition started the engine first time. A rear wheel rode over the man's legs as Zoby drove away. Across Park Lane he turned for Marble Arch. Thirty-five minutes later he was on the A1.

"Zoby to Colonel. Limo secured. One hostile down, no hits taken."

"Roger that, Zoby. Return to base. Long day tomorrow."

Zoby switched off his head radio. "A busy day costs money, Colonel."

Zoby awoke before first light, checked the perimeter boundaries then exercised for two hours. At 0700 hours his mobile beeped with a text message.

Check hotmail, Termination Road. 2 + 1 TQW. ASAP.

"That's a cyber café job," he said. "TQW. Top quality women 2 + 1. Hey babe, that's so neat. I get three of 'em."

Zoby took the van and left the Jaguar hidden behind the hedges of Hollyoaks. He would have to work on that one and change the number plates. A secure vehicle was essential. Parked in Stevenage town centre, he fed the meter, feeling good and confident. Three women, all he needed now was his money.

Zoby was the first customer at the cyber café. He tapped on keys and downloaded the jpeg file. A girl at the counter looked disapproving when he swore. "A fucking alien." A child stared out from the picture. It was the same stare as the boy in the hall. He recognised that stare, it went right through him, like she saw into him, saw him hiding deep inside. He hated her, fucking alien bitch. When she was his, he would cut her in half, exhibit her at Tate Modern.

He flicked to the second picture. The same Morrison Hotel lobby, but this time it was hot pussy, young, tender, good tits and a neat figure. She would make up for the alien. He flicked back a picture and examined the younger one in more detail. If she was cute, he'd keep her a day. If she was some whinging brat, then off with her head.

He read the text while printing off the contents.

Mission target. School girls, hostile. Location, foyer of Red Lion Hotel, Dunstable. See map for location. Today, 1600 hours sharp. Approach as Zoby taking both to photo session. Secure and hold captive. Do not harm until ordered. Repeat, do not harm until ordered. Crystal will deliver money personally. Execute him immediately after. Colonel.

Zoby cleaned the driver's seat of crumbs. He hated to drive a messy limo. Limos were meant to be pristine, clean and smart. They were for rich and important people. He had changed the number plates and filled the tank with sixty pounds of premium petrol. It hurt to spend his own money, he hated spending his own. He wanted cash. He waxed the car exterior with polish found in the boot, shined it like he owned it. He checked and stowed equipment next, ropes, belts, masking tape, clingfilm plus two sealed bags with chloroform soaked pads. He figured that would keep them quiet. The boot was large enough to squeeze two inside. No problem. With hours to spare he plugged laptop to mobile and checked for messages.

Rendezvous confirmed. Targets will be there. All systems go.

No mention of money or the third girl, Zoby thought. Maybe she'll be with them. Trussing up three at once would be tough, would need a quiet spot. He re-checked his maps. He needed somewhere near the pick-up point, a quiet lane with no-one around. Couple of smacks would quickly quiet them down, chloroform would do the rest. He hoped they wore skirts. He loved wrestling when they wore skirts.

He checked the camera and unsheathed the sword. Braced with legs apart, he cleaved the air above the chair backs in one whistling sweep, wondered if he could behead both with a single swipe. That would be a first, two in one. "So neat."

CHAPTER 17

In the morning Sean kissed Victoria goodbye before they went their separate ways. He figured they had one, maybe two more nights before returning to their normal lives. If by choice they met after that it might be the start of commitment. Did she want it? He realised now that her loneliness matched his own. Both were vulnerable to the other, both human. He blew out breath and walked to his car.

After driving in a five-mile loop checking no one followed, he headed for St Albans, knowing the war would always be there, circling his life, hammering in his mind, in his face. Always giving an excuse.

Jan greeted him with a chained door then waved him in to the smell of fresh coffee. She looked neat and scrubbed, boyish in tight jeans and polo shirt, girlish with a slight whiff of scent. She led him into the kitchen. There was no sign of Danielle.

"A meter reader came yesterday morning," Jan said. "He stood in the hall. Something about him unnerved Danielle. The guy was young with long hair and brown eyes."

Sean considered the possibilities. "Doesn't fit the description of our burglar."

"You can't jump at every shadow, boss. Meter men have to call. Do you want a couple of uniforms outside?"

"If John Cobbart thought for one instant my domestic situation was compromised, I'd be off this case immediately. I have no reason to suspect any threat. The girls are staying the weekend with their mother. It's just the connection via the agent's address. I'm responsible for Danielle, so I'm playing safe."

"Danielle's real nice. If you want me sitting again tonight, no problem."

"If you could stay the weekend, at least until I return, I'd appreciate it." He went quiet as Danielle wondered into the kitchen. She was wrapped in a bathrobe, her hair spiky, her eyes defiant. She folded her arms and looked straight at him.

"Jan says she stays at university with me. But there is no need. In university I have friends, some big men, I am safe. From what? You don't tell me, but I am safe."

"She's right, boss." Jan cracked an egg. "I'm more use to you on the job than sitting outside a lecture room."

"What about lunch? When you go out?"

"I stay in canteen. I stay with my friends. Jan and I, tonight we have meal together. That I enjoy, but not at my tutorial. I insist." She put hands to hips.

Sean recognised French defiance. "A compromise. Jan takes you to uni, picks you up this evening, OK?"

Danielle smiled and nodded. "OK. Jan helps you during the day. You need good women to help, Monsieur, then you catch this man."

"You sure?"

"Of course, a woman knows."

Sean passed through the op's room and looked around the activity as nightshift switched with day. Blue and Red Teams were swapping information. Heidi and Diane were busy collating, making sure everyone had a brief. Phones sounded as Sean greeted them. Carole sat near Heidi's desk, her face pale, her blonde curls newly sprung.

"Nightshift found six Mark Harrisons currently in army service but none with a recent bereavement or relevant address," she said.

Dead end. He thrust his hand into pockets.

Diane came across and put papers on the desk. "List of suspects is now down to ten. Two high profiles in Birmingham, five in London, three not so interesting."

"Head of the list?" Sean asked.

"Still Mark Harrison. Mainly because he remains an unknown entity. We have virtually nothing on him. The photofit from the office manager is poor. He doesn't match

our burglar or the description from the clerk at the car hire
company in Dublin. Mind, her description is basically
worthless. The neighbour's description is more like the
manager's."

Sean raised both hands and growled in frustration. "One
way or another this guy must be eliminated. Take a police
artist and find Cindy Bradshaw," he told Carole. "Work her
'til you get a portrait she can positively identify. Go to
Travelpath, get all Harrison's colleagues to verify or change
for an exact likeness. Then check again with the neighbour.
Check the image against CCTV footage on Dublin flight
arrivals from the time the car was hired backwards at least
three hours. He may have sat around for a couple of hours in
order to disrupt any time check. By the end of the day I want
Mark Harrison eliminated or busted. Game?"

"I'm rolling, guv.

When Victoria entered the café in Kensington she felt Alice
Sibree's disdainful glare over the crotch-cutting trouser suit
Victoria wore for Caswell. The material followed detailed
contours like a second skin while the jacket sculptured itself
over a platform bra and V-neck sweater. Victoria bought
coffee and joined the older woman who sat at a table, her
back to the wall and facing the window.

"It's for the benefit of the target," Victoria said by way of
explanation.

Sibree's smile was cynical. "Most becoming my dear.
Let's hope it drives him to distraction, time is now limited.
According to our source, Dr Klass at Milton Keynes, the SPI
programme is completed and the master file taken to
Shoreditch. During the last few days Caswell, Snibbard and
Faulkner have been scrubbing SPI from all public sources.
Evidence will still be scattered around with people who have
illegally burned games onto disks. But unless they are aware
of SPI and know what they are looking for, that evidence will
never materialise. According to our banking info, Caswell has

been busy juggling money to offshore accounts. A lot of it belongs to his partners in PKL. He has also twice visited his safety deposit box where I'm sure he keeps duplicates of the SPI files."

"He's skipping?" Victoria asked.

"Almost certainly. We know that yesterday he bought four airline tickets to New York, all leaving later today. He may have bought more tickets. I would say this is a man planning for immediate but uncertain departure. So, completely off the record my dear, I need you to lift the master files and copy them at the first opportunity. I'll have a van outside with men should you run into trouble."

"If I'm caught, where does that leave me, Alice?" Victoria asked.

"In a precarious and delicate situation. I'm asking you to steal. Any time now, Fagan will close on them. Removal of the files has to be done before or immediately after police engagement. All of which makes your action immediate and imperative."

Victoria suddenly realised why colleagues and subordinates called her the Witched Witch. "And what of Zoby, what of the Colonel and Crystal?"

"You may leave them to the judicial system to prove murder by remote hypnosis. Or if you successfully copy the files, then extract a just revenge. I wouldn't blame you. In fact with the rest of womankind I'd thank you. Just don't get caught."

"What if it's Caswell?"

"Then you have no choice but to leave him to our American cousins and trust in God." Alice gathered up her handbag. "Are you armed?"

"Yes."

"Discharge of a government-issued firearm will make the action official. Could you please pass it under the table as surreptitiously as possible."

Victoria glanced around the almost empty café, pulled the Glock from its rear holster and passed it as instructed. A second later it was in Alice Sibree's bag.

"Aren't you going to take my clothes while you're at it?" Victoria asked.

Alice smiled and raised an eyebrow. "No point, there is already little left to the imagination of what lies beneath. Just make sure Faulkner, Snibbard or Caswell don't physically get to look. One or more are dangerous," she paused and placed the handbag in her lap. "I know you are out on a limb, Victoria, but believe me, if you come out of this clean and with a copy of the files, then your career and future are assured. Within parliament and the Civil Service, within 5 and 6, the Box and the Firm, there is an elite community, members of an inner group, those who go the extra mile. Those who really control and protect this great nation. You can join them, Victoria. All you have to do, is do it. If it's any reassurance, I've had Caswell followed for three days. I followed him to your house in Watford and we'll also be outside Shoreditch. Nevertheless, you'll be inside, so do take care." She rose from her seat and left.

Victoria sipped at her cold coffee, her mind full of apprehension. Having someone outside would do little good if she were attacked where no-one could see. Alice might well have taken her clothes for all the protection left.

Snibbard came in early as expected, and called by phone to the flat. "Where is everyone?" he asked. "Patricia is the only person here."

"I'll be out in ten minutes and explain," Richard said, looking at Jovana Zellar. She had showered and dressed and was applying her makeup. All Richard needed now were Faulkner and the Fagan woman.

Zellar snapped closed her lipstick and glanced across with distain. "I tried. So not my fault. May be you should eat stronger Viagra."

"Maybe."

"Good job you have a long tongue. Now, my shares, then I give you cheque." She placed one hand on her hip and compressed purple lips to smugness.

"Your shares are waiting in the office downstairs, is my cheque in your bag?"

The smile faded. "It takes time to arrange, let me see my shares."

He knew then for certain. No money. Disappointing, but the plan would still work. "You've got to earn them. Snibbard wants you next."

"I will not." Her eyes flared.

"Then Faulkner. If you want shares for nothing, Jovana, then you pay the price. It's good wages. Snibbard won't last twenty seconds. That's one thousand shares per second."

She stared at him, her eyes dark and narrow. He knew she would comply. It was called greed. She hissed and walked back to the bed.

"When he's finished, stay with your legs open, because that's where your future lies." He smiled for her and wondered if Vicky could make him rise. There was something special about the Fagan woman. If she lived, maybe he'd find out.

In the lounge he removed the two shotguns from their locked cupboards. The Remington 870 pump-action was powerful enough to blow a body apart, but he preferred the old-fashioned side-by-side 12-bore, favouring it as a gentleman's gun and more in keeping with his assumed image. He dismissed future troubles that might arise concerning the Remington. Living alone in a large city building gave understandable, if inadmissible excuse for possession. If the police charged him they would also develop a false sense of security in believing they prevented him from leaving the country. That belief would fit nicely into the plot. He unplugged the master phone from its socket, ripped the jack from the cable end and coiled it under the phone.

After placing the Remington in a cloakroom by the front door of his apartment, he passed out of the flat and walked twenty-feet along the corridor into the conference room. Next was the empty accounts department, then Snibbard's office. Downstairs on the lower floors and out of sight, he knew Patricia would be fussing alone with her computer, waiting for Faulkner and the Fagan woman.

Richard checked his watch and entered Snibbard's office at the far end, his adrenalin surging. Faulkner and the woman were both due at 10.30 a.m. He had a maximum of forty minutes to set the scene. This was Harry Boy against the world. The lad from Hackney slotting himself into history. Snibbard sat rattling keys at a computer terminal.

"Snibbsy, me old mate. So you've come in for her too?"

Snibbard's nose screwed up in question. "Come in for who? Where is everyone? What's going on?"

"Faulkner gave 'em all the day off on account of the Zellar woman. That's why I phoned, to get you here early. You'll want her before Faulkner. With SPI finished and Zellar available, it's party time without gossip. Get in there now, mate. Give her one."

"Me?" Snibbard's screwed up expression became fixed on his features. "What on earth are you talking about?"

"Jovana Zellar, she's in the flat, yours for the taking."

Snibbard stared open-mouthed. "Fuck off, you're having me on."

"She's got a cheque from her backers in Russia. But to hand it over she wanted twenty thousand for herself. Faulkner's done a private deal. He said OK, providing he could fuck her. She agreed, but then she came complaining to me. I said OK, but if that's the deal, you and I want her first. Your turn, Snibbsy boy." He bunched his fist and jerked his forearm. "She's along the corridor waiting on you."

Snibbard stood. "You jammy bastard. Is this for real?"

"I'll tell you something else. I told her you do it rough and she said fine. You know, skirt yanked, blouse ripped. She wants, you can give. Just like you did to that bird in Glasgow."

Snibbard's face changed as his skin became infused with heat. "You don't mean that?"

"I know how you like it, Snibbsy. I was there, remember?"

"You said we'd forget it. It wasn't my fault. It was years ago."

"Twelve years, Snibbsy. I know it wasn't your fault, her mucking us about like that, pretending she was going to give when she wasn't. I mean, you thought she wanted it rough. Some girls are like that, like Zellar."

"You helped."

Richard shrugged. "Yeah, but I couldn't do it, not unless I took the pill. You did though, I held her for you."

"But I didn't mean to hurt her."

"Never mind, Snibbsy. I looked after you then, like I'm looking after you now. She's waiting." He pointed down the corridor. "Waiting for you to rip her clothes off. Special treat for my old mate."

Richard watched Snibbard blow out his cheeks. "I'd hurry before Faulkner gets in first. You wouldn't want to go where he's been."

Snibbard went to the door, looked at Richard as if in question then walked down the corridor. He turned once for encouragement then entered the flat.

Richard shook his head. "Stupid sod."

Alone, Richard unplugged the telephone server for the office then felt over the pockets of Snibbard's jacket hanging on the back of the chair. Using his handkerchief to avoid prints, he removed a mobile from inside and placed it in a drawer.

Within ten minutes Snibbard came back, his expression sheepish.

Richard rubbed hand over forehead, waved it, put it back to the arm of his chair and shook his head as if in agitation. "Is everything OK?" he asked.

"Couldn't believe it, she just lay back for me. She didn't like it when I ripped her blouse, mind. She slapped my faced, told me I was ..." His voice trailed off. "She still let me though," Snibbard smirked.

"Well, while you've been there, Faulkner was here, standing right behind this chair, raving that he was meant to get in first. Then he stormed back downstairs." Richard covered his face, looked to the ceiling. "Snibbsy. We got a serious problem. Something you and I need to sort. I know we did bad things at uni, but we were young and, as you say, it was long ago. The problem is, Faulkner's found out. Now he's looking to pin us with bad things he's done."

Snibbard's face grew questioning and Richard tried to fill his own expression with concern and reassurance. "Snibbsy, Faulkner killed Sarah and the others because they discovered SPI. The bastard has involved our work and this company in murder. We need to cover ourselves very carefully or we've got big trouble."

"Derek? No, never." Snibbard's nose screwed up even further as Richard inserted a memory stick into the computer.

"I wasn't going to show you this, Snibbsy, but I want you to understand what has happened. You have to understand the danger we're in right at this moment. While you were indulging, I went down to see Patricia. Faulkner was there, so was another bloke. I'd never seen him before, a hard, nasty looking geezer. Soon as I appeared he hid behind the screens. Faulkner followed me up here. I thought at one point he was going to hit me. He's up to something." Richard began to click with the mouse until a display of photographs appeared on the monitor. He set the programme to slide show allowing each frame to fill the screen. "A couple of days ago I found this memory stick in our main safe hidden amongst the master files for SPI. I didn't say anything because I was shocked and thought maybe it's you. Tell me on your mother's life, Snibbsy, tell me it's not you."

Richard watched the man's mouth come open, watched his head shake from side to side, then watched him shiver when the programme clicked to start. Both stared at the naked and disembowelled body of a woman.

"Did you, Snibbsy, tell me the truth?"

"Jesus Christ, I could never, ever … "

"Then if you didn't it's Faulkner, because he's the only other person with access to the safe. You see what he's doing?" Richard said, pointing to picture after picture that filled the screen. "He killed these women and now he's trying to incriminate us so he can grab SPI for himself."

Snibbard stood starring in fascinated horror at the changing scenes of carnage, then he began to shake. "My God, that's Helen Carter. Call the police."

"No! I'm not going to let him get away with it. If we call the police we'll be blamed and everything we worked for will be ruined. He knows that and he's relying on it. We fight this, Snibbsy, and we don't take chances."

"Derek, he wouldn't, he couldn't do that." Snibbard had hand to mouth, his face ashen.

"Maybe not, but the other bloke downstairs looked vicious enough for it. Faulkner's brought Zoby here to kill us both."

"Don't fuck about, Rich. Call the police." Snibbard grabbed the desk phone and leant forward to press buttons as he listened. "The system's down," he squeaked, throwing the phone, grabbing for his jacket and fumbling in the pockets. "It's fucking gone. My mobile's gone," he said, scrabbling over the lining.

"So that's why the bastard stood behind me. He was nicking your mobile."

"Where's yours?"

"In the flat. The bastard, he's trapped us." Richard stood, walked away and then came back as if undecided. "Look

Snibbsy, we'll get out of this OK. I looked after you in Glasgow; I'll look after you here. You extract the memory stick and keep it on you. We need to show the police what he's done. Stay here with the office door closed. I'll get a message to Patricia, tell her to fetch help. Then I'll go back to the flat and see if Zellar's OK. Stay hidden and don't move." Richard pointed his finger. "Don't leave this room. There's a shotgun in the flat, we need it."

Snibbard nodded, mouth open, his eyes still on the changing pictures of carnage.

Richard left and closed the door. In the conference room he slipped on a coverall boiler suit, pulled long latex gloves from the pockets, then crossed to his flat and shut the door.

"You OK, Jovana?" he called, passing through the lounge to the kitchen, carefully sealing the gaps between his waterproof coveralls and gloves.

"The idiot ripped my blouse." Her voice sounded from the bedroom. "It was designer, expensive."

Richard selected a ten-inch carving knife he'd bought specially for the occasion, really expensive. He figured nothing but the best for Jovana Zellar.

"I don't do this for the other guy unless he's more careful," she shouted. Dressed only in bra and pants she was leaning towards the mirror as he entered the room, one arm behind his back.

"What are you now, fancy dress?" She turned to face him. "What about my blouse? He tore my underwear and made mess all over me. Ughh!"

"Don't worry about it. You're heading for a much greater mess." He put a hand to her shoulder, pulling her to him, the same time he plunged the blade deep into her lower abdomen. "This is for what you made me do," he said, hissing breath the same time her guts hissed gases.

Her eyes clouded with shock as her mouth went wide in a jagged squeal. Richard was conscious of euphoria over his instant erection, a state he had believed impossible. Hugging her body close his free hand clasped on her back, he moved the blade gradually upwards cutting through womb and intestines. Not until it caught the sternum and rib cage did he withdraw the knife and step backwards. Holding her neck at arm's length he watched the lower viscera disgorge onto her upper thighs. When he let go, her knees slumped forward and her torso dropped backwards. With legs bent beneath and her mouth in a wide silent scream, he watched steam rise from her cavity as if she had given Caesarean birth to some diabolical alien. Better than Zoby, he thought.

For seconds he shivered in rapture until a smell so foul made him gag and choke. Revulsion restored his survival instinct. He stepped out of the blood, removed his shoes and returned to the kitchen.

He washed his hands, arms and the knife under a running tap, then cleaned the soles of his shoes before drying them with a kitchen towel. Blood discoloured the front legs of the coverall and he removed it with extreme care before placing the garment into a plastic bag along with the gloves. Under the kitchen sink he lifted the bottom of a unit and pushed the bag out of sight. It would be found, he was sure, but by then he would be gone. The knife he left in plain view on the work-surface. Checking his watch he discovered the murder had taken seven minutes. Worth doing again, he thought. Worth doing to the Fagan woman? He replaced his shoes, collected the Remington pump-action shotgun and ran down the corridor to Snibbard, crashing open the door as he entered.

"For fuck's sake, he's killed her. Faulkner's fucking killed her!" He looked at Snibbard who still sat ashen-faced before the computer.

"Who?" He stood. "Who's he killed?"

"Zellar. He gutted her. Come on, we've got to barricade ourselves in the flat. It's the only safe place." He grabbed Snibbard's arm and dragged him out to the corridor, running him back towards the flat.

"Where's Patricia? We should tell her. Call the police," Snibbard said, trying to turn his head as he was dragged along.

"She's one of them. I went downstairs to warn her and saw her with Faulkner and Zoby, laughing with them. You always said he was fucking her. Well he is, right now." Richard slammed open the flat door and bundled Snibbard inside. The man immediately grabbed the hall phone and held it to his ear.

"It's dead," Richard said. "They also took my mobile."

"Oh for fuck's sake, Richie, this is madness. Let's shout out the window."

"That would be madness. Who do you think would take notice of us? We gotta barricade ourselves in. There's no way they can get into the flat without coming down that corridor. Then we blast them, unless …" Richard turned to the flat's interior. "Unless they came when I left. My God, maybe they're in here already." He beckoned, whispering as he crept towards the lounge with Snibbard following.

Richard pointed and whispered again. "Straight across and into the kitchen, you have to arm yourself." He watched Snibbard nod agreement. Richard moved smartly over the open floor then turned to let Snibbard through the door. "Grab the knife on the worktop, it gives you a chance."

"Look, Richie, I'm no good …"

"Grab the fucking knife, we got to search the flat." He turned away as Snibbard complied and hid his smile when the man came behind him. "They won't be in my bedroom, that's for sure. So you check that. I'll check the two spares and the second bathroom. Go for it." He slapped Snibbard's shoulder then ran, half-crouched, to a small inner passage across the lounge. Entering the first spare bedroom he looked back and waved encouragingly. Snibbard stood holding the serrated knife, his mouth open, then moved slowly into the master bedroom.

Richard leaned against the wall and waited until he heard a half-choked scream, then returned silently across the living room. Snibbard stood in stunned shock, his mouth now gapping, staring at Jovana Zellar's viscera spilt out on surreal display. Then he abruptly retched his breakfast onto the carpet.

"I told you," Richard said. "And if you don't want to end up the same you'd better just listen carefully."

Snibbard moved in a daze, his face was pure white, his body visibly trembling.

"There's three of them down there, so I'm relying on you to help. Can you do that, Snibbsy?"

Again he nodded.

"OK, let's go." Richard went back to the front door, opened it wide then tipped the hall table onto its side before ramming it across the entrance.

"She let me fuck her," Snibbard said. "They'll think it was me."

"I can vouch for you, Snibbsy. That's why we have to look out for each other. Where's your knife?"

Snibbard looked at his empty hands. "Must have dropped it. Oh God, that's worse."

"I saved you in Glasgow, Snibbsy, I'll do the same here." He handed Snibbard the shotgun. "You know how to use it? The safety is off. Just point and squeeze the trigger. Pull back on the barrel grip and fire again. You have seven rounds." He stepped over the table into the hall.

"Where are you going? I'm not being here alone." Snibbard made to follow.

"Stay." Richard pointed his finger. "The Fagan woman is coming this morning, if Faulkner gets hold of her ... " He shook his head.

"You didn't tell me. I didn't know about this." Snibbard was staring at him and for a moment Richard had doubts.

"With all this I'd forgotten about her, OK! But if you want to go down to meet Zoby, you do it, I'll stay here." He reached for the shotgun.

Snibbard shook his head.

"All right, I'll go," Richard said. "But if for any reason when I return with Mrs Fagan and Faulkner is behind us, it's a trick. It means he has a gun at our backs. When we duck you shoot him, Snibbsy. And don't miss. You've seen what he can do. It's your life, my life and the woman's life against Faulkner and Zoby. They know we're up here and if you don't shoot on sight we'll end up like Zellar. Understand?"

Snibbard nodded.

"Good man. I'm relying on you, Snibbsy." Richard squeezed his arm and started down the corridor. When he reached the stairs he looked back and waved in fortitude.

Snibbard was now crouched behind the table, shotgun pointed at the ceiling. Richard turned the corner out of view and stopped. He needed to compose himself and regain his calm. He smoothed down his hair, checked his clothes carefully for any traces of blood then looked at his watch. The Fagan woman and Faulkner were due any minute. The timing was tight but still within margins of what he had allowed. Success now depended on Mrs Fagan and Faulkner.

At 10.25 a.m. Victoria stepped out of the lift onto the fifth floor of the office block. Handbag hooked over one shoulder she paused and made ready to perform, then pushed through entrance doors to smile at the PKL receptionist. The room had changed since Victoria's previous visit. Screens now formed a closed passage to the stairs and blocked any view of the inner open plan office. At the opposite end chairs were set out in a waiting area.

"Vicky Fagan. Mr Caswell is expecting me at 10.30," she said.

The receptionist smiled with professional detachment. "I'll call him, Mrs Fagan. Perhaps you would care to take a seat." She indicated and led Victoria towards the chairs. "Coffee?" she asked on the way.

Victoria shook her head and was left to occupy a chair, gently easing the tight stretch of her trousers against her body.

For the sake of modesty she laid the handbag in her lap. Behind the screen a phone began to ring, then a second. Victoria felt reassured by the people around her, reassured that she was not alone with a murderer. She lifted a magazine from the chair opposite and flicked the pages, one eye on the receptionist at her desk, the other on the magazine contents. The phones stopped ringing. Seconds later another started. The place was busy and that was good. She relaxed.

After five minutes a tall, nerdy guy arrived whom she recognised as Faulkner. He had a thin, sharp face with intelligent eyes and the same weird introvert expression as Snibbard. She put this down to something inbred between computer and human. But unlike Snibbard or Caswell, he did not appear predatory. He glanced once in her direction then back at the receptionist who shrugged. Moments later Caswell appeared down the stairs, talked briefly to both, then approached Victoria with his hand outstretched.

"Good morning, Mrs Fagan." His smile was sheepish but not contrite.

"So glad we're back on a business footing, Mr Caswell." She barely touched the fingers of his offered hand as she stood and re-hitched the handbag to her shoulder.

"About last night," he raised his eyebrows. "What I did was unforgivable, can you forgive?"

She allowed a small, contemptuous smile. "Never take until given, Mr Caswell," she said, producing an envelope from her jacket. "Inside is a cheque for one million pounds. But due to your behaviour, I want to view the master tapes of WorkWell Snibbard told me about. I need reassuring you are all telling me the truth." She watched hesitation creep into his expression. He glanced towards Faulkner waiting at reception. "Of course. But you will only find computer language. Just page after page of numbers and letters. There are twenty-five programmes in all. To look through would take days. They're insignificant to PKL."

"I'll flick here and there, Mr Caswell. You may consider me brainless, all tit and arse, but I have a degree and know how to write software. If you want to touch my body, you and your work have to regain my respect. Only then do you get my money."

He smiled, but she saw no mirth or light, just the return of the predator, as if revelation of an education only increased her desirability.

"As you wish." He ushered her forwards. "You may have met Derek Faulkner," he said as they stopped beside the desk. "Mrs Fagan wishes to view the master file of WorkWell before she makes a heavy investment in PKL. Snibbsy told her all about them. So," he raised both hands, "let's show Mrs Fagan exactly what we can do."

Faulkner shrugged. "Sure, I'll fetch the wallet. But be careful, it's our only one." he said and disappeared through an overlap gap in the screens. Caswell stood looking uneasy and restless which she guessed was his annoyance at having misjudged her character. The receptionist returned to typing, the clatter of her keyboard the only sound besides the London traffic. Behind the screen a phone started to ring. Only then did Victoria realise. There were no other sounds, no voices, no sense of movement, no people.

Faulkner returned through the gap. "The WorkWell master files, written by the professional, for the professional. If you can understand them you are welcome." He raised a leather wallet.

"Mrs Zellar and Snibbard are in the conference room. We have computers up there." Caswell indicated the stairs.

Victoria glanced at the receptionist who kept her eyes on the monitor. Faulkner pointed forward in expectation. With the prize so close and with no alternative other than to break her cover, Victoria fell into step, Caswell beside her and Faulkner behind. She felt a fluttering across her chest and stomach, a sudden quiver of apprehension. She was now where Alice wanted, at the centre of the web.

Zellar's presence offered no safety. Zoby's e-mail from the Colonel made reference to two women. Were they Zellar and herself? Was this the killing ground? She continued upstairs with dread. It seemed probable the top floor would be as deserted as the floor below. What if all three men were involved, Caswell, Snibbard and Faulkner? Victoria maintained her false smile and firm step, her handbag tight over her shoulder and locked against her body. Inside, her MI5 mobile gave a constant signal letting Control and Alice know her exact location. Faulkner carried the prize that Alice wanted, and the Wicked Witch stood waiting. The opportunity might not happen again. It would not be easy for three men to kill her and Zeller simultaneously and if they tried, she was quite capable of retaliation. Or she could snatch the flash drives and run … just run.

A step ahead of her Caswell left the stairs and turned the corner.

"What the hell?" he said, and glanced momentarily back.

Behind her, Victoria sensed Faulkner hesitate as she followed Caswell towards the wide open door of his flat. He stopped opposite the empty accounts office and she came beside him, leaving Faulkner to linger.

"Someone's in my flat," he said. "Zoby! He's going to kill us." Caswell screamed the words at the same time turning to grab around her waist.

Victoria felt herself half lifted, half thrown through the open office doorway. The same time a crack of explosion in the confined space shocked her eardrums. Her feet off the ground, Caswell hurled her into the room so she sprawled across the floor. A second report came almost simultaneously. Under Caswell's weight Victoria fell heavily and lay stunned, her ears ringing. Only after moments did she realise Caswell was lying full length on her back, his groin tight against her buttocks. Instantly he rolled away.

"My God, my God, Snibbard's shot him," Caswell screamed and crawled beneath a table.

Victoria twisted herself over and scrambled for the door. Faulkner lay in the corridor, his body half propped by a radiator, his face and upper torso torn open by buckshot.

The after-burn of gunfire lingered in the air, smoke drifting with a smell of cordite. The leather wallet with the flash drives lay a few feet away but too far for her to reach without exposure. She looked back to Caswell who crouched on elbows and knees, his hands clasped over his head. Kneeling there, she thought he looked ridiculous, too ridiculous. She retrieved her bag and fished out the mobile, immediately opening a line to MI5 Control. Tight against the doorframe she peered towards the flat but at such an acute angle was unable to see. A third gunshot sent her shying backwards. It came with a woman's scream. The sound of terror mixed with hysteria. For moments Patricia's voice filled the corridor then slowly receded as she fled.

Again Victoria looked at the leather wallet, so close yet so far. She rolled back to a sitting position. Caswell crawled across the floor towards her, his eyes wild. "Faulkner?" he asked.

"Dead."

"Are you OK? Did I hurt you? When he pointed the gun I didn't know what else to do."

"I'm fine." The guy had saved her life but she couldn't bring herself to thank him. "What's going on, Caswell? What's this about?"

"You wouldn't understand." He sat back, his mouth open as if in exhaustion.

"Try me, I'm MI5."

She saw a flutter of shock, then panic, then cunning.

"Thank goodness, get help quickly."

"Tell me the truth. Who's Zoby?"

"Snibbard is Zoby, Faulkner was both Crystal and the Colonel. I've suspected them for a year but how do you prove it? The police would have laughed at me."

"Try them. They'll be here any minute. You want to tell me about anything else?"

He shook his head. "I left Jovana Zellar and Snibbard in the conference room. For him to behave like this I can only think he's done something terrible to her. Faulkner controlled him by SPI. They developed it between them but Snibbard never realised Faulkner had used subliminal induction on him. Ironic, is it not?"

"The police may believe you, Mr Caswell. I'm not sure I do." She folded her arms.

He came to his feet. "Sorry for my honesty, but if that's what you think I will distress you no further." In a second he was out the door, his voice resounding in the empty corridor. "Snibbsy, don't shoot, don't shoot."

Doors crashed then came silence. When she peered out the leather wallet had gone.

"Shit." Victoria rolled back to a sitting position. From the distance came the wail of sirens.

With Snibbard so hyper, Richard threw himself into the doorway, rolling across the floor of the empty conference room before scrambling towards the cupboard and his 12-bore shotgun. He checked first for cartridges, then hid the wallet containing the flash drives he had snatched from the hall in a drawer. The find would keep MI5 happy. Keep the Home Office happy and leave him to walk away with the original kept in his deposit box. Back in the doorway he flattened himself against the wall. At this angle and closer than the accounts office where Fagan crouched, he saw Snibbard peering over the table edge no more than twenty feet away. To show unity Richard lifted his own shotgun and indicated for Snibbard to stay down. Snibbard's exophthalmic eyes disappeared until only the bald dome of his head occasionally showed above the table. Richard was happy with that, the skull was visible enough for him to blow a hole in it, if the police did not do so first.

From her more acute angle along the corridor, the MI5 woman had no view unless she stuck out her head. A dangerous move for anyone at this moment. She had felt good beneath him. In seemingly saving her life he had been unable to resist the opportunity to lay claim on her body. She could say nothing against him. That she proved to be MI5 only heightened his sense of power. Richard smiled. Everything still stayed within plan. He thought of Zellar lying on the bedroom floor, her butchered carcass ready to create fear in every woman who learnt how she'd died. Wileman would disown all association. Once he had the SPI file he'd banish Richard Caswell forever. Harry's day had arrived. All he needed was for the police to shoot Snibbard. If they did not, then he would do so himself in a pretence of self-defence.

He watched Snibbard's skull rise into view again, that little round dome of computer technology. Then his hooded eyes appeared.

"Zoby's downstairs, we're trapped." Richard spoke in a harsh whisper, hopeful the woman did not hear. "They gutted Zellar, now Zoby is coming to gut you and me. For Christ's sake, shoot him on sight. It's our only chance."

CHAPTER 18

Immediately the bell rang for mid-morning break, Sophie was out of her seat and heading for computer club. First in the room, even before the prefect, within two minutes she had hotmail on screen.

Hi Sophie, hi Becky. Got your e-mail and arrangements are confirmed, 4 p.m. sharp, foyer of the Red Lion Hotel, Dunstable High Street. Zoby will arrive to whisk you away for your photo session with PKL and party, A..A..A..AND presentation of your two thousand pound cheque! Don't forget your sweatshirts so Zoby can easily recognise you. Of course, you'll know Zoby. Everyone knows Zoby. See you there, Crystal. Please confirm.

Sophie tapped We'll be there. She logged off and leapt from her seat. Obey Crystal, trust Zoby.

In the corridor Miss Nathan walked with a clipboard, her loose floral dress revealing a white and freckled neck.

"Did Mum send a message saying we could go shopping?" Sophie asked, digging her nails into her palms.

"I don't know, dear. Ask in the office. Don't you have games?"

"It's Mum's birthday, Becks and me, we're buying her a present. I'll ask." Sophie started to run, then stopped on Miss Nathan's shrill command.

"No running in the corridor."

Sophie walked, her legs taking long exaggerated strides.

Mrs Thrower, the house administrator, sat at her desk. "Nothing here, poppet. But mail for you and Becky." She handed over two packets.

"Sweatshirts!" Sophie ripped open the paper, tearing the enclosed cellophane and card until able to shake out the contents. She held the royal blue shirt up to her shoulders. Princess Kay-ling was shown in dramatic pose, legs and body braced, arms and sword held horizontally and ready to strike.

"Cool," Mrs Thrower said.

Sophie rushed to the dorm. Becky and Julie sat with a laptop.

"They're coming at four and Mum hasn't texted back. What are we going to do?" Sophie asked.

"'S OK, she texted me."

"But she hasn't told the school."

"Don't worry, she will. She likes presents." Becky took her package.

"I'll ask Dad."

"No, he'll start questioning. You can't tell that many lies. Mum will do it, don't worry."

"But when?" Sophie leant forward, hands splayed in question.

"When she lands. She can't use a mobile on a plane."

"Oh." Sophie stood straight. She desperately wanted a wee. "When's that?"

Becky checked her watch. "About 2.30."

"But we have to catch the bus to Dunstable. We have to leave at 3."

"We'll have plenty time."

"But will we?" Sophie asked, gesturing with both hands. Why couldn't her sister understand the importance?

"If we're late, he'll wait. You can trust Zoby. Anyway, if we've won two thousand, we'll get it. They'll post it. The photos are only a PR gimmick. There's no such person as Princess Kay-ling."

Sophie snapped her teeth and ran out the room. Sometimes her sister was just too stupid for words.

Sean felt admiration for Carole's efforts, the resulting portraits of Harrison were first class. Others came to look over her shoulder.

"That's your man," Carole said, laying together two identical sketches of Harrison, one from Cindy Bradshaw and one from Harrison's work colleagues. "Drawn from the perspective of totally different witnesses."

"Doesn't really match our other descriptions." Sean thrust his hands into his pockets. "Could be he used disguise."

"That did cross my mind." Carole looked up, her pale grey eyes on his. "When Zoby collected his flight ticket and passed through security, he needed photo ID," she said. "So he used Darley's passport and driving licence. It's easy for a close resemblance to be mistaken for the real person."

"Any similarities between Darley and Harrison?" Sean asked

Carole swivelled the drawing and traced with a finger. "Face shapes are similar, Darley has a heavier jaw, wider cheeks. Different colour eyes, glasses, shaved head and a slight touch of acne on one cheek."

"Nothing too difficult for a competent makeup artist to change. Carole's right," he said to those around him. "We could be looking at the wrong man. Go over the video footage at the check-in gate. Look for someone resembling Darley, check facial structure and dimensions, anything similar to Harrison."

Simmy tapped his shoulder. "Victoria's on the line, boss. PKL Shoreditch has gone zappy. Someone's shot Faulkner and fired on a female staff member. It could be Zoby. He's holed up, armed and dangerous. Situation, priority one."

"That doesn't gel." Sean took the phone. "You cornered Zoby?" he asked. Victoria's voice came back, slightly breathless and with a touch of tremor.

"He's cornered me. I'm trapped in the accounts office of PKL. Snibbard's barricaded himself into a flat and is firing on anything that moves. Caswell is next door, also under threat. I hate to say it, but the man saved my life. Zellar maybe a prisoner or dead, we don't know. SO19 are here but they're waiting on developments."

"No communication with Snibbard?"

"No mobiles and the land lines are out. I've been told by the local boys to stay put and concealed. When I arrived there was only one member of staff here. I think Zellar's dead and I think I was being lined up as the next victim. In my opinion these guys are seriously weird, including Caswell. But he saved my life. He says that Faulkner was Crystal and Snibbard is Zoby. Somehow he guessed what was going to happen and tried to prevent it, though I have no proof."

"Two women, top quality, you and Mrs Zellar. It was in the Colonel's e-mail."

"It certainly looks that way, though I don't care for the compliment."

"You OK?"

"I wish I was out of here." Her voice quavered on the last word and he heard the sniff of control. "They were going to kill me. My guts spewed out like the other women. The more I think, the more it hits me. Faulkner and Snibbard ..." Her words trailed off. He imagined her biting down on her lower lip.

"It will be OK. Stay tight, I'm coming. I love you." Sean replaced the receiver. When he looked up the others were staring. He drew breath. "We have ourselves a situation at Shoreditch. Zoby possibly cornered. One, maybe two dead. Two others trapped."

"ID on Zoby?" Diane asked.

"Snibbard."

"How was he in Ireland?"

Sean spread his hands. "No evidence, but it's not impossible. The two women, Zellar and Victoria. It fits the e-mail, two top quality females."

"Kill someone in their own office?" Carole shook her head. "It doesn't make sense."

"Where's the sense of a psychopath?"

"Shall I leave this?" Carole flicked the drawing. He saw her expression, her glory gone.

"No, there may be two Zobys. And as yet we've no firm proof Faulkner was Crystal, or Snibbard Zoby."

* * *

Sean sat in the car and tried to rationalise while Simmy drove with his normal disregard for passengers' nerves. Headlights blazing, siren screaming, he weaved the unmarked Jaguar through the traffic and red lights with zealous determination. Sean covered his eyes. None of what had emerged made sense. If Snibbard was Zoby, DNA linking the Bradshaws and Poor Girl victims also made him an accomplished burglar. Highly unlikely, unless Zoby was using help. He phoned Cobbart.

"We need this guy alive," Sean told him. "What if he's not Zoby, what if he has vital information?"

"Snibbard has murdered one, possibly two people. The guys on the ground will give him every chance but it's not our turf. Snibbard has to be Zoby. It all fits, everything links back to PKL and the games, the other victims, the e-mails, everything. You've done well, Sean."

"This isn't over, John. We are making too many assumptions, it's too tidy a package."

"Have faith. This is the result of your own careful detective work." Cobbart paused. "Report just in that Snibbard fired on one of the SO19 team, fortunately he missed. But these boys won't give a him second chance."

"Pull strings for me, John. I need to question him."

"I'll do my best, but it's really out of my hands."

Sean switched off and again closed his eyes as Simmy gunned the Jaguar passed more red lights.

Sean thumbed through the logic. More than one Zoby was possible. The world was full of psychopaths. If the Colonel controlled one, why not two, three, a hundred? To catch Zoby was not the end. He needed the one who played the Colonel.   Sean sat embroiled in thought, mobile in his lap awaiting the next call. Only near their destination did he remember his closing words to Victoria. They had been instinctive, without thought, words to comfort. Difficult to believe he uttered such a statement. Now it seemed logical, to fall in love was so easy. Only the rest was difficult. Throughout the trip Diane sat in silence, arms folded, lips compressed.

The streets on either side of the building were cordoned off and traffic diverted into a resulting gridlock. Uniformed police stood everywhere. A collective display of badges and Sean's nice-guy smile got his team under the tape and into the ground floor foyer of the building.

Members of SO19 armed with Heckler & Koch MP5s milled around in blue flak jackets looking ready for war. Clearly upstaged, groups of CID in sharp suits and leather jackets affected boredom while they waited for the crime scene to be cleared and made safe. At the centre of this a capped and baton-wielding superintendent held court with a selected group of pressmen. No one seemed visibly in charge.

When Sean approached the stairs two of SO19 at the bottom shook their heads and pointed to the uniformed superintendent. The same thing happened at the lift. Across the foyer someone set up a tea urn that caused a general shift of superfluous CID in its direction.

Sean extracted his badge. The superintendent appeared in age to qualify for the Old Boys' Club. Cobbart had to be of some use here.

"Excuse me, sir." Sean pushed amongst the press and showed his ID. "I need a word."

The superintendent stared stony-faced while he read the badge, then moved from the press so they could talk.

"So, the Serious Organised Crime Agency and MI5 are still holding hands," he said. "What's your interest here?"

Sean ignored the dig. "Victoria Lawless is one of my team players. She was actually visiting as part of our operation. Snibbard, Caswell, Faulkner and their business activities are part of an investigation involving multiple murders and organised fraud. Snibbard could be the murderer and I would like to help extract him alive."

"So would I, Inspector, but my priority is to make this building safe. Unfortunately, Snibbard appears to be highly volatile and erratic. Twice he's taken shots at my men and will listen to no-one. That means he has about zero chance. If he thinks the game is up he wouldn't be the first to choose a police bullet."

"From what I know, Snibbard is probably terrified. If I convince him he won't be harmed, that we don't believe he's a character called Zoby, then he may surrender."

"Zoby?"

"It's a long story, sir. The traffic is building up while the psychiatrists hold meetings. Very soon people sitting round tables will be shouting at us to do something.

"Don't I know it? But I already have a good man up there."

Sean tried the Old Boys' approach. "Snibbard may have murdered Sammy Sinclair's daughter. He may be able to provide evidence relating to Superintendent Sinclair's death."

A muscle twitched in the hard face staring back at him.

"Excuse me a moment." The superintendent extracted his mobile and moved to one side. Isolated, he pressed buttons on the keypad and spoke quietly, occasionally glancing in Sean's direction. When he returned his expression had mellowed. "I'll let you up, Inspector, on the proviso that your actions are voluntary, and your enquiries are involved with evidence which might persuade Snibbard to surrender."

Sean thought the man a politician if nothing else. "The outcome is not guaranteed, sir."

"Unfortunately, that's the way of things. The guy in charge is called Bates. If he needs your services he'll direct you. If not, you come down again."

"Thank you, sir."

"Don't take chances, Fagan. If you or any of my men become casualties, I shall not be happy. Neither will the troll."

The lift carried Sean and one officer of SO19 to the fifth floor. A team of about thirty was installed in an open plan office. Screens were stacked at the bottom of a stairwell to give protection.

Sean came out of the lift to face four men. All wore the dark blue uniform and flak jackets of SO19; all were armed with Heckler and Koch MP5s.

"I'm C.I. Bates." One of them thrust out his hand. "I'm responsible. How can you help?"

Sean found the man's direct talking impressive but it left no room for manoeuvre. He began to repeat what he had told the superintendent. He added, "If the woman in the flat is dead, then a suspect known as Zoby murdered her. If that's not Snibbard, and I don't think it is, he may be traumatised by terror. In which case I can possibly persuade him to surrender by ensuring his safety."

Bates thrust hands into pockets. "Zoby. That's the name he keeps calling. "I'll kill you, Zoby. Bastard Zoby." I get the impression he thinks Zoby is one of us. Let me explain the situation. We've tried first contact and reasoning, but with no intelligible response. We can't use gas on account of others in the proximity and the possibility that the woman he's supposedly murdered is still held hostage and seriously injured. I'm told by the politically correct that anyone held hostage can sue us for not taking appropriate action which might have lessened their suffering. Neither am I allowed to starve him out by denying food and water as it's against his human rights. He shot at a woman staff member who was first on the scene. He shot at one of my men and he shot at me when I stepped out to reason with him. Your player, Victoria Lawless, also tried shouting to him but got no response. Occasionally we pick up whispered conversation between Snibbard and Caswell but our long range listening device is not clarifying what is said. Caswell is close and first in the line of fire should Snibbard do something rash. It's probable he's been talking for his life, trying to convince Snibbard that his situation is hopeless. What are you going to say, Inspector?"

"That I believe he's not Zoby. That I can save him from Zoby," Sean said, knowing that to extract Snibbard alive would earn Bates a commendation. "I'm also a trained negotiator," he threw in for good measure.

Bates was eyeing him with professional detachment and clearly still calculating. His future career hung in the balance, pivoted between his decision and Sean's ability. Sean knew Snibbard's death would black mark Bates' record. But if SOCA entered and things went wrong, then SOCA could be blamed. That was the principal reason he had been allowed up.

"OK, we'll give one final try. After that I've no real choice but to whack the guy."

Sean climbed the stairs and stopped below an armed group of SO19 clustered at the top. On Bates' insistence, Sean wore a flak jacket and body set. While a sergeant checked the body mike, Sean adjusted the earpiece and registered transmission with SO19 control below.

"Once you step round the corner you're in range," the sergeant said. "Unless you have a face hit, at this distance you'll be OK, but the closer you approach the more likelihood of serious injury. So, all initial negotiation you do from here." He pointed to a megaphone and surveillance camera sited in the open passage on attached cable and bogey trolley. "If you look to the CCTV screen," he said, pointing. "You'll see two open doors. The female hostage is inside the first. At the moment she's perfectly safe and we've talked to her over the mobile. But to conserve battery power, she only switches on when necessary. Caswell is in the second doorway. We've also spoken to him over the mobile. He tells us he's tried repeatedly to talk Snibbard out, but the guy won't budge on account he's already murdered a woman in the flat. When you're in the corridor keep to the near wall by the doors and don't block the view of the camera. In that way, if he lifts the weapon to shoot we'll see and retaliate. Then you go immediately to ground, or be in the line of fire. And you know what that means, Inspector." He slapped Sean's arm. "Good luck."

Sean stood three steps down watching the CCTV screen. "Hi, Sidney," Sean's voice reverberated over the amplifier and down the corridor. "My name's Sean Fagan. I'm a detective inspector. I've come to help you. You see, I know all about PKL and the problems you've had with Zoby. I also believe you are not Zoby. I'd like to help if you'd let me. I can prove your innocence. Will you let me do that?" Sean paused. "OK, I'm going to step into the corridor, please don't fire your weapon or it will be fatal for us both."

With no movement from behind the table barricading the flat, Sean mounted the final steps, turning to face the flat as he moved closer to the wall.

"It's my firm belief you're innocent, Sidney. Someone is trying to put the blame on you, but I won't let them get away with it. I'll see to that. I'll make sure you're safe." Sean took three steps down the hall until able to see where Victoria lay prone on the floor at an angle to the doorway. "Put down your weapon, Sidney, and I guarantee no harm will come to you," he said, his words firm and isolated in the confined atmosphere.

Snibbard's domed head and hooded eyes suddenly lifted over the table edge, his expression terrified. Ignoring the sergeant's warning, Sean edged closer. Ten feet from Victoria's doorway he watched the barrel of Snibbard's shotgun appear. Sean raised both arms.

"I can help you, Sidney. Help you get out of this mess and back to your computers. Everything is so easy when you're dealing with computers. Everything is logical, you have none of this craziness."

Snibbard's whole face appeared, his eyes bulging, mouth open. Sean could see threads of saliva between the man's upper and lower teeth.

"Lay down your weapon, Sidney, step over the table. No harm will come to you."

Sean moved forward again as Snibbard slowly rose. First his head and shoulders, then his chest came into view as he pushed to one knee.

"You don't really want to hurt anyone, do you, Sidney?" Sean reassured, glancing to Victoria who lay biting on her lower lip, her eyes squinting. "You've never meant to cause harm. But sometimes it just happens. That's why you hide in your computer. It's safe in there, in there you're somebody. I can help you get back inside. Do you want me to do that for you, Sidney?"

To Sean's relief Snibbard nodded, and continued to rise upwards onto his feet, shotgun level in both hands as it slowly swung round.

"It wasn't me," he said. "She let me. It was Zoby. I know who you are, you're Zoby. I know because he told me." Snibbard looked to the nearest door where Caswell lay crouching. "I bet you killed the girl in Glasgow too."

"Not me. I'm not Zoby, Sidney. Neither are you. Let me help." Sean watched Snibbard's eyes cloud with doubt. His mouth closed but the shotgun barrel continued moving towards the corridor.

"I know who I can trust. Trust Richard, trust Richard," he repeated, his eyes narrowed. "How can you help?"

Sean jumped at the numbing roar of a weapon discharged in the confined space. Instinctively he threw himself sideways through the open door of the accounts office. He hit the floor at full stretch and waited for the engulfing pain of gunshot trauma to rake over his body. In the following instant, the very air vibrated under the repeated whip crack of multiple gunfire, the crescendo of sound hammering into his ears. He could feel Victoria hauling at his dead weight, pulling and twisting him towards her. Then came sudden silence, followed immediately by the clamour of voices.

Sean felt no pain, no wound, no blood. His face was buried in Victoria's lap, her upper body bent over him in a gesture of protection. He kissed where his lips pressed then raised his head.

She touched his cheek and smiled. "Did you mean it, that you loved me?"

CHAPTER 19

"What the hell were you doing with a shotgun and why did you fire?" Sean asked, lacing his fingers together on the tabletop.

Caswell lifted his hands as if in pained confusion. "Because I saw by his expression he was about to shoot, at me, at you, or both of us. Being unable to see you, I let off a round in warning. What else could I to do?"

They sat in the downstairs office where screens, tables and chairs had been gathered to form a small enclosure away from the busy activity of the Forensics teams. The superintendent, a CID inspector, Victoria and Sean were on one side with a woman DC taking notes. Caswell sat opposite, sometimes with his head in his hands, sometimes just staring at the table. His face showed nothing other than what appeared to be genuine grief.

"I've know Snibbsy a long time," he said. "I could see what he intended. I didn't know the police would fire. I was trying to save a life. Your life, Inspector."

Sean watched the superintendent nod his head in silent agreement.

"Regular little hero, aren't you, Mr Caswell? First you save Ms Lawless, then me." Sean stared at the man, saw the flash of hostility, then a return to grief.

"That will do, Fagan." The superintendent leant heavily on the table. "I apologise, Mr Caswell."

"Accepted."

"Who's Zoby? Who's Crystal? Who's the Colonel?" Sean asked.

"Snibbard was Zoby, as testified by poor Mrs Zellar. He was controlled and ruled by Faulkner who played both Crystal and the Colonel. I had long suspected their involvement after I discovered e-mails between them on our main server."

"You knew they had murdered and said nothing?" the CID inspector asked.

"I suspected, but how can you prove murder via the Internet? I may have been wrong. Such allegations would have caused tremendous damage. Call it callous if you wish, but I also had contractual agreements. I needed those guys."

"How did Helen Carter, Lizzie Sinclair and Sarah Finch involve themselves here so that they ended up as murder victims?" Victoria asked.

Again Caswell raised his hands. "I don't know. What I do know is, Helen and Lizzie were friendly with Derek Faulkner. All were prominent in the field of IT. Derek used their body shapes for Princess Kay-ling's figure. Originally I think both were flattered, but it was Snibbard who turned their measurements into computer generated shapes. He created them. He used to say he owned them. They objected to that. As for Sarah, she and I used to be close. She helped by putting money into PKL when I first started."

A detective constable came round the screen and whispered to the CID inspector who in turn whispered to the superintendent. He nodded and looked around the table. "New information indicates Snibbard was definitely Jovana's killer," the superintendent said. "His prints have been found on the murder weapon left adjacent to the body. Snibbard's clothing also contained a memory stick. Forensics have discovered it held graphic photos of the murder victims. Evidence shows that Snibbard killed Faulkner and possibly tried to kill others. It's almost certain he had previously killed Jovana Zellar. The stick implicates him in the murder of four women. At this point we must assume he is our principal suspect."

"What were you doing with shotguns?" Sean asked. "To get a shotgun into the conference room you must have placed it there prior to meeting the others."

Caswell stared back with dead eyes and shook his head. "The weapons are a direct result of police incompetence. I was burgled here. Entry was forced through a private door onto the back staircase. The police did not arrive until one hour after my call. The shotguns were for personal protection. The Remington I keep in the flat. Snibbard knew of its whereabouts because, perhaps foolishly, I showed it to him. The other I keep locked away in the conference room. I am the only key holder to the cupboard. It was safe. If I came home and found the door of my flat open, I would at least know how to protect myself while I waited an hour for help to arrive."

"Enough." The superintendent leant from the table and made to rise.

Caswell looked at Sean and half smiled. "Finished, Inspector?"

"With both your partners dead, what happens to your research?"

Caswell shrugged. "I think our research will stay on the shelf."

"Which leaves you as the principal beneficiary."

"Which leaves me a great deal of worry. For other implications you must ask my lawyer."

"What happened to the SPI you used fraudulently to ensnare shareholders?"

"Ask Faulkner, ask Snibbard. They were in charge. They wrote the software. I had nothing to do with it."

"Leave it, Inspector," the superintendent said, his voice formal. "It is required you make a statement, Mr. Caswell. And you will be held in custody until this is done."

"I have no objection. But you will also understand I wish my lawyer present. Am I being charged with anything?"

"You discharged a weapon under severe duress. You hold shotguns without a licence. I don't see serious charges if any are forthcoming. However, all will be investigated."

"I will help in every way I can." Caswell stood. "Now, you will excuse me, I must call my lawyer, there is much to do."

He met Sean's direct gaze and deliberately kept it locked when Sean stared back. Did he see mockery, or was he being paranoid? Sean watched Caswell leave. Trust Richard, trust Richard. Snibbard has been controlled. Ironic if he had been a victim of his own SPI.

"Before you ask, Inspector Fagan, the answer is no." The superintendent pointed his baton.

"Events here are a viable part of our investigation."

"The Serious Organised Crime Agency don't do murders. This is my manor with my lads on the crime scene. End of story. And I also want a full written statement from you." He pushed back his chair.

Outranked, Sean gambled. "Our own investigation is relevant to what happened here. How about a joint op? Your boys investigate Shoreditch, we look into PKL's computer system at Milton Keynes. You keep us informed of current developments, we give you full info on Poor Girl."

"MI5 would appreciate that, sir," Victoria said. "SOCA and our own department have the equipment and expertise which your division lacks. Looking over computer files can take thousands of man-hours."

The superintendent pulled on his cap and tapped the baton on the table. For the first time he smiled. "OK. But I want a full report on all your finds, ASAP. If you want our findings, let's see your co-operation first."

"Thank you, sir." Victoria smiled, her eyes big and round. "I left my bag upstairs, mind if I retrieve it?" She left without his answer and moved between the screens.

Once alone Sean was immediately on his mobile to Diane. "Get a search warrant and anyone who's spare out to PKL Milton Keynes before the Wicked Witch and her goblins arrive. Get Steve from High-Tech and his team out there also. I want every staff member who was involved with SPI interviewed. Get Steve to search for any SPI evidence which links Poor Girl and any evidence that Caswell might have used SPI to influence his fellow directors, particularly

Snibbard. Give me a sit rep when everything is in motion. I've a statement to make." He called the woman DC with her notepad and sat her in a chair opposite.

When he had finished, Victoria met him by the lift, a closed handbag hooked over her shoulder.

"You don't believe Caswell, do you?" She looked up at him.

"He's playing games with us. But it will be one hell of a job to prove."

"I'm unsure about Faulkner, but the facts pointing to Snibbard as Zoby are damning." She touched a finger to his chest then drew her hand away as if unsure. He made no gesture of encouragement. He had made his move, the response must be hers.

"Trust Richard. Snibbard repeated it twice."

"Caswell's a weirdo, a creep. But he saved my life and seemingly saved yours. Why do that if he isn't genuine?"

"To deflect blame. If he controlled Snibbard, he could control Zoby. Maybe Snibbard was a victim of his own SPI without him realising. Does MI5 want a lift to Milton Keynes? Or are they calling it a day?"

"I've no doubt we'll be there." She touched him again, but only with her fingertips. He sensed the tension and indecision in her as she stepped back. "But, I have to see Alice first, she's called me home."

"Then there's no need for our cover house any more, Mrs Fagan."

"No." Her smile held sadness. "Goodbye, Mr Fagan," she said and stepped into the lift.

Something was wrong, he knew. Something just didn't gel. Victoria and the Witch were playing games.

Jan went back to the Kilburn office after dropping her charge at university. A pickup was arranged for 7 p.m. in the student bar. She had clicked with Danielle the moment they both recognised a mutual preference. Each had given the other space while enjoying friendly, tactile touch, no connotations. Jan thought time might change that.

Carole sat in a chair viewing video footage of Luton airport. Half a dozen Red Team members manned the phones.

"Any news?" Jan asked.

"Shootings over. Half the team have gone to raid Milton Keynes. Got something here, though." She reeled back the footage and lifted a photograph scanned from the airport tape. "The guy who had his driving licence stolen, Darley. I've been on to him, persuaded him to e-mail his photograph. He's turned up on three different videos."

"Can't be." Jan peered over Carole's shoulder.

"Not him – but I'd take bets it's Zoby. Once checking in, once going through security, again by the check out gate. There!" She froze the screen as the target sat back, unaware he stared directly into a camera.

"Looks like Darley." Jan leaned closer.

"But it's not. I took a scan of it." She picked up three printouts, laying them side-by-side. Each showed a face of identical proportions. "This one's Darley, that's from the video, and that's from the drawing of Mark Harrison. All very similar in facial shape, but if you take measurements between the features, Darley and the video don't fit, Harrison does. The video shows Harrison disguised as Darley."

"You're a genius. Does Sean know?"

Carole shook her head, blonde curls bouncing. "Last I heard Zoby had been killed at Shoreditch and Sean was up to his neck in it."

"Men, all guns, no brains." Jan took out her mobile and dialled. "This was your find, love. You want to tell him?" She passed the mobile.

"A definite ID?" Sean repeated over the earpiece.

"Ninety-five percent."

"Don't mess, Carole, I want a full hit on his flat. Get a search warrant and take a couple of boys from Red Team to help."

"What if he turns up?"

"Hold him on suspicion."

"We've got a raid," Carole said, handing back the phone.

"Yoo." Jan lifted her fist.

Big Nose was eager to advise when a couple of Red Team boys took the door from its hinges. So as not to disturb forensic evidence, only Jan and Carole entered. Jan went to the kitchen and Carole to the first door on the left.

"The guy's army mad," Jan called over her shoulder. "Books, posters, the place is more like a field unit." When she received no reply she went back into the hall and looked into the opposite room. Carole stood cradling herself, rocking slowly before a display cabinet containing a pegged out section of a vagina and uterus. She was shivering.

"The bastard!"

She took Carole's shoulders and guided her back outside.

The neighbours had gathered and school kids were arriving like locusts.

Jan beckoned a DC and whispered, "Get this place sealed off. No one in but Forensics. There're human body parts inside." She led Carole to the car and sat with her in the back seat.

"I'm sorry," Carole said, brushing a hand through curls. "I could never stomach that kind of thing. What sort of mind commits such atrocities for self-gratification? They want to make us victims. I don't want to be a victim." She leant against Jan's shoulder.

"We'll get him, but whoever they shot at Shoreditch, it wasn't Zoby." Jan cradled her, took out a mobile with her free hand and punched in Sean's number.

Sean briefed Steve Rawlings in the back of a high-tech operations van parked outside the PKL industrial unit at Milton Keynes. When he re-emerged the area outside was seriously crowded with official vehicles. The plates on several told him they were government owned, Home Office. More fingers in the pie. He went into the foyer and found Victoria with a thin woman wearing a long pencil slim suit, her face austere and without make-up, her haircut like a helmet.

"I'd like you to meet Alice Sibree," Victoria introduced him. "My boss."

"To what do I owe this privilege?" Sean asked, thinking she really did look a modern-day witch.

"The HO are here," Sibree said over Victoria's hesitation. "I just wish to inform you that whatever you uncover regarding SPI is now classified. That includes statements from PKL staff whether here or Shoreditch."

"Why? What we gather is evidence. It will be used in court."

Sibree shook her head and handed him a Home Office directive. "Eventually, perhaps," she said. "But the possible involvement of Starways has given this incident political significance, which for now, is guided by MI5. Your murder enquiry is not our concern, only SPI. So, all evidence until cleared, is restricted."

"If Caswell is involved, I want him."

"Mr Caswell is currently a hero. He saved Victoria's life and probably saved your life."

"Don't believe it." Sean looked to Victoria who had folded her arms, pressing the ground with the toe of one shoe, not meeting his eyes. He blew breath. "If Caswell has anything to answer, I'll find it."

"No doubt, Inspector. Meanwhile he's in custody," Sibree said. "And Zoby is dead."

"Snibbard was not Zoby," Sean said to them. "My team has positive ID for Mark Harrison as Zoby. But of course, there could be two Zobys. My mind's open. I'm just about to find out, at Harrison's flat."

Sibree kept her smile. "I can assure you, Inspector, MI5 will give every co-operation on this. We're all team members in a joint effort."

"Good, because it's my belief Caswell has contrived a complex alibi. If I find evidence against him, he'll go down."

"Well, as we're a team, I'll come to the flat with you," Victoria said.

During the journey to London, Sean drove in silence, feeling both tension and magnetism grow steadily between them. Eventually he broke the deadlock.

"How long has MI5 known of the SPI programme?" he asked.

"We're not stupid."

"Neither is SOCA," he said, thinking love was a bitch. He glanced momentarily from his driving to take stock of her expression and wondered what she had hatched with Sibree. Faulkner and Snibbard were set up too conveniently. MI5 seemed keen on that, a convenient closure of events.

Outside Harrison's flat, journalists clustered around as Sean pushed through and under the tape.

"We're technicians," he told the reporters. "The CID are following."

They looked at him disbelieving and to his annoyance some took photographs. Victoria had split, moving in from the side, her head down.

Jan stood outside the door sharing a thermos of coffee with one of the blue clad Forensic girls. Two uniformed constables kept kids and neighbours back.

"Place is a regular Aladdin's cave," Jan told him. "Pieces of bodies, photographs, porn, weapons, chemicals, uniforms, theatrical disguises."

"But do we have a DNA link?" Sean asked.

"Positive. Michelin man has details." She looked in through the door and called, "Dr Martin."

Dr Martin appeared from the kitchen giving full justification for his nickname. Short, rotund, bald and heavily bespectacled, his over-sized zip suit hung in bulbous folds. He grinned sparse teeth. "Hair and skin from the bathroom match with other crime scenes," he said.

"Then we have our target. S'OK if we go inside?"

"My guys are still in the kitchen, rest is yours."

Before Sean moved, Jan put a hand on his arm. "Big Nose called the press. He's already given three interviews. They want you. The rats are piling up and becoming a nuisance."

"Active SOCA don't do press, you know that. We're supposed to be covert. Get the local boys, give them the glory."

Sean moved into the flat and stabbed buttons on his mobile while watching Victoria head for the computer. Heidi answered.

"I want a warrant out for Mark Harrison, ASAP. National coverage, priority one. Call everyone back. Harrison is prime target, possibly armed and certainly dangerous. Get Chad and some of the team to Travelpath; interview all staff. I want every address where Harrison might be, that's every address of every customer away on holiday. And I need that nationwide."

"Understood, boss." Heidi paused. "A report just in from Shoreditch. Evidence indicates that Zellar was probably raped prior to her murder. DNA found inside the vaginal tract, on torn clothing and the remains all match Snibbard's sperm. Met CID now believe he raped and then murdered her."

"Then we have two Zobys. Or one Zoby and one very crafty Crystal."

"What about Faulkner?"

"I wonder if he trusted Richard."

"Sorry, boss," Heidi's voice came back. "But you've lost me."

"Just thinking aloud, Heidi. Stay with it." Sean switched off and looked for Carole. He found her in the bedroom with a crime scene photographer. Her eyes were rimmed with red and her face grim.

"You OK?" he asked.

"Just angry, boss."

"This was your raid." Sean tried a smile for her. "So I'm leaving you in charge of the crime scene. Collect all the evidence and get it back to Cricklewood."

"Will do, boss." She gave a tight but proud smile in return.

He understood her anger, understood now a little more about Victoria's anger. With people like Harrison, every woman was a potential victim, so every woman who knew of his existence became mentally vulnerable. He was a predator hunting their sex for the sake of their sex, and providing they satisfied his lust, it made no difference which one of them he used. Zoby's freedom was personal to all women. Their sex was the reason he killed them. Sean had no doubt the man would be caught but equally important, and more difficult to capture, was the person who controlled him, the Colonel, Crystal. Somewhere another victim might be lined up. Did Caswell know who?

Sean found Simmy standing by the entrance accepting a cigarette from one of the Forensics girl. "Simmy, interview the neighbours," Sean said. "I want a profile of Harrison's character. Anyone who knows him or his possible whereabouts. Get some lads from the office down." Sean moved to the living room where Jan stood making notes. The walls were pinned with posters of Paras, SAS and American Special Forces, the shelves stacked with combat magazines, books and military memorabilia.

Victoria sat at the PC attempting to open e-mails. "He has everything covered by double access codes," she said. "Who the hell did he expect to read them?

"Military mind, military procedures."

"Probably deleted anyway."

"Could still be on hard drive. Another job for Steve Rawlings."

"He's stretched. MI5 can go through the service provider."

"For themselves or us?" Sean asked.

Victoria swivelled round in the chair and stared at him with hard eyes, her lips tight and thin. "I stood over the butchered bodies of Helen Carter and Lizzie Sinclair. I want this man as much as you."

"I also want the man who controls him."

"Faulkner is dead."

"Caswell is not."

"Proof points to Faulkner."

"Crystal and the Colonel are one. If they lead to Caswell, WorkWell will be exposed and SPI will hit the press. Every government and software company will develop a virus remedy. Starways will suffer huge financial loss if suspected of involvement, and the covert use of SPI will be gone forever; particularly for interested governments."

She continued to stare at him, eyes hostile. "Subjective speculation. Rank amateur. You disappoint me."

"Logical deduction and configuration of relevant facts. Look to who will benefit most. Caswell is taking you for a ride." He pressed buttons on his mobile. "Steve, I have a hard drive which needs urgent examination."

For seconds he watched Victoria breathe muted fire before she swung from her seat and left. Jan stared from the window, lips pursed in silent whistle.

"You're kidding, mate," Steve answered. "I've enough work at Milton Keynes to last a month."

"This is Zoby's personal computer."

"Life was so much easier before PCs," he answered and called to someone in the background. "The quickest way for immediate info is through his service provider. Is the computer on?"

"Yes."

"Start typing – this is what I want."

Sean pushed Jan forward, sat her in the chair and began to repeat what Steve requested. She clicked keys and jotted notes in her pad.

"Service provider, Pacific On-Line, URL, sas.1000mh.com, line number," Jan read it off the phone beside her.

"Pacific On-Line, I know them," Steve said. "I've good contacts through the FBI paedophile directive. I also know that e-mail address. I've recovered e-mails activity sent to there, sent by Crystal and the Colonel out of Milton Keynes."

"Two different people, or the same?"

"All went through the main server. Some were from Faulkner's terminal, some from T3, Snibbard's terminal. Possibly the same guy. I'll e-mail any info to Cricklewood. Leave Zoby's computer online. I'll access through the Net until I can send someone to pick it up."

Outside Victoria leaned on the balcony, her arms folded. Sean leant beside her and allowed a moment of silence to establish peace.

"If it makes you feel better, they've found e-mail between Snibbard, Faulkner and Harrison," he said.

"When will you believe me?"

"When I'm proved wrong. I can guarantee Zoby's computer is awash with SPI. Little suggestions like kill, rape, stab."

"I don't believe SPI could make someone kill."

"Neither do I, but it could tip a psycho already halfway there and it could also direct him towards victims without him knowing why."

"You think Caswell did that?"

"Greed is a great motivator and someone using SPI on the commercial markets could make a lot of money."

"Speculating again."

"I've an open mind."

She turned, leaning her back to face him. "Was it open this morning when you spoke to me over the telephone?"

"So, what's your reaction?"

No smile, but a softening of the eyes. "Why don't you trust me? Love and trust go together."

"In a perfect world." He pushed off the rail. "But the world is not perfect. You coming?"

"So, I'm still part of the team?"

"I like you where I can watch you."

Sean clambered up the stairs to the warehouse office. New desks, equipment and people were everywhere. Centre stage John Cobbart lorded over the activity in a crumpled pinstriped suit, glasses perched, his finger pointing as he gave orders. Sean was glad to see him. He needed muscle that would open doors.

"Getting juicier by the hour," Cobbart said, as Sean approached. "Well done, Sean. You'll get chief inspector out of this."

"I need Caswell for an in-depth interview, John. Although Victoria disagrees, I think Caswell is central to all this."

"At the moment, he's hailed a hero. That makes him untouchable. If you want him, Sean, you'll have to produce substantial and irrefutable evidence."

"Evidence at present is zero," Victoria said, folding her arms. "Snibbard, is responsible for murder and according to your own men out at Milton Keynes, Faulkner is responsible for Zoby. Be that Harrison or Snibbard, or both. Caswell is a victim in this."

"Until we get Harrison. He's the key to Crystal, the Colonel. Harrison is the connecting factor."

"Steve's lifted dozens of e-mails from Harrison's computer," Heidi said over his shoulder. "Want me to print them off?"

"Cheers, Heidi." Sean raised his thumb for her. "How do we keep Caswell in custody?" he asked Cobbart.

"Without substantial reason, we can't even keep him in the country. But why chase Caswell when the evidence indicates Faulkner and Snibbard?"

"Money, power, twisted lust. But mostly because Snibbard said, "trust Richard", the same way our female victims trusted Zoby. Snibbard was under the influence of SPI. "

"Try making that stand up on News Night, never mind in a criminal court."

Sean accepted the A4 sheet from Heidi. "When I have Zoby," he said, glancing at what Steve Rawlings had sent him. Then he read more closely. "Jesus, Zoby has my home address. Meter reader. He was there yesterday." In the following silence Sean felt a pulse in his cheek. Cobbart was staring, eyes full of concern, then detachment. Sean stood helpless until his brain returned from frozen dread.

"Jan," he grabbed her arm. "Phone Danielle at university, tell her under no circumstances must she go home. Take her to your place, a hotel, anywhere, but not home."

"Where are your girls?" Victoria asked.

"At boarding school in Buckinghamshire. Their mother picks them up later this afternoon."

"Sean," Cobbart's voice was deadpan "If there is personal involvement, you're out of it. No ifs or buts."

"Having my address is not involvement," Sean said, knowing his argument was already lost.

"Having your address makes you a potential victim."

"Boss," Jan was listening to her mobile. "Danielle's switched off. She's probably in a lecture. Want me to phone college admin?"

"Yes, but only as a precaution. I don't want them panicking her."

CHAPTER 20

Sophie thought Miss Nathan a bit blustery so stayed saintly silent in case the teacher changed her mind.

"I disapprove," Miss Nathan said, and sniffed. "However, headmistress and your mother consider it acceptable. She picked up your text after landing and phoned from the airport. You may leave at three. Your mother is going home first but will collect you from the Red Lion Hotel between six and six-thirty."

"Yes, miss." Sophie spoke in unison with Becky.

"And you stay in school uniform."

"No, miss."

"Yes, miss. You wear your uniform in the local town not only with pride, but also as a means of security. Do you have your mobiles?"

"Yes, miss."

"Leave them switched on, phone Mrs Thrower when your mother arrives. And don't leave your homework until the last minute."

"Yes, miss."

Both girls walked at speed. They had twenty minutes to pack weekend bags and catch the bus.

Sophie thought it better to stay in Becky's shadow when they entered the Red Lion Hotel's lobby. Big people were best dealt with by big people. The atmosphere had a comfortable plushness. An elderly couple sat over tea, they smiled and Sophie grinned back. A purse and T-shirt for their mother had been bought in ten minutes. Now they had twenty minutes to spare.

"We've arranged to meet someone here at four," Becky told the receptionist. "OK if we wait?"

The woman was young, plump and bespectacled. She looked down at Sophie, Sophie gave her best grin. The receptionist glanced over to a porter then indicated a window seat. "All right, but quietly please."

"Can we use the loo?" Sophie asked the question essential to their plan.

"I suppose so." The receptionist fussed with papers. Sophie followed Becky to the Ladies, watching the porter watching her sister.

Inside both went for separate cubicles. Sophie unzipped her sports bag and began to shed the school uniform. She heard Becky doing the same.

Sophie had brought her best jeans, PKL sweatshirt and new trainers. She changed with record speed, sitting on the lavatory to lace her shoes. She heard Becky head for the washbasins.

Sophie swung the door, Becky was bending forward applying makeup. She wore a white micro skirt and yellow, button through top.

"I can see your knickers," Sophie said.

"No you can't!" Her sister tugged the skirt and straightened a little.

"Dad would go ballistic. Where did you get that?"

"From Julie. It's perfectly decent." She wriggled herself, stretching the hem to maximum length. It made no difference from Sophie's viewpoint. Becky's top was barely buttoned over a new uplift bra. Sophie moved beside her.

"I can see your boobs."

"Will you shut up?"

"Can I use your lipstick?"

"If you behave." Becky pushed the makeup bag towards her and went back to applying mascara.

Sophie selected flame red and began to press it over her lips.

"How do I look?" Becky asked.

"Like you'll catch a cold."

"You're such a child." Becky patted her hair, fluffed it with a comb before preening, smoothing hands over her figure. Sophie did the same, then was forcibly turned to face her sister.

"My God, you look like Dracula." Becky fished a tissue from her bag. "Bite your lips on that," she said, offering a folded edge.

Sophie did so, leaving a scarlet imprint. Standing patiently she allowed her sister to dab at the corners, then comb and fluff her hair before spraying her with perfume.

"That's better," she said. "Now, if you want a wee, this is the time."

Sophie hesitated, then ran back to the cubicle. "How long we got?"

"Ten minutes. See you outside."

Sophie listened to the swing of the door. She always wanted a wee at the last minute, never knew why.

Becky sat staring from the window. Sophie checked her watch for the fourth time in two minutes. Zoby was late. The receptionist glanced across, her eyes questioning. Sophie went over to her.

"He's late," she said. "Is it really five past four?"

"Yes, dear. Who's late?"

"Zoby."

The receptionist looked to the porter who was watching Becky as she shifted willowy legs.

"You mean Zoby from Princess Kay-ling? You know Zoby from PKL?" The porter asked. "I play the games. Why's he coming here?"

"We won a prize. Going for a photo session with the princess herself. But it's probably only an actress, unless she really is true. You think she is?"

"Who knows?" The porter winked, then looked back to Becky. "But if Zoby said he'll come, he'll come. You can trust Zoby."

"He's here!" Becky sprung from the window, smoothed her skirt and patted her hair. A long silver bonnet drew up outside.

Zoby was all Sophie had imagined, handsome, muscular, perfectly tailored. Better than a pop star.

He looked to Sophie in her PKL sweatshirt and bowed. "Ladies, I am Zoby, charioteer to Princess Kay-ling. She awaits your pleasure not twenty minutes drive."

"We have to be back by six sharp," Becky said. "Our mum's coming."

Sophie watched the slightest frown move on Zoby's face.

"No problem, ladies." He bowed towards the door.

Everyone was smiling, Sophie waved. "See you later," she said and followed after Becky. Her stomach was churning, like prize-giving at school.

Zoby played PKL tunes on the sound system, the volume loud enough to deter conversation. He didn't want stupid questions, he needed concentration to sort out static circling inside his head. He adjusted the rear mirror. Observation for primary assessment was essential. He liked most of what he saw. He thought the alien looked wild-eyed, excited, bopping her head to the music. The older one played Miss Cool. She stared from the window, legs crossed, one hand touching the buttons on her shirt. She sure had nice tits. Couldn't wait to get his hands on them. After five minutes he cleared the last buildings and headed for open country. He needed them strapped up before the motorway. The lay-by chosen was partially hidden by trees. Not the best spot, he thought. If someone stopped he'd have problems. He didn't want hostiles nosing, asking why he'd strapped a couple of females, but then he had a heavy bar, good for cracking heads. He hummed quietly to himself as he pulled over.

Only one empty car stood in the lay-by. A little thing, all polished and clean, probably old people out walking. Both girls sat forward, looking around, unsure of the surrounding country, but still eager.

"This it?" the elder one asked.

"Sure is," Zoby said, taking a sealed chloroform pad from the glove compartment. "Let me open the door so you can get out away from the road side, much safer." Both girls waited on him. He liked that, no questions, just obedience. He flicked the pad from its bag and held it in the same hand he used to open the door. His right fist coiled, he watched the elder one struggle to stand. He saw all she had, couldn't help otherwise in a skirt that short. When she finally came out of the car, he smacked the coiled fist hard into her upper midriff, dropping her like a corpse. The alien had slid to the open door waiting for her turn. Now she just sat there, jaw gapping. He rammed the pad into her face, his other hand behind her head. She kicked for a while, twisted, then went still.

Zoby bent down to the elder one who had puked where she knelt, doubled up and clutching her stomach. He yanked her hair back, pushing the pad over her mouth and nose, watching the terror in her eyes until they closed. He liked that, terror, obedience. The mission was looking good. She sure had a nice body.

He taped their mouths; tied wrists and ankles with plastic pull straps then lifted both into the boot. He felt over the elder one, happy with what he found. Top quality, that one. Shame about the alien. He checked the bags they had left on the back seat and found two mobiles. Once they were switched off he threw both into a hedge. Back in the driver's seat he tuned in his head radio. "Zoby to Colonel. Hostiles secure. Heading for base."

"Roger that, Zoby. Wait on my signal."

Wait, why wait? Why not start straight away? Cut the alien in half, play doggy with the other. Where's my money? Where the hell is my money? He drove out of the lay-by and headed for the motorway. Wondered if he should go back and pick up the French female. 2 + 1 TQW. Two women, one alien. Is that what the Colonel meant?

Staying within the speed limit and laws, it took him forty-six minutes to reach Hollyoaks. He parked up across the back lawn, whistling tunelessly as he opened the boot and looked inside. Both girls stared back, both had fight and anger in their expressions. It showed fire and he nodded approval. Discipline gave more pleasure when resisted.

He hauled out the alien first. She kicked and squirmed like a cat, blocking with her legs as he forced her through the back door and into the living room. He tied her arms round the back of an end chair in the row, then strapped her ankles to the front.

The older one tried to head-butt, then thrashed and wriggled until he got her on his shoulder, his hand under her skirt and over her rump. She went quiet then and stayed quiet, even while he strapped her up, her arms behind the chair back, her legs spread. She had fear, he liked that. He took off her gag. She bit him.

"Bitch!" He smacked her face. She screamed once, then went silent.

"Try that again and you pay," he said pointing, feeling heat inside his head like his brain was boiling. "The prisoners will remain silent and obedient. Failure will result in your severe punishment."

"Fuck you. You're mad!"

He struck again and her head jerked. He knew he'd hurt her because he saw the flush of red bruising. She made no sound, not a whimper.

"That's better." He pointed to the alien. "If you start whining, you get the same." He stood in front and ripped the tape from her lips.

She squealed once then sat staring at him, the same see-through stare the boy had fixed on him at Cindy's flat. He hated that, hated she might see him hiding inside. For a moment, uncertainty hovered on the black void. He picked up his sword.

"Don't! Please! I'll do anything. Leave her." The older one was wriggling, jerking at her ropes.

Zoby placed his sword to the alien's neck, feeling some gratification in big sister's panic, feeling it ease the pressure in his head. He grinned, looking between them. "You'd better do that, pretty thing, because if either disobeys, I'll cut the other."

"Our dad's a policeman, he'll get you." The alien spat her words, cheeks flaming.

"You mean I got myself real hostiles? Pig's daughters, and sisters with it!" Now he realised what the Colonel had meant 2 + 1. "Now that's real neat," he said. "I ain't never had sisters. I bet big sister is the juicy one who gave me the come on when I went calling. The Colonel's playing games here." He lowered the sword, switched on his head radio and made instant contact.

"Zoby to Colonel. How do you read me, over?"

"Loud and clear, Zoby."

"Two hostiles ready for interrogation, sir. But you said plus one. Do I think, right, it's three sisters?"

"You got it, Zoby. That's the game plan. Three females, all sisters. Play one against the other. TQW. How long do you have base?"

"Five days, I guess. Plenty time for three hostiles. Shall I go now, pick up the big one in St Albans?"

"Go to it, Zoby, over and out."

Both were staring at him like he was crazy or something. The older one looked real scared. Sisters always protect one another. Three sisters could make the best fun of his life. Zoby lifted his hand to the elder one and started unbuttoning her top, pushing the material until her bra was exposed.

"Have to leave you awhile, go find your big sister. Maybe play with her, maybe bring her back. One thing's for certain, if either of you move I'll cut this little rat straight down the middle, head to arse. You understand me, pretty thing?"

She nodded, the alien just stared. It sure fucked him up that stare. When he got back he'd slice it off her shoulders and make the other one watch. He put down the sword, checked their bonds and re-taped their mouths. They weren't going anywhere.

"If on my return I find you've made any attempt to escape, the alien will be immediately executed. And you, sister, you'll be fucked stupid, then executed. Do I make myself clear?"

Both prisoners nodded.

Zoby felt good on that. He picked up his mobile and went for the van. He found it strange the Colonel hadn't texted him. He usually did on a mission, wanting details like, were they squealing, was he cutting them? Zoby would have preferred to talk but the Colonel wouldn't have it. He parked outside the house 5.30 p.m., put on the rudiments of his gas worker disguise and placed the second sealed chloroform pad in his pocket.

The old Citroen remained on the drive same as last visit. Big sister home alone, perfect. He rang the bell. No one answered.

"Fucking shithead." Zoby kicked the door and tried his head radio but static jammed reception. He could feel the void coming, the black void. He didn't want that, not here. Damn stupid bitch. What the fuck was she out for? He went back to the van and sat waiting.

Danielle left her lecture and wandered to the canteen. She bought iced tea with lemon, then sat on her own, idly flipping notes she did not read. Her last lecture started at 6.30, the talk on programming; boring, boring. The whole day her mind had been elsewhere. Jan had stirred her, now she missed Frankie and wanted the cradle of her arms. She flapped the collar of her dress and blew on a trickle of sweat between her breasts. How cool the garden would be if she lay on the grass, the sun flecking through the apple tree, the birds singing. She folded her notes and slipped them into her bag.

Sitting in daydream, Danielle watched from the train window, her thoughts on Frankie, then Jan, then Monsieur Fagan. Poor Monsieur Fagan, she pouted lips. So many sensual women unavailable. How the world had changed, allowing female tenderness to embrace female desire without shame or guilt. She felt the intensity of sunlight through the carriage glass, the air hot and oppressive. When she arrived home she would shower, lie naked in the privacy of their garden and feel the air caress her skin. She would enjoy the fragrance of blossoming flowers, the sensual pleasure of being.

Walking from the station to home, her bag of books grew heavier with each step. By the time she entered St Albans' leafy suburban avenues she had walked ten minutes. Perspiration beaded her brow and upper lip, tantalised her spine as it trickled to the small of her back.

She dropped the bag and closed the front door. Coolness and shade brought relief, more so when she undid buttons at the front of her dress. In the kitchen she poured limejuice and lemonade into a glass. She sliced lemon with a kitchen knife, kicked off her sandals, shrugged the dress to her waist and slipped off her bra. Opening the back door a small breeze fanned from the garden and for moments she stood in the frame, eyes closed, cool glass between breasts.

The shrill ring of the doorbell sounded over her retreat like an angry irritant. She ignored it, hoping someone would go away. Only on the second, persistent ring did she relent. Putting the glass aside she shrugged first one then both arms into her dress, holding the front together as she walked.

Peering through the spy hole she saw no-one.

"Stupid people." She opened wide and looked out. The figure against the side of the wall came as if from nowhere, thrusting with great force as he pushed through and slammed the door shut, confronting her body to body.

Danielle reeled backwards, conscious of a masked head, eyes circled, teeth bared as he rammed a pad to her face. The stench of chemicals was in her mouth, her nose, choking her. She knew then she was to be raped. Hysteria consumed her, she lashed at his neck and chest until he pulled her body against him. She remembered Frankie's lesson. Fight rape with rape. Her hand went down, her fingers clutching over the fabric of his trousers, feeling for his testicles, ensuring she grasped a firm handful. He grunted surprise until she squeezed, gritting her teeth while twisting and pulling with all her strength. The grunt turned to screech and he dropped the pad to grip her wrist. She head-butted, made stars before her eyes, but it sent him back against the stairs. Free of his grip she ran, making half way to the kitchen before he grabbed the neck of her dress, ripping it from one arm as she twisted free. He snatched her trailing hand, wrenched it up her back, forcing her through the door and face down over the kitchen table.

She screamed, she could hear her scream as he banged down her head then lifted her skirt. She took the kitchen knife feeling his fingers search into her pants, groping for entry to her body. She plunged blindly backwards, felt pain in her own leg and pulled out the blade to jab again. This time he screamed, his hands suddenly gone as she struggled beneath him, pushing in the knife with all her strength, scraping it against bone. The obscenities spat into her ear drew back and his weight eased, allowing her to lift and jerk free. Her own voice split the air along with his wail of disbelief. Running out the back door, she gathered her torn dress, sprinting the full length of the garden, glancing only once to see him in the doorway, knife protruding from his thigh. She made for a gap at the bottom of the hedge. Elderly neighbours were already there, staring wide-eyed.

"Fucking bitch!" Zoby threw the knife to the ground and for moments stood staring as blood spread over his combat trousers. He felt the clutch of panic as his thigh became gripped by a dull, aching pain.

"Colonel, I've taken a hit, I'm bleeding."

"Get out of there, Zoby."

"The bitch, fucking bitch."

"Get out of there, that's an order."

"Yes sir, yes sir." Zoby grabbed a tea towel and wrapped it round his leg, tying it in a knot before hobbling for the front door.

There was only one person in view, a woman on her driveway. She looked scared, unsure. "Did I hear screaming?" she asked.

"Fucking bitch." Zoby got into his van and drove. He couldn't believe what had happened. How could this one be so different? He had never taken a hit before. Now he had so much pain, tears welled in his eyes. Someone would pay. "You fucking bitches, you'll pay, all of you."

"They went shopping!" Sean sensed the first kick of fear, then rationalised. He was overreacting. He heard Miss Nathan explain arrangements at the Red Lion. He clicked the receiver and began to redial. Stay calm, stay calm. He repeated it mentally and waited for the duty sergeant at Dunstable police station to answer. Cobbart was staring, talking to Heidi, his expression dead-faced as he crossed the room.

"St Albans police have you on file as a serving officer," Cobbart said. "They've been on to Pimlico. There was an incident at your home. A young woman attacked."

A sheath of dread descended, clawing over Sean's skin and mind. "Is she alive?"

"Leg wound, no other details."

From the earpiece Sean heard the duty sergeant asking after his enquiry. Cobbart took the phone away. Eighteen people stared in silence. Sean looked to Cobbart and saw compassion, also resolve. "You know the rules, Sean."

"Check the hotel, Red Lion, Dunstable. Now! My daughters should be there, so should their mother"

"Sir," Heidi called. "Your wife's already on the phone, she's hysterical."

Sean sat and listened to his wife, then rested head in hand while he talked to the receptionist. Dark panic was feeding in a frenzy and threatening his mind. No one moved, the air was static as he replaced the handset, an isolated click of plastic on plastic.

"A man fitting the description of Mark Harrison and calling himself Zoby drove away my daughters. They've not been seen since." He looked to the surrounding faces.

No one answered, only stared at him. Heidi bit her lip; Jan placed one hand over her mouth. Victoria reached out, then dropped her arm.

Sean stood, fists clenched, his rage agonising to bear. He called up all mental strength then centred it into cold, tense calm, to lose it would destroy him. He looked at John Cobbart. "These are my children, I'm not letting go."

"You have no choice, you're too close. Your mind and judgement will not be rational. I'm taking over. I'll listen to your advice, everything you say, but from here the decisions are mine. You can do no more. Every copper in Britain is behind you. We'll get your girls back."

"Alive, or dead?"

"Go see their mother, calm her. Check up on the housekeeper. I'll keep you informed."

Sean slumped to a chair and Cobbart turned on the room, everyone was suddenly active.

Jan put an arm round his shoulder. "You want my help, boss?"

"Go to St Albans, find where Danielle's been taken." He looked up and saw her tears. "Cradle her 'til this is over. The house will be full of cops, she can't stay there. Tuck her up somewhere. Give her my love."

"I'll take care like she's my own."

Victoria came over holding a computer printout from Heidi.

"Want to drive with me?"

He shook his head, unsure of anything.

"What about your ex-wife?"

"She chose Bradley."

"So trust me. MI5 is not under Cobbart's jurisdiction. You want to ride, you're welcome."

Cobbart stood in full swing, jacket off, sleeves rolled. He looked the part, good leader showing the way, phone in each hand. As if conscious of Sean's scrutiny, Cobbart spoke from where he stood. "I have a nationwide alert, I need photos, Sean."

Sean opened his wallet and slipped out a school portrait of both girls. "It was taken three months ago. I'll get others." The words came dead and hollow as he placed the photo down.

"There's a witness to Danielle's attacker, he drove a black van," Cobbart said. "They're taking her statement now. I'll have teams linking up from all over; the Met, Hertfordshire, Bucks and Essex constabularies, the whole South East police force if necessary."

"I need air, space to think."

"Stay in touch. We'll find them," Cobbart paused, as if wanting to say more, then went back to his phones.

Sean followed Victoria outside to her BMW and stood hands on roof.

"So give me something good," he said.

She held the printout. "From Zoby's hard drive, a mobile number sent to the Colonel. No mention why. Heidi checked. It's stolen, pay as you go."

"Impossible to trace unless it's switched on. A long shot, way down the list for Cobbart."

"If Zoby uses it, MI5 have resources to track the signal and location within four minutes."

"He may never use it and if he did and smelt police, he might panic." Sean covered his face, not wanting to speculate further.

"I wasn't thinking we make contact as police," Victoria said. "He takes instructions from the Colonel. The Colonel, if he was Faulkner, is dead, but Zoby doesn't know it. We could mimic the Colonel."

Sean paid little attention. He could hear her but he was looking into the face of Caswell. "He knew. When we interviewed him at Shoreditch, I saw it in his eyes. He was mocking me. He knew what was to happen. He set this up."

She touched him, caressing his shoulder. "Why do that? What possible reason?"

"A diversion. Where is my attention now? Where is everybody's attention?"

"You're being paranoid, Sean."

She was looking up at him, her eyes searching over his face. "He used us to shoot Snibbard and he's getting away with it," he said.

"Cobbart was right, you're no longer rational."

"Fuck Cobbart, I want Caswell. If my girls are dead, he is the one who murdered them." He pushed up from the car, centred now. He had a quarry, all he needed was firm evidence and a weapon. He began to walk towards his car until she ran in front and thumped his chest.

"Listen to me, please. Do it my way. We can save your girls. Don't destroy yourself by doing something crazy."

He kept his target, kept Caswell in vision and saw the eyes mocking him. "I have no time to waste. Caswell is the key to Zoby and my girls." He looked down at her, placing his hands on her arms. "If they are alive." He moved her gently aside and opened the car door.

"You can't go near him, Sean."

"If I have evidence they can't stop me and I'll get evidence."

She stood aside as he drove off and stayed in his rear view mirror until he turned into the early evening traffic.

Zoby parked in front of the house and limped around the back. The pain in his right leg was a dull ache and he hated it, hated all pain.

He checked his prisoners first. They were still trussed like chickens. By the red around her eyes, the alien had been crying. He liked that. She'd cry a lot more before dark. Ripping the tape from their faces brought yelps of pain. He liked that too, their pain. They were female. He wanted to give them pain from the boy inside. They would never have children, never, ever!

"Let us go, please," the elder said, her eyes wet.

"Shut up. I've been hit in combat and all you do is whine. You want me to take a belt to you?"

She shook her head. "Please, don't hit us. Let my sister go and I'll let you do it to me."

"Do it to you." He leaned close to her face. "You'll let me do it to you. I'll fuck you whenever I want, bitch. Your big sister cut me, and you're going to pay. I'm going to gut your baby sister while she's still alive, understand? Bitch. Why should I suffer pain? Why always me?" He struck out at her, feeling the crack of his knuckles on her cheek. When her head sagged he limped to the bathroom and looked into the mirror for the soldier.

Static burst over his head radio. "Fucking Crystal. Where's my money?" he shouted, and hit his head so it jolted before he switched the radio to send. "Zoby to Colonel, I made it back to base. But I've been hit in action. I'm hurting, Colonel. Where the fuck's my money?" He twisted up the volume but only static came back. "Do I start on the hostiles? Why the fuck don't you answer? Fucking Crystal." He switched off in disgust and stripped to his shorts.

Blood matted over the wound and his thigh was sticky with congealed blood. It surprised him the hole was so small, it sure hurt for such a small cut. His balls hurt too. Bitch! He felt the void in his head open. Felt it space his brain and saw the floor come up towards him.

CHAPTER 21

Driving a Vauxhall car from the pool, Sean locked himself in the vacuum of isolation, scrutinising details in logical sequence. Time did not allow for failure.

Whoever killed Jovana Zeller did so in a manner that gave perverse satisfaction, a copy of Zoby, someone who knew Zoby's work. Snibbard was a backroom wanker, not a front man. Zeller's death had flipped him. Probably because he believed the same fate awaited himself. That left Caswell or Faulkner as the killer. Faulkner had arrived late and been shot by Snibbard within minutes. It had to be Richard Caswell. Trust Richard, trust Richard. Snibbard had said it as if on auto-speak. In the event, Caswell had successfully put Faulkner up as the Colonel, even made mockery over what he knew was to happen outside. That required black perversity, a brain as crazy as it was greedy. Gutting Zeller showed his lust for gore. What better way to satisfy that lust than to witness from a safe distance? That had been possible with Sarah Finch, very probably with Lizzie Sinclair. Now Sean realised why her father had investigated a top floor council flat and a rent boy called Danny. Half an hour later he parked in Stoke Newington.

The caretaker was dressed in a silk blouse and baggy shorts, his hair spiked and tinted.

"You lied." Sean held the door wide. "What happened to Danny after Sinclair went out the window?"

"He went home."

"Where's home?"

"Where black people come from. Why ask me? He gave favours, that's all. Creech knows." The man retreated trying to close the door.

Sean pushed in after him. He was conscious of his fists in tight knots, conscious he must stay rational. "Before he left, what did he tell you?"

"Ask the female fuzz, I told her."

Victoria knew, he felt shocked. Was that MI5's secret? "When?"

"Couple of weeks ago."

Sean stared down at him and saw fear creep into his expression. "Tell me the truth, Malcolm, because there's no-one here to save you now, no-one but me."

"Danny saw someone in the flat watching the girl being murdered. One of those flash city boys."

"You said nothing."

The man swallowed. "Creech said not to. You know how he is."

"So why did you tell the woman?"

"She had some photographs. Said the boy was under age. Not true, I never touch anyone under eighteen, he wanted to, he wanted my help. Gay people do help each other you know. The police aren't meant to blackmail."

Sean loosened strong fingers around the caretaker's neck. "Someone is hurting my children. I'm angry. You don't want to see that anger, do you?"

The man shook his head.

"You scared of Creech?"

This time he nodded. Sean leaned close and whispered. "Be scared of me, Malcolm, be very scared of me and be scared now, because your life depends on truth. The old boy who went out the window, did he know what Danny saw?"

"Yes, he took Danny's statement."

"When the old boy died, was Creech here?"

"No, but some of his men were. There were dealers around."

"Was the window-sash in place?"

"No. Someone, I don't know who, took it out. I put it back afterwards. The policewoman knew that, she asked me a long time ago."

"What really happened to Danny?"

"Men in suits took him away. Honest, that's all I know."

Sean grew conscious of his own staggered breath. The guy was a pawn and except for lies, without blame. "Time you moved on, Malcolm, some place other than here." He let go leaving finger marks imprinted on the man's neck. The caretaker's eyes watered, his epiglottis shifting as he swallowed.

Walking back to the car Sean kept his fear shrouded by anger. Anger and purpose fed him, gave him hope and strength. He dialled Creech on the mobile number given by Victoria. The response was instant.

"This is Fagan, I want a meeting."

"The Queen's Head, Church Street. Surgery every Friday night between six and eight. Any villain in the neighbourhood has a problem, they can talk direct. SOCA included."

The bulk of Creech's body occupied a single table, his shaven head glistening, his stubby ringed fingers clasped round a beer glass. Two of his boys sat close, looking like smaller versions of their boss. Creech pointed to a chair with a shovel hand, index finger stretched.

"Take a pew, Mr Fagan, tell me your problems."

"Who took Danny the rent boy?"

Creech put hands to expansive belly and drew breath through clenched teeth. "Now, let me see what I recall of that incident. Poor little black boy rents his arse to make a living. Unfortunately, it doesn't feed his habit so he grafts on the side as a police informant. Now, in this neighbourhood, that's a dangerous occupation."

"Don't fuck with me, this is personal. Is he alive?"

"My, my, Mr Fagan, we are in a strop. Truth is, I don't know. He's no longer under my care and protection. Yardie gangs operate here." He clenched teeth again and shook his massive head. "If they're not shooting each other, they're shooting informers. Last I heard, your lad ran back to the Caribbean. Unfortunate move. That's Yardie home turf with Yardie law. My guess, he got eaten by a shark."

"But you have his statement, he saw Caswell witness the graveyard murder?"

"No, Mr Fagan, Goldilocks has a statement."

"But it would be in your station file?"

"Wrong again. Goldilocks told me Sinclair had a statement. It was in his file. How good that statement was I don't know because it never reached my station. Ask Goldilocks, she was the investigating officer."

Sean stared, his cold anger rising. This man was telling him lies. Had to be telling him lies. "Who murdered Sinclair?"

Creech hooked thumbs to braces and let go an expansive sigh. "Nobody."

It raised a laugh from his boys. Sean never shifted his gaze from the tight little orbs staring out of Creech's face.

"Sinclair was a copper, one of us."

"Sinclair was a piss-head. He also went undercover as a wino looking for witnesses. He found your rent boy, paid him, got a statement, foolishly believed it, so wanted more. A meeting was arranged in the flat. The boy never turned up but he told some dealers a copper was spying on them from there. My guess is, they threw him out the window. Sad."

"Not suicide. You knew that."

"One of the dealers was an informer. I needed him to bust a ring. Unfortunately, both got killed in the process. Justice and convenience for all."

Sean stood and kicked back his chair, snapping his words. "The death list in your manor seems more than convenient, Superintendent."

Creech leaned on the table and pointed with a stubby finger. "Before you cast aspersions, Mr Fagan, Sinclair poached on this manor against my advice. He was warned what would happen if caught by the opposition. He chose to ignore that warning. I'm here to fight crime, not nanny a jug head."

"Where's his statement?"

"Ask Goldilocks. Go back to your own manor, Fagan. You don't belong here."

Victoria had lied, lied to him from the start, stayed with him not to corner Caswell, but to protect the guy. She was still doing it. He could not believe her betrayal.

With Danny missing there was only his statement. Possibly, just possibly, if confronted by that statement, Caswell might strike a deal to save himself, give up Zoby, name a location. Zoby had kept the Carter woman alive for three days. Would Victoria deny truth for a chance to save his children, this woman to whom he had declared his love? He phoned the warehouse. Victoria had gone. Cobbart came to the phone.

"The black van was stolen. We also have witness reports on a silver Jag which was possibly the abduction car. Information is coming in fast. We'll find them."

Sean saw no point in being less than direct. The facts stood there even without proof. "Caswell witnessed Lizzie Sinclair's murder. To do that he must have known it was to happen and where. He arranged it."

"OK, I'll put it on file. We'll get to it."

Sean recognised the patronising tone, knew he was not believed.

"Fuck you, John. He knew."

"You're stood down, Sean. Now chill out."

Sean threw the phone to the car floor and clasped head in hands, fingers dragging at despair. It took a minute, but frustration and anger subsided. Calm crept to the edge of his brain and he held it there. I mustn't lose it, mustn't lose it, he thought. Outside people passed on the pavement, going about their lives, smiling, chatting, people without cares.

He picked up the mobile, checked it still worked then phoned Victoria's personal number. The auto reply told him she was switched off. He left a message on voice mail. "I know of Danny's statement. I want the truth."

Sean turned on the ignition and started to drive. He needed to win back Cobbart's confidence, not have him believe he dealt with a crazed father. Three days, Zoby had kept Helen Carter alive for three days. A chance hung there. He needed Danny's statement.

He redialled the Met CID and asked for the Shoreditch enquiry team. He kept his voice calm, listening as he was transferred through different office numbers. He ended up with the CID inspector from that morning's interview.

"I know of evidence linking Caswell to a London murder. Can you keep him in custody 'til I raise a warrant?"

"Not my problem, Inspector Fagan. After his statement Caswell was released without charge. He left in the company of his lawyer and two Home Office senior civil servants."

Sean switched off. "Bastards, what are they doing?" he shouted, shouted to no-one.

If someone had spirited Caswell from police custody, then he was certain who. On contact with MI5 switchboard at Thames House, he gave his name and rank then asked for Alice Sibree. The operator took his mobile number. He waited five minutes for Sibree to return the call. In those minutes he confronted his isolation and realised he had been pushed outside of the normal world. This was the victim's world, the helpless world. He had to go back, or lose.

When finally she called, her voice was dry and bureaucratic. "How can I help you, Inspector Fagan?"

"I want Caswell."

"He's gone."

"Where?"

"I have no idea."

Lies, he thought. She knows. Calm, he had to stay calm. He swallowed. "Caswell is involved with murder. He used subliminal psychotic induction over the Internet directing a psychopath to chosen victims."

"Inspector Fagan, the use of SPI on the public is illegal. PKL were researching SPI to build a firewall against its use in virus form. However, this work was not completed and has no significant value or interest to anyone."

Sean drew breath and let it out slowly. "Ms Sibree, would you please tell me where Caswell is at this very moment?"

"I could find out, but it may take time."

"Zoby has kidnapped my daughters. He attacked and tried to rape their nanny. I know of Danny's statement. I'm not interested in SPI, I'm interested in the lives of my children."

He listened to her start of words, then silence. When finally she spoke again, her voice was uncertain, shocked. "I'll check with the Home Office then phone you back." Her change of manner said everything. How long had she known Caswell was the Colonel? How long had the spooks kept it all under wraps, hoping Caswell would not commit more murders before they struck a deal? For what, for covert use of SPI in the WorkWell programme without Starways realising, without the American intelligence service realising? Would they still protect Caswell for SPI while Zoby killed two children?

The warehouse remained in full operational activity. Cobbart stood central. Sean zeroed himself, took Cobbart's arm and led him aside. "I'm sorry for my outburst, John, but time's running out, I need to find Caswell."

"Alice Sibree's been on the phone asking why in the current situation, we are so concerned with Caswell, and what your involvement is." Cobbart raised eyebrows. "I explained you were stood down, but you've certainly rattled her."

"There's a witness statement that Caswell watched Lizzie Sinclair being murdered."

"Give it to me and I can do something."

"Victoria has it. She took it from Sinclair's file. Sinclair got it from a rent boy called Danny."

"The word of a rent boy won't survive against the lawyers Caswell could hire."

"I don't have the time to argue. For God's sake, John, every second counts." Sean raised his hands, desperate for him to understand.

"But how can it help your daughters?"

"I can confront him, he may trade Zoby for a deal and give us a location."

"You believe that?" Cobbart shook his head.

"I have to." Sean tightened all his nerves. At the first lack of control Cobbart would walk away.

"Is this wise, Sean? Other official agencies are not seeing it your way."

"If Caswell witnessed Lizzie Sinclair's murder, he knew of it in advance. It's my belief the Home Office had MI5 monitor Caswell's research all along, using him to carry out experiments on the population which they would never dare touch themselves. Now it's finished, they want it. Awareness of Caswell's control over Zoby gives them leverage. But if he'll trade with them, he may trade with me."

Cobbart shook his head. "Wild. You'll need all sorts of proof to verify such statements. No agency would allow itself to sanction murder."

"They didn't. The murders had already occurred when Sibree found out. She's been pulling strings to make sure no-one else did, at least 'til the SPI programme was finished and the Home Office had its prize. Now they want him safe, unable to give evidence on the extent to which he used SPI and its influence on the public. But I'm not interested in that, I'm interested in my daughters and the small time we have. Don't you realise? That's why Caswell did this, to distract us."

Simmy interrupted. "We got visitors, guv." He nodded over his shoulder. Victoria Lawless stood in the doorway, hands behind back, not meeting his eyes. Alice Sibree strode towards them, her sharp nose cleaving the way. She met Sean eye to eye.

"Due to the distressing circumstances of this incident, I've come to offer MI5 resources, at least those at my disposal. I won't deny previous involvement, but this cuts through all of us, Inspector."

Sean looked to Victoria who remained behind, eyes still lowered. A sense of betrayal, anger, despair, all boiled at once. Was this atonement, or further deceit?

"Where's Caswell?"

"The Home Office inform me he is currently on an aircraft to America, presumably to visit Starways. It was an amicable departure. There was no reason to hold him, and he gave his word to return if requested." She cupped her hands and posed, prim as a schoolteacher.

"Bollocks he will." Sean watched the hatchet smile appear. Her eyes never faltered.

"Inspector, it is your family we are concerned with here, not Richard Caswell."

Sean looked to Cobbart, then back to her and knew he faced a wall. She had outmanoeuvred him and endangered the lives of hundreds of women worldwide. She had left his daughters in the wilderness with time evaporating. Zoby had kept Helen Carter alive for three days. Oh God, what suffering did he inflict on children? Sean felt the surging of rage. He shouted, pointing. "Witch, you are the darkest evil." The whole room turned, shocked to silence.

"Sean, you're stood down for good reason," Cobbart said. "Victoria, take him for coffee." He gestured Sibree away. "We appreciate your help," he told her, guiding her across the room.

Victoria stayed, head bowed. Sean waited for her to burn, instead she looked up at him, eyes steadfast. "Come ride with me," she said.

"I can drive my own car, thanks."

"No you can't. Sibree has her car deliberately blocking yours. The driver won't budge without her say so."

"What's her game?"

"Bluff. She's obeying orders from unseen mouths. My car is free. Whatever you think, you must trust me, please."

"I wish I could." Emotions came and he shivered his breath to contain them. She was the one person he wanted to trust, but of those he had believed in, she worse than all others, had betrayed him.

"They've bought time for Caswell but not enough," she said. "He's at Heathrow. His plane doesn't leave for an hour. We put a tracker insider his case."

Sean stared long and hard but her gaze never faltered. She didn't lie.

"What about the statement?" He watched her draw a letter from her pocket and pass it to him. His doubts wavered. Time was ticking again.

She shook her head. "Tomorrow is too late. I never realised that before. It's too late because now I know tomorrow never comes." Moisture glistened her eyes.

She followed him to the door, waited while he stopped at Heidi's desk to hand her the statement. Heidi looked up at him, pale eyes tired and drawn.

"In ten minutes hand that to Cobbart," he told her. "Do it when Sibree's not close. Tell him I've gone to arrest Caswell at Heathrow. Get an arrest warrant on grounds he illegally possessed dangerous weapons."

He whisked away Victoria's car key the moment she had pressed the lock release on her BMW. Time needed speed. "You handle the mobile," he said, then waited until she sat beside him. "Once we're clear of here switch on the klaxon."

She nodded and clicked over her belt. "Love sure is a bitch," she whispered.

Sean took every back turn he knew towards the M4, headlights glaring in the dusk, siren screaming. Victoria sat silent, feet and hands braced against the speeding car.

"OK, what's his flight number?" Sean asked.

"I don't know. Only that he's there."

"Then hassle the airport, use MI5 clout. Try flight desks, security. Find out what's going to the States. Find out who has Richard Caswell as a passenger in one hour. Buy me time." He glanced as she dialled and felt the relief of doing something positive. Zoby had kept Helen Carter for three days. If Caswell knew the location, there was a chance.

Waiting in the shuffling queue for security clearance to the departure lounge of Terminal 3, Richard Caswell sensed a growing state of anxiety. Throughout the day he had gambled and won, now the last hour seemed to drag for an eternity.

That afternoon he had sat in some grey building belonging to the Home Office. On the table between Richard and two bespectacled Home Office officials were the flash drives found as intended, and then stolen from the conference room by the MI5 woman.

Richard thought the woman clever to realise what he had done and steal the evidence from under the police, but not as clever as himself. No woman could outsmart Harry Woods. It was why he found them all such easy prey. Even now, his manipulation of her created deception and through it, he had outsmarted even the Home Office.

"We advise your immediate departure out of the EU. In reciprocation, we will look after this research until your safe return," the balding man had said.

"I'll need clothes, I'll need documents," Richard protested. "I'll need … "

"A suitcase has been packed from your flat, it's waiting downstairs with your passport," the woman cut in.

"Most convenient." He tried a tight smile. "The contents of the files are under license from Starways. Until I hand them over they remain my property."

The man had spread his fingers on the table. "Allow me to be explicit, Mr Caswell. The use of SPI on the public is illegal. The police are very thorough and if they had these files you would find to your regret that no person is above the law. However, in a few months when things have settled down and reasonable answers have been found for difficult questions, your presence may not be of such interest. Particularly if the police remain unaware of these files. Also, as they are in our safe-keeping, neither will the Secret Service be further involved."

Richard had smiled with genuine pleasure. He was winning. "Starways will want their property back."

"I'm sure we can come to an amicable arrangement," the woman said.

"In other words, you want the goods while I piss off with nothing."

The woman had cleared her throat.

"I'm sure you have assets, Mr Caswell," the man said.

"I need to visit my bank."

"Granted."

Richard travelled by cab and removed all contents from his safety deposit box. They included five flash drive sticks containing the full and final results of SPI and the WorkWell programme, a laptop with copies of the programme on its hard drive, some cash, and the life of Harry Woods via passport and credit cards. The files on flash drive were for Oscar Wileman. He was a dangerous man not to satisfy. The laptop was for himself. The files left with the Home Office Richard shrugged off. They contained only traces of SPI, simple stuff first used at the hotels. It would take time for anyone to discover, ten, fifteen hours. But just in case, he intended to leave Richard Caswell in the departure lounge. All Richard had to do was get Harry Woods on an aircraft.

After half an hour on the tube ensuring nobody followed, he went to Heathrow's Terminal 3. To hide the time of his departure he had previously spent a small fortune with American Airlines booking five flights to New York. He had also booked seats for Harry Woods on Virgin Atlantic to

Boston. Watching the board, he saw all flights were on time and within close departure of each other.

The queue had gone when he finally made the American Airline's check-in desk. With his boarding pass secured for flight AA107, Richard Caswell watched his case trundle up the luggage ramp and flop onto the conveyor belt. He hoped they had planted a tracking device inside, that way MI5 would know exactly where he was; where he was supposed to be. But they wouldn't know where Harry Woods was.

"No luggage, sir?" the check-in clerk asked.

"Just cabin luggage." Richard smiled, as he showed Harry Woods' passport and received his boarding card for Virgin flight VS019 to Boston.

Sean was on the M4 when Victoria finished on the phone. "American Airlines know of Richard Caswell. He booked five flights, missed four but made the last one. His case has been checked onto flight AA107, Gate number 31. Richard Caswell is on the passenger list. Departure in thirty-five minutes."

"I have him! How fast does this thing go?" Sean pressed his foot down on the BMW's accelerator, shifting between lanes, taking any gap as he streaked through traffic, cursing when it closed around him. "Tell airport police to hold the flight and arrest Caswell."

"Sean, we've got nothing with which to stop him. We may confront him, maybe get some information but we can't hold him without reason."

Sean glanced at her then back to the road. "For fuck's sake, Victoria. Get on to Cobbart. He must have read that statement by now." He banged the wheel as the traffic bunched in front. Victoria started on the mobile again. Cars on the inside thinned, allowing him to push through onto the emergency lane. He put the BM to a hundred.

"You've done it, Sean," Victoria said. "Your boss is drafting an arrest warrant. He'll fax it to the airport. He is not happy."

"What about Alice?"

"She'll know, like the evil witch you called her, she'll know."

Richard smiled politely at the woman on Passport Control. She smiled back, punched numbers on some hidden keyboard inside her booth and returned his passport. That was one obstacle down but it did not remove the unease as he shuffled forwards to the security gate and placed his laptop into the mouth of the x-ray machine. Neither did the shrill ring of the metal detector when he stepped through the arch. Two security men were immediately on either side. Compliantly, Richard raised both arms, turning as they frisked him then waved a handheld detector over his body. He swallowed and found his throat dry. Hands brushed over his jacket, over his two passports and two boarding cards. There was no reaction, no more electronic sounds.

The man nodded and stood back. Richard looked to retrieve his laptop.

"Something wrong?" he snapped at the security woman who had his computer half out of its case. Instantly he calmed himself and tried to smile. Losing his temper or showing fright would only cause suspicion.

"Fine, sir." She pushed the computer back and squiggled a blue chalk mark on the exterior.

"What's that for?"

"So we know it's been checked." She held the bag out, all smiles.

Richard contained his relief and walked slowly, trying to appear relaxed. In a corner of the departure lounge he sat and switched on the laptop. The screen eventually displayed the coded rows of numbers and letters. The same with two of the flash drives which were stored in the outer pockets of the computer case. He let the tension ease on a long whistle of breath. He had done it, Harry Woods was free with WorkWell and full SPI modifications, except he was uncertain about the blue chalk mark. Why him? It singled him out.

In a discount shopping arcade he bought a brown leather briefcase with gold trim, a type sold by the dozen, inexpensive and inconspicuous. He slipped the computer case inside along with the flash drives and entered the nearest public convenience. Locked in a cubicle, he removed his jacket, rolled up his sleeve and pushed Richard Caswell's passport and boarding card under the trap of the WC bowl. Outside in front of the mirrors he washed his hands and straightened his tie. Now Caswell really was in the shit and Harry Woods left free to roam. The tannoy system announced the last call for American Airlines flight AA107, Gate 31. Ten minutes later whilst he sat in a coffee lounge, an announcement came for Richard Caswell to report immediately to Gate 31. It was followed by the boarding announcement for Virgin flight VS109. Richard picked up his briefcase and strolled with other passengers towards the allocated departure gate. Harry Woods was about to fly economy class to Boston. The flight monitor screens were now showing American Airlines Flight 107 as delayed. Richard smiled. Some arsehole had checked in his case then bunked off. Richard Caswell would not be well remembered.

Outside Terminal 3 Sean threw open the car door and entered the building at full run. Warrant card in hand, he pushed through Security and Passport Control. Uniformed and plain-clothed police began shouting, chasing behind with Victoria.

The waiting area for gate 31 was filling with disgruntled people leaving the aircraft. Sean went to the nearest stewardess.

"I'm looking for one of your passengers, Richard Caswell," he said. "I have a warrant for his arrest."

"We're looking for him too, sir," the woman said. "Because he's not on the aircraft and he's not in this room, but he's sure causing us problems."

Sean felt the whole of his inner body contracting into knots. Zoby had kept Helen Carter alive for three days. Three days of abuse. How long would he keep two schoolgirls alive?

Richard shuffled down the aircraft with other passengers and found his allocated seat in premium economy. Two Chinese businessmen occupied the window and middle seat. With passengers in the aisle still pushing and lifting bags into the overhead lockers, Richard sat with the briefcase in his lap. His adrenalin began to surge, he was out of there. He was going.

The black man who pushed up to the seat came with the last passengers and towered like a mountain, his body draped in a black leather jacket, his neck hung with gold. He looked down at Richard through wraparound shades.

"You're in my seat, Mr." He showed his boarding card and beckoned a stewardess.

She came across and stood with a set smile examining both boarding cards. "They've over booked," she said and fixed her smile on Richard. "Don't worry, sir. I'll find you an upgrade. Follow me." She whipped the briefcase from his lap and pushed back into the aisle against the last incoming passengers.

"I'll carry that." He tried to reach for the case, but she was already ahead. Richard stayed close, his eyes on her every move until they reached the door and stairs which led to the upper deck. Other cabin staff, passengers and gantry crew were suddenly around her, all seeming to congregate as she pointed up.

"After you, sir."

"I'll take the case."

"It's OK, I can manage."

Richard went up and turned immediately to watch her carry the precious briefcase. She indicated two empty seats side by side. "Take your pick," she said, lifting the brown case into the baggage locker and closing it. "Please fasten your seatbelt. Our departure for takeoff is imminent."

Richard felt the aircraft move and smiled for the stewardess while she fastened him in. He smelted her perfume and sensed her body. He was safe. No one could touch him now. He had even managed an upgrade. Reasonable, he thought, considering all the money he had spent covering every seat available for his unknown time of departure.

CHAPTER 22

"He could be anywhere by now, anywhere!" Sean punched the dashboard and slumped back in the BM passenger seat, his mind jagged, his anger defeated by despair. Victoria took an envelope from a woman PC who passed it through the open window.

"Arrest warrant for Richard Caswell," Victoria said. "If he's still in this airport, they'll find him."

"He could also be helping Zoby cut up my children."

She shook her head. "Don't think like that. What I said before you left the warehouse, we can still do it."

"Wait on Zoby to use his mobile?"

"That's one way. Sibree maybe a witch, but she'll do anything to save your daughters. If Zoby switched on and gave a signal lasting four minutes, MI5 could cross-reference the beacons and find the spot within five metres. It's cleared with Thames House, they're listening right now."

"Thanks, I appreciate that, but I can't just sit and wait." He put his head back and stared at the roof. He felt his insides chewing up, felt utter despair.

"There's an alternative. We check addresses from Travelpath."

"Cobbart's doing that already. He's got two thousand nationwide, eight hundred in the Home Counties alone. In case they spook Zoby, each check has to be done covertly." He closed his eyes. He felt tired, trapped.

Victoria touched his hand and twisted in the seat. "Has anybody considered that Zoby abducted your girls and attacked Danielle in a time gap under two hours? Time he spent driving a black van."

Sean nodded, eyes still closed. "Probably had the girls in the back. Who knows where he is?"

The full weight of her punch to his chest brought him back to the car. Her eyes were glaring.

"Will you fucking listen to me. Don't give up. The van's not been seen since. If he dropped the girls first and came back for Danielle, he's within thirty, forty minutes drive of the crime scene. I'll be brutal, Sean. He's sadistic, your girls will scream. He'd need isolation."

"He gags his victims."

Her eyes never faltered, locked to his, no mercy, only frustrated rage. "I've talked to expert psychiatrists. All agree he would enjoy it more if he heard their screams."

He wanted to hit her. Every nerve in his body was tense again. She kept eye contact while fishing in her handbag before producing a folded sheet of A4.

"Printout from Heidi's computer. Travelpath list. Three remote properties are within forty minutes drive of your home. Zoby could be using one of them. It's a chance good as any. That and the mobile location may find them. You going to sit there?"

He knew she was right and was thankful for her strength. He raised a hand to touch her, then fastened his seatbelt instead. "Let's go."

"There's a map in the glove compartment." She turned on the klaxon and headlights, then drove out into the airport traffic, cutting light through darkness.

Once the aircraft had levelled, Richard listened to the background whisper of the engines. The seatbelt light went off and moments later a trim stewardess passed by on her duties. Richard stood and removed his briefcase from the overhead locker to place it on the seat beside him. He had to check, to be certain.

The laptop case remained inside. The blue chalk mark on the front told him it was real. The flash drive files from WorkWell sat in their pockets. Everything was as it should be except something, he wasn't sure what, but something made him slide the computer from its case and open it on his lap.

For a few moments he tapped the keys then sat staring at the screen. Mickey Mouse stared back.

The numbing cloak of hopelessness which had coiled round Sean's mind slowly loosened its intensity. It didn't go away but he began to think rationally again. Urgency became paramount, so did news. He called Jan first.

"How's Danielle?"

"At my place. Sexually molested but no penetration. Got stitches in her leg. Mood swings from anger to tears. Needs a lot of re-assuring."

"Does she know about the girls?"

"I've said nothing."

"Don't. I want to give her good news."

"I know you been pushed into touch, boss, but if you want me out there, I'm kind of available."

"I appreciate it, but stick with Danielle, she needs you. This guy is still loose." He switched to redial then had a better idea. "I'm going to text Zoby and lay bait."

"Use this." Victoria reached to her door pocket and extracted a silver mobile. "It belongs to the department. They have constant monitoring locked onto the mobile number found in Harrison's flat. You'll find his contact number sent by e-mail to the Colonel, it's top of the address list." She turned on to the M25 and began to weave through traffic, her full attention back on the road.

For moments Sean watched her profile, the small sweep of her nose and delicate chin. Her eyes glowed like black reflection of the night. He knew then that his daughters were part of her vengeance, part of her silent fury and determination. She was formidable now, and for that he gave back his trust. He switched on the mobile and began to text.

Location and sit rep. Note my new contact no. and report.

"If he answers we keep him on line," Victoria said. "So long as he's switched on, so long as his phone pulses for four minutes we have him. Base can also re-route any calls he makes to reach the mobile you hold." She checked her watch. "First address thirty minutes."

They drove for twenty before a bleep sounded on the silver backed instrument Sean held in his hand.

Where's my money?

"We have contact." Sean pressed buttons.

Money ready. What location? Col.

He watched the message send, watched the screen flicker, then fade to save.

Victoria slowed to the inside lane and pressed to his shoulder, glancing down at the tiny screen. He sensed her energy and strength and again drew comfort from it. He waited, keeping his eyes on the phone as it lay in the palm of his hand like the dead husk of some giant beetle. Nothing happened. "He's gone."

"But we made contact. We know he's there and using that number. Think positive. The moment he switches back on the office will bleep our phone. I'll turn off the klaxon. Try him on voice. I know it's dangerous, he may not recognise you as the Colonel, but we have to risk it, we have to draw him out."

She leant to the glove compartment, searching with one hand to produce a small, sealed packet. One hand still on the steering wheel she ripped open the cellophane with her teeth, stuck a button mike over the back of the silver mobile and clipped the receiver behind her ear. "MI5 goodies. I can listen up to a hundred metres," she paused. "And Alice gave back my automatics.

Richard stared at the screen in dumb horror, realising somewhere, someone had switched laptops. He extracted a flash drive from its case. It appeared to be the original. He started to slot it into a port then stopped. If this was not his laptop, then it might be programmed to corrupt the master files. He sat in hesitation as full realisation dawned. If they had swapped briefcases when he mounted the stairs to first class, then they knew which aircraft he was on. They knew of Harry Woods.

He sighed despondently, the same time a passenger in front stood in the aisle and turned to him.

"Hallo, Richard. Remember me?"

Richard looked at the legs, the short, tight skirt and strutted hip. He remembered her all right.

"Stella. As if I could forget."

"Mr Wileman sent me to make sure you had a comfortable trip, to make sure his files were OK."

"How did you know I was on this flight?"

"Business efficiency, Mr Caswell. It's my job." She reached for a black laptop on her own seat then sat next to him, juggling her skirt to semi modesty before resting the computer on her thighs. Finally settled, she undid her jacket to display a stretched blouse. Small, rimless spectacles perched on her nose and the same loose hair hung in wisps against one check. "You don't mind if I try them?" she asked, extracting a flash drive from Richard's briefcase.

Richard stared out the blackened window into the darkness of night and listened to her try each file in turn. Eyes closed he pondered over his best way out. They had cheated him, stolen his work. SPI could have made him a multi-millionaire. By remote hypnosis, he could have killed any person, anywhere; had a dozen Zobys following his directions. He felt satisfaction over the killing, watching from the sidelines, knowing it was his work. He had money still. He would survive. He snorted breath thinking of Zoby with two schoolgirls, wondering what he'd do to them. Serve the coppers right, always interfering.

"These are real good, Richard," Stella said, pushing the flash drives into her own computer bag and then replacing it on her seat.

"They are?" He sat up in surprise.

"Perfect. Mr Wileman will be real pleased."

"You understand them?" he said, doubting her capability.

"Perfectly. I have my doctorate in computer science now. Recently I tried your early research on our own staff. Efficiency improved by fifteen percent and job dedication by twenty. We're on to both a commercial and political winner." She hesitated and gave a tight smile. "Providing it's kept secret. Under the circumstances, I'm to ask if you would like to rest up at Casco Bay. The house is empty except for a maid. I have encryption facilities in the Beach House. We can make copies of the master files and then insert them into our main programme."

Richard looked into the gap between the buttons of her blouse, then down at her legs. She eased herself which hitched the skirt higher. What he wanted most was to get the files back. This gave an opportunity to copy them at the beach house. Wileman and the girl would never know.

"Am I to assume you are available for other activity?"

The smile narrowed and her lips compressed. "The maid will take care of your sexual requirements. I've since risen in the ranks." She passed him a flash drive of her own. "This is Mr Wileman's new project for you. A lot of money is involved. He wants you to study it during the flight and let him know what you think. Afterwards you get paid a great deal of money." She slotted the flash drive into his computer. "You start working, Richard. I'll drink the champagne."

The mist lifted and Zoby pushed himself up to lean against a wall. His leg throbbed with pain as he removed the towel and cringed at the congealed mess underneath. He washed the wound plus the surrounding dark and purple skin.

"Has to be a bullet wound," he said and pulled open the bathroom cabinet smashing bottles to the floor as he scrabbled amongst the contents, searching for ointment which he smeared over the discolouration before covering it with gauze and plaster strips. What he wanted most was distraction. Money, women. He picked up his mobile and keyed in a message. Where's my money? "You hear that, Colonel? I´ve never been wounded before, I want my money. I want another woman. You can't count the alien as a woman. Fucking hostiles, shit man, I'm going to give those bitches hell." He switched the phone off and slipped it to his shirt pocket.

They sat as left. The elder one had been crying, the left side of her face now red and puffy. The alien had her lips clenched. The floor under her seat was wet.

"You pissed yourself!"

She looked away from him.

"Shitbag! Disregard for hygiene is a disciplinary offence." He lifted the sword from the table. He could feel his mother strapping him, saw the belt coming down and down on the flaming skin of his arms, his shoulders and his back. No one listened to his screams as she forced him down, rubbing his face into the stinking floor, pushing him deep inside, making him hide where no-one could see.

"She couldn't help it, we've been here hours. Please."

"Please what?" He turned to the elder, edging the sword under the hem of her skirt.

"Please don't hurt us." She was shaking her head, crying again.

He flicked upwards, slicing the material. "Sir, you call me sir," he shouted it into her face. "Understand that? Hostile!"

"Yes, sir."

He stooped and licked her. She tasted sweet and salty which gave him an instant hard on. "Prepare yourself, pretty thing. I'm getting ready to fuck." Straddling her legs, his hand in her hair, he jammed her forward, mouth to crotch. Then remembering she bit, he stepped hurriedly back.

Her eyes were closed, her face screwed up, her lips clamped.

"Get used to it, girl. It's tough in the Marines. See that?" He pointed to scars on his arm. "That's from 'Nam, that one's the Gulf, that Afghanistan."

"Liar."

He looked down to the alien, not believing what she had called him as he lifted the sword. "Who the fuck asked you to speak? You stinking, little shitbag. You're gonna die, now. One swipe." He placed the sword blade on her shoulders, standing back to measure his stance and settle his feet. The head rose clean above the chair back, just perfect. She had her eyes jammed tight, her body shaking. The older one sat like a stretched stork, her eyes wide as she mouthed silent words. Then they came tumbling in a torrent.

"I'll do anything, I promise. Don't kill her, I beg you. I'll suck you, anything!"

Zoby laughed and found the boy inside was laughing too. He pointed the sword to her chest. "Only playing, pretty thing. See, I don't really want to kill her, not yet awhile. We got four, maybe five days of fun to go and before I'm finished you'll both be sucking like piggies at the sow." He unzipped his flies, switched on his head radio then waited for the static to clear. "Colonel, this is Zoby. Mission proceeding as ordered. Hostiles under control, I'm about to start the fun."

"Proceed on my order only."

"Combat conditions don't allow that, Colonel. I'm a hostile short and I need distraction from the pain. I'm going to check your command with headquarters." He switched on the mobile. "If they say go, the alien gets first treat, then you, pretty thing." Zoby banged his head to close down the combat radio. Almost immediately his mobile rang. It filled the silence of the room. He couldn't believe his mobile rang. It kept ringing. This was no text. He pressed to answer.

"This is the Colonel, Zoby. Give me situation report."

Zoby opened his mouth but no sound came. He didn't need his head radio, he had real time now. "Prisoners secure and ready for interrogation, sir."

"Well done, Zoby. What is their condition?"

"Loosened up, sir. Ready to go."

"Just keep it on hold, don't do anything."

"Then how do I interrogate them? I have my systems." He listened to a moment's silence.

"They're under the Geneva Convention."

Sean looked into the black night. Somewhere out there his babies were still alive, somewhere close. He felt tears on his cheek, felt the burn of rage. He waited on Zoby's answer.

"You're kidding me, Colonel. This mission is covert. What's the point of risking my neck for hostiles if I can't do anything?"

Sean closed his eyes, doubts pulling in every direction. "I got your money."

"All of it, double bubble?"

"Double bubble, plus bonus."

"How come you're calling? You never called before."

"I need your location for the drop." Sean clenched his teeth, waiting.

"It's the interrogation compound, same as always. I told you over the radio. I want it here now, not in the bitch's grave."

Sean paused, listening to his own breath. "Bad reception, I didn't pick up your signal. Tell me that again."

"Can I start on the hostiles? I need to go for mission objective."

Sean looked to Victoria and indicated for her to slow. "It's different this time, you didn't get the last hostile so I brought another for you."

"A proper female? These two ain't much. One's OK. The other's just a piss-pants alien."

"Don't bother with them, Zoby. Wait for the real one. This one is class."

"Decent body?"

"Perfect. Want to talk with her?" He glanced at Victoria and slotted the mobile to hands-free, checking his watch for length of call.

"Hallo, Zoby." Victoria's voice purred like velvet.

"Hope you're getting yourself ready woman, 'cos once I'm into you, you're mine forever."

"If you say so, sir."

"I like that. Respect, obedience. When will you be here?"

"When I know your location, sir, I'll be there."

"Off the A1. Now put me back to the Colonel."

"Off the A1," she repeated. "Whereabouts?"

"Give me the Colonel, bitch."

Sean retrieved the phone, switching eyes between motorway and map, tracing a finger to the second address. It had to be. He showed Victoria and was pressed back in his seat as she came out the slow lane under maximum acceleration. God, he had hope, at last he had hope.

"ETA twelve minutes," he whispered and put the phone to his ear. "Like the sound of her, Zoby?"

"I'll like it better when she's squealing. Sure wish I could warm up on these two."

"No, Zoby. That's an order."

"Where's my fucking money? Crystal was meant to bring my money."

"It's coming. A real woman too. You're going to have it all, Zoby. Just wait a few minutes."

"I'm dumb sick of waiting! I want action."

"Shit!" Victoria glanced to her rear mirror the same time the wail of sirens reached the car. The motorway patrol was a quarter mile behind, struggling to keep pace.

Sean covered the mouthpiece. "You have to stop, can't have that blaring up to the house. Christ knows what he'd do." Victoria began to slow.

"Hey, Zoby. I'll be back in a minute."

"You got problems? Do I hear sounds of pigs approaching?"

"I'll deal with it, Zoby. You talk to the woman, take a smoke."

"Smoke! I'm physically A1, combat proficient. I don't smoke."

Victoria stopped on the hard shoulder. Behind them the siren slowed and faded. Sean thrust the mobile into her lap.

"Keep him sweet." He opened the door, took out his badge and pushed it into the face of the patrol constable.

"Serious Organised Crime Agency, priority operation. Now fuck off. Quietly." Sean returned to the car. Victoria sat shaking her head, her faced flushed as she listened. "Colonel's back," she said, handing over the mobile, blowing her cheeks in relief. She shot the car to speed. Her own mobile buzzed and she lifted it to answer, whispering into the mouthpiece as Sean listened to Zoby.

"Is this situation red, Colonel? Shall I execute the prisoners now?"

"No! Situation normal. I got a top quality female for you. She gets first hit."

"What the fuck's going on, Colonel. I'm hearing over my combat radio you're back at base. You fucking with me?"

Sean screwed up the ham of his fist, pressing it down against his leg. "Zoby, no-one fucks with you. You've done the campaigns, put in the sweat, taken the knocks."

Victoria slowed and cut across lanes for the next turn off. "Mobile watch gives cross-reference to second address. Four minutes," she whispered. Top of the ramp she turned left, kicked the car to eighty, then a hundred, skipping both sides of the road, braking, taking any gap between traffic. She turned again on to a minor road, headlights blazing into darkness. Ahead lay a cluster of street lamps and the concrete strip to an industrial estate.

"I sure have, Colonel," Zoby said. "And I got the medals to prove it. That faggot, Crystal, he's got shit all. Soon as I get my money, I'm going to chop him."

"You do that, Zoby. He deserves it."

"Sure does, fancy streak of shit, walking round like he's somebody."

"You seen him?" Sean asked.

"Course I seen him. Except he don't know it. I hid when he put money in the bitch's grave. Flashy bastard in his pinstripe."

Victoria slowed and cruised past industrial buildings. No house until a hundred metres down the road. An old gate lodge. "Has to be," she whispered and stopped the car.

"Now you got more money, and the woman. You got it made, Zoby."

"You said that already, Colonel."

Victoria took an automatic from her bag and handed it to Sean, then a second Glock 9mm from the glove compartment before she left the car. Sean followed.

"You're sharp, Zoby. You don't miss a thing."

"You can say that again, shit head. Because I know Crystal and the Colonel are the same. You think you fool me? Where's the money? Where's this woman?"

"I got her, Zoby. I'm bringing her right now."

"Listen, Crystal, I just raised the real Colonel on my combat radio. You streak of shit. He just gave a direct order for me to take mission control. I'm losing patience, Crystal. I want my money, now!"

"Here it comes, Zoby. Few more minutes, it's all yours."

Sean followed Victoria into the front garden. The black van was evidence enough. Lights showed at the rear, garden lights and window lights, meaning whoever was inside could see out.

The silver Jaguar was parked askew over the back lawn. It gave some cover but a bad angle of approach. Crouched on the dark side with Victoria beside him, he peered over the bonnet into a set of French windows.

Zoby stood central to the room holding something by his side. Two heads were silhouetted above the chair backs. The angle of fire was bad, the range too far for certain accuracy. Sean took aim, his heart hammering with taut nerves.

Victoria put up her hand. "Don't, the glass may deflect the round. You might hit one of the girls."

"Give me an alternative?"

"Diversion," she began to unbutton her blouse. "You said you were bringing a woman. Let's show him one. Try the kitchen door. If it's open, you take him from inside. I'll only fire if necessary. My weapon is unofficial." She took off her blouse and bra, then unzipped her trousers. "Go," she said, standing in a half crouch while jamming the whole lot to her ankles, wriggling her feet out of shoes and trouser legs.

Sean ran, his head low, staying from view on the edge of light until he could turn along the wall of the house.

"OK, Crystal," Zoby said, over the mobile. "I'm fucked off with you. Time to execute the hostiles."

"Look out the window, Zoby. The woman is there. You can see her. I brought her for you, Zoby. Don't do anything 'til you see her."

The back door creaked open with slight pressure on the handle. Immediately he could hear Zoby's voice. The kitchen lights blazed and the furniture gave no cover as he crept forward to the hall. He tried to hold his breath, tried not to make a sound.

"What fucking woman?"

Through the open door of the back room, he saw his girls. Both stared up at Zoby, their faces shocked by fear as he lifted a sword shoulder high and braced himself, the blade poised to swing. In those seconds he became motionless, staring to the window. Victoria stood naked, one hand behind her back, preening. She had Zoby's total attention.

Sean kicked the door. "Armed police, don't move."

"You're not Crystal. Who the fuck are you?" His hand momentarily loosened on the sword, then tightened again.

Sean fired three rounds into Zoby's groin and blew away his genitals. He spared his life, he had a living witness to Caswell. The fourth round came from outside and smashed Zoby's head open.

CHAPTER 23

Sean sat in the ambulance and held both girls to his chest. Amidst their quiet sobs he whispered words of reassurance. He left Victoria to phone his wife and Danielle, left Victoria to do everything. The squad car from the motorway had arrived within ten minutes, sirens blaring. Helicopters came next, then an ambulance and more patrol cars. Within forty minutes the place was ablaze with portable lamps. Everyone was there but the SAS. Sean allowed no-one near his daughters. Finally, Victoria came to the ambulance door. She sat on the step half in, half out, as if uncertain whether to approach further.

"Formalities taken care of," she said, looking up at the stars.

With the girls present he had no chance to ask the questions. Both knew she had murdered Zoby, the last witness to Richard Caswell. "What you did took courage and fast thinking, stripping off like that," he said.

"The nature of the diversion won't be in my report. Our secret, all of it." She looked to him.

"Our secret, but what about your unofficial weapon? Forensics will realise two weapons were used."

"Alice will take care of it." She clasped hands, pressing her fingers, holding them to her chin as if in prayer. "Richard Caswell was born Harry Woods, an East End boy from Hackney. I've just been told that during our time at the airport, Harry Woods flew out on a flight to Boston. Alice had no choice but to let him go so he could deliver the SPI files without raising suspicion. I'm informed our American cousins have arrangements for him. Try not to hate me." She stood slowly on his silence and walked away. He felt cold inside. Cold and bitter.

When they entered the house, Camilla threw herself into full-blown hysteria, which sent both girls into screaming trauma.

Only Danielle's comforting voice calmed them. Sean watched the four clustered in a group of mutual support then went to the kitchen.

Bradley mooched around with waiting psychologists and counsellors. Sean poured him a large whisky before retreating to the study, bottle in hand.

Silent rage sweated on his skin and burned any tears from his eyes. He felt inadequate as a father, inadequate as a policeman. The darkness of another world had touched his family and he could not forgive. He wanted his report to have effect, to ask the pertinent questions that could not be denied. He poured another drink and stared at the computer screen for half an hour before Cobbart arrived.

"Operation over. Well done." His boss accepted a whisky and sat by the desk.

Sean maintained eye contact, hoping for a reaction to truth. "Zoby was a paid killer, directed by a third party. He killed for pleasure and profit. So did the third party."

"Snibbard or Faulkner – perhaps we'll never know which," Cobbart said.

Sean searched his eyes, the troll was in residence. "Caswell orchestrated and controlled everything. Even his carefully planned exit."

"During your family's abduction, Caswell was voluntarily assisting police with their enquiries. The CID were impressed by his concern, particularly at the devastating misuse of PKL research by Faulkner and Snibbard."

"That's bollocks and you know it. The Home Office wanted the SPI research and they've got it. What they didn't want was Caswell in court talking about it. Caswell's real name is Harry Woods. The Witch knew and let him go. If you check the passenger lists, you'll find that sometime while we were searching, one Harry Woods flew out of Heathrow. Victoria told me."

"If Caswell ever did control Zoby, then he had lost that control. The recordings of your phone proves it. He could not have helped you, Sean."

"Maybe, maybe not. Who will ever know? But I do know, that in letting him go, an evil has been let loose on this world. Caswell used SPI over the Internet to induce a psychopath to murder selected people. He used SPI to encourage those victims to their place of execution."

"Say that in court, Sean."

"But it happened. Caswell influenced investors to part with millions. Spread subtly, the power of SPI is immense. What if a paedophile used it? Get into a stranger's car, little girl, take sweeties, little girl. Walk in the woods, big girl, like Sarah Finch, like Lizzie Sinclair, like a helpless nun."

"Subjective science fiction. We all know it's possible, but how do we prove it? Even if we knew for certain he was guilty, and we don't, we have to produce evidence."

"Morrison Hotels. Kids go from all over the country. What he could have done mentally to those kids is horrifying."

Cobbart shook his head. "All hard drives at those hotels show only the regular PKL Games. Our high-tech unit have checked. There are no subliminal suggestions and certainly no chance of prosecution."

Sean heard the departure of counsellors and psychologists, heard Camilla gushing her patronising thanks. He poured more whisky.

"What of Milton Keynes? There has to be something there."

"There is no evidence of SPI. Steve Rawlings has been through the lot. The new PKL games were all clean. We've interviewed every staff member. All were aware of SPI but research was to protect the WorkWell programme against an SPI virus. True, that defence does have the potential for abuse by those who control a trusted file. Accepted as official, the SPI can pass anti-virus software and hide in the operating system. It is untraceable, does no apparent damage, can be sent, altered or deleted at any time. PKL is a legitimate research company engaged in controversial work, but there is no proof they broke the law. Neither is there proof that Caswell contaminated the WorkWell programme. There are no master files, only hearsay."

"You telling me we have nothing?" Sean hit the table, causing Cobbart to sit back. "What do I have to do? Give my resignation, go over there myself and put a bullet in Caswell's head? This man is setting himself up as a mass murderer, yet money and bureaucracy allows him to remain free."

Cobbart raised his hand. "It's been a long day, Sean. But we can still only look at the evidence."

"What about my girls? They were influenced to trust a killer."

"Caswell was in custody at the time of their abduction. Zoby was operating alone and independently."

"Whose side you on, John?" Sean gulped his whisky. "You issued an arrest warrant on evidence of a witness statement."

"Against my better judgement, on a wild hope it would help your family. Viewed rationally, it's only an uncorroborated statement collected by a drunk from a rent boy." Cobbart shook his head. "There are occasions in policing when no matter what you feel, you can only consider what is possible and what is not. What will bring a conviction and what will not. Snibbard, Faulkner and Harrison were our killers. Caswell is not on the list. It's hard, but that is fact."

"You disregard everything I told you." Sean took a deep breath, restraining his anger.

"I didn't say that. Politics and policing have always been unethical traders." The troll smile flashed briefly, then Cobbart's face became shallow. "Caswell has what others want. In result, he's gone. If it's any consolation, I have it on good information that the Home Office did not receive what they expected. Someone cheated them."

"Caswell will find other Zobys, he'll kill more women," Sean said. "Will the unseen faces live with that?"

Cobbart spread his hands and for the first time looked troubled. "I understand your feelings. Your daughters were abducted. But don't destroy yourself. Let others deal with him. For you the case is closed."

"Not for me. Not 'til Caswell is put away. I will not turn my back."

"You're tired Sean, think carefully before you act."

When Cobbart left, Sean heard him talk briefly with the duty patrolman outside, then silence, followed by car engines and the measured pacing of the patrolman. Sean reached for his phone and dialled Cricklewood. Diane picked up. Her words were boisterous.

"It's the boss," she shouted. "Come over, boss. We've having a party. Everyone's so relieved for your girls. Give them a kiss from Blue and Red Teams."

He listened to background voices, cheered by alcohol. "You did a great job, all of you," he said.

"Come over. Celebration time. We won, we won!"

"Did we? Give everyone my thanks." He replaced the receiver and buried his face in his hands.

Danielle sat at the kitchen table wearing a loose towelling robe, a glass of untouched wine before her. Sean put his whiskey down and placed a hand on her shoulder.

"Where are the girls?"

"Tucked in bed with their mother. It is good they are close."

"How about you?"

She squeezed his hand. "Hours ago I fought on this table trying to stop the violation of my body. Now for some, it is a safe, family home again. But for me, never. I have been shown an existence amongst us so dark it suffocates life. To know it is there destroys all confidence, all trust. To know that any woman can be hunted simply for her sex reduces her to an animal existence. That is so hard. How I weep for what it has done to your girls."

Sean closed his eyes. Her loss of faith, her loss of belief in the world gave him cold determination. How many years before his daughters recovered? If ever. Caswell would not escape.

"You're a strong lady. Your world, my daughters' world, it will return, I promise. It is also why I must continue."

Danielle stood, tears glistening on her cheeks. "You must find yourself a good woman, then I go back to France." She left quickly, heading for her room.

Sean returned to his study and switched on the computer. Numbers flickered over the screen, the computer box gently thumping its way through start-up. Images, icons and system codes rattled before him. He saw only Victoria, her ivory skin shimmering like a ghostly spectre from the darkness. "A good woman," he repeated.

His hand rested on the telephone. What he wanted most was to be in her bed, in her arms, in her body. He was drunk, he knew it, drunk, maudlin and stupid. The screen settled and a metallic female voice welcomed him to Starways Processing Systems. Every software package showed a Starways icon.

"You won't get away." He pointed to the screen. "You made me a victim. But your world doesn't frighten me. I can also kill, and I'm coming after you."

He lifted his glass, drained the contents and crossed the silent hall. He dropped heavily onto the living room couch, lay there, pushing off his shoes, one against the other. From outside came the click of a lighter – the patrolman, puffing on his cigarette. When Sean closed his eyes, Victoria reappeared and stayed in his mind as he drifted in turbulent dreams.

Richard felt it imperative to have Stella's trust. Unrestricted access to the master files would only come if Wileman believed in him via Stella. Pretending dedication to

Wileman's orders, he examined in detail the contents of the file she had provided, only stopping for meals and to sip orange juice.

"What's your reaction?" she asked after several hours.

"Interesting," he said, unsure how deathly boredom could be given praise. "It has a lot of graphics. Are they necessary?"

"Yes. I wrote the programme," she said. "It's part of my thesis. Would you trust me to write something for you?"

"I trust you," he said, without thinking.

"Good." She smiled. "Then if you trust me maybe you would like to see another?" She passed him a flash drive. "Mr Wileman said you should take notes, he wants your opinion. So do I. The moving graphics and figures are for a reason."

"Do you want a complete analysis?"

"The sooner it's done, the sooner you have a pocketful of money. Trust me, Richard, Mr Wileman does."

When they touched down at Logan International Airport in Boston, he watched Stella bracing herself in the seat, her eyes tightly shut until the 747 ran smoothly along the runway.

She smiled for him and pushed the spectacles up on her nose. "A car is waiting," she said. "It's a three hour drive to the house, but don't worry. I have more files to pass the time."

"Thank you, Stella, that's most considerate of you. Perhaps when we arrive we can get straight down to putting my SPI on to WorkWell ready for incorporation into your system? You don't have to get involved, I can do it myself."

"Sure." She glanced sideways. "If you want to burn your butt, it's fine by me."

"It'll take most of the night. You can sleep, this is my baby."

"We'll see."

He smiled and watched the tight set of her lips. During the night he would recopy the master file and hide it off the Beach House premise. Wileman would never know.

The man mountain who had claimed Richard's seat on the aircraft followed them out of the terminal building, his face still blanked by dark glasses, his body dapper in the long leather coat. Stella called someone on her mobile and ten minutes later a silver Mercedes 500 was delivered to passenger pick-up.

Stella drove in concentrated silence and soon had them on the freeway, heading north. Richard chose to sit in the back, ostensibly to concentrate on the software programme he analysed, but in reality to fall asleep, which he did after an hour. He awoke when they stopped outside the house in Casco Bay.

Stella opened the car door for him and smiled. He felt safe. You could trust Stella.

"The computer facilities are down in the Beach House," she said. "You want to work the night, you can." She hoisted the laptop bag onto her shoulder. Richard followed as she walked, watching the quivering strut of her stride beneath the tight skirt. The main house was in darkness save for outside lights. Around the back and passed the pool, strings of lanterns lit the path leading towards the turbulent Atlantic. The way ran over rock then descended towards trees that quickly isolated them from civilisation. It seemed longer than he remembered, but up ahead he heard the pounding of waves followed by the suck of surf over beach. Guided by lights strung between poles, he kept his concentration on Stella and the sway of her hips. She kept a good stride but slowed when they came to the last cluster of pine trees. He watched as she bent momentarily and retrieved something from the bench, the same place where Oscar Wileman had sat contemplating the ocean and his pet cemetery. Then she turned back to him.

"Something wrong?" he asked

"No, Mr Caswell, I'm very positive. I've been given this opportunity by Mr Wileman to show my ultimate commitment. He's a hard taskmaster, but he's fair. You were chosen because greed motivated your success and drove you to experiment on the public in a manner no reputable company would dare. In a reputable company, staff may have spoken to the press, but you kept everything secret because you wanted it all for yourself. You see, he knew you would try to double-cross him. He knew you had those women killed so he would dissociate himself in case of legal connection. But unluckily for you, his dissociation is in sending me to collect the SPI files, allowing me revenge for you raping me."

"We're alone here, Stella. That's not good for you."

"Not quite alone, Mr Caswell." She beckoned and the man mountain stepped from the trees, a shovel over one shoulder. Richard saw the white of his smile and the reflection of light on gold. "Mr Wileman promised you sanctuary, deep and permanent sanctuary. He's a man of his word and I'm here to help," Stella said.

Fear came instantly to Richard. He lifted his hands in protest. "What the fuck's going on? I've done everything that was asked. I brought the files. Only one set." He began to retreat, looking back along the path to see a shadow of someone moving down. "I want to see Wileman." He pointed to Stella. "I trusted you."

"I know. SPI is so subtle, so simple when used on those who think they are so clever."

"Look," Richard raised an arm. "You want money?"

"No," she said. "I want revenge. You ain't going to rape me or the maid, Harry Woods. You ain't going to rape any woman, even though it's the only way you get an erection. Welcome to your sanctuary, your permanent sanctuary beneath the ground."

He watched the bull nose revolver come up and for an instant looked into the end of its barrel, at least until the sharp flash of its discharge.

Sean woke long before dawn and listened to the silent house, his mind momentarily at peace before the return of memory. It came without mercy. In the end who had allowed his daughters to be kidnapped and Danielle attacked? Who didn't see the emerging dangers? He could blame Victoria, Cobbart, MI5, the Home Office, but in truth he knew the blame was his. He had screwed up and left Caswell to spread his murder on the web, left him with the ability to butcher other human beings by manipulating the minds of deranged people. Unless he removed that evil, Sean could never forgive himself.

In his study he found the computer still running, the screen saver twisting Escherean shapes through impossible three dimensions. He clicked onto Starways Business Centre and began his report. He spent two hours in deep concentration. He praised the operation teams and damned all others. He tore up the printed copy and switched to a new file. His letter of resignation took minutes, less to ball it up and start another. Each time he gave a reason for his failure, he stopped, dissatisfied. Their way, his way, Zoby would have lived, would have one day walked free. It left only a justice that was beyond the boundaries, beyond the law; Victoria's justice.

In the room overhead he heard Sophie wake, heard the tremors of fear in her voice as she called for her mother. On the desk his mobile buzzed. The world was still there, still demanding.

"I'm sitting outside in my car. Can we talk?" Victoria asked.

"Sure." Sean stood and walked through the litter of paper. Inside he felt emotion and resolve battle for supremacy.

When he opened the door, Victoria looked up at him, her eyes steady, her voice soft.

"Confession time. Forgiveness time too, I hope."

He stood back and let her pass into the study. Who didn't have confessions?

"I intended to kill Zoby from the start," she said. "I wanted to ever since I saw the bodies of Helen Carter and Lizzie Sinclair, since witnessing what he did to them simply because they were women. When I resigned from CID because of Creech, MI5 took me into their fold for my silence. In return they promised Zoby, but Caswell had to stay clean, least 'til the WorkWell programme was completed. Then the Americans would deal with him."

"These were orders?"

"Of course not, informal, off the record suggestions. But they might have been printed in stone. Zoby in exchange for Caswell. I sold my soul for revenge."

"Not for the witch?"

"No, I did it for the dread and humiliation Zoby caused to women, for Sarah, Helen and Lizzie Sinclair. For the young nun in Ireland. In other words, for myself. Involvement made me a victim. You should know that place of entrapment. It's a dark hole full of cold anger. Alice thinks I killed to protect Caswell. She never realised my rage." Victoria shook her head as if in disbelief. "I'm the golden girl and in reward the witch has favoured me with the truth, or at least the truth so far as her conscience allows. She left it to my conscience whether I tell you. Under the circumstances, it's the least I can do." She paused and spread her fingers. "Caswell is dead. He was a danger to all society. His termination was arranged and carried out by other interested parties"

"Outside of lawful justice, I assume," Sean said, watching her sit as he leant back on the desk and folded his arms. Staring down at her hunched figure he became conscious of his relief that he would no longer need to pursue retribution.

"I call it peoples' justice." Victoria gave a wry smile. "Other than renewing his passport, Harry Woods has not been heard of for years, and no-one is looking for him now. The real Richard Caswell died of an overdose twenty-five years ago after a fellow pupil at Westminster, one Harry Woods, sold him heroin. Both were orphans and both had won scholarships. When Woods came out of prison he assumed Caswell's complete identity, including his educational record. He was so successful he even managed a passport. With Caswell's 'A' levels, he gained entry to a Glasgow university. At the same time so did Snibbard and Faulkner, all of them studying computer-related courses. Snibbard became a suspect in a series of sadistic rapes but Caswell provided alibis. Due to lack of evidence no-one was charged. Examination of the victims' computers showed signs of SPI. That's when the Box became interested and Woods, alias Caswell, entered their files. Six years ago Caswell took SPI to Wileman. Starways funded his research on the pretext of producing anti-virus software, but when it came to experimenting on people, Oscar Wileman drew the line. If caught, Starways would have been globally damaged. But Oscar saw the potential. Caswell was sent back to Britain with the benefit of PKL instead of Starways to fund his research. PKL was also listed as a minor sub-contractor to a Starways subsidiary. However, in reality, they designed WorkWell to accept SPI and through computer games, used the British public as guinea pigs."

"Wasn't Wileman worried using someone with Caswell's background?" Sean asked.

Victoria shook her head. "Caswell was the leader in his field. He was also crooked enough to work outside the law. Our American source tells us Caswell had been set up for sexual blackmail after he raped one of Wileman's female employees. If Caswell had stepped out of line, he would have ended in an American jail. As it is, he ended dead."

"And MI5 just watched?" Sean shook his head in despair.

"There was nothing else they could do until Sarah Finch was murdered. Alice raided police files and saw links between Sarah, the Glasgow rapes, Caswell, PKL, Starways and SPI. She immediately guessed what they were doing. When the government of the day read her report, they also saw an opportunity. Alice was placed on the dark side. She became the buffer between politically correct bureaucrats and their desire for public control via mass subliminal hypnosis. Never again was Harry Woods alone. During the last years he's been continuously monitored. But Alice could never prove his involvement in murder through SPI, so she let the research go forward and waited to grab the results. Then along comes Victoria Lawless, closely followed by Sean Fagan and that really messed things up."

"You're telling me we have a government agency sitting on a fence outside the laws of a society they are meant to protect."

"Alice would call it inactive surveillance. Ethics are one factor, evidence before an enquiry something entirely different. The Box was staying non-committal. Elements within the Home Office wanted access to SPI. Everyone was waiting on Caswell's completion of the files, including Caswell, because he wanted it for himself. Hence the violent end of his partners. Murder of the Irish girl was meant to divert all attention to Zoby. But he went too far in the abduction of your daughters. That hit Alice. So she did a deal with Wileman. She agreed to let the research go providing he took care of Caswell."

Sean buried his head in his hands. "Alice Sibree with a guilty conscience, I don't believe it."

Victoria shrugged. "Witch or not, she's still a woman. Children mean something to her. To satisfy the Home Office she gave them the file Caswell had left in the conference room for me to steal. When Caswell was released she had him followed but soon realised Wileman's people also followed, a big black guy and a young white woman. He was tailed to the bank, then to Heathrow. She checked which computer he carried when he passed through Security, then replaced it with an identical one after he had boarded the plane. She took a calculated risk in assuming that the hard drive contained the SPI software, but she won."

"So neither the Home Office nor Wileman know she has it?"

"That's correct. And no-one can ever prove possession. That's why she told me. I don't know if I should have told you, I just thought you deserved the truth. And I swear to God, until after last night's events, I never knew the existence of Harry Woods."

"You both went outside the boundaries, you know that?" Sean said.

"Yes. I executed Zoby. But who would you have executed, Sean?"

"Caswell. I would have hunted him. Exterminated him."

"The witch knows that. It's why she told me the truth, knowing I would come here. The truth implicates us both. Within the SIS, the police, parliament, the Civil Service, there is an inner force, the Community. It's a group beyond the Old Boys' Club, a group both secret and powerful. It's composed of people who arrange justice for the right of justice. People who would behave like you and I, Sean. People like the Wicked Witch. That is where she has taken SPI. Where she always intended it to go. Not to the government but the inner circle, to the unseen."

"What is wrong remains wrong. Once WorkWell is implemented by Wileman, what is to stop your community from using SPI for their own benefit?" Sean asked.

"They would never be caught, so who would know?" She paused, raised her eyes. "What I want to know, by telling the truth, do I cast us both into their eternal darkness?"

Sean looked across to her. Her eyes were wide and questioning.

He shook his head. "Perhaps that darkness is here already."

About the Author

As a child, James McKenna travelled extensively throughout Europe and the Far East with his military parents. He joined the UK army at 15 and attended the Royal School of Military Engineering. After passing selection he served with the Paras in Europe and the Gulf. He has since run his own security companies providing electronic and physical protection before expanding into construction and development. He is now a full-time writer living between the UK and Portugal.

The Uncounted

Another crime thriller by James McKenna

Is the girl on the train beside you a free citizen or trapped by debt bondage, one of many thousands illegally trafficked into Britain from Eastern Europe? The slave trade is alive and flourishing.

DI Sean Fagan of SOCA investigates the Agency, a criminal fraternity trafficking illegal immigrants. Trapped in a wretched world of modern slavery and barbaric killings, Jelena, an illegal from Kosovo dreams of freedom, but violent forces which shaped her adolescence still dominate her life. Jelena is given to an Islamic terror cell as a disposable chattel and finds herself locked in a luxury flat with millions of virus contaminated bank notes. Death seems certain until events reunite her with Gavrilo, the boy she had known and loved when both were adolescents. As Fagan closes, a bomb containing enough Anthrax to kill thousands is unwittingly carried by Gavrilo into Central London. Fagan and team desperately search as the timing device ticks to detonation.